MW01492758

Advance Prais

"Ally Walker's thriller *The Light Runner* captivated me from start to finish. The imagery is vivid and other-worldly, and the storytelling is done in a way that makes it impossible to put down. The characters are unique and compelling and made the whole ride fun."

—Katey Sagal, actress

"I've known Ally Walker as a gifted storyteller—as an actor, director and screenwriter—and this novel's debut still knocked my socks off. *The Light Runner* is propulsive, thoughtful, incisive—the kind of thriller that stands out in a crowded field. It pinned my attention from the first page and held it deftly through the riveting ending that I truly did not see coming.

—Sarah Wayne Callies, actress

"Ally Walker has crafted a compelling read. The fascinating prologue immediately hooks you, and the expertly drawn, flawed characters pull you deep into their world. This is a masterful weaving of past and present, where every carefully placed sentence feels like a vital clue in a gripping murder mystery. A powerful and thought-provoking exploration of the prisons we build for ourselves, both within and without."

—Tim DeKay, actor

"Ally Walker is a writer who brings the same laser understanding of character, human motivations, and storytelling that she displayed as a brilliant actress. She has planted her flag in the crime genre, as her new book *The Light Runner* will attest! So, grab a drink of your choice and get ready for a novel that feels like cinema! Vivid storytelling, imagery, pacing, and character development, true cinematic storytelling…. A great actress and now a great author! Congrats, 'Sam'!"

—Robert Davi, actor, singer, and filmmaker

THE
LIGHT
RUNNER

ALLY WALKER

RED RABBIT
PRESS

Published by RED RABBIT

Paperback ISBN: 978-1-966981-06-0
E-book EISN: 978-1-966981-03-9

Printed in the United States of America

10 9 8 7 6 5 4 3 2 1

Produced by GMK Writing and Editing, Inc.
Managing Editor: Katie Benoit
Developmental Editors: Randy Ladenheim-Gil and John Peragrine
Copyeditor: Randy Ladenheim-Gil
Proofreader: Lissette Lorenz
Text design by Libby Kingsbury
Composition by Joanna Beyer
Cover design by Vicky Vaughn Shea
Printed by IngramSpark

For Nita, Lou, and Babe, who led the way.

Special thanks to my husband, John, and our sons Walker, Will, and Cal for filling my reality with love.

I'd also like to thank all the good witches who've guided me on the journey.

"If you feel pain, you're alive. If you feel other people's pain, you're a human being."

— Leo Tolstoy

Prologue

One-Seven had never ventured out of the building this far, and he was becoming increasingly worried that the man-with-the-kind-eyes, who had woken him up from a deep sleep, was doing something that wasn't exactly OK. So, his body did what it always did when he was nervous and froze up.

He snuck a look up at the man-with-the-kind-eyes again, trying to understand why he kept muttering to himself, and why he seemed so frantic. Usually, he just held One-Seven and gave him treats. And that was great. But today was different. He sure hoped the man knew what he was doing, because now he was making One-Seven sort of scared. Very scared.

The man had visited One-Seven and his relatives with that other man, and One-Seven had grown somewhat fond of him. Mainly because he brought treats, but also cuz he was gentle. Very gentle. But he didn't like that other man. He was cold. Like most of the humans he had known.

But the man-with-the-kind-eyes seemed to want to be his friend, so One-Seven sorta looked forward to his visits. But today was different. The man-with-the-kind-eyes seemed very different. He was running now, and it suddenly got a lot darker. Of course, One-Seven could see just fine. Probably a lot better than the man could. And once again, he sure hoped that the man-with-the-kind-eyes knew what he was doing.

But suddenly, the man stopped and gasped. He didn't move a muscle for a long time. So, One-Seven, who'd remained frozen for what seemed like an eternity, looked up at him and followed his gaze. One-Seven wasn't sure, but he thought he saw something running out of the corner of his eye, but it was the human lying there sleeping that caught his attention. Apparently, the man-with-the-kind-eyes didn't like this one bit, cuz he went to the human sleeping, and he began to cry and mutter even louder.

And One-Seven didn't know what he was saying, but he could tell it had nothing to do with treats.

And now something smelled funny. When One-Seven looked closer, he noticed that there was a lot of black stuff coming out of the human sleeping on the ground. He had smelled this black stuff before, and seen it a few times when humans hurt one of them. One-Seven knew the black stuff was a bad sign, and he decided that the time to move was now. So, when the man-with-the-kind-eyes touched the human on the ground, he saw his chance and took it.

He pushed off with his strong hind legs and virtually flew out of the man's hands.

Wow! he thought as he sprang toward freedom. *This feels fantastic!* And he never looked back.

He set off toward green bushes that didn't look green.

Toward a place they couldn't catch him.
Toward a new life.
He set off . . .

Toward the light.

FOREWORD

I f you've ever flown into Baltimore's BWI Marshall Airport, you've probably seen Bainbridge Psychiatric Hospital sprawled below you as you landed. Its three large, brick buildings border a lush forest to the south and, as you descend, you can just make out the train tracks that wind their way through the woods like a serpent crawling to and from the city and beyond.

Some people in the area know that in the mid-1800s, this land belonged to the Western Maryland Railroad Company and housed a railway station and train factory, with the largest brick building on the property serving as the passenger station. But, as the planes overhead so clearly attest, the days of the passenger train are long gone, and Western Maryland's tracks are restricted to the transportation of freight between neighboring states.

Others are aware that the two smaller buildings were added during the First World War, when the property was used as a training base for the Army before the men were deployed to Europe. But there aren't many who know what happened to it after that, or how long it stood desolate and barren before becoming a psychiatric hospital.

Fewer still could tell you exactly how the hospital came to be or how it got its name. It just seemed to have appeared one day. For many, it was considered a stigma by the sheer nature of its purpose, and to others, it never crossed their minds to think about it, for they couldn't remember a time when it wasn't there.

Wayne Bainbridge, who came from a wealthy logging family in Minnesota, was born with a deformed right leg that disqualified him from service in the Second World War. So, Wayne studied medicine instead, and upon his arrival in Baltimore in 1945 with his wife, Marie, he took up practice at the city's Presbyterian Hospital. Wayne became known for his kindness and devotion to his patients, as well as his love of gardening. It was rumored that between shifts, one could always find Wayne pruning, fertilizing, or watering the hospital's garden.

Wanting to be a part of the war effort in any way he could, Wayne used his family money to buy the old railway yard and its three buildings with the intention of turning the property into a convalescent home for soldiers returning from the war.

Shortly after the renovations began, Wayne and Marie welcomed a baby girl to their family, whom they named Mildred Rose. Mildred Rose was the apple of Wayne's eye, and in between working at the hospital and overseeing the renovations of the railway buildings, he doted on the little girl he called Millie.

But as Mildred Rose grew, her temperament began to change. Her once happy countenance was marred by tantrums and periods when she couldn't sleep, only to be followed by days when she could do nothing but. Exhausted, Wayne and Marie took her to a specialist in Washington, DC, who diagnosed the five-year-old as having manic-depressive disorder, and the Bainbridges' lives were changed forever.

Not much was known about the illness then, and the treatments were very limited and somewhat barbaric. Because of her mood swings and tantrums, Mildred couldn't go to school and was kept at home with a revolving door through which nannies came and went. This was particularly difficult for Marie, who felt ostracized from society as well as isolated by her daughter's illness. Wayne stopped the renovations on the railway property and worked less often at the hospital to help Marie care for their daughter. But as she got older, Mildred's condition became so bad that Marie could no longer handle the stress. Acutely aware of what kind of life lay ahead for her child, Marie became an alcoholic and died in 1959, when Mildred was only twelve years old.

Unable to care for her alone, Wayne began the arduous task of admitting his daughter to various sanitoriums. Mildred Rose never lasted long at any one place and seemed to grow worse from one facility to the next, and it was these experiences that ultimately led Wayne to take what family money he had left and turn the railway property into Bainbridge Psychiatric Hospital. He vowed that at Bainbridge, those with mental illnesses would be given the care they needed and, more importantly, the dignity they deserved.

Wayne threw his heart and soul into finishing the hospital, with the intention of bringing his beloved Millie home. But that was not to be. In

1968, just before Bainbridge Psychiatric Hospital opened, Mildred Rose hanged herself in the showers at a sanitorium in Virginia. She was twenty-one years old.

Devastated by her loss, Wayne sank into a depression, and the hospital floundered. In the mid-1970s, he was forced to sell one of the buildings to the State of Maryland to keep the hospital's doors open. The state building, known as C Wing, was then used to house Maryland's criminally insane. Shortly after that, Wayne Bainbridge suffered a heart attack and died. Many say he died of a broken heart.

Members of his staff came together to form a Board and kept the hospital going in the 1980s by catering to the addiction needs of the upper class, which Betty Ford had made so popular. In the 1990s, with the destigmatization of mental illness, Bainbridge became regarded as one of the best psychiatric hospitals on the Eastern Seaboard, and the State allowed the hospital's Board to direct the care of the inmates in C Wing as well.

As with most things, time and progress have erased much of what was known of Wayne Bainbridge. In fact, if you visit the hospital today, you will only see a few pictures of him in the C Wing lobby, as well as a small statue of him with the inscription *Wayne Bainbridge (1918–76), founder of Bainbridge Psychiatric Hospital, who dedicated his life to the ethical treatment of those suffering from mental illness* as you enter the grounds.

But there is very little mention of him in history books and almost nothing of his wife, Marie, who was a casualty of her daughter's illness. As for Mildred Rose, whose suicide brought shame to the family and somehow invalidated much of what her father accomplished, her name was never mentioned. Hence, she was completely forgotten.

But if you make your way out the east entrance of one of the smaller buildings, you will come to a garden where many of the patients take a turn to bask in the morning sun. And if you are very observant as you walk by the rose garden near the east wall, you will notice a plaque fitted into that wall, nestled behind the birdbath. It is hard to see in the summer as the blackberry vines grow and twirl all around it. But if you are there in the winter, you will see the plaque in all its faded glory. And, if you look carefully, you will see that it has one word inscribed on it.

A word surrounded by an explosion of color in the spring and summer but quite desolate by November. A word that Wayne Bainbridge undoubtedly put there as he tended to his beloved roses.

And that word is *Millie.*

Chapter 1

I t was always the same. She was in her aunt and uncle's house, the house she grew up in, looking for the little girl.

Outside the wind howled as a mounting sense of dread propelled her down the hall. There was her room, with the pink pony on her bed; there was the TV in the den, where her uncle's big chair held court; there was the old green sofa in the living room, tired and worn, as if the weight of the world was on its weary springs.

But just then there was a noise, and she cocked her head to listen. There she was. The little girl's cries were coming from her aunt and uncle's room at the end of the hall. She moved quickly and cautiously, and as she entered the room, a wave of longing hit her. There was the old afghan her aunt crocheted; the pictures of her as a child on the bedside table and her aunt's slippers at the foot of the bed, as if to guard it.

The windows in front of her rattled loudly, and the wind howled as if in pain. She saw the trees bend to its will and behind them, two stars shining brightly. They seemed too close to be real. So close you could almost touch them, and they looked more like Easter eggs, nestled into the night sky. But then she heard a whimper, and she turned her attention to the closet, where it came from. She saw the light seeping out from under its door, and as she moved toward it, it seemed to grow brighter, beckoning her. She reached out to open it and was stopped by what she saw: dark red specks of blood spattered all over her hand. A chill ran through her, and she noticed her other hand and her arms were covered in kind. She stared down at her appendages in shock, almost as if they'd betrayed her. And she couldn't help but wonder, *whose blood was it?*

Her reverie was cut short when suddenly the windows flew open, and the wind filled the room with dust. Until it was everywhere. Until there was nothing to do but let it swirl all around her. Until there was nothing to see but the red, red dust . . .

Ella's eyes flew open as she gasped for air. Sunlight assaulted her consciousness, and she was forced to pull her pillow over her head to ward it off. Her heart raced, and she bit her lip as she tried to calm it. She felt cold beads of sweat run down her neck. *It was just a dream*, she told herself. *Just the stupid, Goddam dream . . .*

She took a few deep breaths when suddenly there was the splutter and pop of a lawn mower outside the window. It was so loud, she pulled the pillow even tighter over her ears and from underneath it lamented, *Why?* Why must the gardener start so damn early? Every time she stayed at Clyde's on Sunday night, she was confronted with yard work bright and early Monday morning. She really could have used another hour of sleep, but between the dream and the lawn mower, it wasn't meant to be. So she tossed the pillow, rolled over, and saw that Clyde was already out of bed.

The clock read 7:30 a.m. Her first session was in an hour and a half. She stretched her arms above her, yawning, and felt the dull ache behind her eyes that greeted her most mornings when she'd forgotten to take her medication. Why hadn't she put the damn pills in her bag? She could see the bottle in her medicine cabinet, laughing at her. *You forgot us again!* it squealed. Fuck. Her medicine was the only thing that staved off the dream, or the nightmare, as she had come to know it. The term *dream* was usually reserved for something pleasant, wasn't it? And hers was anything but.

She heard the shower running and realized that she had a few minutes to kill, so she grabbed the remote and turned on the TV. A chirpy newscaster done up to the nines popped up on the screen. Prepared to be greeted by the political catastrophe story of the day, Ella was surprised to see that it was something about a war hero's wife being killed in a parking lot.

But the next image on the screen surprised her even more, because it was a picture of Bainbridge Psychiatric Hospital. The very hospital where she worked. Ella leaned forward and listened to the details of what seemed to have transpired the previous evening.

"Captain Oliver Haskell was taken to Bainbridge Psychiatric Hospital last night upon hearing of his wife's murder in the parking lot at Wellglad Pharmaceuticals. Captain Haskell is a decorated Iraq war veteran who planned a daring escape from the Taliban after being captured," the reporter continued, but Ella was lost in thought.

Was that why Clyde had come in past midnight last night? Had he been tending to the war hero?

Clyde Westbrook was the chief psychiatrist at Bainbridge Psychiatric Hospital and happened to be Ella's boyfriend, as well as her boss. She'd heard the rumors about his affairs with other residents when she'd started at Bainbridge and so had kept her distance from him. But he was so inquisitive and kind and didn't seem anything like the lothario she'd heard about, and soon she was captivated by him.

She kicked off the covers and headed into the bathroom, where he stood before the mirror, furiously fixing his tie. His face looked haggard from lack of sleep, which only accentuated the age difference between them; Clyde was twenty years her senior. Suddenly, the newscaster in the next room got his attention, and he shot Ella a nasty look, as if to say she knew better than to turn on the TV, and he headed to the bedroom to turn it off.

It was one of *those* mornings, she thought. Best to be quiet and give him his space. So she went to the sink, put some toothpaste on her toothbrush, and began brushing her teeth. Clyde reentered a moment later and decisively cleared his throat.

"I have some news."

Ella spat into the sink. "Uh-huh."

"I'm giving you a fairly big case."

Ella looked at him, still brushing.

"Did you hear the news last night? The war hero whose wife was murdered?" he asked.

Yes, she'd just heard, as a matter of fact. Captain Oliver Haskell had lost his wife to murder in the parking lot of Wellglad Pharmaceuticals, where she worked.

"Well, he was brought into Bainbridge late last night for observation and stayed on a volunteer basis—a wellness watch. The admitting doctor saw no signs he was suicidal, but the friend who brought him in was worried about that and thought it best to be on the safe side. Probably just shock and anxiety. Anyway ... I've decided you should handle the case. You'll have to start immediately."

Ella was stunned. She'd only recently ended her residency and was not as experienced as the other doctors on staff who would normally take on something like this. The scrutiny would be intense.

"That's pretty high profile, Clyde," Ella said, spitting out some toothpaste.

He looked at her, disappointed. "Well, if you're not ready . . ."

That stung, and it wasn't what she'd meant at all, so she scrambled. "It's not that I'm not ready, it's just . . . Aren't you worried about what people will say? That you gave it to me because of us?"

He looked at her pointedly. "I really don't waste my time with others' opinions, and I thought we agreed to keep *us* under wraps for the time being?"

"Well, I have, but it's been over four months. . . . I just thought . . ." she stumbled.

Clyde's brow furrowed. "I'm the chief psychiatrist at one of the more pre-eminent psychiatric hospitals on the East Coast and you are fresh out of your residency. Not a good idea to share with your friends. Who've you told?"

"No one," she said, somewhat put off by his insinuation.

He looked into her eyes and, seeming satisfied, said "Good." Then he kissed the top of her head and quickly walked out, saying, "You want the case or not?"

Ella looked at herself in the mirror and flushed with excitement. "Of course I want the case. I'm not an idiot!" she said, and then rinsed her mouth.

"Good. And don't worry. If there are any problems, just come to me."

He walked back in, ready for work. "I've gotta go."

Ella couldn't believe Clyde was giving her this chance and silently vowed to show him that his trust was well-placed.

She went to put her arms around his neck and kiss him, but he spoiled the moment and intercepted her hands, saying, "My jacket." As in *don't get it wet*; then he kissed her quickly. Ella felt a wave of disappointment at his unsexy behavior but quickly shrugged it off.

"I have to run. Can you lock up?" he asked, on the move.

Ella nodded and watched him go. She heard the door shut as she started the shower and went into the closet, where she'd fortunately stashed a change of clothes. She would have to hurry to Bainbridge and prep for her new case before her regular rounds. Stopping by her apartment was out of the question.

She pulled the handle on the dresser drawer, but it stuck. After some jiggling, it opened, and she grabbed her bra and panties. When she went to close it, it stuck again, which resulted in a framed picture on the dresser falling to the floor. She bent to retrieve it and stopped to study the photo.

There was Clyde amid several men on a boat, holding up a sacrificial fish. Smiling faces in hats and dark glasses to ward off the sun as they celebrated the murder of an unsuspecting tuna. As she scanned the faces, she recognized most of them as colleagues at Bainbridge. But there was one man standing next to Clyde who she didn't recognize. He was the only one not wearing sunglasses and not smiling. His gaze was quite intense. In fact, it was a bit like that of a vulture.

Maybe fishing just wasn't his thing, she thought as she put the picture back and hurried into the bathroom.

Chapter 2

Detective Paul Moran sat in his office and looked out at the clouds threatening to dump even more water on the drenched, dismal city. He was already tired of winter and it had barely begun. It must have something to do with his age, he thought. He had turned sixty-two last month, and all sorts of aches and pains had developed, as if on cue. His bones began to echo their discomfort as he shifted uneasily in his chair and loosened the metal brace that encircled his leg.

Moran was sort of a mythical figure in the Baltimore PD. Not just because he'd closed more cases than any homicide detective before him, but because he'd almost died doing it, and the tale of his injury was the stuff of legend.

He'd been tracking down a killer who had a predilection for young prostitutes, and had narrowed it down to one suspect. On the day he went to bring that suspect in, he was ambushed in a dark alley outside the man's apartment. After the man shot him, he approached Moran, who lay in a pool of his own blood. Once he was just a few feet away, Moran, with a bullet in his back, flipped over and emptied his gun, killing the suspect. He then dragged himself fifty yards to his car and called for help before he passed out and almost bled to death.

The bullet lodged next to his L6 vertebrae, and Moran had to make the difficult choice between using crutches the rest of his life but walking, or having a surgery that, if unsuccessful, would render him completely crippled. He chose the former, as the crutches against the wall behind him innocently attested.

His reputation after that preceded him wherever he went. Even though he stood just five feet six inches, had a bad leg, and was more bookish than bold, he was the best that the Baltimore PD had to offer. But right now, none of that mattered. He just ached.

It also didn't help that he'd spent half the night in Wellglad Pharmaceuticals' parking lot and only gotten about three hours of sleep before he came back to work this morning. But it couldn't be helped, he thought, and looked down at his notepad, perusing what he had so far.

Hannah Lloyd Haskell—born September 14, 1985. Lancaster, Pennsylvania. Father was a high school English teacher and mother taught science.

In 2003, Hannah attended Yale on a full scholarship and graduated summa cum laude. PhD in microbiology from the University of Pennsylvania in 2010. Worked for Wellglad Pharmaceutical 2010–present.

Captain Oliver Haskell—born May 20, 1982. Mother Barbara Haskell, deceased. Father Jerry Haskell, whereabouts unknown.

Enlisted in the Army after high school for two years (Army paid for undergrad and postgraduate studies).

Accepted to Yale undergrad in 2003. 2007 went to Penn Law School. Reached the rank of captain in 2010, served in Afghanistan and Iraq. Received a Purple Heart for his bravery in leading men out of Taliban capture in 2015. Discharged with distinction 2024. Running for US Senate, Maryland, 2024.

So, Hannah Haskell was thirty-nine years old. Young, thought Moran. Too young to die.

He sat back when his partner of twentysome-odd years, Detective Alonso Scarpetti, glided into his office. Scarpetti was a handsome man in his late fifties with an enormous zest for life. A ballroom dancer with quite a few competitions under his belt, he cut an elegant figure for a detective. He was also blessed with a wicked sense of humor that fended off his colleagues' jokes about his aforementioned hobby. This made him the perfect partner for Detective Paul Moran.

"Got a few things," he quipped.

Moran nodded, ready to listen.

"As far as Wellglad, there are cameras on the front and sides of the building that cover the perimeter and entrance, but as you know, there is a wall around the perimeter that blocks the view. We see Hannah Haskell on the front entrance camera entering the building at 4:19 p.m. and exiting the building at 4:43, but once she's beyond the gate at the wall, there's no street or parking lot view. So, no help there.

"Also, it seems there are no cameras on any of the streets around that area since it's still pretty remote. I checked with traffic, and the only camera up on State Street isn't functioning, so—there's that. And since I knew you would ask, I checked, and there are no cameras on the street from Haskell's house to Wellglad. Both are on the outskirts of town.

"As for the garage itself, anyone could have gotten into it. It has the main gated entrance for cars on the west side, but the north and east sides have a three-foot wall that anybody can jump over. The south side has an entrance for a few cars, but the rest is completely walled off."

Moran nodded. He'd canvassed the area when he was there last night and realized it was wide open.

"What about Captain Haskell's timeline?" he asked.

Scarpetti gave him a look, then flipped through his notes. "I only have what he told us last night: that his wife left the house for Wellglad about four p.m. and he left half an hour to forty-five minutes later, so four thirty or four forty-five p.m. Talked to the valet at the fundraiser cocktail party, who said he arrived around five ten p.m."

"That's a bit strange," Moran interjected. "He's the guest of honor and he's late?"

"I knew you were gonna say that, so I had Ross look into it, and given the traffic last night, it being Sunday, he probably could have driven from his house to the party in as little as twenty minutes, but it probably shouldn't have taken him forty minutes unless he made another stop he didn't tell us about."

Moran nodded. "So, there could be as much as twenty minutes that he hasn't accounted for."

Scarpetti frowned. "Yeah, but come on. He'd just been told his wife was murdered, so unless we interview him again—that time's not going to hold. And even if what you're saying is right and he left at four thirty, then—what? He drives to Wellglad, kills his wife, and then gets back into his car and drives to a cocktail party? I don't know. Seems a little far-fetched to me, Paul."

Scarpetti looked through his notes again. "Oh, the security guard said that they've been seeing more vagrants recently, and let's not forget the train passes directly behind Wellglad. So, if some freighthopper decided to get off there, we could potentially be looking at someone from outta state."

Moran remained quiet but frowned slightly. He didn't relish the idea of it being someone from out of state. But it was more than that bothering him. Something just didn't feel right. He knew the consensus at the department was that it was a mugging gone wrong—that a homeless crack addict had tried to mug Hannah Haskell. That she had fought back or tried to get away and had been thrown down, hitting her head against the pavement, killing her.

The fact that her credit cards and phone were still on her pointed to someone just wanting to score some quick cash. Normally, Moran would agree with that, but after meeting her husband, he just didn't know.

People handled things differently, but most relatives of crime victims literally fell to pieces on being told a loved one had died. And in fairness, it wasn't that Captain Haskell hadn't seemed upset hearing about his wife. No, he was so distressed he'd gone into the entryway bathroom and said he'd been sick. Only to reappear a few moments later with the water he'd splashed on his face still dripping onto his dress shirt collar. But when he spoke, he'd seemed so detached that Moran wasn't sure exactly what was going on inside his head. It had felt as if the captain was not there but quite aware at the same time.

Moran had put it down to shock. Not exactly shock to the point where he couldn't function. Quite the contrary, in fact. He was lucid and capable. But his eyes seemed somewhat dead for lack of a better word, and gave away no emotion.

Perhaps it was Captain Haskell's many years of being in the service and dealing with things most people should never experience. Civil War General William Sherman had coined the phrase "War Is Hell," and Moran agreed with that. Too often, he'd seen firsthand what combat had done to those returning home. And it was never good.

But something about Captain Haskell made Moran feel oddly uneasy. It was as if he was taking everything in quite carefully but giving no hint as to what his reason for doing so was. And it bothered the detective.

"Look, I trust your hunches," Scarpetti said. "You know I do. But I think it's far more likely that she was the victim of a meth fiend than her husband. I mean, think about it: Is he really going to kill his wife in her office parking garage? He doesn't strike me as dumb, Boss. And if it was a crime of passion, it probably would've happened at their home."

In murder cases like this, law enforcement always looked at the boyfriend or the spouse first, and Moran felt that this case wasn't any different. But he had to agree with the logic of what Scarpetti was saying, and so he nodded reluctantly.

"Don't you think it's kind of weird that he called Levine to come over last night? And after Levine spends some time with him, he asks us to escort him and the captain to the psychiatric hospital?" Moran asked.

Arthur Levine was head of one of the big law firms in Baltimore that catered to the very wealthy. He also happened to be an excellent litigator.

Scarpetti shrugged. "Said he's a friend of the family, works for his campaign. The guy probably didn't know what to do and was glad we were there."

He looked at his notes. "Levine came at nine p.m., and we went to Bainbridge around ten. Just FYI."

Moran nodded. "Did Captain Haskell seem emotionally unhinged to you last night?"

Scarpetti thought about that. "Not so you'd notice, but he was a little edgy. And you know, somebody suffers something like that, they can go down at any time, right?"

"I suppose," said Moran. "I just can't help but wonder if Levine's setting things up for a temporary insanity plea."

Scarpetti shook his head doubtfully. "I don't see it, Boss."

Moran sighed and changed gears. "Did you speak to any friends or family?"

Scarpetti flipped through his notes again. "He doesn't have any living family. She was an only child. Mother's deceased. Spoke with the caregiver for her father, who has MS. She was very upset when I told her. Said Hannah was a wonderful daughter. She had only good things to say about Haskell too. Said they had a good marriage. I mean, I didn't ask much about it since he isn't a suspect. Right?"

Moran nodded, frowning. No, he wasn't a suspect. And if they wanted to pursue him as one, they would need solid evidence because he was a popular public figure, and Moran would be in the middle of a political shitstorm if he started making accusations he couldn't back up. Ah, well, it would all be revealed, he thought. Things usually were in the end.

Scarpetti continued, "Forensics confirmed death by blunt force trauma to the head. Looks like she was pushed, hit her head on the concrete, and bled out. They found what looked like a partial print on her neck, and there was bruising on her arm, as if someone had grabbed her. Uh . . ." He flipped his note over to read the back of the paper: " . . . there were a few hairs, and they'll try to grab some DNA and will get back to us."

Moran nodded. "Thanks."

"You got it," Scarpetti replied, closing his notebook. He then did a pirouette and headed out the door.

Chapter 3

Ella's headaches started when she was ten years old, and they had put her on a migraine medication that, fortunately, alleviated the pain. But it did a lot more, too, that Ella could never quite tell the doctors. Sometimes, she experienced auras with the headaches, and her vision would blur or be lost altogether. When that happened, a strange sort of shift occurred, and she felt as if she wasn't in her body, even though her senses seemed to become much more acute in a strange sort of way. It was like she was floating and able to feel everyone and everything around her—just not herself.

Even stranger, when the headaches were over, she was always shocked by how long they'd lasted. For some reason, it felt as if they'd gone on for an hour or so when, in reality, they could last for days. This loss of time made Ella feel as though she was tethered to the here and now by a very thin thread, and that scared her. But the medication had changed all of that, as well as halting the nightmare she was prone to having. God bless modern medicine. But of course, she'd forgotten to bring her medicine to Clyde's, and now her head was throbbing.

Her appointment with Captain Haskell was in just under an hour, and she needed to prepare. This was a big case and very high profile, and she found herself marveling in the Uber on the way over that Clyde had given it to her at all. To make matters worse, the damn press, with their cameras and vans, had camped out at the hospital's front entrance, so Ella had to go in the back way through the C Wing of Bainbridge, where the criminally insane were kept, and it had taken her an extra ten minutes to get through the guarded checkpoint. Ten minutes she really didn't have.

As she walked up the stairs toward the old brick entrance, she looked around at the hospital grounds nestled in the woods and felt a sense of belonging that she didn't really feel anywhere else. She'd noticed it the first time she came here, when she was interviewing for her residency. It was an incredibly strange feeling, as if Bainbridge had some magnetic power over her.

She walked past the small statue of Wayne Bainbridge and entered the building. She'd read a little about the man's tragic life and thought it terribly unfair. He'd done a lot for the field of psychiatry, yet you rarely heard anything about him.

She made her way down the hall toward the receptionist, Jenny, who was talking on the phone. Jenny had been here as long as anyone could remember and seemed to run the place, which she didn't mind letting everyone know. Ella prayed she could slip quietly past her but, unfortunately, she hung up the phone at that moment and locked her eyes on Ella.

"Dr. Kramer! I guess congratulations are in order. I understand you landed your first case!" she said with syrupy sweetness.

Ella felt like a trapped rat. "Oh well, yes. Thank you."

"Poor man," Jenny continued. "Can you imagine the pain he's going through? He can't even suffer in privacy, poor thing. We're getting a billion calls from news outlets every hour. What a nightmare. God, that poor, poor man."

Ella cringed slightly and got the feeling that Jenny was more impressed with the news outlets than she was concerned about Captain Haskell.

"Yes, it's very sad. Well, I really need to get going, Jenny," Ella said, moving off.

"Good for you, Dr. Kramer. Just out of your residency. Way to take the initiative!" Jenny called after her, making her cringe again.

She suddenly worried that Jenny knew what was going on between her and Clyde, which sent a jolt of panic through her. If Jenny knew, then everyone did. *Christ.*

She entered her office, picking up the mail from the letter box on the door, and pulled out Captain Oliver Haskell's case file left there by Clyde.

She quickly scanned Captain Haskell's psychological and medical workups and saw that they both looked normal. His Army psychiatric discharge showed no sign of PTSD either, which was uncommon among veterans. That was impressive.

She then looked at his Bainbridge admit referral. He'd broken down and become despondent upon hearing of his wife's murder from the police. Was admitted by a Mr. Levine, who informed the charge nurse that Captain Haskell had said more than once that "he felt like dying."

Ella went through the night nurse's notes: *Vitals: good. Shock/Depressed affect. Administered Klonopin, 5mg. Slept fitfully. Woke at three a.m. and became aggressive. 10mg Klonopin administered.*

The aggression was a little weird. It didn't quite fit with his shock and depressed affect, but maybe it was because he was a soldier. Or it was simply a result of his wife's murder. To understand what Captain Haskell was going through, she needed to know exactly what had happened to his wife last night to better approach him.

This was where she and Clyde disagreed, theoretically speaking. Ella liked taking a broader look at a patient and wanted to know the precursor of their psychological response in order to address it. Clyde looked only at how the psychological response manifested and dealt with those manifestations regardless of the patient's history. Ella secretly worried that psychiatry had become less about caring for patients and more about medicating them, and she disagreed with this standard approach.

She pulled out a bottle of Advil Extra Strength from her drawer and took four of them. If she doubled the dose, the ache at her temples would diminish for a while.

She powered up her computer and began scrolling through news sites for information on Hannah Haskell's murder and stopped at an article with the headline:

HANNAH HASKELL, WIFE OF SENATE HOPEFUL, CPT. OLIVER HASKELL, MURDERED

Above the headline was a picture of Oliver and Hannah taken some years before. The two had their arms around each other as they smiled at the camera, the sun on their faces. She looked so happy, Ella thought. As if the whole world lay before them, with nothing but promise.

She scrolled down and saw another picture of Hannah. This time, she was surrounded by a team of scientists with a caption that read:

Dr. Haskell is known for leading the team at Wellglad Pharmaceuticals that developed Lyprophan, a revolutionary new antidepressant. Lyprophan has only been on the market for a few months but has met with huge success.

Ella looked at the picture and noticed the man standing next to Hannah was the one she'd seen in the photograph in Clyde's closet. The one with the sour expression on his face on the boat. She glanced at the names in the caption and saw that he was Edward "Ned" Dowd, the CEO of Wellglad Pharmaceuticals. What a small world, she thought. Coincidences like this always fascinated Ella, who paid attention to them almost as if they were messages.

But right now, she needed to focus on Hannah Haskell, though, so she scrolled until she saw a picture of Captain Haskell with the caption:

She is survived by her husband, Captain Oliver Haskell, a Purple Heart recipient who served in Afghanistan in 2015. Haskell is up for Senator Hewitt's seat in the midterms. He could not be reached for comment, and it is questionable if he will continue with his bid for the US Senate.

Chapter 4

Sebastian Crown sat in the La-Z-Boy recliner in the TV room, which faced the window where he took his sun. He'd done this every morning since he came to Bainbridge some thirty years ago. Of course, in the beginning he was housed in the C Wing with the criminals, even though he was just fifteen at the time and saw himself as more of an avenging angel for killing the father who had beaten him and his mother almost daily for most of his young life.

Fortunately, his mother, who hailed from Savannah, Georgia, had made a considerable donation to the hospital, and the doctors moved him to the men's ward for nonviolent offenders, known as B Wing.

Right now, no one else was in the TV room, and Sebastian had the luxury of thinking his thoughts without interruption. It was bad enough the *Others* crowded him out and made him lose time, but to be surrounded by nothing but idiots all day was just the outside of enough. Why, he thought, could insane people not live up to their film-inspired reputations and be highly intelligent like him, or at least passably interesting? He'd found most of the patients here at Bainbridge incredibly dull.

Of course, there were always exceptions. One was an arsonist named Fletcher, who he'd met in C Wing many years ago. Fletch, as he called him, had looked out for Sebastian during those early years and had just a wonderful sense of humor. And, as Sebastian had come to find out, he also had a penchant for watching people burn to death.

Another person who fell into the exceptional category was his resident doctor, Ella Kramer. First off, she was a woman, and he liked women. Not in that way, of course. No, in that way he'd always preferred his own sex, but what with all the drugs they'd given him over the years, it was a wonder he had any preference left at all.

Dr. Kramer was a breath of fresh air here at Bainbridge, with its stuffy collection of shrinks who talked down to him. He could really speak to her, and she always made Sebastian feel seen. She made him feel as if they were equals and, sometimes, in small ways, he could tell that she looked up to him and even celebrated his "uniqueness," if there was such a word. Dr. Kramer was just wonderful, unlike that horrid receptionist, Jenny. How he wished ol' Fletch could set that nasty woman alight. That'd be a barbecue worth attending.

The sun began to wander higher in the sky, and he realized that he didn't have much time before the lunatics descended. As if on cue, he heard voices in the hallway just outside. One belonged to Eddie, the head nurse, speaking with someone whose voice Sebastian didn't recognize. He poked his head around to get a better look and saw Eddie typing on his tablet with a new patient at his side.

Eddie, looking confused by what he saw on his screen, gestured to the couch in the TV room.

"Why don't you rest there a minute while I go find out exactly who you are supposed to be meeting with this morning? I'll be right back."

The new patient did just that, and Eddie lit off down the hall.

How unprofessional, thought Sebastian. Unprofessional but fortuitous. Sebastian loved meeting new people, and this was someone he would like to meet, so he pushed the hair off his face and stood. All six feet three inches and 250 pounds of him. He tucked in his shirt with some difficulty and wished he'd lost some of the holiday weight he'd sworn to shed. Then he turned and approached the newcomer.

The man sat on the couch fiddling with the TV remote and didn't seem to notice him. So Sebastian cleared his throat before saying in his thick Southern drawl, "Good morning." He extended his hand. "I don't believe we have met. Sebastian Crown at your service."

The man looked up, and Sebastian got the distinct impression that he'd seen him before. He couldn't place him, but it wouldn't surprise Sebastian if he were a movie star or something. He certainly had the looks for it.

They shook hands, and Sebastian was struck by how blue the man's eyes were. Eyes the color of the water Sebastian so loved to splash in when he and his mother, Earline, summered in Key Biscayne all those years ago.

"Oliver Haskell," said the stranger.

"Do you mind?" asked Sebastian, gesturing to the seat next to him. The man shrugged and turned his attention back to scrolling through the channels on the TV, which was blessedly muted.

What a wonderful distraction, thought Sebastian. He loved figuring people out, which probably stemmed from being his mother's closest confidant at a very young age. After all, who had Earline had to talk to about their shared abuse? Him! And only him since, for she had forbade him from telling anyone. Appearances were very important to Earline. Appearances and money. Lucky for her, she now had Sebastian's entire fortune, *his birthright*, because of what Sebastian had done. And how had she thanked him? By locking him up in a mental hospital out of state. That was how!

She'd barely visited him during his first decade here, and after that, all it took was one outburst from Nadine and Earline had never shown her face at Bainbridge again. Now, granted, Nadine had tried to strangle Earline on that visit, but that wasn't her fault. No! She was just doing what she'd always done, which was to protect him. Someone had to!

But he mustn't think about his mother now or Nadine would make an appearance and he'd be put on restriction again. So, he made himself comfortable on the couch while Oliver struggled with the Volume button on the remote. Suddenly, the TV blasted loud cartoon music, and it was obvious the newbie needed help. Sebastian put out his hand for the remote, which the man handed over, gently brushing Sebastian's hand, which thrilled Sebastian more than he could say.

"Idiots in this place have completely destroyed the damn remote. But Sebastian Crown seems to have just the right touch."

After a few seconds of fiddling, the volume went down to a consumable level, and he handed it back.

"Be forewarned—do not lose the remote or give it to Petey, because he will hide it, and then the other monkeys will go apeshit!"

He laughed at his little play on words. Hadn't even intended to say it that way, but that was just the way his mind worked.

"Many a fight has ensued over the precious remote. Full-scale mutinies!" he added. "Sometimes Petey takes it, and the entire floor gets involved. It's a kook-fest! And all the nurses come running, syringes at the ready!"

But the man didn't seem to be listening as he proceeded to go from one channel to the next.

Sebastian watched him, intrigued. How the hell did he know this guy? He didn't want to be rude and just blurt out, *Hey, who are you?* No, Sebastian Crown was too polite to do anything that tacky. So, he continued with polite chitchat.

"Well, Oliver, let me be the first patient to welcome you to the B Wing of Bainbridge Psychiatric Hospital, where the patients are harmless, but the boredom is lethal!"

He smiled, because that usually got a good laugh. But Oliver just kept scrolling.

Jeez, he thought, this guy was tough. Then something occurred to him: Had they overdone the Klonopin? Sebastian just hated the way they doped up the new arrivals at Bainbridge. It was so unfair, and had the unfortunate side effect of making them virtually unreachable at times.

Then, to add insult to injury, the poor things would be given another drug, and then another drug, until their minds were absolute mush. After which they would start the process of weaning them off those drugs, only to find new drugs to give them. The whole cycle was ridiculous. Half the people in there should just be put down anyway. If you could do it to a perfectly good dog for the crime of getting old, surely you could do it to some of the droolers in this place.

Drugged out or not, this man didn't seem like your average drooler. He just seemed very interested in what was on TV, and Sebastian was having a helluva time trying to engage him. So he decided to try a new tack.

"Let me start," he said pleasantly. "Why am I here? Well, many, many years ago, my father, who was horribly abusive to me and my mother, died. And of course I was the one they blamed. Even though it was Nadine. But anyway, the stress of the whole thing led to my coming somewhat *undone*, and that's why you find me here, where they've diagnosed me as having dissociative identity disorder with paranoid tendencies. Which is just a nice way of saying I have a split personality problem. My grandmother always referred to it as *losing time* when I was a kid, because I guess I would black out and one of the *Others* would take my place."

Oliver continued to flip through the channels.

"Anyway, it sounds worse than it is, and I prefer to look at the upside, which is I am always the life of the party because I bring the party with me!" With that, he threw back his head and roared with laughter.

The man turned and looked at him, amused for a second, but then quickly went back to flipping channels.

Defeated, Sebastian decided he would just have to wait until after Oliver watched a little television or the Klonopin wore off, whichever came first.

Suddenly, the CNN music came up, announcing a breaking story and, weirdly enough, he heard the announcer say something about a Captain

Oliver Haskell. Sebastian turned toward the TV, where he saw a picture of the man sitting next to him!

What happened next felt like it came straight out of a tragic novel, because Captain Oliver Haskell's picture was replaced by that of a woman named Hannah Haskell, who was obviously the captain's wife. Then, sadly, the newscaster started talking about how Hannah Haskell had just been killed.

Sebastian gasped audibly and said, "Oh my God! How awful!" and stared at the captain. "I am so sorry. So very sorry," he stammered.

And that was when things seemed to change. It was like a flip in the energy field, for Captain Haskell turned to him, and those blue eyes seemed different. They were now a dark gray and had a look in them that warned Sebastian to stop talking without the captain ever having to utter a word.

Sebastian sat there frozen. The exchange lasted a nanosecond, but he'd gotten the message loud and clear. Sebastian Crown had been around long enough to know when to be worried, and if the hair on the back of his neck was any indication, that time was now. For there'd been no expression on the captain's face yet Sebastian had felt his rage.

Sebastian's gut started writhing around in knots. He hadn't felt like this since he'd been around those men in C Wing all those years ago. The men who pretended to be friendly one second only to hurt him in terrible ways the next.

One thing was for sure: Captain Hottie here was not what he seemed.

Sebastian felt his eye begin to twitch, which was always a bad sign. A sign that he was in danger, so it would not take long for Nadine to show up. *Christ*, he thought, he had to get the hell out of there. So he sat there with his twitching eye and tried to come up with an exit strategy.

He couldn't just stand up and run, which was what he wanted to do. He'd just have to calmly make his excuses and exit as gracefully as he could, but given his size, that'd be difficult. Just getting off the couch was going to be tough. He simply had to stop eating so much!

But before he could do anything, he heard a loud banging coming from across the room. For a moment, he was grateful for the distraction, but when he turned, he felt his stomach drop in horror. At the other end of the room stood Dan, a very tall man with red hair, smacking his palm on the ping-pong table while he muttered expletives.

"No, no, no. I motherfucking cock-cock-cocksucking ... Van! Van! Van!" Dan shouted.

Oh God no, Sebastian thought, as if things could get any worse. Dan was about to have an enormous meltdown! He couldn't let that happen, not after the confusing exchange he'd just had with Captain Hottie.

"Damn it, Dan! Stop freaking out or we are all going to our rooms!" Sebastian hissed.

He turned to the captain and attempted to diffuse the situation. "That's just Dan. He's a paranoid schizophrenic with a nasty case of Tourette's. Thinks we're all out to get him and throw him in a van. He'll stop in a minute."

But Dan didn't stop, and Sebastian noticed his eyes locked onto Oliver. Clearly, something about Captain Hottie had set him off.

"No! No! No! Motherfucking Van! Van! Van!" Dan yelled angrily.

Sebastian's twitch went into high gear as he tried to reason with Dan.

"Dan, the captain is a guest, OK? And he's been through a horrible ordeal, so—knock it off!"

He turned back to the captain to apologize, but the look on his face stopped Sebastian. He was white as a ghost and his eyes were like lasers piercing the distance to Dan, studying him. Almost as if he was looking at Dan like . . . *prey*, for God's sake!

"He's really harmless," Sebastian said frantically.

The captain didn't seem to hear a word Sebastian said, and things went from horrible to hideous as other patients filed in to see what was going on. One even began to cry, pleading, "Stop it, Dan."

Not only did Dan not stop, he also began to walk toward the captain, pointing his finger accusingly. "You! You! B–bu . . ."

Dan looked like he might cry as the words stuck in his throat, but then he became enraged and started yelling, "Goddam fucking Van! Van! Van!" at the top of his lungs.

It was at this point that Sebastian realized he might end up in the middle of a full-on brawl. Dan wasn't usually like this. What the hell had happened to him? Why would he go after a complete stranger like this?

Sebastian stood, holding out his hands to ward Dan off. "For goodness' sake, Dan! Calm down!"

Instead of calming down, Dan lunged at the captain, and they both fell to the floor and began grabbing at each other. The other patients began to hoot and howl as Sebastian backed away, horrified. It was exactly these types of situations Sebastian liked to avoid, but he had to do something or Nadine would arrive and there would be hell to pay.

Fucking Dan! Captain Hottie didn't deserve this, no matter how weird he was, and if Dan got Sebastian put on restriction and stuck in his room for the rest of the day, he would just kill him, or rather, Nadine would.

The captain seemed to be handling the attack quite well, probably from all those years of training, when fortunately, an orderly entered the fray and dragged Dan off of him. Unfortunately, Dan proceeded to throw the orderly off like a rag doll and headed back to the captain, who stood there staring intently at him.

Wow, thought Sebastian, *this guy is something else!* He didn't seem scared at all. No, it was more like he was formulating a plan as he stood there quite still. *Very impressive*, thought Sebastian.

Dan, on the other hand, burst into tears, yelling, "Go back! Go back! Van! Van! Van!" And that was when another orderly arrived and hit him in the arm with a syringe.

Eddie came running in, huffing and puffing. "What the hell happened?"

Before the orderlies could answer, Dr. Westbrook entered.

"What's this?" he demanded.

Eddie stood there speechless, so the orderly explained, "Dan was attacking the new patient."

Westbrook looked at Captain Haskell, horrified, then snapped his attention back to Dan and said, "Take him to his room."

Dan began to sob loudly, saying, "But Dr. Westbrook! Make him go back! Make him go back! Bu . . ." But the orderlies dragged him out of the room as his body began to go slack from the drugs.

Westbrook turned to the captain, shaken. "Captain Haskell, I can't tell you how sorry I am. This sort of thing never happens. Are you OK?"

The captain nodded, looking at his arm, which had a scratch on it. "I'm fine."

Westbrook shot Eddie an accusatory look. "Why is he in here?"

Eddie stammered helplessly, "I left Captain Haskell here for a few minutes while I made sure of the arrangements with Dr. Kramer. I'm sorry. I should have left him in his room, but I thought you were meeting him. When I couldn't find you, I went to find Dr. Kramer."

Sebastian noticed Westbrook's face tighten. *Eddie's gonna get it now*, he thought.

But Westbrook said simply, "Very well," and turned back to the captain.

"I'm Dr. Clyde Westbrook, the chief psychiatrist at Bainbridge. Again, I cannot tell you how sorry I am about this."

He extended his hand and did something that Sebastian had never seen him do before: He looked at the captain with such trepidation that one would think he was afraid Captain Haskell might throttle him.

Sebastian had never seen Westbrook look so scared. No, never. Not once in all the years he'd known him had Dr. Clyde Westbrook ever looked at someone like he wished he could crawl under a rock and hide. Maybe he was afraid of the public relations ramifications because, let's face it, SENATE HOPEFUL BEATEN AT PSYCH HOSPITAL isn't exactly the kind of newspaper headline you'd want to see.

The captain, meanwhile, seemed to have recovered and shook Westbrook's hand with a silky-smooth composure. "That's OK," he said.

Sebastian couldn't help but notice how relieved Westbrook looked.

"As Eddie has said, Dr. Kramer will be meeting with you, but I am also here at your disposal," Westbrook said.

Then he looked to Eddie and snapped, "Have him wait in his room and I will send Dr. Kramer *to him*." Meaning that was how it should have been handled in the first place. And then Westbrook left.

"Of course, Dr. Westbrook," replied Eddie, still in a state of shock. And he led Captain Hottie back to the room he should never have let him leave.

Sebastian stood there in disbelief at what had just transpired and said to no one in particular, "Well, shut my mouth! The mighty Westbrook quaking in his boots! I never thought I'd live to see the day."

And as he watched Captain Oliver Haskell being led down the hall, his eyes narrowed and he murmured quietly to himself, "You somethin', honey."

Chapter 5

Ella was still going over Oliver Haskell's file when there was a knock at her office door and Clyde walked in. Ella had never seen him look so—freaked out—for lack of a better term.

"You OK?" she asked.

But it was as if he didn't hear her, he was so preoccupied with whatever had happened to him.

Ella got up and went to him. "Clyde, what is it?"

He looked at her anxiously. "Eddie left Captain Haskell alone in the TV room and Dan physically attacked him."

Ella'd witnessed her fair share of squabbling between patients at Bainbridge, but physical altercations? Those were very rare in the B Wing. And they usually did not involve someone like Dan, who was known as a gentle giant.

"What happened?" she asked.

"Who the hell knows? He was in there with Sebastian, and the orderlies had to subdue him!"

Ella became alarmed. Sebastian was her patient. She hoped he hadn't done anything to get Dan's goat. He could be mischievous at times.

"How is Captain Haskell?" she asked.

"Fine. He seemed calm, but of course this will get around." Clyde ran his hand through his hair. "Christ, why the hell is he *here*?"

Ella gave Clyde a funny look. What did that mean? Haskell had obviously suffered a breakdown. That was why he was here.

"Clyde, calm down. It does no good to get worked up," she said. "It's going to be OK." And she kissed him softly.

He stared at her strangely, then returned the kiss hungrily, pulling her to him, which surprised Ella.

"Clyde …" she timidly protested. But he didn't stop, and she felt a weird kind of desperation driving him.

"Clyde, stop," she admonished him again when suddenly the door was opened by one of Ella's colleagues, Dr. Gary Lester, who stared at the two lovers, unsure what to do.

Clyde immediately jumped away from Ella and began talking about the Haskell case.

"So, you should have everything you need. I told Eddie you would meet him in his room. Let me know how it goes."

This confused Ella, who thought he would want to be present for the initial meeting. "You're not going with me?" she asked.

"No, it's your case. I'll just be there for backup. Give me a report later."

Ella was thrilled and terrified all at once. "Of course," she said.

Clyde exited, mumbling, "Dr. Lester," as he went.

Gary stared at the floor and mumbled back, "Dr. Westbrook."

But as soon as the door shut, he looked at Ella incredulously. "Oh my God! You and Westbrook?"

"Shh! No one knows, and I'd like to keep it that way," she pleaded. "You can't tell anyone, Gary. OK?"

"Oh, this is huge!" he said, teasing her.

Ella looked at him imploringly, and he mimed zipping his lips.

"Sealed. Steel vault."

Ella nodded gratefully.

Gary eyed the file on her desk. "He gave you the Haskell case? I had no idea you were such a clever little minx!"

She whacked him with the file, joking, "Gary! I mean it."

He held up his hands. "No. Hey, listen—I'd sleep with him if he would give me a prestigious case like that!"

Ella gathered up her things to go. "You might wanna tell your wife that."

Gary nodded. "She knows."

He picked up the newspaper from her desk and glanced at the article. "War hero's wife. Juicy stuff. The nurses were all atwitter this morning. Apparently, he's a real looker. Not in my league, of course."

"Is anyone?" She laughed.

"Exactly." He scrutinized the article. "Bet he was having an affair and she caught him and things got ugly. What say you, my little alienist? Temporary insanity?"

"Him or you?" she answered, heading out the door, Gary close on her heels.

"Well, I for one am not about to let an opportunity like this go to waste. Since you two are an item, can you ask him to look at my proposal on binary light treatment again? He's had it for months and keeps putting me off. And we both know you're nothing if you aren't published. Well, of course *you* are, you little tart."

Ella laughed again as Gary opened his office door.

"I've reminded him a couple of times, but I will again. Wanna get lunch later?" she asked.

"Can't. Giving a lecture at the university today. Wish me luck."

"Good luck!" she said, continuing down the hall. And as she walked, she felt as if a weight had been lifted from her shoulders. She was so tired of the secrecy about their relationship that Clyde demanded. She understood why, but it was annoying.

Maybe being discovered was a good thing. Maybe now Clyde would be more inclined to be open about their relationship. With those happy thoughts, she turned the corner and was about to open the hallway door when she stopped.

Through the glass pane, she saw Clyde talking with a pharma rep with the WELLGLAD logo emblazoned on her rolling drug case. That was weird, she thought. Another strange coincidence.

The woman was about Ella's age, maybe a few years older, but perfectly coiffed. She stood very close to Clyde, laughing at something he'd just said, and Ella felt herself flush.

But it was Clyde's face that made her heart stop. She'd seen that look before. It was a mixture of curiosity and lust that always sent Ella reeling. Here he was, moments after kissing her hungrily, looking at the pharma rep in much the same way. Ella's gaze remained transfixed on the two as they flirted.

So this was why he hadn't wanted anyone to know about them. So he could continue to play the field. Christ, what a fool she'd been. Everything she'd heard about him was true after all.

She watched as he put a hand to the small of the woman's back, then turned and pointed toward her as he gave the pharma rep directions. Ella jumped away from the door, hoping they hadn't seen her. And then she heard their voices getting closer, and she realized they were headed her way.

She quickly ducked into the room across the hall and held her breath as they passed by, the pharma rep tightly gripping Clyde's arm. Ella's blood boiled. What a fool she'd been, she thought again, and fought the urge to be sick. She couldn't be this person, this cliché. She took a minute to catch her breath and was about to leave her perch when she heard a voice behind her.

"Dr. Kramer?"

She spun around and saw Annie Chu, the admitting property nurse.

"Can I help you with something?"

"Oh, hi, Annie," Ella said, fighting to regain her composure. "Well, yes. I've been assigned a case and thought I would look at the patient's belongings, if that's OK. You know, to sort of get a sense of who I'm dealing with." Suddenly, she realized how bizarre that must've sounded and wanted to flee. "But if it's too much trouble . . ."

Annie chimed in eagerly. "No trouble at all, Dr. Kramer. Not at all. And may I say, well done. A lot of doctors don't take the time to understand their patients, and a person's belongings are an integral part of that, if you ask me." And without missing a beat, she asked, "Now, who is the patient?"

Ella answered haltingly, "Haskell. Oliver Haskell."

"Oh! The celebrity! He came in last night." Annie turned to her computer and scrolled through her files. "Here we go. Just gimme a second." With that, she took out her keys and opened the door to the adjoining room. Ella heard her shuffle around for a minute, only to return with a white envelope that she handed to her, as well as a bag of his clothes. "This is it."

Ella took the envelope and pulled out Haskell's wallet. She felt foolish performing this charade, and guilty for going through the captain's things.

Inside the wallet, she found his credit cards, driver's license, and what looked to be a worn picture folded and tucked into a little side pocket. She pulled it out and unfolded it. It was a worn photo of Hannah and him at their wedding. They were laughing at the camera and pointing to the wedding bands on their hands, à la, *We did it!* Ella looked at the two young faces and felt horrible that she had intruded on their privacy.

Annie leaned over to see the photo. "So sad. I heard her head was bashed in."

Ella quickly refolded the photo and tucked it back into its hiding spot, then poured out the remainder of the contents in the envelope: a piece of spearmint gum and a chain with his dog tags on it. She looked at the dog tags for a few seconds, then decided she'd seen enough. She returned his things to the envelope and handed it to Annie.

"Thanks so much, Annie. That was very helpful," she said, and turned to leave.

"Kinda odd, don't you think?" Annie asked suspiciously.

Oh Christ, thought Ella. She just wanted to get out of there. "What?"

"No wedding ring." Annie shook her head, disgusted. "Walter used to do that to me. Take off his ring when he'd go out to meet the slut he was having an affair with. Took me a few times finding it left in his sock drawer before I confronted him. Of course he lied straight to my face. Couldn't lie his way out of it when I followed him to her apartment, though. That was a scene, I can tell you."

Ella was sure it was, but this admission by her colleague left her embarrassed and sad. She'd suddenly caught a glimpse of Annie's life, and it felt like an omen.

What women had gone through because of men. Fucking unfaithful men.

"Have a good day, Dr. Kramer," Annie said, scooping up the envelope and bag of clothing and heading back to the room where they had come from.

Chapter 6

She made her way to Captain Haskell's room and took a few deep breaths to clear her mind before she knocked. She heard a low, "Come in," and pushed the door open to find him standing by the window.

Captain Haskell was a tall, good-looking man with broad shoulders and muscular arms. His sandy hair was disheveled, though in a way that made him look more vulnerable than pathetic. But it was his eyes that disarmed her: pale blue pools that looked at her intensely. Almost as if he was looking through her for a truth she was unaware of.

She felt herself flush but recovered quickly and extended her hand only to drop her pen, which he quickly picked up and handed to her.

Ella flushed again. "Thank you so much," she said, willing herself to get it together. "Captain Haskell, I am Dr. Kramer. I will be working with you during your stay with us."

He nodded, his brow furrowing as he seemed to study her, which only made Ella more nervous.

"Shall we sit?" she heard herself chirp and was immediately aware of the octave her voice had just increased.

He followed her to the table and planted himself across from her.

"How are you feeling this morning?" she asked.

"I feel calm," he replied.

"Yes," she said. "They've given you some Klonopin to make you more comfortable."

Haskell seemed to take this information in stride and said nothing.

Ella continued, "I understand there was a bit of a scuffle in the TV room this morning. Are you all right?"

"I'm fine," he said.

"This sort of thing rarely happens, and I'm sorry you had to deal with it," she said, waiting for a response. But none came.

She flipped through his file and zeroed in on something with her pen, which she noticed shook a tiny bit.

"I wanted to ask you if you or any member of your family has had a history of depression?"

He shook his head.

She noted that down.

"Any history of mental illness?" she asked.

He sighed, as if somewhat annoyed, and said, "No," and before she could go on, he added, "Nor have I ever been diagnosed with PTSD or GAD*."

And the way he said it was as if he knew those questions were coming and he wanted her to pick it up and move on. She felt the dull ache move back into her temple, while a few beads of perspiration sprang up on her neck. This hadn't started well.

She put down her pen, took a breath, and decided to tackle things head-on.

"Well, first, let me say how sorry I am about your wife. An experience like that is truly devastating."

He nodded but gave no reaction save for his jaw tensing.

"Would you like to share with me what you're feeling?"

He stared out the window for a moment, and the sunlight gave his blue eyes a translucent quality that seemed otherworldly. He looked down at his hands for a moment, then shook his head. "I don't know," he said, and went back to looking out the window.

And that was it. His silence was resounding. She looked down at his admit report and decided to dive in.

"When you were brought in last night, the nurse said that your friend was worried you could hurt yourself. Is that what you felt like last night? Hurting yourself?" she asked carefully.

"I felt horrible last night. But no, I wasn't suicidal. My lawyer and the police apparently thought so, but I don't think I am capable of that."

And it was said in a way that almost made it seem as if he was the one doing the assessing.

"Can you tell me more about how you felt?" she pushed gently.

He met her gaze and shook his head, and Ella suddenly got the feeling he was standing ten feet behind his gaze somewhere, watching.

_____

* Generalized Anxiety Disorder

Oh dear, she thought, flustered. This was going to be tough. She looked at the admit report again.

"Do you remember saying that you 'didn't feel like living'?" she asked gently.

And that's when those beautiful blue eyes darkened and he snapped, "I'd just found out my wife was murdered!"

Ella jumped involuntarily, and he quickly apologized. "I'm sorry. It's just been . . ."

"I understand," she said quickly, wanting to kick herself. She was blowing it, she thought, still a little stunned by his anger. And now he was a million miles away again, staring out the window. *Great.*

She had thought being direct was the best approach, but she'd obviously miscalculated. It almost seemed as if he was hell-bent on shutting her out. He didn't seem like he was in shock. Nor did he seem dissociated. It was more like he wanted to keep whatever he really felt concealed, and she didn't understand that. He had come here voluntarily, so one would assume he came for help, which made this silence of his kind of baffling.

Perhaps being in the military had made him excessively stoic. Or maybe it was because she was a woman. Or maybe the fact that he was a public person made him second-guess his coming here.

He didn't seem suicidal to her, at least not in the typical way, and his admit report made no mention of anything that would cause very much alarm. Just flat affect. He was dealing with a terrible loss, so of course he was depressed. It all seemed straightforward to her. But apparently it wasn't.

Christ, she thought, *what if he continued to stonewall her?* Then she would have to tell Clyde. The thought of this caused a wave of fear and anger to pulse through her. That was not happening. She'd struggled against tremendous odds to get to where she was now, and she wasn't going to let the captain's silence derail her. She would just have to change course.

"Captain Haskell, would you mind if we went over yesterday's events? Would that be OK?" she asked calmly.

He looked somewhat wary but nodded.

"So, you woke up . . ."

He responded carefully, "I got up around eight."

"And then?"

"And then I went for a run."

"And after that?"

"I came home and made pancakes for Hannah. That was her favorite." Here he took a moment to remember. "Been doing it since we were in college."

"How long were you and your wife together?" she asked.

"Twenty-one years this March. Married for seventeen. We met at Yale, when we were freshmen," he answered.

"Twenty-one years. That's a long time."

He nodded. "I was away for a lot of it. I enlisted in the Army after high school. I retired nine months ago."

He was relaxing. Now she was getting somewhere.

"And so, after you ate breakfast, what did you do?" she asked.

He stared off, remembering. "We read the papers, showered, and then left around noon and ran some errands."

"What kind of errands?"

"We're redoing the entryway bathroom , so we went to a tile place and picked up the tile she wanted. Then we grabbed some burgers and headed home about three."

She took note of the fact that he used time to anchor his recollections. Captain Haskell was probably a very punctual person.

"And then?" she continued.

"I worked on my speech—I was speaking at a fundraiser that night. And she just did stuff around the house."

She nodded for him to continue.

"Then Hannah went to work at around four or so, and I got dressed and headed out for the fundraiser at about four thirty."

"Your wife worked on weekends?"

"Sometimes. She was very dedicated to her research," he said, his jaw tensing.

Ella waited, thinking he wanted to say more, but he didn't. "So you went to the fundraiser without your wife?"

He got very quiet, looked down, and shook his head guiltily. "She didn't want to go." And for the first time, his face began to betray sadness.

"Why not?" Ella pressed gently.

"Because it was Sunday, and she didn't like doing campaign events. She wanted to spend the weekend alone, like we had in Hawaii. We were there a week ago. Just the two of us. Looking forward to the future and our lives together."

There was something about this last statement that landed oddly to Ella, yet she wasn't sure why.

"I called her. On my way to the event," he continued. "I wanted her to change her mind and come, but she never called me back, and now . . . I'll never see her again."

He turned his head away, fighting back tears, and it was clear to Ella that Captain Haskell, like many family members of victims, was dealing with the guilt of remaining alive after his wife had been killed.

"I understand," she said softly.

Ella breathed a little easier, relieved she was able to break through his defenses and get him to this point. But for some reason, she still felt off or underwhelmed, for lack of a better word. She hadn't connected with the captain the way she normally did with patients and she didn't know why. He was a different breed, that was for sure, but Ella worried that it was because of what had just happened with Clyde and the pharma rep in the hall. Thinking about Clyde made her heart ache, and she suddenly felt very sad and alone.

She looked up at the captain and reflected on how sad and lonely he must feel right now. What he'd gone through was immeasurably worse. Overcome with empathy, Ella did something she never did; she reached out and took his hand.

"It's always a shock to lose someone we love," she said gently. "But this kind of tragedy is so painful. It's hard, but try not to blame yourself for what you did or didn't do."

He wiped his eyes before turning back to her and nodded gratefully. But then he looked down at the table pointedly. And when she followed his gaze, she saw that he was staring at her hand, which was still resting on his.

Suddenly, Ella felt very foolish. It had been a natural gesture on her part. A kind one. She'd wanted to comfort him. Perhaps she'd been a little too familiar, she thought, as her face flushed with embarrassment. She pulled her hand away quickly, leaving his alone on the table and, strangely, she found herself captivated by it.

His was a delicate hand, with long, elegant fingers, which she found somewhat dissonant with his very rugged masculinity. But then she noticed something else: his lovely caramel-colored tan. The same tan that set off the blue in his eyes so beautifully was there on his hand, too. Probably from Hawaii. And it was uniform, except for what appeared to be a lighter ring of skin on his wedding finger.

Ella flashed to the property room and remembered there was no wedding ring in his belongings, and Annie's words echoed quietly somewhere in the back of her mind.

She was abruptly brought back from this reverie by Captain Haskell's voice.

"Thank you, Dr. Kramer. Thank you for helping me."

And there was something so strange about his acknowledgment that suddenly her antennae went up, and her gut seemed to pronounce that this was a red flag moment. But it was the look in his eyes that troubled her even more.

Gone was the feeling that he'd been struggling to find his emotions, only to be replaced by the notion that he was quite satisfied with their interaction and, even stranger, with his part in it.

It wasn't smugness, but there was something she couldn't quite put her finger on. It left her feeling something akin to the way one would feel if they were playing checkers and took their eyes off the board for a second only to find that when they looked back, they had been playing chess.

"Of course," she said, taking her cue to end the session. "I think that's enough for now."

She stood and moved to leave when he stopped her.

"Would it be possible for me to go outside? I hate being cooped up in here."

"Of course. I'll tell the nurse to let you take a walk after lunch, but you'll have to be accompanied," she responded.

He gave her a sad smile in response. A smile that would melt the most doubting of hearts. Such a simple response, she thought as she entered the hallway. But her gut told her that the captain was anything but simple.

She closed his door and eyed Nurse Bennet at the nurse's station. "I'm going to let him take a walk in the garden after lunch, but you have to stay with him."

Nurse Bennet nodded, and Ella quickly made her way down the hall when it dawned on her what had bothered her about the captain's statement that he and his wife were looking forward to their lives together. If you were part of a couple, wouldn't you say, "we were looking forward to our *life* together" and not "our *lives* together"?

But she dismissed the thought as quickly as it came. She wasn't in the right frame of mind to make any judgments. Not now. She had to get out of there and think. Something wasn't right. Her feelings and thoughts were at war with one another, and she couldn't trust either.

She had to go to see her aunt. Had to be around someone who loved her.

And it wasn't until she reached her office that she realized that she probably should have checked with Clyde before she gave the OK for Captain Haskell to take a walk after lunch. But at this point, she really didn't give a damn what Clyde thought.

Chapter 7

Dan lay on a surgical table, electrodes attached to his head while restraining straps held him in place. Separated from his patient by a glass partition, Dr. Westbrook and a technician sat controlling the panel in front of them.

"Let's go again," Clyde said.

The technician did as he was told, and Dan's body convulsed as electricity poured through his system.

Dan didn't know why Dr. Westbrook thought electroshock was necessary. He hadn't had one of these treatments in years, hadn't done anything to deserve it, either. He had just been trying to warn them that they were in trouble. If the trap in his throat didn't catch his words all the time—his real words and not the silly garbage he spewed—oh, the things he would tell people! All the energy dancing around them! Playing with them! Flowing through them that they didn't even know existed. It was a damn shame, he thought.

His grandmother had always told him that he was ahead of his time, and that God didn't want Dan to reveal everything he knew. She said God put some people on this planet to keep secrets and that he, Dan, was one of them. That the special trap God put in his throat was a blessing, because it was usually the truth tellers on this planet who were reviled and killed. And because it was God's way of protecting him, no matter how hard he tried he wouldn't be able to get around it.

Now, Dan loved his grandmother very much, but frankly, what she said didn't make much sense. First of all, if God didn't want him talking, why had he made Dan so aware of all the energies? The ones people never knew existed. That was weird.

And second of all, why had God given Dan such a good memory? Dan remembered everything! Every life he had ever lived. Dan's memory was endless! But what was the point of having all these memories of different lives if you couldn't share them? It just didn't make sense.

His grandmother always said history repeated itself, which was arguably true. But Dan didn't know why it had to be that way. He figured that if he could tell others God's secrets, people would stop causing all this destruction and pain. But when he'd mentioned this to his grandmother, she'd laughed and said, "You're counting on way too many people not to be stupid. But trust me, they are. Nothin' you say will change that."

Talking about how dumb people were always gave her a good laugh. And as he lay on the table, he imagined her soft chuckle and began to remember the woman who'd meant so much to him.

He remembered her kneading bread on the counter in her kitchen as he sat on a stool and watched. She would look up and give him a wink every now and then that thrilled him, for they had a secret. The rest of his family just wanted him out of the way; he was a crazy schizophrenic who spoke gibberish to them. But not her. She'd made him feel seen and loved, and when she died, he wished he could have gone with her.

But to his surprise, he never stopped feeling her around him. And he found that if he was calm and focused, he could feel her next to him, offering her pearls of wisdom.

So, as he waited for the next volt to rocket through his system, he closed his eyes and focused on his grandmother: her thick gray hair twirled up in a bun, her gnarled hands, caused by years of needlework and gardening, and her eyes that seemed green, yellow, and blue all at once. Just then, another volt shot through his system, and every muscle in his body clenched in response. And as his jaw tightened down on the rubber plate they'd stuck in his mouth, he could have sworn he heard her voice before he completely blacked out.

Chapter 8

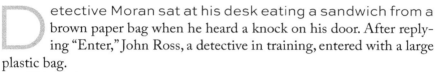

Detective Moran sat at his desk eating a sandwich from a brown paper bag when he heard a knock on his door. After replying "Enter," John Ross, a detective in training, entered with a large plastic bag.

"Here's her purse," he said, and Moran gestured for him to set it on the desk.

"Forensics dusted it?" asked Moran.

Ross pulled out the purse, which was covered in black dust. "Looks like it," he said, which earned him an annoyed look from Moran.

He would never have dreamed of being sarcastic with his superiors when he was in training. No one would have tolerated it if he had.

But today's young person seemed different to Moran. Most of them seemed completely devoid of respect for those who came before them, which annoyed him to no end. They also seemed completely enamored with fame and trying to achieve it. When you combined this with the prevalence of social media, Moran felt the beginning of the end had begun. The social fabric of the world was being obliterated, and not by nuclear bombs, as he'd always feared, but by selfies.

But he had work to do, so he put on his latex gloves and proceeded to take Hannah Haskell's belongings out of the bag. Moran opened her wallet, studied her license, and noticed how pretty she was. Not today's kind of pretty, but there was an honesty to her face that struck him.

"Didn't take her credit cards, but there's no cash in the wallet, so I figured it was some druggie doing a bash and grab," Ross offered.

Moran stopped what he was doing and gave the young man a withering look. "A bash and grab?" he asked.

Ross turned red, and before he could correct himself, Moran continued. "May I remind you that this woman has lost her life, Detective Ross? If you have no respect for what you are doing here, that's on you, but at least show some respect for her."

"Sorry, sir."

Moran took out Hannah's phone. "Were you able to get into this?"

"No, sir. She had it locked with a passcode. We asked Haskell's lawyer, Levine, if he could get us the password, but apparently, Captain Haskell didn't know it. I tried a couple of his suggestions, but we only get six tries and then we're locked out. Apple's putting up the usual wall about privacy."

Moran clocked that the captain didn't know his wife's password and moved on. "Let's see if we can get her cell phone records."

"Yes, sir," Ross said.

Moran looked at her license again. "Do we know if she was wearing any jewelry?"

Ross went through his notes. "No, sir. There was none found at the scene."

"Very well. That's all for now," Moran said.

Ross quickly made his escape, with Moran giving the door an irritated look before returning to Hannah Haskell's wallet. He pulled out an older picture of Oliver Haskell in his Army fatigues and looked at the captain. This young man with his bright smile was a far cry from the gentleman he'd visited last night.

Finding nothing else of much interest in the wallet, he turned his attention back to the purse and removed a hairbrush, a small bag of makeup, a Kleenex packet, and breath mints. He was about to abandon it when he felt something stiff inside the pocket and pulled out a small piece of paper. He unfolded it and saw that it came from a prescription pad with the letterhead of *Dr. Morris Kimmelman, Pediatrics, 531 Highpoint Ave., Suite 700,* on it. And underneath it, scribbled in the perpetually horrid handwriting of a doctor were the words, *AJS/8 Yetz et al.*

Moran scribbled down the information on his notepad. What did that mean exactly? And why would she go to a pediatrician? She and the captain didn't have children, and if she was trying to conceive, wouldn't she see an OB-GYN?

Even the address was strange. That part of Highpoint wasn't in a very nice area. It wasn't just that it was known to be run-down, it was also known to be rough. Surely the wife of a US Senate hopeful could afford better than that?

Just then, the phone rang.

"This is Detective Moran," he answered.

The person on the other end was a young woman. Or at least she sounded young.

"Detective Moran, this is Dr. Kramer from Bainbridge Psychiatric Hospital. I'm handling the Haskell case?"

Moran frowned slightly. "Yes?"

There was a slight pause on the other end, and he could hear the wind, but then she plowed ahead. "I know this is unorthodox, but I was wondering if I might be able to ask you a few questions about your interaction with Captain Haskell before he came to Bainbridge."

Moran had never had a doctor reach out to him like this. "What kind of questions?" he asked.

"Just some clarification on a few things. I have the intake report, but I would like to get your impressions of a few things. Would you be able to do that?" she asked.

Just then, Scarpetti poked his head in the door. "Forensics is ready."

Moran held up his finger indicating to wait, and Scarpetti ducked out of the room.

"I'm very busy right now, Dr. Kramer."

"You could call me later," she blurted out. "It wouldn't take very long."

Moran's curiosity was piqued. Why would Haskell's doctor want information from him? Clarification as to what? Had Haskell done something? Said something?

Against his better judgment, he heard his voice saying, "Very well. Do you have a pen?"

"Yes, of course," she replied quickly.

"There is a place called the Bell Jar on Delgado Avenue. I can meet you there at eight p.m."

He heard her hesitate for a minute.

Then, "Uh, sure. That's fine. I'll meet you there. Thanks." And with that, she hung up.

Moran looked at the phone for a second, then pushed back from his desk and tightened the brace around his leg. He swiveled around and grabbed his metal crutches, which were propped against the wall behind him. He took a moment to steel himself, took a breath, and, with some difficulty, pulled himself up. He fit the metal braces around his forearms, securing them in place, and thought to himself, *That was getting harder to do.* Then he left to join his partner.

Chapter 9

Malakhi worked in the garden tending the few tomatoes he had planted. He wished that Dan was here. Dan was always a help in the garden, and the two worked quietly, side by side, which Malakhi enjoyed and Dan seemed to find relaxing. Nothing like dealing with the Earth to restore oneself.

Malakhi had heard Dan's grandmother speaking to him when Dan thought he was alone and knew how much he missed her. Malakhi often heard people's deceased loved ones speaking to them, even if they themselves could not.

Sometimes, the dead asked him to convey things to those loved ones, and he obliged. But a lot of the time, they simply ignored him and kept trying to get whoever it was they were hovering around to pay attention to them.

Most of the patients at Bainbridge, at least here in B Wing, were sensitive enough to recognize the souls speaking to them. And if they didn't, Malakhi would intervene and help. But every now and then, he would see patients being tortured by a lost soul, a person who had crossed over whom the patient didn't know. A soul who just wanted to speak to anyone in this realm who would listen. That was when Malakhi would address the deceased directly through Ahura Mazda, who then sent them on their way.

Malakhi wasn't sure when he first started hearing the voice of Ahura Mazda, the benevolent deity of Zoroastrianism, but his mother had always told him it was after his brother accidentally pushed him off the roof when they were youngsters. Shortly after, his mother noticed that he began talking to himself when no one was around. When she asked him who he was talking to, he told her it was the God of Light and Creation, Ahura

Mazda himself. Afraid others would think him crazy, she warned him that he must always whisper with the deity, and never in front of others.

He had done his best, but somehow word got out; stories of his ability to converse with the divine quickly spread, and that was how he became the soothsayer for Cyrus the Great in the sixth century. He stayed with Cyrus for twenty-five years, but alas, those days were gone, and now, here he was, an old man full of wisdom and stories with very few people to share them with. He knew it was his fate to be here, for Ahura Mazda had told him so. He'd just never thought his fate would be so dull.

Everything was colorless and drab at Bainbridge. Especially the doctors and nurses. They were constantly trailed by their deceased loved ones trying to make contact, and were completely oblivious to them. This frustrated and angered many of the dead family members, and Malakhi spent an inordinate amount of time praying to Ahura Mazda to clear their energy so that they—and he—could get some peace.

Normal people didn't know that the living and the dead were still occupying the same realm but were operating on different frequencies. And therefore, these people never understood one very important thing about life, and that was that it didn't end with death.

And so Malakhi decided that Dan's grandmother was right; that God had put some people on Earth to keep His secrets, and he, Malakhi, was one of them. But the time was coming when that would change and the truth would be known, he thought, as the wind ruffled his hair. The time when all would be *one* again. But now was not that time, and he decided to focus on saving his tomato plants from the impending rain.

Just then, Captain Haskell exited the building, Nurse Bennet trailing behind him. He looked around and, recognizing Malakhi as Sebastian, decided to walk over.

"It's too late," he said, eyeing the tomatoes.

Malakhi looked up at him. "Excuse me? Did you say something?"

But instead of answering, the captain looked at him, baffled. Perhaps it was because the Southern drawl that had dripped from Sebastian's lips earlier, in the TV room, was now replaced with a soft Middle Eastern accent. Or maybe it was that the boisterous charm Sebastian exuded had given way to a somewhat weary wisdom that belied a much older man. Either way, the captain was speechless.

Most people at Bainbridge knew that of the three personalities inside Sebastian Crown, Malakhi was the least offensive and probably the most beloved. But Captain Haskell knew none of this and simply continued to stare.

Malakhi said, "Excuse me?" again.

Haskell's eyes narrowed, as if something had dawned on him. Probably something having to do with a comment the man in front of him had said earlier about multiple personalities.

"For tomatoes," he offered. "It's too late in the year for tomatoes."

Malakhi gave a little chuckle. "Ah, yes. It would seem you are right. But one can always hope for a miracle. In fact, it's a prerequisite for living here." He dusted off his hands and stood. "I have not seen you here before. Allow me to introduce myself: I am Malakhi Hindrasi, and I would shake your hand, but mine are filthy."

Malakhi waited politely as Captain Haskell's stare turned from one of confusion to one of utter fascination.

"Oliver Haskell," he replied. "Nice to meet you."

"I had hoped for another crop, but I guess that isn't in the cards," Malakhi said, indicating the plants. He was about to say more when, suddenly, he heard a woman crying, and he cocked his head, looking just past Haskell. He half-expected to see a woman weeping behind him, it was so loud. But, of course, he didn't.

Not wishing to offend his new acquaintance, he shifted his focus back to the man and was unnerved by something in his eyes. *Something he didn't see.* But now the woman's cries were getting louder and becoming very distracting. So, he did what he always did: bowed his head, folded his hands, and whispered a prayer asking Ahura Mazda to clear her energy and give her peace.

Unsure of what to do, Captain Haskell began to back away, muttering "OK" under his breath.

As if on cue, Malakhi looked up and said, "Yes, take a turn around the garden. It will do you good."

The captain nodded in agreement and walked off.

As Malakhi knelt down to tend the soggy tomato plants, a worried expression crossed his face. He looked back at the man with the crying woman following him. She seemed very reticent to be healed and didn't seem to want to leave the man. He would have liked to pray for her some more and was about to when he suddenly felt a finger jam into his chest, and he turned to see Elvis kneeling beside him, furious.

Chapter 10

told you not to put those fucking plants here!" Elvis spat out angrily. "The moisture creeps into the building, and poof! We're all covered in fucking fungus, you idiot!"

Elvis was widely regarded as *unpleasant* at Bainbridge. A short, wiry man with tattoos covering his arms, he was put into Bainbridge by his family, who'd found him trying to have sex with his five-year-old niece. After beating him to a bloody pulp, his brother-in-law agreed not to press charges if he was locked up for good. And so he was brought to Bainbridge, where he lived a much better life than he would have in prison, where he may not have lived at all.

Elvis couldn't figure out why he was the way he was, but he had a sneaking suspicion that it had something to do with mushrooms. He hadn't acted on his *urges* until after he had gone shrooming with Karl Radcliffe in the eleventh grade.

It was after that psilocybin trip that the urges became overwhelming, so he lay the blame for his problem squarely at the fungi kingdom's feet.

He began to obsessively study the fungi world and realized what a lethal opponent it was. Sending out its armies of spores to colonize, these creepy invaders caused anything from diarrhea to death, and he, Elvis, was no longer going to be their patsy. He hated that they'd made him this way. He also hated weirdos like Malakhi.

This idiot was endangering his health by encouraging fungi to grow inside the hospital. And Elvis was simply not going to stand for it. He began pulling out the plants from the ground.

"You fucking little shit! Are you trying to kill me?! Is that it?!" Elvis hissed.

"But this is where the sun is the strongest. Please, Elvis!"

As Malakhi reached over to intercede, Elvis grabbed his hand, stopping him. And within seconds, everything changed.

The moment Elvis touched him, Malakhi's eyes rolled back and he snapped his head down. His body seemed to straighten as his remaining hand curled into a fist.

Suddenly, his eyes flew open, alighting on Elvis with an icy rage that was startling. Well, not really, for it belonged to someone else entirely: Nadine, the third member of the trifecta that inhabited Sebastian's body, and by far the most dangerous.

"You wanna hold my hand, do ya?" she asked quietly. Her voice was reminiscent of a 1940s gun moll, replete with a heavy Brooklyn accent.

Before Elvis could react, Nadine's hand clutched his collar and she thrust her face inches from his and hissed, "You wanted to know if I was trying to kill you?"

But instead of answering, Elvis began to turn beet red as Nadine quietly twisted his shirt collar tighter and tighter, choking him.

"You think you can mess with me? Is that it?" she leered. "Now, why is that?"

And, without waiting for Elvis's response, she yelled, "*WHAT KIND OF A GIRL DO YOU THINK I AM? A FIVE-YEAR-OLD?!*"

The orderlies heard that and looked over in time to see Elvis, now a pale shade of blue, slump to the ground.

Suddenly, Nadine turned, scanning the crowd until her eyes locked on Captain Oliver Haskell.

"And you!" she called as she jumped up and headed toward him. "Don't think we don't know what you are! You stay away from us, you hear me! Suck the light out of someone else but not this boy!" she said, closing the gap between them.

That was when Nurse Bennet, who was shadowing the captain, tackled her like a linebacker and held her on the ground. Still struggling, she looked up at Captain Haskell and hissed, "Go back to your moons! We see you here!"

Reinforcements soon arrived in the form of an orderly with a syringe, who stabbed Nadine in the thigh, and after a second or so, she went out like a light. Two more orderlies joined them, and they gathered her up like a rag doll and dragged her into the hospital. All 250 pounds of her.

Another orderly ran over and helped Elvis, who was so shaken by the altercation that he had to lean on the man as they headed into the hospital. All the while whining hysterically about being infected with mold spores.

Chapter 11

Ella rode in the car, worried that she'd just made things worse for herself. She'd decided to make the call as she waited outside for her Uber, and at the time it seemed like the right thing to do. Of course, calling the detective on the case was unusual, but it was permitted according to the legal guidelines she'd looked up. Doctors were allowed to ask first responders about their patients, and that was all that she wanted to do. The detective asking to meet in person was a real monkey wrench, but there wasn't much she could do about it now.

Ella'd gone into the Haskell session off her game, but she'd left it feeling as if she wasn't even in the same ballpark when it came to the captain. What had gone on the previous night to so alarm the people around him? She was certain he wasn't suicidal. But maybe she'd missed something. Hopefully, the detective could clarify a few things.

The Uber pulled over and came to a stop, and Ella got out and ran into Seaside Memory Care Facility just as the rain began to come down. Usually, she took the bus, but thank goodness she hadn't today. The stop was two blocks away and she didn't have an umbrella.

Polly Martin had been a registered nurse for most of her life and always made people feel that everything was under control. This came in handy when dealing with Alzheimer's and dementia patients.

Polly looked up as Ella walked in. "Well, hey there! We missed you last night."

Ella liked to see her aunt every other night, but since she'd started seeing Clyde, her visits had become more and more irregular.

"Work is crazy, and I couldn't get away."

"Isn't it always crazy?" Polly quipped, referring to Bainbridge. "You'd better hurry. She might be taking her nap already."

Polly's comment bothered Ella, who'd heard it all. "You work at the nuthouse? The loony bin? The crazy house?"

Would they make fun of people with cancer that way? People with mental health issues were so marginalized in society. They were treated as if they were idiots, which Ella'd found to be anything but true.

She headed down the hall and knocked quietly on a door. When there was no answer, she entered and saw her aunt in bed, looking out the window, watching the rain.

Moira Kelly had aged well for someone who'd had a difficult life. And it was her hardships that gave her the indomitable spirit she still possessed. One that not even Alzheimer's could erase.

"Hey there. How are you, Aunt Moira?" Ella cooed as she took off her jacket and put down her things.

Moira looked at her blankly.

Ella was used to her aunt having difficulty recognizing her as time had gone on. It made her sad, but she'd prepared herself for Moira's impending loss years ago. Because she'd lost her parents at an early age, Ella was quite secure in the inevitability of death. But losing Moira while she was still alive was a different kind of pain; it was a constant reminder of what she was losing, almost as if her own past was being erased along with Moira's memory. And that was hard to take.

"It's me, Ella," she said gently.

Moira smiled a smile of recognition. "Hey, Sugar! How are you? I love you," she answered.

Ella sat on the bed beside her and took her hand in hers before kissing her on the cheek.

"I'm good. Been busy," Ella said.

"Well, it's a lot of hard work, but when you get your degree, you'll see it was all worth it," Moira answered. "Shouldn't you be in class now?"

Ella, used to this confusion with time, simply answered, "I had a break right now, so I thought I would come to see you."

"Well, I'm not going to argue with that!" Moira laughed.

She looked Ella up and down. "You look thin. Are you eating? I gained weight in school, but then, you have your mom's figure, not mine, lucky girl!"

Ella felt a familiar sting at the mention of her mother and changed the subject. "What did you do today?" she asked.

"Well, let's see. I walked outside . . ." and then she stopped, unable to recall anything else.

Ella quickly looked around the room for something to fill the void and noticed Moira's painting easel set up across the room.

"And it looks like you painted."

Moira had taken up painting a couple of years ago and it had a calming effect on her. It was almost as if she meditated when she painted, seeming to go somewhere else.

Ella went to the easel to get a better look. The new canvas was a small watercolor but was very different from the flowers and sunsets she normally painted.

It appeared to be a small abstract landscape with a gold pyramid shape in the center and two stars, one slightly larger than the other above it. Even stranger, the tableau's exact mirror image was painted just beneath it. Almost as if there was a pool of water reflecting the scene. And the whole thing was finished with a thin patina of red glaze.

"Wow," murmured Ella. "I've never seen you do anything like this before."

She gazed at the landscape's surreal quality. It looked like something one would find on the cover of a science fiction novel and not on her aunt's easel.

"Is it a pyramid? Did you ever travel to Egypt, Aunt Moira?" And the minute she said it, she bit her lip. She wasn't supposed to ask questions about the past like that; they could cause frustration.

But today was a good day, and Moira said confidently, "No. Most of the traveling we did was in the RV, from horse show to horse show. Your uncle and I spent a lot of time in that RV."

At the mention of her uncle, Ella's face looked pained. She had been in therapy for the last few years and had begun to remember things about her uncle. Things he had done to her. She couldn't say if the memories were real or not, but they haunted her. She'd never told anyone except Dr. Farber, her therapist. Obviously, she couldn't talk to her aunt about them. Not now, anyway.

Suddenly, she felt a stab of pain behind her eyes and rubbed her temples reflexively.

"I hated that RV," she murmured.

"You did a lot of vomiting in it, that's for sure!" Her aunt laughed, and then her mood changed quite suddenly and she looked as if she was going to cry. "Poor girl. Just a little ol' kid and you lose your parents . . ."

Before the first tear fell, Ella took her in her arms and whispered, "Don't cry, Aunt Moira. I had you. You were a great mom." She hugged her aunt tightly, but her eyes drifted to the little watercolor again, "It's a beautiful painting."

"Well, then, you keep it!" Moira said, wiping her eyes. "Nothing would make me happier! Go get it and put it in your bag," she said.

Ella smiled and did what she was told. She tucked the small painting into her backpack when she heard her phone ding. She looked back at her aunt, who was gazing out the window sleepily, and quickly unzipped the front pocket of the bag and pulled it out. There was a text from Gary Lester that read "911." *Oh dear*, she thought, *what happened now?*

She quickly texted back, "What's going on?" and stood waiting for a response, but none came. "Gary?" she texted, trying again. But he was clearly away from his phone.

"On my way," she typed and turned back to her aunt, who had shut her eyes and was falling asleep. Ella watched her quietly, remembering who her aunt used to be. Hard to think that this was all the family she had in the world. She leaned in to kiss her cheek, hoping to make a stealthy exit, but suddenly, Moira's eyes sprang open and she grabbed Ella's wrist.

"I'm not gone," she whispered urgently. And there was a wildness in Moira's hazel eyes Ella had never seen. "Not yet. I'm riding out front, Ella! Far ahead, looking for a place to go!"

Ella looked at her, confused. What was she talking about?

"They're here!" Moira gasped. "They're taking over! They steal your soul! The poor babies . . . They don't have souls!" she wailed, as if in pain.

Ella had never seen her aunt like this before. Nor had she ever heard her say things like this. It was as if she were possessed.

"Aunt Moira, it's OK . . ." Ella stuttered, trying to calm her down.

"Otis knows! *He's a drifter too!*" Moira cried.

Ella had worked with autistic children when she was first in training, and Otis was her favorite. She used to regale her aunt with stories about him, the bright, clever child locked away in a world that most people couldn't get to. But Ella had. He'd trusted her, and they had worked together for a few years.

"Ask him! Ask Otis!" Moira said, becoming desperate. "They can't see us! We hold the space! And the children! So brave! So brave! Especially the children who aren't really here! They're the bravest of all!" she cried.

Ella felt a wave of apprehension flow through her. *Children who weren't really here?* What was she saying? Was she talking about Otis? What had she meant by calling him a *drifter*?

Moira began to cry out in frustration. Ella stroked her hair to calm her, but her aunt batted her hand away and stared at her aghast, as if some horrible realization had dawned on her.

"You're surrounded by them!" Moira hissed. "You don't even see it! You don't see it! They take your soul right out of you!"

Ella felt a wave of panic hit her. What the hell was happening?

"Aunt Moira, it's OK," Ella soothed.

"No!" Moira yelled. "You don't even see!" she wailed, struggling.

A couple of nurses rushed in. "What happened?" asked the first one, who pushed Ella out of the way while the other loaded up a syringe.

"I don't know. She just became upset and . . ."

"You have to see them!" pleaded Moira loudly. "You have to see them, Ella!"

The nurse looked at her. "You should wait outside. We'll take care of her."

As the second nurse gave her the shot, Moira's eyes locked on Ella desperately. "They'll suck the soul right out of you—just like they did to Skeeter! Just like Skeeter!"

But the drugs took effect, and Moira began to drift away.

Ella stood there in shock. The nurse patted her shoulder gently. "You know these episodes happen, Dr. Kramer. It's part of the progression."

Ella nodded but didn't move, haunted by what had just happened.

The other nurse looked back at her. "Who is Skeeter? Never heard her mention that name before."

Nor had Ella. Not for a long time.

"Skeeter was a horse we had when I was a kid," Ella murmured.

She wasn't sure what had happened to the big old bay horse. Just remembered that he had been sold and she never saw him again. She felt a tug at her heart that she hadn't felt in years. Why had Moira invoked his memory? And what did she mean, *they'll suck your soul out—just like Skeeter*?

"I'm sorry, hon. But you know how it is with Alzheimer's. Time just doesn't make sense to her anymore. The memories are all fragmented and mixed up now," the second nurse said kindly.

Ella nodded, staring at her sleeping aunt. She wished Moira was the aunt she remembered, the one who danced with her and taught her how to ride horses. The one who went wading in the creek with her and taught her how to bake. But that was all gone.

As she stepped out into the rain and into the Uber she'd called, she pulled her jacket tightly around her and felt a shiver run up her spine. It was a wonder her head hadn't exploded, she thought, and then it dawned on her that her headache was gone. It had been there all day. Even when she was looking at her aunt's little painting. But it had disappeared completely—when Moira began to rave. Almost as if Ella's body was listening to her aunt even though her mind couldn't fathom what was being said.

She pondered this for a moment, then shook her head. It must have been an adrenaline rush, she thought. The fear that came with witnessing her aunt's meltdown.

But somewhere deep inside of Ella, something began to stir. A part of her that she hadn't acknowledged in a very long time. That part was awake now and had heard her aunt's warning.

Chapter 12

"What happened?" Ella asked as she rushed into Sebastian's room in the infirmary.

"The dreaded Nadine happened," Gary responded, helping her get out of her coat.

"Oh no," she said, looking down at Sebastian sleeping peacefully. "He's been doing so well."

Ella loved working with Sebastian and his two *Others*, as he liked to call them. Sebastian kept her on her toes; he was so clever, and Malakhi's knowledge of history and astrology astounded her. He also had such a calming presence that Ella found herself looking forward to his *visits.*

She hadn't worked with Nadine much but found her to be honorable in a weird sort of way. The dreaded Nadine protected Sebastian and only came around when she felt he was being threatened. Even then, she usually just screamed at the perpetrator and never really hurt anyone. But she was scary, Ella'd give her that.

Each of the trio served a purpose, and Ella thought of them in the following way: Malakhi was the id, Sebastian the ego, and Nadine the superego. All working together to take care of the whole.

"Don't worry, Ella. I think we stopped things in time," Gary offered.

"What happened exactly?" she asked.

Gary looked down at the report he had been composing. "Well, apparently he . . ." he said, indicating Sebastian "was gardening and speaking to another patient when Elvis came over, and they had words. Elvis ripped out some of Sebastian's plants and then everything went to hell."

"If he was gardening, then it was Malakhi," she surmised. "But why would Elvis rip out his plants?"

"You know Elvis. If he can mess with you, he will. But apparently, Nadine got really mad, and grabbed him and cussed him out."

Ella immediately became worried. Sebastian could be moved to a higher level of risk if he was felt to be a threat.

"She grabbed him?" Ella asked.

Gary nodded. "And, unfortunately, she pushed him down."

"Oh no," Ella murmured.

"Sorry, El."

Ella mulled this information over before asking, "Who was the other patient Malakhi was talking to?"

Gary sighed, hating to be the bearer of even worse news. "Captain Haskell. And it looked like Nadine was heading for him too."

Ella's face paled visibly. "Oh God."

This was very bad. Very bad indeed. Clyde was going to lose it with her for allowing Captain Haskell to leave his room. Her headache returned with a vengeance. She dug through her bag for some Advil and took a couple.

"He wanted to go outside, so I said he could take a walk after lunch. He didn't seem to be at risk. I asked Bennet to watch him," she said defensively, preparing for the storm that was to come.

"Bennet was with him and nothing happened to Haskell. It's nothing you did. If it's anyone's fault, it's your boyfriend's. He should have helped you with this," Gary said.

"Don't call him my boyfriend," she snapped.

She felt her anger at Clyde grow. How could he leave her alone on such an important case? He said he was her backup, and yet he hadn't even discussed the case with her. Just left Haskell's file for her to read. Every case she'd done with him before, he had been looming over her shoulder, never letting her make a decision or even talk to the patient without him. Granted, she was in her residency then, but that was just a few short weeks ago.

Gary interrupted her train of thought. "Wanna hear something weird and kinda funny?"

"What?" she asked with trepidation.

Gary chortled a little, then, mimicking Nadine's Brooklyn accent, said, "Nadine told Captain Haskell to *suck the light outta someone else!*"

Her brow furrowed. *Suck the light outta someone?* Hadn't her aunt said something almost like that an hour earlier? Something about sucking people's souls out of them? Ella rubbed her head at her temples, trying to ward off the pain.

"What the hell does that mean?" she heard herself ask.

"I stopped asking questions like that a long time ago, El," Gary said as he looked at his watch. "I will say one thing about the captain, though: He's not exactly popular with the other patients."

She nodded, contemplating that. No, the captain wasn't doing well there, and of course that would fall on her.

Gary's phone dinged.

"Christ," he muttered under his breath, reading the text. "I gotta go. The remote's missing and there's a fight. Petey's hysterical. Shit! You're not the only one with difficult patients!" he said. "You OK?"

"I'm fine. Thanks, Gary."

"Sure thing," he said, and sprinted down the hall.

She watched him go, then leaned over Sebastian and took in his cherubic face.

"Why today of all days?" she asked forlornly.

But the only answer she heard was Sebastian's soft, steady breathing.

Chapter 13

Ella decided she'd better speak with Clyde before she saw Captain Haskell again.

She nodded to his nurse, Alana, who pointed to Clyde's door, meaning she should go directly into his office. Ella steeled herself for the storm that was sure to happen.

Clyde was on the phone at his desk, trying to insert himself into what sounded like a very one-sided conversation.

"I understand. No, of course, not. . . . Mr. Levine, if I could . . . Yes. That will work. Yes, of course."

He hung up the phone and looked at Ella angrily. "Do you know who that was?"

"Clyde . . ." But that was as far as she got.

"That was Captain Haskell's lawyer friend, coming to take him home because he might be in jeopardy here!"

"I know. I should have been here, but . . ." Ella began but got no further.

"But nothing! After what happened in the TV room, you should have sequestered him! Why the hell was he allowed to roam the halls? To come and go as he liked? Why wasn't someone with him at all times?!" he yelled, and Ella realized she had never seen him this undone.

She took a breath to steady herself. "After I spoke with him this morning, it seemed to me that he was doing well. I agreed with the admitting doctor's report—he didn't seem suicidal. So, upon the captain's request, I said he could take a walk after lunch. I probably should have spoken with you, but . . ."

"You're damn right you should have!" Clyde snapped angrily.

Ella continued, "He was lucid, responsive, and didn't seem agitated at all. He asked if he could go outside and I said he could take a walk if he was accompanied by a nurse."

"Oh, it was the nurse's fault, was it?" spat Clyde.

"No, that's not what I'm saying. It's my fault, obviously."

"Yes! It is!" Clyde fumed.

Ella decided her best course of action was to be quiet. And so she watched silently as Clyde stood and walked around the room like a caged animal before blurting out, "And if that isn't fucking bad enough, we have paparazzi out front waiting to get a shot of him. Christ, this whole thing has been a nightmare!"

After a few more minutes of pacing, he sat down. "I never should have given you this case. It's my fault."

Ella felt like she'd been smacked in the face. "What?"

He looked at her. "This is a high-profile case. I left you alone on it and shouldn't have. It shouldn't have been your first case out of your residency. It's not your fault."

To Ella's surprise, he seemed to mean it. She didn't know what to say. She couldn't tell him that she happened to agree with him. Or that she couldn't help it if the other patients decided to pick today to have melt-downs. Elvis wasn't her patient. Nor was Dan. As a matter of fact, Dan was Clyde's patient.

But it didn't matter. It had all just sort of happened, an unfortunate confluence of events that created the perfect storm. A storm that had hovered over her visit with her aunt as well. She couldn't tell Clyde how much this day had unnerved her. How her aunt had warned her of beings sucking the souls out of people. Or how hurt she'd been to see him canoodling with the pharma rep, or how weird she'd felt about her meeting with Haskell. She couldn't tell Clyde any of that, so she remained quiet.

Clyde took out a notepad. "How was your interview with him?" he asked dismissively, as if she was now an afterthought that he had to contend with.

Ella swallowed the bile rising in her throat. "It went well. He answered all my questions. After a slow start, he was communicative, if not somewhat unemotional. Very . . . capable."

"No breakdown or confusion?" Clyde asked.

"No. None. He doesn't really seem like the type to threaten suicide and made it clear that it was the people around him who were worried about that."

"What about PTSD, memory issues?" Clyde continued.

Ella's brow furrowed. "Not really. Oddly enough, he offered up that he hadn't been diagnosed with PTSD or GAD."

"Why is that odd?"

"It was just the way he did it. Like he wanted me to move along with the questions. I don't know. It was just weird."

"Those guys are guinea pigs for the VA when they come home, so that's not surprising. Domestic violence?" Clyde continued checking off the boxes.

"No. He said they'd had a disagreement about going to the campaign function that night, but he was very contrite about it. Survivor's guilt, I assume."

Clyde nodded and put the pen down, signaling that he'd heard enough.

"There's something about him, though," she continued. "Something that I couldn't quite get. He seemed forthcoming, but it felt very . . . I don't know—hollow. And even when he displayed emotion, it just felt . . . off somehow."

Clyde sighed. "Obviously to be a captain in the Army for that long, he would have to be a strategic thinker and probably have serious issues with control. Dealing with this would make him feel inadequate, so he would resort to coping skills that have worked before, such as becoming unemotional and careful with what he shares."

He looked at her condescendingly. "I will write up the report and handle the discharge. Levine should be here in an hour, so I'll need the notes."

Ella nodded, understanding that she was being dismissed. "I'll go get them." Then she added, "I should probably go and speak with the captain."

Clyde looked up quickly. "No. I've already done that. Just bring me the notes and I will handle things from here on out."

And that was it. No caring words. No understanding smile. Just *go get the notes*. And so she stood, walked out of his office, and decided then and there that she would never put herself in this sort of position again.

Chapter 14

The electroshock treatment made Dan feel as though he'd been run over by a truck, and he knew that he would end up feeling groggy for a few days.

Earlier, while he was still sleeping, he'd dreamed that the captain had come into his room, and Dan woke with a terrible start. It felt so real that he'd looked under the bed and even checked the closet, but there was no one to be found. He had, however, felt the cold emptiness that was always a sign that they were around, so his dream might not have been a dream at all, he decided, and got out of bed.

Dan also knew that if he didn't get some food, he'd wake up in the middle of the night with a knot in his belly, and since dinner was only served from five to seven p.m., he decided he'd better go.

He entered the dining hall and grabbed a tray. The servers plopped his meal on a white ceramic plate and handed it to him. Tonight, they had turkey meat loaf, potatoes, and vegetable medley, which was really just peas and carrots.

He scanned the room groggily. That *person* better not be here, he thought. If you could call him a person. Dan had known it the first time he'd seen him staring with that weird stare. Dead eyes like a shark's, he thought, and shivered a little. "Goddammed van!" he muttered involuntarily as he looked for a place to sit. Well, if Shark Eyes thought he would get away with it with Dan, he was sorely mistaken.

Suddenly, a white-haired old man began waving him over. *Oh no*, Dan thought. *Not Clark.* He just wasn't in the mood for him tonight. Probably wanted to talk about his stupid book. Or even worse, his dead wife.

Dan looked around, trying to act as if he hadn't seen him, but that only made Clark call out to him by name, and suddenly everyone began looking at him. *Shit*, he thought, he'd just have to go sit with the old coot.

Clark Van de Hout was a seventy-year-old, mild-mannered schizophrenic who loved to remind people that he was the only patient at Bainbridge with a PhD. And in physics, to boot.

Clark had been a professor at Yale and, upon retiring, moved to Baltimore, which was Ava his wife's, hometown. One evening, he and Ava were experimenting with LSD in the jacuzzi, and Clark didn't seem to notice that Ava had suffered a massive brain hemorrhage and died. Clark managed to remain oblivious to her demise in the days that followed and hauled her around the house, propping her up at the dinner table for meals and on the couch to watch TV at night. It went on this way for about a week, until a friend came over and witnessed Clark speaking with his very dead wife while she sat on the porch *watching* him trim the wisteria. Ava's death was ruled accidental, and Clark ended up in B Wing, where he loved to lord it over the other patients.

He'd told Dan more than once that although he wasn't a great conversationalist, he was an excellent listener, which apparently made Dan a good dinner companion in Clark's book, and probably explained why Clark was waving at him now like a lunatic.

"Dan!" Clark called out again as he waved.

Dan headed his way, scouting the area for anyone who might be trouble, and sat down by Clark.

"How's it going, old boy? Haven't seen you all day," Clark said, buttering his dinner roll.

"Restriction," mumbled Dan.

"Oh, I'm sorry to hear that. What for?" asked Clark.

Dan, suddenly startled by something behind him, spun around only to see a patient setting down his tray. Satisfied all was well, he turned back to Clark, who repeated his question.

"Why were you on restriction?"

"Because they're here," Dan said quietly, eyeing the entrance to the cafeteria.

Clark looked around. "Who's here? I just see the regular crowd."

Dan shook his head vigorously, his face contorting as the trap in his throat again strangled the words trying to escape him. It was such a shame he couldn't tell the truth, and was always forced to talk around things. Almost as if he were leaving breadcrumbs as to what was really going on. It made him feel like an idiot.

"Van, van, van . . ." he whispered anxiously.

Clark sighed, feeling genuinely sorry for poor ol' Dan. "Now, Dan, stop that. You cannot be terrified of everyone trying to throw you into a van! We were all brought here by a van. A white one, as I recall," he said, pondering the color. "And if you think about it—you are already here, so you don't have to worry about the van getting you! I daresay you will never have to ride in a van again if you don't want to. You just have to calm down and get ahold of yourself, for your own sake!"

Clark was such an arrogant bastard. The way he talked down to Dan really irked him which made Dan even more determined to get his words out.

"Van, van . . . van! Motherfucking fucking . . . ffff . . ."

Clark stared at him, shaking his head. "Dan, you are going to drive yourself crazy if you don't focus your attention on things outside of this issue with vans."

Dan pursed his lips like a small child about to have a tantrum and realized that trying to talk—especially to Clark—was futile.

"Did you read any of my book that I gave you? I shouldn't say *book* as it really isn't that. Yet. My thesis, then. Did you read it?" Clark asked, happily changing the subject.

Dan knew that was why Clark wanted to sit with him. What the hell was it with that stupid book of his, with all its drawings, graphs, and talk of black holes?

"You've had it for a month, Dan," Clark continued, "and I was hoping that you would be finished by now. I don't think the material's beyond you, even though the math might be. And I was thinking you might have some questions." Then he lowered his voice ever so slightly as he confided, "Not to brag, but I speculate my ideas will finally do away with this ridiculous discussion about quantum mechanics not meshing with Newtonian physics—which, you'll see, was a complete waste of time."

Dan couldn't get over what a horrible day this had been. It was astonishing that not one person realized the enormity of what was going on around them. That none of them realized that they were all in terrible trouble.

And not just here in B Wing. Everywhere! It just wore him out, trying to warn them. God certainly was doing a bang-up job of making him keep his secrets, he thought.

"How much more of it do you have to go?" asked Clark.

"I don't ffff . . . want to read it!" Dan answered, surprising himself.

Clark's face was crestfallen. "Why the heck not?" he asked. "It's fascinating stuff, and we could have some great conversations instead of just sitting around on the lookout for some phantom van that's never coming to get you."

Dan wanted to laugh. That was exactly what was happening. Only Clark was too blind to see it!

"Fucking fu . . . no!" Dan muttered.

Not to be deterred, Clark leaned into Dan conspiratorially and whispered, "I am going to tell you something, and I want you to keep it to yourself. It's a spoiler of sorts, but here's the thing, Dan: It's a hologram. This whole universe is just a giant hologram that could be a thought of God, or—who the hell knows what—pierced by a very high beam of light, and we are all existing in a two-dimensional universe instead of the three-dimensional one they would have you believe. It's all preordained! You get my drift?"

Dan's whole demeanor suddenly changed and he looked at Clark fearfully.

"Light?" he asked as little beads of perspiration began to adorn his forehead.

"Yes! The link between *all that is seen and unseen!*" marveled Clark.

Dan began to sweat. What was Clark talking about? Had he heard something? No, that was impossible, he thought, and he shook his head again.

"I hate the light," Dan said adamantly.

"Don't be ridiculous, Dan. Light is the key to everything. Just read my damn book! It will explain who you *are,* and you won't have to put up with all this psychobabble that we are being bombarded with on a minute-by-minute, mind-fucking basis!"

Dan really didn't want to talk about the Goddammed light. Especially not with Clark! He wanted to tell Clark to shut the hell up, but now all his damn words were getting stuck, and all he could do was grunt.

"What is it?" Clark asked, trying to make sense of the grunting.

"I do not want any more fuck fuck fucking light in my eyes!" Dan finally spat out. "I have to wear this hat, and I feel like . . ." his face contorted, "I'm trapped! And then the light starts, and I hate it!"

Clark looked at him, absolutely dumbfounded. "What the hell are you talking about? I'm trying to explain the universe, for God's sake! The light is key!"

"But the light is different colors and makes noises! And I can't feel my thoughts with it in my eyes!" snapped Dan.

Unbeknownst to Dan and Clark, Dr. Gary Lester was behind them, pouring himself a cup of coffee, and had overheard this last bit of their strange exchange. And for some reason, it seemed to make his face blanch.

"Then just pull down the damned hat or wear some sunglasses!" Clark said, exasperated. "Don't you want to know who those voices in your head are, Dan? It's you! From different points along the hologram! You *are reaching out to* you!"

"The light's coming *from* the hat, Clark! So just shut the hell up, you Goddammed fuck fuck fu . . . cker!!!" hissed Dan, and that was when Gary stepped in.

"You OK, Dan?" asked Gary, pulling up a chair, which made Dan even more paranoid.

He quickly looked back down at his meat loaf and nodded, thinking, *Goddam Clark! Always pestering me about his stupid book!*

Gary turned to Clark. "How goes it, Dr. Van de Hout?"

Clark could barely hide his contempt for Gary. He found psychology a field that was completely unremarkable. *A bunch of egoists passing opinions off as science. And if they all agree—well then, it's a fact!* he'd said.

"Fairly well, Dr. Lester," Clark answered smugly. "I think I might be ready to leave this fabulous establishment. Get back to teaching once my book is published." Then, to make sure that Gary knew he was dealing with a real scientist, he added, "You know, I ran the physics department at Yale, and I'm sure they'll want me back."

To which Gary nodded. "Sounds good."

"Well said, Dr. Lester." He stood to go. "In my opinion, those two words, when uttered together, explain the entire basis of your profession."

Then, without waiting for a reply, he added, "I think I will see what kind of sugar formation they're pushing tonight," and took off.

Which left Dan there alone, wishing, probably for the first time, that Clark had stayed.

"We missed you in Dr. Culma's art class today, Dan," Gary said kindly.

Dan nodded, locking his eyes on his plate.

"Some of your paintings are very good."

But again, Dan said nothing.

Then Gary asked pointedly, "I heard you talking with Clark just now about the light. What did you mean, *the light comes from the hat?*"

Dan felt his heart might explode. If he complained about that hat to Lester, Dr. Westbrook might find out, and that would be very bad. He simply couldn't risk being treated with the damn electroshock again.

"Nothing," he said, never taking his eyes off his plate.

But Gary pressed him further. "You know, I saw a hat once that emitted light. It covered your head and made these weird noises as different lights passed before your eyes."

Dan felt trapped and decided his best course of action was to finish his meal. He began to shovel peas, carrots, and meat loaf into his mouth.

"Did you ever see a hat like that?"

Dan very vigorously shook his head no.

"You sure?" Gary persisted.

To which Dan nodded just as vigorously.

Suddenly, Dan wished that Malakhi was here. Malakhi always made Dan feel calm, unlike that awful Sebastian. Too bad they shared the same body, he thought. And just when it seemed Dr. Lester might ask another question, Dan blurted out, "Where's Malakhi?" And watched as a few peas hit Dr. Lester's face.

Gary stared at him for a second, then wiped his face and said, "I think he's resting. You and Malakhi had a very tough day."

And to Dan's immense relief, Gary stood and picked up his coffee. "Maybe we can talk some other time about the light hat, Dan. I think it sounds really cool."

Dan nodded, desperate for him to go away. And as it began to look like he was about to do just that, Lester asked, "By the way, Dan, who is your primary?"

Westbrook would be furious if he thought Dan had talked about something he'd told him not to. But what was there to do? Lester could very easily answer this question himself at any time. "Westbrook," he said in between bites. And for some reason, Dan got the feeling that that was exactly the name Dr. Lester hadn't wanted to hear.

Chapter 15

Ella arrived at the Bell Jar with the rain still coming down. She'd forgotten about her meeting with Detective Moran after the confrontation with Clyde, and by the time she remembered, it was too late to cancel. There wasn't any point in doing it now because Clyde had taken the case away from her, so she would make up some excuse and get out of there as quickly as she could.

It was Monday, so there were very few people there, and Ella soon noticed a man in the back raising his hand and giving her a little salute.

"Detective Moran?" she asked as she approached his table.

He gave her his business card and extended his hand toward the seat across from him without getting up. "Please."

She slid into the red booth. "I'm sorry I'm late. The Uber driver got lost," she lied.

"You don't drive?" he asked.

This question surprised Ella. "No," she answered.

"May I ask why not?"

What a strange man, she thought, and then surprised herself by answering. "My parents were killed in a car accident and I just never wanted to learn."

He nodded, as if he'd known there was more to it. "I'm so sorry. How old were you?"

"I was eight," she answered, starting to feel his forthrightness bordered on being rude.

The waiter descended, and Moran ordered a cognac and Ella a glass of wine. This was unusual for her, but after the day she'd had, she decided to throw caution to the wind.

"What can I do for you, Dr. Kramer?" Moran asked, coming to the point.

Ella was about to make excuses and extricate herself from the situation when her curiosity got the better of her. Why *had* Captain Haskell ended up at Bainbridge? She hadn't seen the reason for it, and what was the harm in asking a few questions?

"You were the one who informed the captain about his wife?" Ella asked.

"Yes, my partner and I went to the captain's house, where he had just returned from a fundraiser, and informed him of his wife's murder."

"How did he respond to the news?"

Moran hesitated, choosing his words carefully. "He seemed upset. Said he felt ill and went into the bathroom. He returned after a few minutes and seemed . . . composed."

She found it odd the way he'd phrased this. *He seemed upset* as opposed to *he was upset*. And *seemed composed?*

"He didn't say anything about hurting himself?" she asked.

"No, not to us. We didn't get to speak with Captain Haskell very long, though. His friend, Mr. Levine, arrived shortly after we did and made us aware that he was worried about Captain Haskell's frame of mind. He was concerned as to what he might do. So I would suggest you speak with Mr. Levine."

Ella'd already read what Levine had told the admitting doctor and couldn't talk to him now that she was off the case. And hadn't Captain Haskell said the police thought he was suicidal?

The waiter arrived and set their drinks in front of them, and they each took a sip.

"So, you didn't really get a chance to talk to him?" she asked.

His brow furrowed. "I'm not sure what you are looking for, Dr. Kramer."

Ella felt herself beginning to wonder the same thing. "I'm just trying to ascertain what his state of mind was at the time of his wife's death, Detective. I want to be thorough in my evaluation."

"I'm not sure I can answer that. I can say that Captain Haskell seemed upset. But not hysterical."

There was that word again, *seemed.*

"Well, he is someone whose seen death before, so perhaps he's just good at keeping his emotions in check."

"Perhaps," conceded Moran. "My experience of him, however, was not that he was trying to maintain control over his feelings. To me, the captain simply seemed . . . *detached.*"

Yes! That was it, she thought. The perfect word to describe Captain Haskell.

"Perhaps he was in shock," she answered.

"Perhaps," said Moran, sipping his cognac. After a moment, he added, "Am I to assume you don't feel that Captain Haskell was a danger to himself?"

Ella's alarm bells went off. "I didn't say that."

"You're implying it," Moran retorted.

"No, I'm merely being thorough as to his state of mind," she said, flustered.

"I see," he said, and took another sip of his drink. "Then I really think you should speak with Mr. Levine. Since he is his friend, he would know best how the captain was handling things. Now, if he was acting as the captain's lawyer, that would be a different story."

A chill ran up Ella's spine. What exactly was Moran trying to say? That Captain Haskell might *need* a lawyer?

"May I ask you a question?" Moran asked, interrupting her thoughts.

Ella nodded nervously.

"How long have you been doing this?"

Ella flushed. That was rude. "I've been at Bainbridge for three years," she answered defensively.

"The reason I ask is that I have never had a doctor call me like this about a case."

"Doctors are allowed to speak with the first responders on cases like this," she said a bit too quickly.

"Indeed they are." he answered. "And have you had many cases like this?"

Ella took a slug of her wine, desperately wishing she could disappear. This guy was relentless, and she was terrified this would get back to Clyde.

"I have worked with my boss on cases like this, yes."

He scrutinized her for a moment and then said, "I see. And who is your boss?"

Ella felt like fainting. Time to shift gears and get out of there.

"Look, Detective, I'm not insinuating that I doubted Captain Haskell was in trouble. He was clearly struggling. I'm just trying to do the best evaluation I can and be . . ."

"Thorough," he said, finishing her sentence for her.

Ella had to do something. She couldn't let the detective leave there thinking she doubted Captain Haskell's need for help. *Crap.*

"Captain Haskell has suffered tremendously, Detective Moran. He's lost his wife. The man's life has been ruined."

Moran spoke quietly. "You're right. He has suffered a terrible loss." It looked like he wanted to say more but thought better of it. Then he abruptly picked up his crutches, which were lying underneath the table, and stood, preparing to leave. *That was it?* she thought. *He was leaving?*

"Why did you want to meet with me, Detective?" Ella asked. " We could just as easily have spoken over the phone."

He looked at her and smiled. "I delight in curious people, Doctor. As I am curious myself." Then he scrutinized her for a second and added, "That gut of yours is pretty good. But be careful. You're swimming with sharks now."

Then he left, and Ella was left alone in the Naugahyde booth in the dimly lit bar to wonder exactly who the sharks were in this scenario. She sat until the *whoosh-thump* of his crutches could no longer be heard and finished her wine.

On her way out, she stopped at the bathroom, which was small and dimly lit, and she cursed the darkness as she struggled with the stall door. Afterward, she made her way to the sink to wash her hands and noticed that her mascara had smeared.

"Great," she mumbled as she put her face over the bowl and tried to wash it off. The whole time she'd spoken with the detective, she'd looked like one of those guys in that old rock band, KISS. Worse still, her roots were growing out, and Ella hated her natural hair color.

She finished washing her eyes and reached over to grab a paper towel when she caught the reflection of someone standing behind her. Christ, she'd been hogging the sink. She turned to apologize, but to her surprise, there was no one there. She stood for a second, staring at the empty space.

The makeup in her eyes must have impaired her vision. Or maybe it was the wine. After all, she rarely drank alcohol. But it had been a hell of a day. She wasn't going to begrudge herself one glass of wine, visions or not.

Chapter 16

Dan lay in his bed staring at the ceiling. Dinner with Clark and Dr. Lester earlier was the cherry on top of another perfectly terrible day, or so he thought. He liked Dr. Lester, but not enough to tell him things that Dr. Westbrook had sworn him to keep secret.

Truth be told, Dan was terrified of Dr. Westbrook and never could understand why he wanted Dan to wear that damned light hat.

The hat sorta made him wonder who he was after he'd worn it, and he felt so dizzy with it on that once he'd even thrown up. The worst thing was, he couldn't feel his grandmother around him afterward, which really upset him. And the more he'd worn it, the harder it had become to feel her presence. It was like a part of him was being erased by that damned hat, and when he tried to tell Dr. Westbrook that, he seemed pleased! Yes, he seemed very proud of the light hat, and Dan couldn't fathom why.

But it was his little friend who Dan really felt sorry for. If only humans knew how impure their energy was compared to that of other species, he thought. It sure made sense why man was feared by every other animal that walked the planet. Yes, their ability to be cruel was ubiquitous, and Captain Haskell was certainly proof of that. A Goddammed Van if ever there was one.

When Dan returned to his room after dinner, he tried to stay awake in case ol' Shark Eyes decided to come back, but he just couldn't. He'd fallen back to sleep only to dream about his grandmother. She was sitting right there on his bed. And she felt so real to him, it made him want to cry. She looked the way she always had, and he could feel her love even though it was just a dream. But there was something different about her. An urgency that Dan had never felt before. So, when she told him that he had to listen to her very carefully, he did.

And that's when she started to tell him the story about the girl with the red hair. She said that the girl was young, no more than fifteen, and she was dressed like Dan, in the clothes the hospital gave him.

"Was she from A Wing?" he'd asked her, cuz that's where the ladies lived.

And that's when the dream got strange, cuz his grandmother answered that she was from *the outside of the world,* and that she had a very important mission to complete, and that Dan was going to play a part in it.

"What kind of mission?" He'd never been involved in a mission before.

And what she said next really floored him, cuz she shared everything the red-haired girl had told her, and said that if Dan helped her, he'd be helping the whole world. *Wow,* thought Dan. That would really be something!

But the strangest part was that when he thought about what she said now, it all made perfect sense, and he had to smile, cuz, in a way, she'd vindicated old Clark Van de Hout. What a hoot! Too bad Dan would never be able to tell him.

His grandmother explained that there would be a few steps, and that it wouldn't be easy, but she would be there with him. One of the steps even involved Dr. Westbrook's car!

Dr. Westbrook let Dan wash his car occasionally, cuz he knew Dan had worked at a carwash before he came to live at Bainbridge. Dan knew a lot about cars and would have been a good mechanic given the chance, but that chance had never come. Anyway, he especially liked Dr. Westbrook's black Mercedes, cuz Mercedes was the cream of the crop in his book, and Dan worked hard to keep it very clean. And when he was washing it, he remembered all the good times he'd had at the car wash, working with the guys. They were all nice men with families and weren't cruel like his sister. They made life fun.

But then Dan pulled his thoughts back to the dream and remembered what his grandmother said next. She'd taken his hand and told him that the first step was going to be the hardest part because for the girl to complete the mission, he would have to be outside of the world too. But only for a short while. And that he needn't worry, cuz she would be with him every step of the way.

And then he woke up.

And here he was in his room, staring at the ceiling, wondering if it was a dream or if she'd really been there. He could almost smell her perfume wafting in the air, and it made him wonder. But most of all, he wondered if he would really get to see her again, because that's what he wanted more than anything.

And since there was only one way to find out, he sat up, pulled the sheet off his bed, and worked quietly, fashioning it into a noose that he threw around his neck before heading to the closet.

He wondered if he would ever see the redheaded girl. He hoped so. She sounded very brave, and Dan hadn't met many brave people in his life. Truth be told, even though the girl was young, she inspired him.

So much so that he had no qualms looping the sheet around the closet bar and tying it in a knot. All the while, concentrating on what his grand-mother had told him to do. He was *to bring it to a certain spot by the wall on a certain day and at a specific time and leave it there for the girl to find.* His grandmother said she would remind him when the time came. And he'd smiled and told her not to worry, that he would remember. Cuz Dan had a good memory. He remembered everything.

He stood there by his closet for a minute and noticed that his knees felt terribly weak, and there was a lump forming in his throat. Of course he was nervous. Who wouldn't be? But then he took a deep breath and could swear that he felt his grandmother's presence, even though the light hat had tried to take it away.

And at that moment, Dan realized something that all the Westbrooks in the world would never understand: *that nothing ever could or would defeat love.*

So he tightened the noose around his neck and thrust himself forward toward the ground.

And soon he found himself looking up into blue-green eyes flecked with yellow that smiled lovingly at him, and he heard her whisper, "It's time, Dan. It's time."

Chapter 17

Dr. Eleanor Farber sat across from Ella, listening patiently as Ella went over the events of the previous day. In her midsixties, with glasses and gray hair worn neatly in a bun the way Aunt Moira wore hers; Dr. Farber was a woman who inspired trust. Ella described the terrible time she'd had the day before. She didn't talk about the strange visit with her aunt but instead concentrated on what had happened with Captain Haskell and her meeting with Detective Moran.

"Sounds like you've dug yourself into a bit of a hole," Farber said.

Ella frowned. Of course, she was going to say that Ella had created the whole thing for a reason, and prod her to figure out what that reason was. Farber was keen on the idea that one created their own destiny.

"You knew that Clyde wouldn't be supportive of you speaking with the detective after what happened in the garden. What did you hope to accomplish?"

Ella shifted uncomfortably. "I wanted to help him . . . I don't know."

Dr. Farber waited, but Ella had nothing to add.

"From his campaign commercials, Captain Haskell seems like the all-American hero. Getting away from the Taliban like that?"

"Yes. He's very enigmatic, but there's something else. He's guarded for the obvious reasons, but it wasn't that. I just couldn't peg him," Ella said.

"What do you mean?" Farber asked.

"I couldn't get a read on him. I thought it was me because I was nervous, the case was high profile, and I was handling it alone. Obviously what happened with Clyde in the hall didn't help. But there was . . ." She stopped, unsure how to express it.

"Keep it simple. Tell me what stuck out. What bothered you," Farber encouraged.

"Well, it was all weird. At first, I felt as if he was sort of bored by some of the questions and wanted me to move along."

"That is odd," Farber said.

"Then, I decided to confront him about what he'd told his friend, the lawyer, the night before, which was why he ended up at Bainbridge."

"Which was?" asked Farber.

"Something to the effect that he *didn't feel like living*. And his reaction was very defensive and angry. I was just trying to find out if that feeling still resonated with him. But he took it . . . as if I was . . ."

"Criticizing him?" Farber finished.

Dr. Farber was very good at this—drawing the truth out of Ella. Even when Ella didn't see it, Farber would find it. Even worse, Farber would sometimes pick up on things Ella was thinking and vocalize them. Almost as if she were psychic. Theirs was definitely a unique shorthand.

"Yes," Ella said. "Which I can understand; he's a very stoic guy. But then he apologized right away and just sort of checked out again."

"So, what did you do?"

"I went over the day his wife was murdered. Asked him to tell me what he did leading up to the event. He did. Very succinctly. He ran through it using time as an anchor. He was pretty clear."

"Did you find that odd?" Farber asked.

"Not really."

"Do you think he's a suspect?" Farber asked.

"No," Ella answered. "I don't. Why?"

"Well, if he did have something to do with her death, he would want an airtight alibi. Perhaps he was practicing that alibi on you."

Ella remembered Moran implying something similar by saying the captain's friend, Levine, might have been acting as his lawyer. But Ella'd gone over the case again last night and thought that impossible.

"He was at a function at the time she was killed. It's just his style. I think it's because he was in the military. For him, structure, punctuality, means everything. It's a way of maintaining control."

"I suppose," Farber said simply. "But what was your sense of him, Ella? What did you *feel* when you were around him?"

Ella became quiet and thought about that. "I don't know. I definitely don't think he was suicidal. But it was like I couldn't find him. Even when he became emotional after recalling his trip with his wife. I thought he'd accessed his emotions, but then I patted his hand to comfort him and he gave me the strangest look. I know it was a bit improper of me, but afterward, it just seemed . . . like he knew me, but I didn't know him at all."

Farber nodded her head, as if to say, *well done.*

"In our line of work, feeling and perceiving are our greatest strengths. It's hard to work in a vacuum, Ella. I think the reason you wanted to meet with the detective was to see if you had missed something. You wanted to be validated. That you weren't the only one who couldn't *find* him, so to speak." And then she paused before saying, "But I'm not sure that the captain is someone who is easily found."

It didn't matter if he was or wasn't, Ella thought. She still should have handled things better.

"Well, he isn't in my care anymore." She shrugged.

She'd heard Captain Haskell had left Bainbridge sometime after the scuffle in the TV room. Clyde had told her to stay out of it, and she had. She hadn't even said goodbye to him. And now here she sat, feeling like a complete failure.

"Perhaps if you ever do have to deal with the captain again, you'll be the wiser," Farber offered quietly.

Ella found that comment strange. Why on Earth would she have to deal with Captain Haskell again? Clyde certainly wouldn't allow it.

"So, let's get back to you," Farber said. "Any more memories or flashes about your uncle?"

"No. Nothing recently," Ella answered.

"What about the dream? Have you been having the dream?"

Dr. Farber always made Ella go over her dream. She knew it was important, especially given what had happened with her uncle, but constantly rehashing it had become annoying. And the more she tried to avoid discussing it, the more Farber pushed.

To top it all off, Ella felt exhausted. Dr. Farber had kindly agreed to meet at an early hour for Ella's sake, but right now she could have used a few more hours of sleep. Farber's accommodation had basically saved her sanity through the last two years of her residency, though, so, she wasn't complaining.

"Ella?" Farber nudged. "The dream?"

"Yes. I had it last night. Even though I took my meds when I got home. I guess it was the wine," she said begrudgingly.

"Let's go over it, shall we? Tell it to me like you're in it. Like you're experiencing it," Farber directed kindly.

Ella thought of refusing, but that would just lead to a standoff. And Farber was very patient.

"I'm running through the house."

"Which house?" Farber interjected.

"The house I grew up in. My Aunt Moira and Uncle John's house," and she sighed, annoyed.

"Specificity is important, Ella. The more specific we are, the more we're able to release the trauma, and on a much deeper level."

Ella loved how Farber tossed around the word *we*. So far, it had just been her dumping her shit all over the place.

"What room are you in?" Farber continued.

"The living room. Then I hear the girl crying, so I run down into my aunt and uncle's bedroom."

"And . . ." Farber started.

Tired of being prodded, Ella quickly continued. "There are these weird stars and there's a storm, and the wind is loud."

"Go on," Farber urged.

"I hear the little girl again. She's crying."

"Where is she?" Farber asked.

"She's in the closet. And when I go to the closet to get her, I see the light . . ."

Dr. Farber continued gently, "And?"

"I see blood on my hands . . . on my arms . . ." Ella said quietly.

Dr. Farber pushed her. "Can you open the closet?"

"I go toward it, but then . . . the storm gets worse, and the windows blow open, and there's dust . . . and I can't see . . ."

"Why can't you see?" Farber asked.

"Because there's too much of it!" Ella snapped, frustrated. "There's too much Goddammed dust! Or *rust*! Or whatever the hell it is, and I can't fucking see! OK?"

This wasn't helping. It was making her feel worse! What the hell was Farber's fascination with her dream? It was as if she was obsessed with the damn thing, no matter what the cost was to Ella. It was unprofessional, and she had a good mind to tell Farber that. But just then the clock chimed, and Ella heard Dr. Farber's calm voice say, "Time's up."

Chapter 18

Moran didn't normally do death inquiries, but when Detective Ross called him earlier saying he'd been dispatched to Bainbridge for a suicide, Moran's curiosity was piqued. Psychiatric hospitals had suicides; that was just a fact. But this hospital had just recently become host to someone who Moran was quite interested in and so he decided to tag along.

He'd been waiting in Clyde Westbrook's office for approximately ten minutes when the doctor entered looking pale as a ghost. Moran stood, extending his hand.

"Dr. Westbrook, I'm Detective Moran. I'm sorry to meet you under these circumstances."

Clyde nodded, shook his hand, then sat across from the detective at his desk.

"I understand that you were the doctor in charge of Daniel Zimmerman?"

"Yes. Yes, I was," Clyde said, looking at Moran, somewhat puzzled. "I'm sorry, Detective, but we've had this sort of thing happen before, and there were no detectives summoned. Is there something else . . . involved?" he asked with trepidation.

"No, no, nothing like that. My trainee, Detective Ross, answered the call earlier, and I arrived a few moments ago to make sure everything was done correctly," he said, and he smiled reassuringly at the doctor.

"This is just a formality," Moran said, taking out his notepad. "I just have a few questions for you."

He couldn't help but notice how distraught the doctor seemed to be. Dr. Westbrook was taking Daniel Zimmerman's suicide very hard.

"Of course," Clyde said.

Moran cleared his throat and then read from his notepad: "Mr. Daniel Zimmerman was found at approximately seven a.m. this morning by one of the nurses, hanging from his closet door by his sheet. We believe the time of death was approximately three to eight hours prior. Do you know who the last person to see him was, Dr. Westbrook?"

Clyde answered, "Well, the nurse on duty would have seen him while on his rounds."

He pushed the intercom on his desk. "Alana, can you bring in Dan's file?"

As if she had been waiting for just such a request, Alana appeared, file in hand. Clyde took it, and she disappeared as fast as she'd come.

"Yes. Nurse Obert said that he checked and saw that Dan—Mr. Zimmerman—was asleep at ten p.m. last night." Then he added, "I hadn't seen him since the morning, but I trust what Nurse Obert has on the chart."

Moran thought that odd. No one questioned when he'd seen him last.

"How long has Mr. Zimmerman been here?" Moran continued.

"About ten years. Here . . ." He looked through his file. "Dan was here for ten years and two months."

"And why was he here?" Moran asked.

Clyde looked a little uncomfortable. "His primary diagnosis was paranoid schizophrenia. Very common here."

"I see. Family?" Moran continued as he jotted down notes.

"There's a sister in Idaho, but I haven't seen her in years. Most of our patients have very few to no visitors."

Moran skipped through his notes. "Nurse Obert mentioned that he seemed off yesterday. That there was an altercation with another patient. Was Mr. Zimmerman violent?"

Clyde paled even more. "Since it's public record, I can tell you that his sister had him admitted because of a disturbance in their home. Apparently, during an argument with Dan, he pushed her very forcefully, and she was hurt. But he's been an exemplary patient here. Everyone on staff loved him. He was a very gentle person."

Moran watched as Westbrook clenched his hands together on the desk.

"So, the altercation with the other patient yesterday was physical?" Moran asked.

The doctor looked as though he'd been caught. But at what, Moran could only wonder.

"Well, we had a new patient, and sometimes when you introduce people too quickly, other patients can react poorly. Dan was given treatment afterward, which left him quite relaxed last night," Clyde stammered defensively.

"So, you did see him last night."

"No. No, I administered the treatment after the altercation, which was in the morning," Westbrook clarified quickly. "And that calmed him."

"What treatment was that?"

"Well, there are many, but with Dan, I used electroconvulsive therapy, or electroshock, as it is commonly called. I know it sounds somewhat barbaric to the layperson, but when a patient is in a highly agitated state, it is the fastest way to alleviate the stress."

Moran's brow crinkled. "Not drugs?"

"Dan was also bipolar and had Tourette's syndrome—most of our patients have clusters of issues like that. Anyway, he was on a very specific drug regimen that we found worked well for him. Sometimes, if you introduce another medication, it can hurt the patient, who then struggles to find equilibrium. With bipolar disorder, I've found electroshock works better."

Moran pondered this information. "You don't think the electroshock would have made him suicidal, do you?"

Clyde shook his head emphatically. "Absolutely not. Electroshock had a very calming effect on Dan. The only downside, if you could call it that, is that it made him sleep for long periods of time after it was administered." And then he added, "Dan wasn't suicidal. If he were, he would have been handled quite differently."

Moran looked at him pointedly. "So, you don't think he was capable of suicide?" he asked, almost as if it was a foregone conclusion. And the doctor's, to boot.

Clyde quickly began to backpedal. "Well, I'm not saying that. I mean, let's not forget this is a mental hospital, and any one of our patients could do something we may not expect. I am just . . . surprised. That's all."

Moran referred to his notes. "Who was the patient he attacked?"

Clyde's jaw visibly clamped down as little beads of perspiration slid down the side of his face. "I'm not sure I am at liberty to discuss other patients with you, Detective."

Moran nodded, seeming to understand the doctor's predicament, but an alarm had now gone off in his head. What was up with him? What was he hiding?

"If I didn't think it pertinent, I wouldn't ask. I really would like to wrap this up as soon as possible, Dr. Westbrook, but . . ." Moran shrugged, implying that he could take other measures to get the information he'd requested.

Clyde quickly held up his hand. "Of course." And then, with some difficulty, he said, "Captain Haskell was here yesterday, as I am sure you are aware, and when Dan saw him, he became very agitated."

Moran waited for more, and when it didn't come, he filled in the blanks himself.

"And there was an altercation of some sort between him and Mr. Zimmerman?"

The way Westbrook held his breath told Moran just how bad it had been.

"Yes. The orderlies got there quickly, though. No one was hurt. Captain Haskell was fine."

"Is Captain Haskell still here?"

"No. He left yesterday afternoon," Clyde said, obviously relieved.

"So, I assume he was no longer considered a danger to himself?" Moran asked.

This was a bridge too far for the doctor. "I cannot discuss that with you, Detective."

Moran acquiesced. "Of course. I understand."

What Dr. Westbrook didn't know was that Moran was the one investigating Hannah Haskell's death and, if his suspicions were correct, he may have more questions for the doctor later.

"Very well, Dr. Westbrook. I would like to see Mr. Zimmerman's room," Moran said.

Clyde looked perplexed and was about to ask why when Dr. Kramer suddenly burst into the room, Alana chasing after her.

"Oh my God, Clyde! I can't believe . . ." She stopped short when she saw Detective Moran looking up at her. "I'm terribly sorry," she managed to say.

Clyde glared at her. "It's fine," he said, and waved his nurse away. "Detective Moran, this is my associate, Dr. Ella Kramer."

Ella stared at Moran, who didn't miss the fear in her eyes. So, Westbrook was her boss, he thought, remembering that she hadn't answered that question last night. He held out his hand and said quickly, "Nice to meet you, Dr. Kramer. I wish it were under better circumstances."

"Yes. It's terrible," she said, and Moran couldn't help but notice the grateful gleam in the young woman's eye.

He turned back to the doctor and said, "And now, if you could escort me to Mr. Zimmerman's room, Dr. Westbrook."

Clyde led the detective out of the office and down the hall, leaving Ella standing at the door watching the strange duo walk away. *Whoosh thump! Whoosh thump!*

Ella breathed a sigh of relief. Thank God Moran hadn't given her away. She didn't know why he'd done what he had, but she was so relieved she could've hugged him. Her reverie was soon broken by the sound of Alana loudly arguing on the phone at her desk.

"I'm sorry, but Dr. Westbrook is busy! No, I do not! Listen . . . listen . . ."

Ella walked over and looked at her quizzically. Alana put her hand over the phone. "This guy keeps calling, demanding to speak to Captain Haskell or Dr. Westbrook. Probably a reporter, the persistent jerk!"

Something about this irked Ella, and since she'd just been saved by Detective Moran, she was feeling rather magnanimous and decided to pay it forward. She reached out her hand for the phone, which Alana was only too happy to give her.

"This is Dr. Ella Kramer. Can I help you?" she said officiously.

The voice on the other end didn't sound like a persistent jerk to Ella. Quite the opposite, in fact. He was speaking in a whisper, and Ella detected a distinct timbre of fear.

"Dr. Ella Kramer?"

"That's right," she said.

"I need to get something to Captain Haskell," the caller said.

"Who is this?" Ella asked sternly.

"You need to tell him that Hannah . . ."

Suddenly, there were voices in the background on the other end, and it seemed as if the caller had put his hand over the receiver and said, "No thanks" to someone before he spoke directly into the phone again. "Look, I gotta go. I'm sending you something. Give it to Captain Haskell."

And just like that, he was gone.

Ella stared at the phone for a second before handing it back to Alana.

Why had the caller jumped off the phone? Almost as if he was afraid of getting caught.

"Weirdo, right?" Alana asked.

"Probably," Ella murmured, and she wasn't sure why, but she didn't think that. No, she didn't think that at all.

Chapter 19

Ezekial Weintraub sat alone at his lab bench, staring at the manila envelope through his dark-rimmed, Coke-bottle-lens glasses. He'd panicked just now on the phone with the doctor because Kim Matsunaga, Hannah's other lab assistant, had appeared out of nowhere and asked him if he wanted a breakfast burrito. *Christ.*

He couldn't help but wonder if he was doing the right thing. He'd thought about giving the envelope to the higher-ups yesterday, but if Hannah had wanted it with them, she wouldn't have given it to him.

Besides that, the other PhDs were wary of Ezekial, and had never really approved of him. But Hannah had. She'd taken Ezekial under her wing when he was at the community college where she'd guest lectured. She'd seen his promise when others discounted him as a druggie, and gave him a chance when no one else would. He owed her. Yes, he owed Hannah Haskell a lot.

His world had been shattered after he'd been arrested for drugs the second time. The first arrest was in high school, when he'd sold pot to an undercover officer. He was seventeen, so his record had been expunged. The second time he was in college, and things hadn't gone as well.

He'd been working a couple of jobs and started using speed to get through the demands being put on him. From speed, he'd graduated to meth, and soon found himself out of a job and failing his classes. One night, after pulling an all-nighter, he had an accident in his car and was arrested for possession, DUI, and vehicular endangerment and placed on probation. He went into a state-funded program and managed to get clean.

After a year's expulsion, he went back to school and was on the path to finish his degree when Hannah Haskell began guest lecturing in his microbiology class, and the two hit it off. He sought her out regularly and eventually confided in her that he, too, wanted to pursue a career in research, to which she responded by offering him a job. Ezekial was at the top of his class and had a 4.0 GPA, but anyone else would have pulled the offer after finding out about his criminal history, but not Hannah.

And he loved her for it.

She'd called him on Sunday afternoon and left him a terse message about leaving something in the lab for him, saying she would explain later. He'd heard the tension in her voice and wondered if he'd done something wrong. Then he got the call from Kim yesterday morning on his way to work, telling him what had happened, and his sense of unease began to build.

He'd looked everywhere for whatever it was Hannah had left but could find nothing. It wasn't until he moved the rubber mat to clean the countertop that he found the manila envelope. In it, he'd found scans. Brain scans, to be exact, with a little sticky note on them that said, *"Z—Hang on to these re: Lyprophan—Hannah"* in her handwriting. He'd noticed the serial numbers on the bottom of the scans and tried to access those files on his computer only to find they didn't exist.

He even checked the X File, the file for people who'd dropped out of drug trials and were X'd out of the data. But they weren't there either.

The media said Hannah's death was a mugging gone wrong, He'd seen the homeless around Wellglad; it wasn't exactly a nice part of town. But the fact that Hannah had called and left such a cryptic message only to be found dead a couple of hours later struck him as odd timing.

It wasn't just that. Hannah had seemed different the last month or so. She was preoccupied and jumpy, but when he asked her about it, she said she was fine, and he hadn't wanted to pry. Now he wished he had.

Last night he'd come up with the idea of giving the envelope to her husband, Captain Haskell. Surely Hannah would have told her husband if something at work was amiss.

He was going to mail it to their home, but then he'd heard that the captain was at Bainbridge, so he decided to send the envelope to the hospital and let someone there get it to Haskell. That way no one would have to know it'd come from him. Sending it anonymously would also shield him from any trouble with the Wellglad NDA he'd signed when he was hired. If Wellglad found out, he probably would be sued, especially because it had something to do with Lyprophan. That would make them all go bonkers.

He pulled out his phone, googled Bainbridge's address, and began to copy it onto the envelope when he was interrupted.

"Mr. Weintraub," Edward Dowd said as he entered.

Ezekial jumped, his thick, dark-rimmed glasses almost falling off his face. "Dr. Dowd," he said, covering the manila envelope with his backpack.

"I didn't mean to startle you. I just wanted to see how you were doing. This has been a horrible couple of days, and I know you and Hannah worked closely together."

"Well, I just do the grunt work," Ezekial stammered. "She was a brilliant researcher and a wonderful boss."

Edward Dowd hadn't said more than two words to Ezekial the entire time he'd worked at Wellglad, and when he did, his eyes always made Ezekial nervous. They were unusually large, and when they were fixed on him, it felt sort of like an owl was tracking him.

Dowd moved closer to Ezekial, and he felt his heart skip.

"You know, I'm aware of your somewhat troubled history, Mr. Weintraub," Dowd continued. "I'm also aware of all the good work you've done since you've been here. I just want to make sure that you can carry on with your duties, and that Dr. Haskell's death hasn't set you back in any way."

"No, sir. I'm fine," Ezekial stammered.

"Good," Dowd said, and then his tone softened. "You're going back to school for your PhD, aren't you?"

"I'm waiting to hear back from universities."

"You applied in town?" Dowd asked.

Ezekial nodded.

"Would you continue at Wellglad if you got in?"

"Yes, sir. If I can. I can't afford not to work," Ezekial explained.

"I know the head of the microbiology department at Loyola. Let me look into it," Dowd said.

Ezekial stuttered his thanks.

"Dr. Haskell believed in you, Mr. Weintraub. That means a lot to me. I take care of those I believe in."

And with that, he turned and left.

Ezekial watched him go, his eyes narrowing. The great Edward "Ned" Dowd was going to help him with school? Something was definitely up.

He picked up his pen and addressed the envelope to Bainbridge, adding, *CPT Haskell, c/o Dr. Ella Kramer.*

Chapter 20

Dan's room was small and ordinary, almost like a college dorm. There was a potted plant beside his bed and a bookshelf just under the window, with some of Dan's favorite reading. A few of his paintings adorned the walls. Clyde watched the detective as he put on latex gloves and moved about.

"He lived in this room for all ten years?" Moran asked.

Clyde nodded, turning on the bedside lamp to help Moran see better.

Moran thanked him and asked, "Everything seem in order?"

"It looks the same," Clyde responded absent-mindedly. Other than Sunday night, he hadn't spent much time in here. And right now, his anxiety was so high, his powers of observation were at an all-time low.

He looked down at the little flowering plant on the bedside table. *A gardenia*, he thought, and murmured, "Malakhi" to himself. He wondered how Malakhi would handle Dan's death. His wondering was short-lived, though, as he suddenly saw something reflected in the window on the other side of the plant. Something small and shiny tucked into the gardenia's soil.

"Did you say something?" Moran asked, turning to him.

Clyde shook his head.

Moran smiled. "My wife, Martha, tells me I need hearing aids. Old age is not for the faint of heart."

Clyde smiled as the detective turned back to the closet and then quickly reached down and snatched the shiny object from the plant's soil, knocking one of the gardenia's buds to the floor in the process. He looked to see what it was and took a sharp intake of breath before he slipped it into his pocket.

Suddenly, his cell phone rang, and he jumped involuntarily before looking at the caller ID. "If you don't need me for anything else, Detective—I have to take this call."

"Of course. Thank you for your help. I will check in with you later."

And just as Clyde was about to sprint down the hall, Moran added, "Oh, if you could have . . ." he pulled out his notebook and found the name, "Nurse Bennet, come down and see me, I would appreciate it."

"Of course," Clyde said. Then he ran out of the room.

Chapter 21

Moran's eyes narrowed as he watched Westbrook leave. He moved to the bedside table and picked up the tiny gardenia bud that Clyde had unknowingly knocked off. "Who . . . is Malakhi?" he whispered.

He turned to place the bud on the night table when his eye fell onto the books on Mr. Zimmerman's bookshelves. Books befitting a child, like *Now We Are Six* by A.A. Milne and *The Very Hungry Caterpillar* by Eric Carle. He then saw a slender book, a notebook really, which he pulled off the shelf. *The Basics of Universal Holographic Design* was written by hand on the front cover. How did one go from a book about a hungry caterpillar to something like this? he thought. He opened the book cover and saw the author's name: CLARK VAN DE HOUT, PhD. He flipped to the first page and saw that this was heady stuff.

"We are living in a universe that is a two-dimensional hologram," it began. "With our past, present, and future all existing at once. And how it held together? By light."

Odd. No one had described Zimmerman as an intellectual, he thought, going through a few more pages before putting the book back.

He pulled out a sketchbook and noticed that Zimmerman was not a bad artist, with a talent for landscapes. He put that back and stood when the painting on the opposite wall caught his eye. He moved closer to it to get a better look.

It was a desert landscape, with a pyramid and a lake beneath it, reflecting the pyramid. In the sky were a couple of stars or planets, and the canvas appeared to be covered in red. *Unique*, Moran thought. Daniel Zimmerman had a talent, no doubt about it.

From behind him, he heard someone utter his name, and he turned to see a very fit-looking young man in white standing in the doorway.

"I'm Nurse Bennet. I was told you wanted to see me."

"Of course, Mr. Bennet. I have a few questions for you about Mr. Zimmerman. Come in," Moran replied.

"Anything I can do to help. This is just awful and so surprising," answered the nurse.

"Yes, that seems to be the consensus."

"Well, it's a mental institution, so it's not unusual, but man, I feel so bad for him. Dan was such a sweet guy."

"You worked last night, correct?"

Nurse Bennet nodded.

"When did you last see Mr. Zimmerman?" Moran asked.

"He'd had a treatment, so he was pretty exhausted afterward. I checked on him before he went down to dinner, so maybe around four thirty. He was in his room, sleeping."

"I understand that there was an altercation with him earlier yesterday morning. Involving Captain Haskell?"

Nurse Bennet nodded. "Yeah. I wasn't there for that one, but apparently, Dan started thinking he was coming to take him away and got real upset. Probably because he was new."

"I'm sorry, *coming to take him away*?"

"Yeah. Dan had a fear of people coming and taking him away in a van. Happened with a few people. Not a lot, but often enough that it was a thing," Bennet explained.

"And he thought Captain Haskell was going to do that?"

Bennet nodded.

And then Moran backtracked to something else Nurse Bennet had just said. "And what did you mean, you weren't *there for that one*? Was there another one?"

Bennet nodded.

"Mr. Zimmerman had another altercation later?" Moran asked.

Nurse Bennet shook his head. "No, Captain Haskell did."

This sent a small jolt through Moran's system. "With whom?"

At this point, Bennet seemed to get a little worried, so Moran waved his hand. "Completely off the record."

Bennet sighed and said, "With Nadine."

"I thought only men resided in B Wing. Is Nadine a nurse?"

"No. One of our other patients, Sebastian, has three personalities. Two are guys and the third is Nadine, and she's mean as hell. Usually takes a lot to get her to show, though."

"What happened?" Moran asked.

"Well, I was shadowing Haskell outside after lunch. Malakhi was gardening, and . . ."

"Malakhi?"

"Oh, sorry, yeah, that's Sebastian's other personality."

That was the name Westbrook had murmured before he left the room. Well, that question was answered. Moran listened, somewhat stunned, as Bennet filled him in on what happened in the garden after lunch the previous day.

He hadn't had a very good feeling about Captain Haskell and, apparently, that sentiment was shared by at least two of the patients here at Bainbridge. Not exactly an endorsement, but still.

"Did she er, *he* hurt Captain Haskell?"

"Nah, she was just talking smack."

"Like what?"

"She said something like *we know what you are* and then told him to go back to the moon." Bennet smiled at that.

When Moran asked him what that meant, Bennet shook his head and chuckled. "Who knows? I was just trying to hold him down."

"What happened next?" Moran continued.

"After we got Sebastian under control, we handed him off to the orderlies to take to the infirmary."

"And Captain Haskell? What happened to him?"

Bennet frowned a little bit at that. "When I went back to the garden to get the captain, he was gone. So I came inside, and I found him in the TV room. He said he couldn't find his room, which was strange because it's right next door to the TV room. I think he was dazed. I mean, it was a rough day for everyone, but I felt really bad for him. He left shortly after, around the time the TV remote thing happened."

Moran looked at him. *TV remote thing?* What was he talking about?

"What TV remote thing?" Moran asked.

"Nurse Obert didn't mention it?" Bennet asked.

Moran shook his head.

"Yeah, yesterday was just a weird day. Really weird," Bennet said, and sighed before continuing. "We have this patient, Petey, and he's always taking the TV remote and hiding it, and it makes the others pretty mad. So he pulled that stunt again yesterday, and there was a lot of arguing, and Petey wouldn't give it up, which is unusual, but . . . anyway, some of the patients became belligerent, and things got pretty loud, and it was all-hands-on-deck time. We had to medicate quite a few of them, and confine them to their rooms."

Moran listened, hiding his shock. "Is all this fighting typical?"

Bennet shook his head emphatically. "I've worked here for seven years and have never had a day like yesterday. I mean, Petey taking the remote? Sure. Maybe there's an argument. But usually, it's pretty dull around here. That's why I felt so bad for Captain Haskell. He came at a bad time. Go figure."

Go figure indeed, thought Moran. "Was Captain Haskell involved in the remote argument?"

"No," Bennet said. "Thank God! That was after the garden. And I was with him in his room until I got the request for help in the TV room. And by that time, he'd already spoken with Dr. Westbrook, who was on his way up to see him. Probably about leaving, because when I finished up with Petey, I was told he'd been released."

"What time was that?" Moran asked.

"Uh, anywhere from three thirty to four?" Bennet said and shrugged. "You can check with the admitting nurse up front."

But Moran wasn't going to do that just yet. He didn't want to call any attention to his suspicions about the captain. Not just yet.

"So, when you went to help with the TV remote argument, the captain was alone in his room?"

"For like a minute or two. Dr. Westbrook was on his way, so I didn't think it was a problem," Bennet said somewhat defensively.

"I'm sure you're right," Moran said quickly, before asking, "Why was Captain Haskell allowed to mingle with the other patients in the first place? He was on a wellness watch, and after what happened in the morn-ing with Mr. Zimmerman, I'm surprised he was allowed to do that."

"Dr. Kramer thought it was OK for him to get some fresh air, and I was shadowing him. It really wasn't her fault," he said, defending the young doctor. "She's a great doctor. She was Dr. Westbrook's resident, and the patients love her. But in all honesty, we were all kind of surprised Dr. Westbrook gave it to her. But you know—it was his call."

Moran found that interesting. And the way she'd burst into West-brook's office. That was a little strange. He wondered what the arrange-ment was between those two.

"So, you last saw Dan at four thirty p.m., and he was in his bed?"

Bennet nodded.

"And Captain Haskell? Around three thirty?"

Bennet nodded.

"One last question: Do you know of any reason why Mr. Zimmerman would do this to himself?"

Nurse Bennet thought for a minute and then answered. "I think they are all capable of something like that, if you want my honest opinion. Having said that, I never saw it coming with Dan."

"All right. Thank you for your time, Nurse Bennet."

Bennet turned to go, then stopped, remembering something.

"Actually, it was 'moons,' not 'moon.'"

Moran cocked his head. "I'm sorry?"

"Nadine. She told Captain Haskell to go back to his *moons*."

Chapter 22

Detectives Moran and Ross walked down the hall on their way out of Bainbridge, discussing the Haskell case.

"So, apparently, the guy who ran the Wellglad parking lot, Armando, had his own camera hidden in the kiosk at the entrance parking gate. Said he was worried about his workers taking money. He was outta town Sunday but brought it in last night. Scarpetti says he's gonna have Berman, the IT guy, see if he can see Sunday night's footage under it. It's digital, so he should be able to," Ross said.

"Anyone other than Wellglad use that lot?" Moran asked.

Ross flipped through his notes and shook his head. "The only people who would have access to it have key cards, which was just Hannah Haskell and the security guard this past Sunday. But apparently, this whole area is up and coming. From here to Wellglad, which is just a few miles down along the train tracks. Lotta businesses and houses going up."

Why anyone would live on this side of town was beyond Moran. Up-and-coming, good grief. His thoughts were quickly interrupted by the low drone of a TV up ahead.

"Go get the car. I'll be down in a minute," he said to Ross.

Moran entered the TV room and saw a couple of patients sitting on the sofa, catatonically watching *SpongeBob SquarePants,* the remote resting on the table in front of them. He glanced around and was about to leave when he heard a voice behind him.

"Pathetic, isn't it?"

Moran turned to see Sebastian sitting by the window, watching him.

"I mean, at least watch a game show or something skewed a little beyond a four-year-old. Am I right?" Sebastian asked sarcastically.

Intrigued, Moran headed toward Sebastian, who stood to greet him.

"Sebastian Crown, at your service, Detective . . . ?" he asked with his Southern drawl as he extended his hand.

"Moran," said the detective as he shook his hand, and remembered this was the fellow Nurse Bennet had told him about, with the three personalities. The one who told Captain Haskell to *go to the moons*.

Sebastian sighed, shaking his head sadly. "Terrible news about Dan."

"Yes," offered Moran.

"It would take a lot of courage, don't you think? Killing yourself?"

What an interesting thing to say, thought Moran. "I suppose. Or quite a lot of distress," he answered.

"Well, Lord knows we are all distressed in here!" said Sebastian, then he threw his head back and roared with laughter.

Moran watched, fascinated. "Did you know him well?"

"Well enough to know he didn't have an ounce of courage," replied Sebastian. "I guess the *vans* finally caught up with him."

Moran cocked his head, feigning ignorance. "I'm sorry?"

"Dear Dan thought anyone new was a van driver who was there to pick him up and take him away. Apparently, he hadn't gotten the message that he had arrived! *Hello, Dan? It's Earth calling, and you're already in the loony bin.*" He threw back his head again, laughing as Moran silently watched. "Probably wasted his brain on drugs and can only remember the van ride here. What an idiot!"

Moran studied him carefully. "You didn't like Dan?"

"Oh, I liked him well enough. Even though he almost got me put on restriction yesterday when he attacked Captain Haskell. And if you really think about it, he probably *is* the reason I got put on restriction."

"Really?" prodded Moran gently.

"Well, let's just say that if Dan hadn't attacked the captain for no good reason in front of me, Nadine probably wouldn't have thought it necessary to visit. And then *I* wouldn't have been shot up with fucking Haldol, which just depresses the hell out of me! Which is probably why I'm so cranky. I apologize."

"Not at all. Sounds like you've been through quite an ordeal," Moran said kindly.

Sebastian looked at him gratefully. "Being locked up with these . . ." He eyed the men on the couch, "baboons is not only dull. It's dangerous!"

"I'm so sorry," said Moran compassionately.

"It's not every day, mind you, but yesterday was a terrible, terrible day. Probably the planets—but still. First Dan attacked the captain, then

Nadine came, then the whole remote thing." Sebastian clucked, looking out the window as he recounted the horrors of the past twenty-four hours.

Then he turned back to Moran, looked him in the eye pointedly, and said, "I warned the captain about the pandemonium that would ensue over the remote being taken. At least he missed that horrific episode. So embarrassing! Fortunately, I was not here at that time either, or I would have fallen into a fit of the vapors myself."

"Well, that is fortunate," Moran heard himself say as he stared at this fascinating creature.

"Isn't it?" said Sebastian with a sly little grin.

He nodded toward the remote on the table in front of the two catatonic men. "As you can see, it was recovered. It was in the bathroom the whole time, which is odd, cuz Petey usually takes it to his room. I just hope they sanitized it. Who knows what he was doing with it in there! Disgusting. Disgusting and strange! Don't you agree? I mean, why on Earth would you take a remote to the bathroom with you?"

And as he asked this, his eyes locked with Moran's again, and the detective nodded in agreement to appease the very strange man.

"Well, I have got to take my constitutional or Eddie will come in and annoy me to no end. It was lovely to meet you, Detective Moran."

"Likewise, Mr. Crown," Moran said, then watched Sebastian trudge down the hall.

And as he went, Moran was struck by the feeling that Mr. Crown was a more fascinating character than he'd imagined. *Three people in one*, he mused. But there was something else about him that intrigued Moran more: The whole time he'd spoken to him, Moran got the distinct impression that Sebastian was saying things without saying them.

It was almost as if Sebastian's other two personalities were whispering in his ear, and that was rather unsettling. Sebastian Crown was like a large Cheshire cat who'd eaten a canary. And the canary—or canaries, in this case—were driving the ship.

"Likewise indeed," Moran murmured.

Chapter 23

Ella finished her afternoon rounds and was on her way to her office when, up ahead, she saw the fleeting figure of a girl with red hair rounding the corner. The girl couldn't have been more than a teenager. Why on Earth was a girl in B Wing? she wondered. Ella sped up, but when she reached the turn in the hall, the girl was gone. Maybe she was a nurse, she thought. But she'd never seen her before.

Ella decided to look through the panes on the patients' doors. Most rooms were empty, or their inhabitants were inside alone. She reached the end of the hall, where she was confronted with one more room. A room that had yellow police tape on its door.

She peered inside and was surprised to see Sebastian sitting on the edge of Dan's bed, staring at the wall. She pushed the door open. "Sebastian? What are you doing in here?"

Sebastian looked as if he'd been crying, and when he turned to her with his kind eyes, Ella realized that this was not Sebastian at all but Malakhi. She sat on the bed beside him.

"Malakhi? Are you OK?" she asked softly.

He shook his head. "I am very sad to hear about Dan. He was my friend."

Ella rubbed his back. "I know you two were good friends. I'm sorry. Who told you?"

"Sebastian knew," he said simply.

Ella had long suspected that the three personalities communicated with one another, or simply knew what the *Others* knew.

As she rubbed his back, she noticed that he seemed to be staring at something on the wall. When she followed his gaze, what she saw shocked her. It was a painting with a pyramid and water beneath mirroring it. There were two orb-like stars shining brightly in the sky, all covered in a thin patina of red. How was this possible? she wondered.

Ella stammered, "Did . . . did Dan paint that?"

Malakhi nodded sadly. Ella went closer to the painting.

It was exactly the same as the watercolor her aunt had given her. She stood there at a loss for words, her head beginning to ache.

"I don't understand. . . . My aunt painted this exact same scene. How could . . ." Her voice trailed off as she stared at the painting. "Is it a famous landscape or something? I've never seen it."

Malakhi looked at her strangely. "Perhaps you have but you don't remember."

"What?"

"Perhaps you just don't remember."

She shook her head, sure she hadn't seen this before. "Where is this?" she asked.

Malakhi said slowly, "It is where we were many lifetimes ago."

"Egypt?" she asked.

"No, not there. Other . . . places," he answered.

Ella looked at him. Why was he being so cryptic?

Malakhi returned her look and seemed to be making a decision before asking, "Do you remember the ages as I have explained them to you? The changing constellations?"

She nodded, not sure what that had to do with anything.

"We have been living in the time of the Fish, Pisces, the Time of the Christ, and the Buddha. But we are transitioning to the Time of Aquarius—the time of unified consciousness. The time to return to One. But there are forces coming into play now that would not have this be so. And because we are in transition and our world is in flux, we cannot protect Earth against these forces." He looked at the painting. "It happened there. Life was ended by the extreme natures of the forces against it."

"Life was ended?" she asked incredulously.

"As we know it, yes. It found new planets to inhabit, but it appears that we are once again in a precarious position, with energies that seem to have followed us here. I fear Earth will pass the way of the others."

She stared at him, dumbfounded. "I don't . . ." but she didn't finish.

"You do. You may not remember yet, but you do understand." And he smiled at her almost as if she were a child.

This sent a chill through Ella. Malakhi had never said anything like this before. Sure, he liked astrology. He'd told her all about her sun sign and what was going on with the planets, and she had to admit it was sort of fascinating. But life ending because of evil forces following it? This seemed less about astrology and more about science fiction.

"Life is composed of many energies, Dr. Kramer. Many are compatible, but some are not. Some are so foreign and so different that they can seem evil to us and can destroy life itself. And as this transition into the New Age happens, we must take care, lest that happen here."

Ella's mind reeled, and she got an eerie feeling that he was trying to warn her. She'd felt that way with her aunt yesterday, when she was talking about babies with no souls, and what was it she'd called Otis? A child who wasn't there? She kept saying *they* were all around her. Who *they* were she had no idea, but she knew intuitively that her aunt was trying to warn her. Was Malakhi doing the same now?

Ella rubbed her temple, took a deep breath, and was about to say something when she noticed that Malakhi was no longer looking at her but just behind her. His head was cocked, as if he was listening to someone.

"Your aunt would like you to know that she is fine. That she is seeking a better place. That it isn't safe here," Malakhi said gently.

"My aunt?" She gulped.

Ella felt her body go cold. Malakhi had explained long ago his ability to hear the deceased loved ones who surrounded people. She'd witnessed an exchange between him and Jenny, when he'd explained to Ella that he'd had to pray to Ahura Mazda repeatedly to get her deceased husband to stop screaming at Jenny, which she'd found amusing. But Jenny did not.

Ella'd read all about Zoroastrianism after he'd told her that he prayed to the deity to give the deceased souls peace and reflected again on what a marvelous mind Malakhi/Sebastian had to come up with that.

"Malakhi, my aunt isn't dead," she said, but then she was confronted with a terrible thought: What if Moira *had* died and she just didn't know it yet?

"No, she has not passed completely," he answered. "But she is going back and forth between realms, for her energy can travel into the realm of death. She is on a quest to seek another place for life. Life as we know it. Full of love and joy." He looked at the painting on the wall. "Life that existed there and was destroyed."

"To seek another place for life?" Hadn't her aunt said something about looking for a place to go?

"Perhaps that is why Dan left," Malakhi added.

Ella stared at him for a moment. "You think Dan killed himself to find . . . another place for life?"

Malakhi nodded.

"I don't think Dan would make a choice like that," she said.

"Perhaps he had no choice in the matter. Our destinies are our destinies, Dr. Kramer. I think we make the choice we must. One need only look to the planets to know that."

Ella sighed and looked at him sadly. He was missing his friend. "I know you place a great deal of faith in astrology, Malakhi. But don't you think sometimes we just make mistakes?"

"There is no such thing as a mistake, Dr. Kramer. Dan was destined to do what he did, just as he was destined to be born with a gift that you could not understand."

Ella's mind swirled. "What do you mean, a *gift*?" she asked.

He looked at Ella pointedly. "You will now be required to *open your mind*, as you like to say to your patients. You will have to listen with all your being, for you truly are capable of that, Dr. Kramer." He took a breath before continuing. "What you called his *mental illness* was actually a gift bestowed upon Dan by the universe. A gift for mankind."

"What are you talking about, Malakhi?"

"Schizophrenia, as you call it—the ability to hear others. Others who you say are not there. You look at this as an illness. But another way of seeing it is that those with this gift are privy to information that you cannot access . . . *but Dan could*."

Ella was dumbfounded. She didn't know what to say.

Malakhi pressed on. "And Dan didn't only have what you call schizophrenia, did he, Dr. Kramer?"

Ella shook her head, not liking where this was going. "Malakhi, Dan was delusional and paranoid . . . and . . ."

"Delusional by your standards, as someone who cannot yet see," Malakhi snapped. "And paranoid? Wouldn't you be paranoid if you could hear things that most people cannot? Wouldn't that make you feel alone and odd? Of course it would!"

Ella didn't know how to respond, nor did she have time to, as Malakhi was picking up steam.

"But Dan did something else. Something you also thought was abnormal, though it was done in the service of those around him. For their protection. And you misunderstood that as well."

"Malakhi . . ." she started but was cut off.

"He was trying to warn you! All of you! But unfortunately, his warnings fell on deaf ears." And then he quietly whispered, *"Van, van, van ..."*

Ella felt as if the air had gone out of the room. She had never seen Malakhi so worked up and decided she needed to calm things down.

"Malakhi, Tourette's syndrome is a neurological disorder that caused him to have many tics, one of which was to shout out at inappropriate times and say things with absolutely no meaning."

But this just seemed to make Malakhi angry. "It was loaded with meaning, but you, Dr. Kramer, you could not understand!"

Ella snapped defensively, "No, I didn't understand why he was shouting *van*, but given his history ..."

"That is not what he was saying, and you would do well to remember in whose company he would say it!"

He said this so vehemently that Ella was shocked. She reached out to calm him down and said, "Listen, Malakhi, you're upset ..."

He pushed her hand away, having none of it.

"No, I am tired, Dr. Kramer! Tired of hiding the truth. And I must now right the wrongs done to my friend. At least the ones I can. And I will start by saying he was not saying *van*! *No!* His *tics*, as you so eloquently put it, did not allow him to finish the word that stuck so painfully in his throat! And that word that he so valiantly tried to utter was *Vanitan!* *He was warning us! His simple cries that you so foolishly mistook were a warning to we, the living! Beware! Beware! The Vanitan is in our midst!"*

Ella sat dumbfounded. She had no idea what he was talking about and could only stammer, *"Vanitan?* What ... what is that?"

Malakhi became quiet, measured, and very deliberate. "There is our universe, and there is a *shadowverse*, known as the *Vanitan* which is now engulfing our universe. The Vanitan's energy is empty. It has no empathy, no love, no light. It is the non-life. What Dan could not explain is that it is this energy that is descending upon us now. For everything is energy, Dr. Kramer. Everything. All around you. You are energy vibrating at a very specific wavelength and frequency. But what if I were to tell you that your vibration can be stopped by another energy that you cannot see, equal to your own but opposite? You would probably not believe me.

"Yet Newton's Third Law tells us that for every action there is an equal and opposite reaction. There is yin and yang; dark and light; life and non-life. Mind you, I did not say death. For non-life is very different, as it has never lived at all. And death is a part of life.

"Now, this energy is on Earth. It dwells amongst us, infecting the living in its path. Infecting humans. It consumes light, taking the light that the living emit. Like a black hole pulling matter into its void. We are in terrible danger, Dr. Kramer. And you would do well to have a care lest it infect you.

"And now, as the constellations change into the time of Aquarius—the Time of the One—we must come together for the energy of the non-life, the Vanitan is upon us. It has seeped in slowly, destroying life on the outer planets, but is descending on Earth now in full force."

He stood there, his soul exposed, waiting to see if she understood.

Her breath caught for a second and she feared she might have a panic attack, but the look in Malakhi's eyes stopped her, and a strange thing happened as she held his gaze: Her head no longer ached, and a deep sense of calm descended upon her. It was almost as if she understood on some level that he was telling the truth. As if his saying this had suddenly made her less alone.

She hadn't felt this kind of resignation for a very long time. Not since she was eight years old, sitting in the back seat of the old Pontiac, when the car wreck that took her parents' lives happened. She knew it was coming right before the metal made contact. She was asleep but woke with a start a second or two before their car slammed into the back of the semitruck. It was almost as if someone had gently whispered in her ear what was to come, so that she wouldn't be scared. She remembered feeling this same calm watching her mother fly through the windshield as the glass rained down all around her. As if she was watching a movie. A movie that she had already seen.

They said the seat belt had kept her in place. That was what they said. But Ella remembered feeling like someone was holding her in place. In fact, she remembered feeling a body go over hers right after her mother flew out that window, as if someone was protecting her with their body. She'd never told anyone that. She knew she'd sound crazy. But she also knew that it was true. That someone had been in that car with her. In the same way, she knew that Malakhi's warning to her now was also true, and instead of feeling panicked and scared, she experienced that eerie calm she'd felt all those years ago. As if she knew it would come to this.

All of a sudden, there was a breeze in the room, and the spell was broken by a voice behind them.

"Dr. Kramer?"

She whipped her head around to see a young male nurse in the doorway. "We aren't supposed to let anyone in here, Dr. Kramer."

Ella stood up quickly. "Of course," she stuttered. "We were just . . ." But she had no idea what to say.

Sensing her confusion, Malakhi stood and took her arm gently, indicating for her to go ahead of him out of the room.

"Shall we?" he said.

And as they went, it struck the nurse that they seemed to have traded roles, with Malakhi helping Dr. Kramer down the hall.

Chapter 24

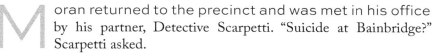

Moran returned to the precinct and was met in his office by his partner, Detective Scarpetti. "Suicide at Bainbridge?" Scarpetti asked.

Moran nodded.

"Anything to do with Haskell?"

"Not directly. But I will say that Captain Haskell wasn't a very popular guest at Bainbridge. He was attacked by two of the patients."

Scarpetti whistled. "Anything serious?"

Moran shook his head. "No, but one of them was the patient who committed suicide."

Scarpetti frowned at that. "You think he's involved?"

Moran shook his head. "Haskell had his lawyer, Levine, come get him Monday afternoon, well before the suicide. So, probably not."

Scarpetti watched him for a beat. "Probably?"

Moran sat at his desk and shrugged. "I don't know. It's just strange. He checks himself in, has two altercations with patients, and then checks himself out."

Scarpetti remained quiet, waiting.

"I spoke with the doctor in charge of his case. A young woman. She seemed somewhat inexperienced, which I found odd," Moran said.

"They probably didn't think he was a serious risk to himself," Scarpetti offered.

Moran nodded. "No, she didn't get the feeling he was a risk to himself."

Scarpetti looked surprised. "She said that?"

"Not in so many words but yes."

Scarpetti nodded and then changed the subject. "I spoke with Armando Garcia, who runs the Wellglad parking lot. He has a hidden camera in the kiosk at the entrance to the lot, behind a wall clock. Put it there because he said he thought his nephew was stealing money. He came in last night and dropped it off. Said he'd been outta town or he would have come in earlier. Said he showed the footage to his boss, Edward Dowd, who told him to come to us."

Moran cocked his eyebrow.

"I watched the footage, and I think we might have someone. At least we have a guy around the time of death," Scarpetti said.

Moran looked at him intensely. "Can we make an ID?"

Scarpetti shook his head. "No. It's just the back of his head. You'll see." He began looking through his notes. "Armando kept referring to him as a *borracho*. Whatever the hell that is." He found what he was looking for and stopped turning pages.

"We were missing about an hour of the footage, when Hannah Haskell would have arrived, because it was taped over by Monday. Berman said he would *get under it* and get us all of Sunday." He looked at his watch. "He should be ready."

Moran shifted uncomfortably in his seat and loosened the brace on his leg. rubbing it.

"A *borracho* is a drunk," he said absent-mindedly.

Scarpetti looked at Moran with a smile, "I guess those Spanish lessons are paying off."

Moran frowned. "Martha's already fluent; I'm still conjugating verbs."

Scarpetti laughed at this. "When does Martha sense the big trip is coming?" he asked, using air quotes to emphasize the word *sense*.

"She says she sees us there in the summer, so I have time," Moran answered.

Moran had met Martha twenty years earlier on a murder case in South Baltimore. A young woman was bludgeoned to death. Moran was sure it was her ex-boyfriend, but they couldn't find anything linking him to the murder, and his alibi of being out of town seemed airtight.

Out of frustration, the department requested help from a psychic. Her name was Martha Wilman, and she was as intelligent as she was pretty. And Paul Moran fell madly in love at first sight.

Martha told them that the ex-boyfriend had come back into town that night and killed the girl, and that they should look for a picture in a picture, because that would solve the case. Moran thought it was all nonsense—What did a picture in a picture even mean? But he agreed to look into it so he could remain in contact with the blue-eyed psychic.

What transpired after that shocked him to his core. The victim had taken a photo for her work ID the day of her murder, and in it, she was wearing the locket her grandmother had given her. A heart-shaped locket with a picture of her grandmother inside it on a gold chain with large links. The police were given the ID, and they used it for the case file.

After weeks of fruitless investigation, Moran paid a visit to the ex-boyfriend. While there, a young woman wearing that exact chain came to visit. Moran left the house, called for backup, and the two were arrested and taken into custody.

The woman claimed she was innocent and told the police that the ex-boyfriend had given the locket and chain to her as a gift. She hadn't liked the locket and had no idea that there was a small picture in it when she handed it over to them.

Moran looked at the victim's ID in the case file, where she was wearing the locket—a picture within a picture, as Martha had said. The detectives now had a piece linking the ex-boyfriend to the murder. And Moran never doubted a thing Martha told him again.

Moran tightened the brace on his leg with a sigh. "I suppose we should go see what's on the camera," he said and reached for his crutches, stifling a grunt. The rain was making his body ache. He wanted to make it to his retirement in three years, but the pain in his back and hip was getting worse, which probably meant that the bullet lodged next to his L6 was moving, and he would have to have the surgery.

His doctors wanted to remove it ten years ago when it happened, but there was a good chance that it would render him unable to walk, and Moran hadn't wanted to take that chance. Now he might have to. To top it all off, Martha had been forecasting his imminent retirement for a few months now.

"You good, Boss?" Scarpetti asked.

"Fine," Moran replied, and the two set off down the hall.

Chapter 25

Gil Berman, the resident IT geek, acknowledged the detectives with a quick hello as they entered his lab. The detectives sat beside him, their eyes on his large computer screen.

"So, I cleaned it up and I now have most of Sunday. There's no sound; he turned the mic off," he said, typing like a madman until the video footage from the garage popped up with the timecode set in the upper right corner.

"So, as you see, there is nothing going on for a few hours," he said as he fast-forwarded the footage. "But then, at two p.m., we see a car."

On the screen, they saw the interior of the kiosk, the entrance to the parking structure with its gate, and a small sliver of the street outside, which allowed them to see the tires of cars passing by but no more.

"So, this car goes by the entrance," he said, pointing to the screen. "We see the tires go by, and then everything is dead for about ten seconds, but then you will notice on the glass of the toll booth . . . there are two red car brake lights reflected. See?"

Moran and Scarpetti nodded, acknowledging the lights' reflection.

"So, I looked up the parking garage . . ."

He brought another screen up to show a Google Earth map. "And you see that there is a small parking area south of the garage that doesn't have a gate. I checked with Wellglad, and they say that it's the lot used for the South Building, and that it's mainly used for deliveries, temporary parking, handicapped, etc." Berman's face flushed a bit at *handicapped*, but then continued.

"Then we don't see anything for a good two hours and fifteen minutes, when we see Hannah Haskell use her card to enter the lot."

On the screen, they saw Hannah in her car, using her key card to gain access to the parking lot.

"And then here she comes on foot at 4:18 p.m., exiting the lot to head into Wellglad."

Hannah Haskell walked by the kiosk with her purse over her right shoulder. She was also holding something close to her chest. As she passed the camera, she looked over her shoulder, almost as if she sensed something behind her.

Moran interjected, "Can you rewind her and slow it down?"

Berman did, and they watched as Hannah walked slowly by the kiosk and then turned and looked behind her.

"Stop," Moran said and stared at her image. "What is that she's holding to her chest? A manila envelope?"

"Looks like it," said Berman.

Moran stared at her face as she turned to look over her shoulder. "She looks worried, doesn't she? Like she's heard something."

Scarpetti nodded. "Homeless guy?"

Moran nodded. "Maybe. OK, continue."

Berman hit Play again and continued with his description.

"Then you don't see anything again for a good fifteen minutes until . . ." and on the screen, they watched Hannah Haskell quickly walk back past the kiosk at 4:31 p.m.

"Stop," Moran commanded as she entered the frame. "She doesn't have the manila envelope with her."

Berman hit Rewind and played it in slo-mo, and sure enough, the manila envelope was gone. She was just clutching her purse with her left hand.

"She's also wearing a wedding ring," Moran said, pointing to her ring finger. "But it wasn't on her when we found the body."

"Nope," said Scarpetti.

This hung in the air for a second, and then Moran motioned for Berman to continue.

Berman hit Play, and Hannah Haskell entered the frame, and then, as she passed the kiosk, she looked up quickly, almost directly at the camera, before she left the frame.

"Stop!" Moran barked. "Back it up and run it slowly."

Berman did as he was told, and they watched as Hannah took two steps into the frame and, just as she walked by the kiosk, looked up toward the camera.

"Stop," said Moran again, and the three of them stared at the woman's face looking at them. Moran leaned closer to the screen.

"Did she know there was a camera there?" Moran wondered aloud.

Scarpetti moved in to get a closer look. "Hard to tell. She could just be looking at the clock. The camera was hidden behind the clock, so . . ."

"But she looks at it pointedly. Doesn't she? Like she's . . . scared?" asked Moran.

"Well, she's in a parking lot. Alone as the sun's going down. Makes sense," Scarpetti said.

Moran made Berman play it back and forth several times, but it was so quick and the quality so poor that he wasn't sure if she was just looking at the clock or trying to signal to the camera that she was in trouble. He shook his head and let it go, but there was something so troubling to him about this young woman's eyes looking up at the camera like that. He couldn't say why, but he felt as if she wanted them to know that she was there, or that something was very wrong. He didn't know why he felt this way; he just did.

"All right, let's move on," he finally said.

"OK, so now it gets really weird," said Berman, and they watched as he fast-forwarded for ten minutes. But at 4:44, something strange happened. A small animal bound through the frame out of nowhere, followed by a man wearing a weird hat chasing it.

Berman stopped the footage. "You can only see it for a second because it shoots through the frame so quickly, but I think it's a rat. I wish it was a better camera, but that's all I can make of it."

"A rat? Pretty fast rat. It's like he's flying through the frame," said Scarpetti.

"You would be too if some nutjob was chasing you," Berman offered with a chuckle.

Moran stared at the rat flying through the frame. "Back it up and play it in slo-mo until the man enters."

Berman did, and the three men watched as the animal flew through the air until the man chasing it entered the frame and obscured the creature. He was a large man, wearing a strange hat that seemed to have buttons on it. His face couldn't be seen, but his red hair peeked out of the cap.

"I didn't notice the cap earlier. What's on it?" asked Scarpetti.

Berman zoomed in on the hat.

Moran leaned in and stared. "It looks like a button or buttons of some kind." He raised his eyebrows and shrugged. Berman was right. It wasn't a very good camera.

"Continue," he commanded, and the three watched the man run out of the shot.

"And now we have nothing else, but give it seven minutes . . ." Berman sped through the footage. ". . . and we see two lights reflected in the glass of the kiosk again. But these lights aren't red, they're white, so they're not brake lights like the ones we saw earlier but reverse lights. So whoever was parked in that temporary parking lot close to the South Building left at 4:51 p.m., right after the guy ran through."

The two detectives watched the screen, perplexed. Who the hell was in that lot? The car leaving so quickly after the man in the hat ran through gave them pause. But what did it mean? Was it just a coincidence?

"We need to see if there was a delivery that day," Scarpetti said.

"On a Sunday? I doubt it," said Moran and turned to Berman. "Is there anything else?"

Berman shook his head. "No, not until 7:45, and we see the security guard come into the lot." Berman fast-forwarded it so they saw the security guard enter. "And then . . ." He fast-forwarded again, and the security guard rushed out of the lot. "He obviously found her body and ran back into Wellglad to call for help."

The men sat there in silence as the camera continued to play. And when they saw the red lights of the police, Moran told him to turn it off.

"Thanks, Gil," said Scarpetti.

"Of course. I'll put this on a drive and get it to both of you."

"Thank you," said Moran as he headed out with Scarpetti.

The two walked the hall in silence until Scarpetti said, "What do you think?"

Moran contemplated the question before he answered.

"I think she was afraid. I'm just not sure of what. I'd also very much like to know what was in the manila envelope that she found so necessary to deliver to the lab on a Sunday afternoon. I suppose I will have to pay Wellglad a visit tomorrow."

Scarpetti nodded. "Whoever it was got her wedding ring."

Moran nodded as they walked in silence before he blurted out, "Why the hell was he chasing a rat?"

Scarpetti shrugged. "That area is filling up with homeless. And most of the people on the street are on meth these days. I'll find out more about the small parking lot and see if I can get any deliveries coming in or out that day."

Moran nodded, lost in thought, and the two headed off in different directions.

Moran entered his office, sat behind his desk, and saw he had a message on his cell phone from his wife, He dialed her back.

"Hola?" she said.

"It's me."

"You're supposed to say *hola* back. We agreed to practice," Martha chided.

"*Lo ciento*," said Moran. He'd gotten that down pretty quickly. "Hola."

"You gonna be late?" she asked.

"Not too late. Just wanted to hear your voice before I headed out."

"Tough day?" she asked.

"No more than usual. How was your day?" he asked.

"Tough. One woman had a tumor she didn't know about until I told her. That's always the worst, because I can't say it. I just have to alarm them, you know?"

"I'm sorry, Marti," he said, calling her by her pet name.

"It's OK. But then I had a weird thing happen. After I finished my last reading, I was sitting there, exhausted, and I got a vision that didn't make any sense at all."

"Oh?" said Moran absent-mindedly as he pulled his things together to leave. "What was that?"

"I saw a rabbit. It just bounded through the room."

Moran immediately stopped what he was doing. It wasn't the first time some of his wife's clairvoyance had spilled over into his work, and he probably would have thought nothing of her statement if he hadn't just seen a small, furry animal jumping through a crime scene.

"What do you make of that?" he asked quietly.

"I don't know," Martha said. "But you know what's even weirder? There was a girl chasing the rabbit. Like a teenager. And her hair was red."

Moran felt the hair on the back of his neck stand up. As much as he preferred cold hard facts, he had learned to take his wife's abilities seriously. The homeless man with the strange hat in the video had red hair.

"What do you think it meant?" he asked.

"I have no idea. It doesn't really relate to any of the people I read today. I was just sitting there, when all of a sudden, this rabbit comes bouncing through with the girl chasing him. Sort of made me think of *Alice in Wonderland*." She laughed. "I must be going crazy!"

"Well, we can talk more about it when I get home."

"Perfecto. See you soon," she said and hung up.

Moran stood there, lost in thought, his wife's words ringing in his ears.

He slowly pulled on his raincoat, grabbed his crutches, and turned off the light to his office. All the while wondering what the hell a rabbit was doing in a downtown parking lot. And why the man with the red hair and the strange hat was chasing it.

Chapter 26

Ezekial Weintraub entered his apartment after what had proven to be another very long day. It was a small, first-floor one-bedroom on a busy street in a not-so-great area, but it was only five minutes to work by train, and it was all Ezekial could afford.

He flipped on the lights, threw his backpack on the ground, and went into the kitchen, where he noticed a breeze coming through the apartment. The traffic also seemed louder than it usually did. Suddenly, he felt very uneasy. Had he left a window open when he left for work? He'd never done that before.

He quietly grabbed his baseball bat and headed down the hall, looking inside the bathroom as he went. As he closed in on the bedroom, he steeled himself, for what he wasn't sure.

He entered his bedroom and turned on the light. Nothing seemed amiss, except for the fact that his bedroom window was open. How could that have happened? He never opened that window, and what with the rain over the last few days, it wouldn't have made sense to do so. Besides that, it was a sliding window that locked when shut. So it couldn't have been blown open by the wind.

There was only one answer—someone had been in his apartment. And if they had, were they still here? He looked at the closet, tightening his grip on the bat, and took a step toward it. His jaw clenched as he reached for the knob, took a breath, and quickly swung it open, ready to attack. To his relief, he just saw his clothes, which he poked with the bat to make sure no one was behind them. He stood there, dumbfounded.

Slowly, he looked around the room until his desk caught his attention. The bottom drawer was slightly open. He pulled it open. Everything seemed to be in order, and he racked his brain, trying to remember if he had been working there last night. No, he thought, he had spent most of the night on the couch, trying to understand what had happened to Hannah Haskell.

To say her loss was devastating was an understatement. She had been there for him in a way few people had. She gave him a second chance at his career. Hell, at his life.

Why had she left those scans for him in the lab on Sunday? And what did they have to do with Lyprophan? For the life of him, he couldn't figure it out.

Everything on Lyprophan had run like clockwork. He'd been at Wellglad the last two years and had done most of the finishing work on it with Hannah and Kim, and they had busted their butts to get it done. Wellglad was ecstatic with their hard work, and Ezekial felt thrilled to be a part of something so innovative. The FDA had approved it after seven long years, and the whole lab had gone out and celebrated with champagne.

But Sunday night Hannah was murdered after she left him those scans and a cryptic note, *Hang on to these. Re: Lyprophan*, and put them in a place she never normally would.

And now his bedroom window, which he never opened, was left wide open on the same day he'd had a bizarre conversation with Dr. Dowd and impulsively sent those scans to her husband.

Christ. Why hadn't he just told the police about the scans yesterday? he thought. Maybe he should just go there now and come clean.

But that was where things got tricky. Ezekial had tried to stay clean and sober and had done pretty well until they had gone out to celebrate the launch of Lyprophan, and Ezekial'd had a drink or two. He'd scored some meth afterward, and had been using for the last two months. Just a couple of times a week, but still . . . If he went to the police, they'd be suspicious, because he hadn't told them about her message and the scans, and they'd probably want to drug test him. And then all eyes would be on him.

He looked up at the window again and wondered how it had gotten open.

And just as he closed it, it dawned on him. What if someone had left his window open . . . *because they wanted him to know they were there?*

And then another terrifying thought assailed his already anxious mind. If they had her phone, the police would see that he had called her back on Sunday night. Why hadn't they asked him about that? Suddenly, he had a sinking feeling they would. Holy shit, he had to get out of here and get clean. Now.

But he couldn't just leave. Not after all Hannah had done for him. He sat on the bed and racked his brain about what to do. And soon he had a plan.

He'd heard on the news that Captain Haskell had gone home. Ezekial would go to him and explain what had happened. He'd tell him how Hannah had left him the scans with the note . . . and here he stopped. *Christ. The note.* In his haste to get the damn thing mailed to the hospital, he'd forgotten to take the sticky note off the scans. So Haskell would know it was from him anyway. That settled it. He would go and tell Captain Haskell what he knew about the scans, and that they should probably look at Wellglad. If anyone could get the police to do that, it would be Captain Haskell.

After that, he would get on a plane and head to his sister's house in Toronto. She'd probably make him drug test, but he didn't care. He'd get into a program again, and get his life straightened out once and for all. That's what Hannah would have wanted. And that's what he was going to do.

Chapter 27

Ella sat in Dr. Farber's office the next morning, feeling drained and out of touch. Farber had been listening carefully to Ella as she recalled her experience with Malakhi the previous day and seemed to be quite invested in exploring what he had said.

"The Vanitan?" Farber asked. Ella nodded, feeling strange at hearing Farber say the word.

"From the Latin word *vanitas*, I presume. Which means emptiness and vanity."

"Funny, there was a movement in the art world in the mid-1500s when paintings were categorized as vanitas paintings," Dr. Farber continued. "Basically, they were still lifes that depicted treasures like gold or jewels, with skulls or people who had died to show that earthly possessions have no meaning when we die and move on to the afterlife."

Ella was only half-listening as Farber mused on.

"Interesting, though, isn't it?" she queried. "To think there is some sort of energy force invading Earth? And that it can infect us humans? The *Non-Life*." And here she stopped pointedly. "And in a way, he's right. One need only watch the news to see how little care we have for our fellow man, let alone other creatures and the planet itself."

Ella nodded, but she couldn't quite explain how disturbing the whole interaction was for her. And not because of the science fiction overtones but because of the way it had made her feel.

She genuinely loved her patients, and often preferred their company to that of the doctors at Bainbridge. Her patients were very vulnerable and once you got past their disorders, their humanity was usually right there on the surface and easy to connect to. And Ella did. She was able to cross the divide and see things through their eyes. And because of that, she had gained their trust and assuaged their fears of being in a world that had ruthlessly left them behind.

Ella also trusted them. Especially Malakhi. And even though it seemed ludicrous, she worried that his warnings had merit. As if she *knew* the truth behind his words, even if she couldn't explain it rationally. She had felt that way with her aunt just two days prior, and she couldn't shake the feeling something was about to happen. It was a visceral feeling she couldn't seem to ignore. As if there were some *underreality* where everything Malakhi had said was taking place.

"Humans with the Non-Life energy infecting others. Sort of like a virus or vampires and zombies," Farber continued. "Perhaps he's referring to people incapable *of feeling or caring.* Those with no empathy; sociopaths, borderlines, psychopaths, or narcissists—although that term is thrown around rather loosely today. We've all had run-ins with those types, and I tend to agree with Malakhi. They're parasites; black holes sucking up all the energy from those around them for their own gain."

A chill ran through Ella. Dr. Farber sounded a lot like Malakhi right now. Her surprise at Farber's comments must have shown because Farber quickly said, "Of course there are varying degrees of the disorders." She then added, "What a clever person Malakhi is. Or Sebastian, rather."

Ella nodded. "Yes, he is."

"In the nineties, only about one percent of the population had one of these disorders in its extreme form, but that number has increased over the years. Now they say it is between two and four percent, but some, including myself, now place it as high as ten percent. Mind you, I have nothing but compassion for those who were abused as children and dealt with extreme violence or neglect. Or even those who fell into drug use, but many of these people were born that way. And since they have poor outcomes therapeutically, neurobiologists are looking at their brains for clues. It's really sort of a fascinating landscape. They've come out with studies showing that the MRIs of people with clinical sociopathy or psychopathy show much less gray matter in the prefrontal cortex. Particularly in the left and right anterior insula of the brain that deal with empathy . . . as I'm sure you know."

As a matter of fact, Ella did know. She remembered this from her studies and knew the anterior insula lay in the cerebral cortex, which was believed to be the seat of consciousness. It was responsible for decision-making, self-awareness, and empathy.

"And now we know these disorders are genetically heritable, which is a terrifying thought," Farber said as she took a sip of water.

Ella knew about the studies tracking the heritability of these disorders, but she still felt that if children genetically predisposed to these conditions were raised in a loving home, the disorders would have much less of a chance to be expressed, if at all.

"It's funny. We used to characterize a person with one of these disorders as having *deficient personality syndrome*," Farber added.

Ella perked up. This was something she hadn't heard before. "Why is that?"

"Because people who have it have no real core. They co-opt the qualities and traits of others to impress and seduce. Wonderful mimics, psychopaths. And they have to be." And then she said rather emphatically, "For whatever made them the way they are, they are utterly empty."

This statement shocked Ella. It was as if Dr. Farber had nothing but contempt for people suffering with these disorders. Wasn't she a psychologist whose mission was to help these very people?

"Wouldn't it be remarkable if one day we just ran MRIs on people before doing therapy to determine if a person had these disorders? Certainly would save a lot of time." And then she smiled and said, "Who knows? Maybe we will."

It was meant as a joke, but Ella found it sort of bizarre. What was going on?

Farber zeroed in on Ella again. "Let's get back to you and Malakhi. What do you think he meant when he said that you should remember who Dan was with when he was saying *van* repeatedly?"

"I don't know. I guess he was saying that Dan was trying to warn me. Or not just me—everyone. That they were around someone bad or . . . dangerous."

There, she thought, she'd said it. It was another warning.

"What about with respect to you? Do you think he was speaking about anyone around you in particular?" Farber asked.

Ella flushed. She couldn't mean Clyde, could she? Dr. Farber didn't like him from the first time she mentioned him, and things had stayed that way, which was why Ella rarely brought him up. Farber obviously thought Clyde was bad for her.

"I know you mean Clyde, and no, I don't think he was speaking about him," Ella said, annoyed.

"No, I didn't. I don't think Clyde is a psychopath. I think he's narcissistic, but I also think he's fairly easy to spot."

Ella was speechless. She would never speak to a client that way.

Undeterred, Farber continued, "Look, I don't mean to be insulting, but he does seem drunk on his own success. There was a marvelous study at UC Berkely that showed that many people in positions of power over time acted as if they had suffered a traumatic brain injury: They became more impulsive, less risk-aware, and, probably most importantly, they became much less adept at seeing things from other people's point of view."

Ella had had enough. Yes, Clyde had hurt her by flirting with the pharma rep, but this character assassination was unnecessary.

"Despite what happened with the woman in the hall, I've learned a lot from Clyde Westbrook these past few years. And giving me a shot at the Haskell case was an enormous opportunity. It was very generous of him to do that for me," she said defensively.

Dr. Farber remained quiet for a second, then said, "Was it? Was it just out of goodwill toward you, Ella?"

That shook Ella. She hadn't confided to Farber that she wondered why Clyde hadn't monitored her on this case as he usually did. She hadn't told Farber that he'd disappeared, as if he had wanted nothing to do with it. Nor that she'd seriously begun to question why he'd given it to her in the first place. But apparently, Farber was wondering the same thing.

Just then, the clock mercifully chimed, and Dr. Farber looked at her and said, "Time's up."

Ella headed to the door, feeling more unsettled than she had when she'd entered. It was as if the ground was sliding beneath her feet. First her aunt, then Malakhi, and now her therapist.

She felt as though a veil was being lifted, and she wasn't sure what was on the other side. Or if she could handle it. She'd had to handle so much in her life. Too much, really. If people only knew the battles she'd fought just to get to where she was, they wouldn't believe her. Well, she thought, not all people. Her patients would.

Chapter 28

Otis Raymond sat on his bedroom floor wearing the red Power Ranger costume his mother had gotten him from eBay a few months ago for his eighth birthday. His room was another world, an escape for Otis with its maps of exotic lands on the wall and the glow-in-the-dark planets and stars his mother had pasted to the ceiling. Otis could think in his room because he wasn't bombarded with all the petty goings-on of other people interrupting him like they did at that awful school. And speaking of school—he'd just heard his brother and sister leave and knew that his mother would be coming to get him ready to go to his school any minute now. All the more reason to finish his picture quickly, he thought.

His face strained with concentration as he took the red crayon and went over his whole drawing with it, not missing an inch. And as he went, the red crayon sort of reminded him of the costume he was wearing, which was weird if you thought about it. Then again, Otis knew that *everything was connected*.

He had asked his brother, Lance, if he minded that he got the red suit, because that would mean that he, Otis, would be the leader of the Rangers. Lance said that was no problem, and because he was fifteen and pretty tall, Otis doubted he could get a costume in his size anyway.

Lance had been a *Mighty Morphin Power Rangers* fan and had shown the TV series to Otis when he was six, and Otis fell in love. So much so, his mom bought him all the DVDs so that he could watch whenever he wanted. At this point, he'd seen them so many times that he'd memorized most of the dialogue and would mouth the words as he watched.

The Power Rangers were superheroes who possessed enhanced strength, agility, and combat prowess. Some even possessed superhuman or psychic abilities, and each Ranger had his or her own unique weapon to go up against the bad guys.

But it was the Rangers' Code that impressed Otis the most, and was one that he himself tried to live by. Rangers couldn't use their powers for personal gain or to start a fight, and they couldn't disclose their identities to the public.

That last one was hard on Otis, but he'd learned that it was necessary to do what he needed to do here, so he just kind of took it as part of the mission.

Just then, his mother came into the room. Carla Raymond looked tired and worn, but her eyes shone brightly when she saw him, which lit up her whole face. Everyone said he looked just like her, with his blond hair, green eyes, and thin face, but Otis didn't really see it. She just looked like Mom to him.

"Hey you." She smiled. "We have to get going. Don't want to be late for school."

Otis's face soured into a frown. He hated those dumb kids and that ultradumb teacher. What he really wanted to do was keep on drawing. His mom must have noticed his reticence and sat on the floor beside him.

"How pretty," she said, tracing the lines of the drawing with her finger. "A mountain—a very tall one with some stars?"

Otis nodded begrudgingly. It wasn't that exactly, but it was OK that she didn't know. He'd learned to make allowances when it came to his mom. Right now, he just wanted to finish his drawing before he went to school, so he began moving the red crayon faster.

"Is that water?" Carla asked, pointing to the patch of blue.

Otis ignored this question. It was pretty obvious, wasn't it?

So she asked another. "Why are you covering it all up with red, sweetie?"

Why couldn't she just let him finish? "Because it's red there!" he said, somewhat exasperated.

As a rule, he wished she'd stop asking questions altogether. It just made everything so difficult. He turned his body away from her, pulling the sketchpad around so she couldn't see it, hoping this would make the questions stop.

And it worked partially, because the questions did stop, but his mom didn't. "Otis, we need to get to school on time today. It's a very important day because we're going to talk to your teacher about how things are going. So I need you to put down the crayon, and let's get you dressed."

Otis felt exhausted just thinking about the day ahead of him. How he wished he could share with his mother what his drawing was and what it meant, but his words wouldn't make sense to her, and that would just make her sad. And he hated it when she was sad more than anything else in the world.

And so, like the Power Rangers, he concealed a lot of who he was. It used to make him angry that no one understood him. But now he knew he just had to do what he had to do here, even if it meant going to school. The people there were just dumb. But it made his mother happy, and Otis would do anything in the world for his mother, because he knew that she loved him more than anything on Earth. And because he couldn't really reciprocate that love in a way she could see, he vowed to do pretty much anything she wanted. And, unfortunately, that included school.

It hadn't always been that way. When he was younger, Otis used to tantrum and scream a lot. But he was just getting used to being here then and didn't realize that they couldn't feel him the way he felt them.

Lance was the one who'd told him that he had to be easier on Mom. Lance was good like that. He wouldn't go so far as to say that his brother understood him, but his brother was not a liar, and more than anything, Otis needed to hear the truth. And so he respected his brother in a way he could never respect his father.

His dad, Guy Raymond, was a nice guy, he guessed, and he smiled at using the word *guy* twice. But his dad's mind was never really on anything but work, and that kind of bugged Otis. Dad's energy was always in his office in that big black building, even when he was home.

His mother used to take him to visit Dad there for lunch, but after one deeply disturbing trip when Otis had felt surrounded by one too many liars, they had never gone back. He couldn't help that he'd had to fight for his life to get away from those awful people with their yucky energy that leached onto him. Nor had he felt bad about kicking that woman who'd touched his cheek.

She didn't think he was cute. She didn't like him. She was a liar.

But he had felt bad on the car ride home, because Mom seemed superupset. It looked like she was crying at one point, which made Otis feel just terrible. So terrible he had rubbed her head when she carried him out of the car after they got home, and he knew that she knew that this was his way of saying he wished she wasn't sad. And he'd been grateful that rubbing her head had worked, and that he hadn't had to say anything like he was sorry. Because that would've been a lie.

But what he really felt bad about—or mad, to be more exact—was the fact that his father had been so embarrassed by the incident. What the hell did Dad have to be embarrassed about? If Otis was his dad, he would be more embarrassed about all the energy being sucked out of him working at that place than he would be of his son for telling the truth. But of course, his dad hadn't seen it that way. And from that day on Otis never really liked spending time with his dad.

But Lance? He liked Lance. Lance made him feel safe. Lance wasn't a liar. You know who else wasn't a liar? Rudy the gardener. Otis liked Rudy a lot. He was old and kind of crabby, and he didn't talk a lot, but when he did, he was funny. And not a liar.

You know who else wasn't a liar? Dr. Kramer. Otis had really liked her. She didn't seem to know what she was or why she was with him, but she would figure it out one day. If only he had had more time with her. She had stopped coming when he was five, and he hadn't really seen much of her since, which was too bad.

Now his mother was looking at him and asking him to put his color down, and because he had promised Lance to be easier on her, he did just that. He'd do what she wanted, he thought, but not without a parting shot.

"I hate that stupid school," he said defiantly.

Carla looked at him lovingly and said, "Of course you do. They don't speak your language, my little intergalactic traveler. But while we are on Earth, we have to go to school."

He nodded, acquiescing, but decided to clarify something she'd gotten wrong about his drawing.

"It isn't a mountain, you know."

Carla, who was looking for some pants for him to wear, replied over her shoulder, "Oh no? What is it?"

"It's a place where we land," replied Otis, thinking this might intrigue her.

But Carla answered absent-mindedly, "Who lands?"

Otis decided to skip that question, because she really didn't seem to mean it, and explained *why* instead of *who*.

"You can see it from space. It's like a sign."

"You mean like McDonald's? Like the golden arches sign?" she asked cheerfully.

This answer really bothered him for all the obvious reasons, so he shook his head vigorously. Why did she have to be so silly sometimes? But then she apologized and told him that she didn't understand what he meant, and so he bit his lip and reached out his hand for the pants. Better to just let it go. That was what Lance would say. That was what a Power Ranger would do. She handed him the pants and gave him a little kiss.

"Good boy. Now let me find a shirt." And she disappeared inside the closet again.

Otis looked back down at his drawing and sighed. Why couldn't any of them remember? It wasn't that long ago.

He looked at the dumb pants in his hand and decided he had better get on with it. So he put down his crayon on his drawing and stood up as he mumbled begrudgingly, "And those aren't stars. They're moons."

Chapter 29

Ella arrived at her office and noticed that Gary Lester had left her two messages. She sat down at her desk and called him, but there was no answer.

As she hung up the phone, she noticed the little watercolor her aunt had done on her desk. She stared at it. How had Dan painted the exact same thing? Down to the color of the wash that covered both paintings.

Ella had gone home after her conversation with Malakhi last night and scoured the internet, looking for landscape paintings that would match what Dan and her aunt had depicted, but to no avail. She did, however, find an awful lot of information on pyramids.

She had no idea there were so many pyramids around the world. There were the pyramids in Egypt but also in Italy, Greece, Sudan, Mexico, Java, Cambodia, and Peru as well. There was even a pyramid in the United States called Monks Mound, built at the site of the ancient Native American city of Cahokia in Illinois.

Many historians thought pyramids were used as tombs for pharaohs and others of noble birth. Often, they were buried with their possessions and animals so that they could make the trip with them, and Ella reflected that the vanitas painters would have a field day with them.

What Ella found most interesting, though, was that the pyramids were built at all. If they were erected around 2500 BC, just how had they been able to move the tons of stone needed to build them? The engineering was flabbergasting, and Ella marveled at their precision.

She was also struck by the important role astronomy and astrology played in their creation. The pyramids were aligned with different cardinal points and celestial bodies. It was all absolutely incredible.

She stayed online for quite some time, until she found herself tumbling down a rabbit hole that was bizarre. There were articles stating the pyramids had been built ten thousand years ago by an advanced civilization that had been wiped out by a global catastrophe. Others said that the pyramids had been built by extraterrestrials who would one day come back to claim their territory.

It was in this rabbit hole in the wee hours of the morning that Ella found herself wondering what if Malakhi wasn't wrong. About the Age of Aquarius and the dark energy of the Vanitan descending? What if Malakhi was right and Ella and normal people were only privy to a tiny bit of information and couldn't go outside their sensory arena for higher forms of knowledge?

Here Ella decided she really couldn't lump herself in with *normal people*. She'd never felt normal. She'd lost her parents at the age of eight, and when she was ten, her uncle died in an accident involving a firearm. Ella'd been present during the accident, and she'd dissociated from herself afterward. It was as if she'd left reality during the incident and couldn't quite get back. They had kept her in the hospital for a couple of weeks under psychiatric observation because she couldn't function, and that was when her headaches began. The episode subsided, but it took her a long time to get any memory of what had happened that night. And even now, she couldn't recall it completely. But she had worked very hard to get better and change her life. And she had. But normal? No, she'd never felt normal.

Now, here she was, trying to figure out how her aunt and Dan, two people from extremely different walks of life could have painted the same tableau so similarly. But her thoughts were interrupted by a short knock on the door, followed by her friend, Gary Lester, walking into the room.

"You busy?" he asked curtly.

"No. I just tried calling you," she said, putting the painting in her bag. "What's up? And please don't tell me something bad." She smiled, but Gary didn't seem amused.

"I hope not," he answered tersely.

She waited for him to tell her what was wrong, but he seemed to be wrestling with it.

"Gary, what is it?" she pressed.

"You know the paper I asked you to give to Westbrook? The treatment for schizophrenia?"

She frowned, confused. "You mean the research on your light treatment protocol? Yeah. I gave it to him months ago, right after you asked me to. Why?"

Gary's face seemed to drain of color. "Well, turns out I may have been scooped."

Ella had pushed Clyde to talk to Gary about his light treatment idea, but he always seemed to sidestep the subject. He didn't seem to think much of Gary, and now that he knew about their relationship, she doubted Clyde would help him at all.

"What makes you think that?" she asked, concerned.

"Just something I overheard," he said cryptically. "You're sure you gave it to him, right?"

Ella felt terrible. "Of course I did. But I'll push him to read it again, OK?"

"No," Gary snapped. "Don't do anything until I find out more. I've made some calls to the *American Journal of Science*; I have a couple of friends there. Let's wait until I hear back from them."

Was Gary insinuating what she thought he was? "Gary, you and I are friends. Tell me what happened," she said.

He looked at her for a second, and Ella got the distinct impression he was summing her up before he said, "I overheard an interesting conversation between Dan and Clark at dinner Monday night."

"About what?" she pushed.

"Clark was trying to sell his holographic mumbo jumbo to Dan, who seemed out of it until Clark mentioned light. Then Dan started talking about a light hat that he had to wear . . . that sounded a lot like the one proposed in my treatment."

Ella felt as if ice water had been poured into her veins. "What?"

Gary nodded. "And Dan's primary was Clyde Westbrook. The same Westbrook you gave my treatment proposal to."

Ella vaguely remembered something Farber had said earlier about power corrupting the mind. "He would never do something like that."

"I sure hope not," Gary said tightly. "I'll find out more and let you know." And with that, he turned and left.

Ella felt as if she'd been hit by a truck. It was hard to fathom someone she cared for—loved, even—doing something so selfish and underhanded. But then she remembered him flirting with the pharma rep after kissing her, and it occurred to her that Clyde Westbrook may not be constrained by any sort of loyalty that she or Gary took for granted.

She had to find out what happened and was about to head down the hall to Clyde's office when her cell phone rang. She looked at the caller ID and saw the name CARLA RAYMOND, Otis's mom. Her aunt had just mentioned Otis, and now here was his mother calling.

This happened frequently to Ella. If she thought about a person or heard someone's name, someone she hadn't seen in a while, invariably that person would either call, or she would run into them, as if it had all been preordained.

She answered the phone. "Carla. How are you?"

"Good, good. We're all just fine," Carla said. But Ella detected the worry in her tone.

"Is Otis OK?" Ella asked.

There was a slight pause, and then Carla vomited up her fear and frustration. "He's—you know—he's Otis. Brilliant and difficult, but the most loving boy. He has an evaluation later today at his school, and I'm worried. His teacher said that he isn't making the progress in socialization that she had hoped to see, and . . . well, I'm just scared that they're going to tell us that we have to leave. I don't know."

Ella realized the enormous stress that Carla was under and said calmly, "Carla, that won't happen. They won't do that. I can reach out to the school if you're worried."

"No, I don't want to do anything yet. Except . . . do you think you could come and see Otis? He would really love that. And so would I."

Immediately, Ella felt awful. He was five years old when she had stopped his occupational therapy and started her hospital residency. She'd stayed in contact, but then life got hectic, and the Raymond family and Otis had drifted away like so many other things.

Memories of the little boy flooded her mind, and she found herself missing their discussions about the constellations, on which Otis was an expert. She missed seeing his prowess with numbers and delighting in how quickly he could solve numerical riddles. Once, he'd confided that mathematics was the only true language, but most people were unwilling to speak it because lying was easier, and that tickled her to no end.

She remembered how he looked the day she'd asked him to stop his tantrums, saying the noise bothered her ears. His little face had become vulnerable, and he had bitten his lip but agreed to do so, and Ella realized that he had stopped *for her*. And this made hearing Carla's sad voice all the harder.

"Carla, I've been meaning to call you for some time now to see if I could come visit. How weird is that?" Adding quickly, "What day works for you?"

She heard the relief in Carla's voice, and they set a time for Friday afternoon.

She hung up the phone and brought her focus back to what had just transpired with Gary. She steeled herself and headed down the hall toward Clyde's office. Her jaw tensed at the thought of him, and her temples began to throb. She wasn't sure if he'd done what Gary thought, but she intended to find out.

Chapter 30

Detective Moran had slept very little the night before and was not feeling his best as he pulled into the parking lot at Wellglad the next day. He'd gone home and had dinner with Marti, who continued to talk about the rabbit jumping through her day with the redheaded girl following it, until he finally told her about the redheaded man with the odd hat chasing something that looked like a rat—or a rabbit. Marti asked why he hadn't told her earlier, to which he'd shrugged. They ate in silence for a while until Marti said, "It was a rabbit," rather definitively.

As he waited at the gate to the parking structure he'd seen Hannah Haskell drive through the day before on the video, he heard what he assumed to be Armando Garcia's booming voice snap at someone. Instantaneously, a young man of about twenty ran into the kiosk and opened the gate for Moran. That must be the nephew, Moran thought as he glided into a space.

"Good morning, Detective Moran. Detective Scarpetti told me you would be coming in," Armando said, heading over to him.

"Buenos días and mucho gusto," Moran answered as he put on his crutches and got out of the car.

"Is everything OK? Did you need something?" asked Armando, closing his door.

"Everything is fine," Moran replied. "I'm going to meet with Dr. Dowd."

Armando seemed relieved and said, "Dr. Dowd is a wonderful man."

Moran then asked quietly, "You said Dr. Dowd knew about the camera?"

Armando eyed his nephew, who was fixated on his phone.

"Yes. I asked him if it was legal to tape, so he checked with his lawyer, and if it isn't in the bathroom, it is OK," he answered just as quietly.

"Did Dr. Haskell know there was a camera there?"

Armando nodded. "Yes. When she was working the long nights for the new drug, the Lyprophan? I told her not to worry, that she was safe because . . . because I had the camera." He looked down sadly, as if he failed.

"Cameras deter break-ins, but not usually this kind of crime, Armando," Moran said, trying to assuage his guilt. He looked around the lot. "Tell me—did you often see vagrants on the camera footage?"

Armando shook his head. "Sometimes. But there are no public bathrooms or places to eat, so why would they be here?"

Why indeed? thought Moran as he headed toward Wellglad's entrance. "Thank you, Armando."

And as he went, he heard the man yelling at his nephew in Spanish. But he couldn't make out a word of it.

Chapter 31

Edward Dowd's secretary, Jane, met Moran at the entrance and escorted him to his meeting. Dowd's office was beautifully decorated and overlooked the railway tracks behind Wellglad, which seemed to stretch on endlessly into the woods behind them. As he waited, Moran found himself contemplating what life would be like on the other side of those tracks, the side Edward Dowd obviously lived on.

He was joined a few minutes later by the man himself, and Moran couldn't help but notice he looked somewhat like a bird. Dowd stretched out his hand and introduced himself, then sat down as the detective said, "I'm sorry to meet you under these circumstances."

Dowd nodded sadly. "Horrible business. Hannah was a wonderful person and an integral part of Wellglad. We've all been shocked and horrified that something like this could happen."

"Yes, it is horrible, and I'm sorry for your loss," Moran replied, and then dove right in. "As you know, Mr. Garcia gave us the camera that he had placed at the entrance to the parking garage, and we were able to see footage of a man running through the parking lot."

"Yes, Armando came to me and played some of the tape. I saw the man and immediately told him to go to the police," Dowd replied.

"And why do you think Mr. Garcia came to you first instead of coming straight to the police?"

Dowd paused before answering. "Armando has family members and friends who came to this country and have not been treated all that well by the authorities. Unfortunately, there is a deep distrust of law enforcement, and I think he was worried that the camera would get him into trouble."

"Yes, he mentioned that you had asked your lawyer about the legality of filming people without their knowledge."

Dowd nodded. "I did, and everything he did was aboveboard. There was no sound involved, which would have made it a violation, apparently."

Moran agreed, "Quite right," and then changed course. "Have you had trouble with vagrants in the parking lot or surrounding area before?"

"Not to my knowledge, no. This is a fairly deserted part of town still, so I do not think we have a problem with the homeless or people of that ilk," Dowd replied. "But surely building security would have more information on that score?"

Moran had always found that people of a certain socioeconomic class were prone to talking down to others either directly or indirectly. Dowd might just as well have said, *Why are you bothering me? Ask security*.

"Quite right." Moran nodded, looking at his notes. "My partner said that apart from a car break-in last year, there wasn't anything that would send up a red flag."

He took a second to write something on his notepad before asking gently, "Were you close to the deceased?"

Dowd took off his glasses and cleaned them, and when he put them back on, Moran felt as if he was sitting across from a giant owl.

"Hannah was a valued colleague," he replied. "But we were not particularly close. We worked together and attended professional gatherings, but it wasn't an overly familiar relationship. I think those can be extremely damaging in the workplace."

Moran feigned enlightenment before asking, "Did you know her husband?" And he watched as Dowd crossed his legs. *Well*, thought Moran, *that's your second tell*. The first was the need to clean his glasses when Moran asked how close he was to Hannah Haskell.

"I have met the captain a few times, but I don't really know him. As you know, he is running for the Senate, and Wellglad has contributed to his campaign—and not just because of Hannah. No, we support his platform, as well as many other politicians, as you can imagine," he said carefully.

"Of course, of course," Moran said, taking notes. Dowd uncrossed his legs and shifted in his seat. *Number three*, thought Moran.

"As a matter of fact, I was part of the hosting committee for the function given this past Sunday night. So I was at the cocktail party with the captain the night Hannah was . . . killed." And here he cleared his throat.

Four, thought Moran, who played dumb but knew that Dowd had been at the fundraiser. Moran had looked at the guest list and the registry of the PAC putting on the party and was surprised to find Wellglad and Edward Dowd among its investors. But what surprised him more was the fact that Hannah Haskell hadn't accompanied her husband to a cocktail party that her company was involved in throwing to support her husband's Senate bid. Now that was odd.

"How did Captain Haskell seem that night? At the party?"

"He seemed fine. He's a very good speaker, very charming. It was quite a successful event," Dowd confided.

Moran frowned slightly. "Why do you think Dr. Haskell didn't attend the party with him? After all, it was Wellglad—at least partially—putting it on. Didn't you find that strange?"

Dowd picked up his glass of water carefully, taking a few sips before replying.

Number five. What would Dowd have to worry about? Moran wondered.

"Hannah was apolitical, Detective Moran. At least with me. We kept our conversations outside of work to travel, film, or art. She'd tell me if they'd discovered a good restaurant—that sort of thing."

"She never spoke of her husband's campaign?" Moran asked incredulously.

Dowd realized his mistake and blinked slowly, which made him look even more like an owl. And the pitch of his voice rose when he answered, but at this point, Moran had lost count of Dowd's tells and firmly decided that he was hiding something.

"Well, she didn't say anything to me specifically. I think she mentioned that she didn't enjoy being on the campaign trail because she had too much work to do. Hannah was working on a new medication the last few years and spent long hours here at Wellglad," Dowd explained.

"I see. Well, that leads me to my next question: Why do you think she came to work Sunday afternoon? We reviewed that tape from Armando Garcia's camera, and she couldn't have been here more than fifteen minutes. What could she have accomplished in fifteen minutes?"

Dowd shrugged and shook his head. "There are any number of things she could have done. Perhaps she needed some data she couldn't access from home. As you can well imagine, we don't allow our system to be accessed from private servers because of the climate we live in."

"Is that right?" Moran asked innocently.

"This is a multibillion-dollar business, Detective Moran. Our research must remain extremely secure. Everyone has to sign nondisclosure agreements, and we have no-compete clauses in every contract down to the lab assistants. 'Knowledge is power,' after all."

"True. So, she could have come just to get some data off her computer?" Dowd nodded.

"What was she working on, if you don't mind my asking?"

Dowd took a slight pause before going on. "Hannah and her team were beginning work on a pancreatic medication, among other things. It's still in the early stages."

"And the one she was working on for the last few years? The one you just said she'd spent long hours on?" Moran asked pointedly.

Dowd hesitated slightly before answering. "She had just completed work on an antidepressant that had taken years to get approved by the FDA. Getting these approvals is rigorous work and extremely time-consuming. She was the consummate professional when it came to her work. Very thorough."

When Moran had researched Hannah Haskell, he'd seen the announcement of the drug and its success mentioned in the newspapers. It was quite the boon for Wellglad, and Moran found it odd that Dowd didn't mention the drug by name.

"I see," Moran said, and then remembered something. "Hannah Haskell was the only person who parked in the lot that day using her key card. Well, her and the security guard. But we saw that there was a car that pulled into the southern portion of the parking lot. It seems to be a separate lot?"

Moran noticed that something seemed to have changed for Dowd. His shoulders dropped, the natural timbre returned to his voice, and he seemed almost eager to answer.

"Oh yes. That's a small lot for the handicapped, or the deliveries and the handlers, of course."

"Handlers?" asked Moran.

Dowd proceeded to explain that most studies were done on human participants in the form of drug trials and tests. Then he went on to add that Wellglad used animals for some of their testing in the South Building, which was directly across from that small lot.

Moran asked politely, "Oh? What kind of animals do you have on the premises?"

"Mostly rats and rabbits. They multiply quickly, and their systems are fairly similar to ours," Dowd answered, and Moran quietly checked *rabbit* off on his mental list.

"Would there be any way I could see Dr. Haskell's laboratory and per-haps take a look at this South Building?" he asked pleasantly.

Dowd cocked his head and answered, "That shouldn't be a problem." But his eyes narrowed as he said it, and Moran got the feeling that he was about to be mauled by a very big crow.

"I'm not sure why you would be interested in Hannah's work if you weren't pursuing an investigation outside of what I thought was a mugging gone wrong. Is it possible that there is something more sinister happening?"

Moran shook his head reassuringly. "No, not necessarily. I just like to be thorough with cases, even though the obvious is usually what took place. And being thorough for me usually means knowing the victim as well as I can. I will say that I've been very surprised by some of my cases. Sometimes something mundane can lead one to extraordinary discoveries."

Dowd looked away as he pulled himself to his feet with his crutches, and Moran was certain this was not done out of compassion but out of disgust. Men like Dowd were bothered by imperfection. The tight smile on his face let Moran know just how uncomfortable his being disabled was making him.

Moran stopped as they headed to the door. "Oh! One more question. Who was the lawyer you spoke to regarding Mr. Garcia's camera?"

Dowd turned to him. "I believe it was someone at the firm who handles us."

"And what firm is that?" asked Moran.

"Levine and Klein," Dowd answered, and turned to open the door. Moran nodded, making another note on his mental checklist: Levine, as in Arthur Levine, Captain Haskell's friend, the one who was so worried about the captain's mental state.

Dowd opened the door, and Jane magically appeared.

"Detective Moran would like to see Dr. Haskell's lab and the South Building. Can you arrange that, Jane?" Dowd asked.

"Of course." She smiled.

Dowd shook Moran's hand as he said, "And just one more thing."

Dowd sighed. "Yes?"

"What was the name of the antidepressant Hannah Haskell worked on? The one she had just *taken to market*, as you said?"

And it was this tell that was the most notable to Detective Moran, for Edward Dowd's breath seemed to catch before he muttered the name of the drug under it: *Lyprophan*. And as Moran mentioned that he had seen the commercials for it on TV, Dowd stared at him like a giant vulture. A vulture who had mistaken his prey for dead.

Chapter 32

Jane escorted Detective Moran to the first floor, and they entered Hannah Haskell's lab. It was eerily quiet, with only one person working at her desk wearing a lab coat. The woman was small and of Asian descent and was introduced to Detective Moran as Kim Matsunaga, Hannah's lab technician.

Jane asked Kim to help the detective to the South Building after he was finished in Hannah's lab. Kim frowned, as if she found the idea of that distasteful, but nodded. Jane said her goodbyes and was gone.

Kim looked at the detective expectantly, and Moran dove in. He found out that Kim had worked for Hannah for the past year, and that she was Hannah's second lab assistant. Her first assistant, Ezekial Weintraub, had called in sick that morning, but Kim was sure that he was devastated by Hannah's death as they were particularly close. Moran made a note that he would have to reach out to Mr. Weintraub later.

Kim showed him around the lab, and Moran politely asked what they were working on. She told him that they were doing some preliminary work on a medication for pancreatic insufficiency.

"Would that be what brought her to the lab on Sunday?" he asked.

"Maybe," she answered, then quickly added, "When we were working on Lyprophan, she was in the lab a lot of weekends. It was pretty crazy." She went on to gush about the new antidepressant. "It's the most revolutionary drug Wellglad's had," she told him, and when he asked why, she waxed on.

"It's not an SSRI, for starters. Those work by suppressing the body's reuptake of serotonin, and they can come with side effects like lethargy and some serious GI problems, not to mention sexual dysfunction," she told him. "Lyprophan is a completely different drug that bypasses the reuptake loop entirely and works on the brain stem directly. This causes the prefrontal cortex to be flooded with serotonin and . . . well, I won't bore you with the details, but it's stronger and twice as effective as the SSRIs," she gloated. "It's in a class all by itself.

"It took Hannah seven years to get it through the FDA, which is kind of record timing for something this revolutionary," Kim exclaimed proudly. "It's like the Holy Grail of antidepressants and is killing on the market right now. Wellglad shares are up 80 percent, and the projected earnings are off the charts."

"Well, quite the superdrug indeed," Moran concurred. "Was it tested on animals?" he asked.

Kim smiled at his naivete. "In order to get FDA approval, a drug has to be tested on people, Detective Moran."

To prove her point, she took the detective to the computer and pulled up the Lyprophan case file, which showed hundreds of numbers.

"Each number is a patient that we tested the drug on and followed for seven years," she explained.

"Wow. That is a lot of work," he said, then noticed that some of the numbers had the letter *P* by their entry.

"What does the *P* mean?

"*P* is for placebo. Those people weren't given the real drug," Kim explained.

Moran then asked her how test subjects were chosen.

"These are voluntary tests, Detective, and, as you can see, we didn't have trouble recruiting people to join."

"And all these people signed up?" he asked.

"Yup. And we had a good representation as far as race and sex are concerned, which you don't always get. Depression seems to cross all population boundaries and is one of the fastest growing health issues in this country, so a lot of applicants responded or were referred by their doctors."

Moran marveled at this world he knew nothing about. She was about to exit the folder when something else caught his attention. On a lot of the entries, there was a star.

"What does the star represent?" he asked.

"Armed forces," Kim answered.

"Is that normal? " He gestured to the computer screen. "There are an awful lot of stars here."

"The military usually has a stipend for these kinds of tests. So those subjects actually were compensated. We do that sometimes with people who work in government. And given what a lot of people in the military go through, their willingness to test antidepressants makes sense," she answered.

Moran quietly reflected that Captain Haskell was also a military man, and wondered if he had had something to do with the large number of the test subjects being in the Army.

He was about to stand when he eyed a file with a red X on it at the bottom of the chart. "And this?" he asked.

Kim leaned in and said, "Oh, that's what we call the X File," and laughed. "That's our nickname for it—you know, like that old TV show? *The X Files?*"

Moran vaguely remembered the show from the nineties and nodded.

"The people in that file dropped out of the trial." She clicked on the file but found it empty.

"Huh. That's weird," she said. "Hannah probably just got rid of them after approval. But I can tell you that there were very few who dropped out of Lyprophan because it worked so well. I think it was like seven people out of about eight hundred. Pretty small number, given that it was a seven-year trial."

Moran asked her why they'd dropped out.

"Various reasons," she said. "A few had allergy issues; I think one went AWOL and two got pregnant. Still—a one percent exit rate is phenomenal."

Just then the phone rang. Kim left to answer the call, and Moran found himself sitting alone in front of Hannah Haskell's computer. He made sure that Kim was out of range, then clicked on the Calendar button, and Hannah Haskell's schedule popped up.

He scrolled back two weeks prior to her death but found nothing that wasn't work-related, but then he noticed a name with an appointment set for two days before her murder. Moran recognized the name as the one he'd found on the prescription paper in her purse. *Kimmelman 6 p.m.* was all it said. Dr. Kimmelman was a pediatrician, and Moran again wondered why Hannah Haskell would want to meet with him. Kim ended her call right then, so Moran hit the Escape button and turned to her.

"I meant to ask—Hannah Haskell was carrying a manila envelope when she came into the lab Sunday evening. Did you find anything like that in the lab on Monday?" he asked.

"I didn't see anything like that. I mean, she didn't leave anything for us that I found."

Moran indicated Hannah's desk drawers, and Kim shrugged and opened them. But there was no envelope.

"Would she usually leave things like that for you in the lab?" he asked.

Kim scrunched her face. "In a manila envelope? No. I mean, she left notes and stuff, but just—you know—on paper. Maybe it was just her mail?"

Moran nodded agreeably. "Very well. Would you be so good as to take me to the South Building?"

As the two made their way there, Moran saw the small parking lot that the car had pulled into on the afternoon of Hannah's death. He asked Kim if she ever used this lot.

"That's for deliveries and visiting researchers," she explained.

"Visiting researchers?" he asked.

"Yes, sometimes we do things in cooperation with other companies, and they usually park over there. I guess that way, Wellglad doesn't have to pay for their parking!"

Moran looked up at the entrance of the South Building and saw that there were no cameras there, unlike in Wellglad's main building.

He turned to Kim. "They don't have security cameras up on this building?"

"I guess not," she said, looking up. "But who the heck would want to come in here anyway?"

Kim opened the door to the South Building, and Moran was immediately struck by the smell. It was like being on a farm.

"This place is gross," Kim said. "There are only two labs, but they smell to high heaven."

She proceeded to lead him down the hall, showing him one of the labs, which was similar in size and layout to Hannah's. Then they passed a small room full of machinery, and Moran stopped and looked in.

"And this room?" he asked.

Kim pointed as she went. "Equipment room. That's a centrifuge for spinning down cells. That's an EKG machine." She squinted as she looked at another machine before saying, "That looks like an EEG machine."

"And what is an EEG machine used for?" Moran asked.

"For measuring brain activity."

Moran nodded, and they moved on to the other lab, where the odor became extreme.

"And this is what we call the slaughterhouse," Kim said as they entered, and Moran suddenly found himself surrounded by cages filled with rabbits and rats.

"Is Randall here?" Kim yelled at one of the workers, holding her nose. The lab tech pointed to a room behind them.

She led Moran back to the room, where a man of about forty was dissecting a small animal.

Kim grimaced. "Randall?"

The man looked up and saw that he had company and took off his mask. "Hey Kim. What are you doing in these parts?" he asked, eyeing Moran.

Kim explained that Moran was the detective handling Hannah Haskell's murder and introduced them.

Randall took off his gloves and greeted the detective with Dr. Randall Thurst. "So horrible what happened to Dr. Haskell. I'm now escorting my female worker, Geena, to her car at night. I can't believe they don't have cameras all over the place. What can I do for you, Detective Moran?"

Before Moran could answer, Kim blurted out, "If you don't need me anymore, Detective, I'm going to go."

Moran thanked her for her help, reserved the right to call on her again, and asked, "Could you write down Mr. Weintraub's contact information for me?"

Kim wrote the information on a piece of paper and handed it to him.

"Here you go," she said, then beat a hasty retreat.

Moran turned to Randall Thurst.

"I'll keep it brief, Dr. Thurst. Do you know if anyone parked in the South Building parking lot across the street on Sunday, the day Hannah Haskell was killed? Any of your workers? Maybe a delivery?"

"That should be easy to answer. Only three of us work over here." And with that, Randall walked over to a large calendar, murmuring, "Sunday, Sunday . . ." staring at the calendar, then shook his head.

"Looks like Geena was here to feed them on Saturday, but that was it. Hang on." He wandered to the doorway and called across the lab, "Geena! Dave!"

Shortly, Geena and Dave appeared, replete with masks and gloves.

"Neither of you came in on Sunday, did you?" he asked them.

Dave shook his head, and Geena explained that she was there Saturday to feed *the critters*, as she called them.

"Could there have been someone visiting without you knowing?" Moran asked.

Randall shook his head. "If there's a visiting professor or research technician, I would know. Whenever someone wants to work with the animals, they go through me. Wellglad doesn't do much animal testing anymore, so I would know if someone were here."

Moran took that in and then asked them how many animals they housed.

"We usually have about one hundred, give or take."

Moran glanced at the poor animal being dissected, and Randall added, "The mortality rate is high, but they breed very quickly, so there's always more on the way."

Moran felt a tad squeamish and decided to ask his final question. "Do any of the animals ever escape?" he asked innocently.

Randall looked at Geena and Dave somewhat strangely. They both looked at Moran as if they had been busted cheating on an exam.

"Not usually, but recently, one of our rabbits from Cage 9 seems to have disappeared. OC-17, to be exact," Dave explained.

"Pardon me?" Moran asked.

"Oryctolagus Cuniculus, which is just a type of rabbit, number 17," Geena explained.

"I see," Moran said. "What do you think happened to it?"

Dave jumped in. "Probably crawled somewhere and died, but we haven't found any remains yet."

"You will in about a week," Randall said, sarcastically holding his nose.

"Has that happened before?" Moran asked.

They shook their heads. "But I doubt it escaped. No windows, no holes in the cinder block walls that we can find," Dave said. "It could have been killed by the rats, but that's a long shot." Then he took a jab at his cohort. "Geena probably took him home because she hates it when the rabbits suffer."

Geena warily eyed Randall. "I would never do that."

Randall nodded. "I know you wouldn't," he said and gave Dave a look. Moran saw none of this, though; his mind was racing.

"When did you notice the rabbit was missing?" he asked.

"Well, he was there Saturday when I fed him," Geena said. "But then, when we came in Monday morning, OC-17 was gone."

Moran felt his skin tingle and asked quietly, "This past Monday?" That was the morning after Hannah's murder.

Geena nodded but seemed somewhat discomfited by the intensity with which Moran was gazing at her. But he didn't see her; he was lost in a world of his own conjecture.

"Is that all, Detective?" Randall asked, breaking the odd silence.

Moran snapped out of it. "Yes. Thank you for your time."

He hurried out of the lab toward the parking lot. And as he walked, he asked himself: *Who had the man in the hat been? And why would he want to take a rabbit from the lab?*

Detective Moran didn't have those answers yet. But he intended to find them.

Chapter 33

Ella had tried to find Clyde after seeing Gary but had been told by Alana that he would be in meetings most of the day. She'd found it odd that Clyde hadn't called her last night or reached out to her in any way today. But if Gary was right and he'd taken his light treatment idea, then Ella knew that Clyde not calling was the least of her worries.

She felt her headache coming on like gangbusters now, even though she had taken double the dose of her medicine. And this time it came with an aura that started in her left eye. It was as if the periphery of things she was looking at shimmered, which was incredibly difficult to deal with.

Ella despised dishonesty almost as much as Otis did. It was probably why they got on so well together. Having experienced the loss of her parents at such an early age had made Ella feel separated from other people. Alone. So trust was no small thing for her. Clyde's flirting was one thing, but stealing? That was something she couldn't fathom or tolerate.

She checked the doctors' lounge again, but Clyde was nowhere to be found. She decided to try the cafeteria, which was a long shot. She entered the dining hall and scoured the room, but again, no Clyde.

She did, however, see Clark Van de Hout conversing with another patient named Hugo. Hugo had barely spoken to anyone in years, and Ella doubted that he would mind if she joined them and asked Clark a few questions about Dan and their conversation about the light hat.

"Dr. Van de Hout?" she said, interrupting Clark. "May I speak with you for a moment?"

It was commonly known that Clark Van de Hout had a thing for pretty women, so it wasn't remarkable when he stood gallantly and pulled out the chair next to him. "I was just talking business with Hugo here," he said.

"Business?" Ella asked.

"About my book on holographic light function. You know, sales projections, that type of thing," he explained.

Clark Van de Hout had been a prolific writer before his ill-fated acid trip and his wife's death in the hot tub, so Ella assumed he was speaking of one of his published books.

"Oh. I haven't read that one. I'm sorry," Ella said politely.

"Well, actually, I'm still working on it. It's a fairly vast piece that requires an inordinate amount of proofing. But I think it's safe to say it will replace all the garbage out there now dealing with the dissonance between quantum mechanics and relativity. Simply put, they can't explain the way things work here on Earth and translate that to the Universe because they're looking at it completely incorrectly."

"I see," interjected Ella, wishing she hadn't opened this can of worms.

"Well, actually, you probably don't see," admonished Clark. "Because you have been fed a steady diet of disinformation about it all. For instance, if I ask you what the unifying factor of everything is—you would probably say . . . ?" Here, he waited for Ella to fill in the blank.

Ella had no idea what to say or think.

But that didn't matter to Clark, who quickly answered his question for her. "The unifying factor is light, Dr. Kramer. With both its wave and particlelike properties. Particles are really the interesting thing here, because you can measure a particle by the value of its momentum or by its position in space, but *not both at the same time.* If you measure its momentum, you can't see the particle's position anymore. It is gone! And why is that?"

Ella hadn't counted on a quiz. "Well, I was never very good at physics, Dr. Van de Hout," she said, rubbing her temple.

Clark, not to be deterred, went on. "I'll make it easy for you. It's because the particle is in two different dimensions at the same time. Do you get that?"

Ella nodded.

"And if it's in two different dimensions at once, then how can that be? Well, it only works if time is two-dimensional. So, without getting too technical, I say the concept of time that we have now—which is that time is one dimensional, which means it only goes one way so that there is a past, a present, and a future—is incorrect. I say time is not linear. No, I would say it's two dimensional as well. If a particle can be here and yet somewhere else, then why can't time? Time could go back and forth and turn around on itself, so to speak. You get my drift?"

Strangely enough, Ella found herself somewhat intrigued by what he was saying.

"You can go between these two dimensions of time when you realize that everything is going on at once and not in a linear fashion. And if I was to take it a step further which, why not? I think time acts sort of like DNA in that it coils up on itself. So that you may have Abraham Lincoln on one coil of time and then, directly above him, in that same position, you have a guy living two thousand years from now named Fred. Wouldn't it be fascinating if you could jump between the two times and Lincoln could meet Fred? If Fred could just reach up and shake ol' Abe's hand? I say he can!"

"That is fascina—" she tried to interject.

"But light also has the properties of a wave, which rolls on and on toward its intended destiny! It ripples along until it spreads out and dissipates. It's sort of like the wave is the soul and the particle is the free will. But a wave can be interrupted by another wave, and it took me a while before I realized that's what Dan was talking about. I mean, if you drop a stone in a pond, it will make little ripples, right? But if you do it during a hurricane, I would bet the waves from the storm would wipe out the ripples from the pond. Know what I mean?"

At the mention of Dan, Ella became alert. "What do you mean, that's what Dan was talking about?"

"Well, that's where my theory comes into play." And here he paused dramatically. "I postulate that we are living in a *hologram*. Do you know what that is?"

Before Ella could answer, he continued. "You've seen them. They're like a picture of something trapped in glass or metal. It's a picture of a light field—a wave front, actually. Well, it's the refraction of the waves of that light field by another wave front . . . well, anyway, simply put . . ."

He struggled to make it simple for her. "People take pictures of the light field of an object. Follow?"

Ella nodded.

"I would argue that everything we see here is just a picture of a light field and that we are just transient beings, particles if you will, playing in this particular picture that, unbeknownst to us, is two dimensional. We just perceive it to be three dimensional, or *real*, because we're in it. But the object that the light picture was taken of exists elsewhere. Does that make sense?"

Ella slowly nodded. It did sort of make sense in a very bizarre way. And now she noticed that the shimmering of her vision was happening in her right eye as well.

Clark went on. "And now let me tell you something that really might interest you: Did you know that if you take a piece of the hologram of the picture and shine a light through it, you can see the whole object again, the whole picture?"

Ella shook her head.

"No, you didn't!" Clark said triumphantly. "And what does this tell us? It first tells us that we contain the whole Universe within ourselves, but it also tells us that *there is such a thing as destiny*. Because the hologram can be seen from several perspectives, but it's still the same object, and even if it's torn apart, within any one fragment is the whole. It is destined to be that object! There might be different perspectives, but within each perspective resides the whole, and the whole is the same!"

He paused and held up his finger, signaling her to remain quiet as he took a sip of his milk before continuing.

"And of course now they think black holes keep all the matter they swallow in a two-dimensional form on the surface of the event horizon! So why not us? What if we are just the matter coded by the two-dimensional information on our world's event horizon? Kind of like a hologram! So of course time is two dimensional! And Clark Van de Hout pointed both those things out twenty years ago!"

His gloating was quickly interrupted by Hugo, who pushed back his chair, muttered, "Fuck you, Clark," and abruptly left.

They watched him storm off, and once he was out of sight, Clark turned to Ella and said, "Good Lord, what has gotten into him?"

Ella saw her opening. "Clark, I wanted to ask you about the conversation you had with Dan. About something he said to you."

But Clark was now totally focused on his meal. His long-winded diatribe had obviously made him hungry. "Dan said a lot of things, Dr. Kramer. Usually unintelligible and having to do with a van coming to get him," he said between bites.

Ella rubbed her temple to soothe the headache, which was getting worse. She had to work to focus her eyes on Clark as her peripheral vision was really being affected by the shimmer now.

"Well, I heard he was telling you about a hat he had worn," she said cautiously. "One with lights on it."

He stopped eating and eyed her suspiciously. "Dr. Lester put you up to this?"

Ella was taken aback by his paranoia and said casually, "He mentioned it, but I was wondering if you could elaborate. Just for clarification."

Clark looked at her for a moment and seemed struck by something. "Your skin is so translucent; it's almost as if you glow. You're like a fairy, Dr. Kramer!"

"Thank you. Did Dan say that the light hurt him? That it made him feel bad?"

Clark smiled slyly. "No, he said that the light hat made it so he, and I quote, *couldn't feel his thoughts*, which is a different thing altogether."

"I don't know what you mean."

"No. You don't. Again, disinformation."

Then he carefully pushed away his plate and wiped his mouth with his napkin.

"Dan didn't have a feeling or lack thereof with the light hat. It isn't about emotional trauma, no matter how hard you try to peddle that psychological drivel. And at the time, I must admit, I didn't give any credence to his complaint, but after thinking about it, I realized he was on to something."

He leaned in and spoke quietly and carefully, as if to a child. "Dan said he couldn't feel his thoughts. Well, one doesn't really *feel* their thoughts, do they? No, they don't. They just think them. Right?"

Ella didn't understand where this was going.

"Let me explain it this way. Have you ever had a gut feeling? Something nagging at you? Something you *know* but don't know how you know it? Someone pops into your mind, and then you hear from them or see them the next day? Or a dream that seems remarkably real to you?"

Ella felt a little rush, and the hair on the back of her neck stood at full attention.

"Of course you have! There are many documented cases of people feeling something may happen and it does! One woman I knew, a chemist, said that once she was driving along the Taconic Parkway, and she had such a bad feeling that she pulled off the road only to witness an accident happen right in front of her at that exact moment! You get my drift?"

Ella nodded.

"Well, I would venture to call that a gut feeling or an inner voice. Wouldn't you?"

"I guess," Ella said, and then suddenly the room got very quiet. There weren't many patients in the cafeteria—maybe a dozen or so—but they all seemed to stop talking at the exact same time.

Clark continued, "As we both know, Dan, being a schizophrenic, heard voices, and those voices were very strong, and he misconstrued those voices to be his *thoughts*. But what they were, were just Dan speaking to himself. Dan was calling out to himself from the future, or the past, or whatever you want to call this coil of time, which is not linear, as I have explained. He was trying to warn himself, teach himself or who the hell knows what, but *those voices were Dan from various points along the hologram!*

"So the act of *feeling his thoughts* was actually him *first* hearing himself reaching out to himself from other points of the hologram, which *then* caused him to feel something. *A gut feeling*, if you will. And it was that process that was disrupted by the light from the hat. The wave of light from the hat canceled the wave of light from the hologram! After all, one wave front can change another.

"Hence, the light hat neutralized his ability to hear himself from other points along the hologram or, which might be easier for you to get, it neutralized his ability to hear himself from other points in time."

Clark took a swig of water and added, "And since I have just explained to you how the holographic universal system really works, what Dan said makes perfect sense, doesn't it?" He smiled, very happy with himself.

Ella sat there, not sure what to say. The shimmering was becoming unbearable.

And, even worse, a part of her did kind of understand what he was saying.

"Shocking, isn't it? To think that the only difference between people like me and you is that I know these voices or feelings are me. Me at various points in my . . ." and here he used the quote signs, "*life* and not some mental illness. Do you get it?"

Nothing moved. Not even the air in the room. And now Ella's peripheral vision was almost gone. Everything outside the center of her vision field was shimmering now. She couldn't see them, but she felt the other patients holding their breath. As if they all were waiting to hear her response. And Clark was waiting for his answer, so answer she did, from a place deep inside, as if she had no choice.

"Yes, I get it," she whispered.

There was a moment of silence as that hung in the air, and then, as suddenly as it had stopped, the chatting in the cafeteria resumed, and all went back to normal. She looked on as Clark started his dessert, and different thoughts began to assail her mind.

Just like Malakhi, Clark had made the case that their mental illness wasn't a deficit, but instead a gift. And in Clark's version, they knew they had the ability to transcend time.

This was all too much to take. She felt as if she was losing it and had to get ahold of herself. More importantly, she had to find out what had happened with Gary.

"Clark, who gave Dan the light hat?" she finally asked.

Clark looked at her and shrugged. "I have no idea." And he continued with dessert.

That was too bad, she thought, and rubbed her temple. And that was when she realized that the pain in her head was completely gone. Her meds must have kicked in. But then, why was her vision still shimmering? She blinked hard a couple of times, trying to correct it but to no avail.

When she looked up, she noticed Clark was staring at her very oddly. Almost as if she was some kind of alien creature.

"What?" Ella asked self-consciously.

"I don't know how to tell you this, but . . . It's like you don't reflect light, Dr. Kramer . . . *you are light.*"

Chapter 34

D etective Moran sat in his office going over his notes when he saw the name Kimmelman, the pediatrician Hannah had the appointment with before she was killed. He pulled out the notes on the prescription he'd read, found the doctor's telephone number, picked up the phone, and dialed. An answering machine picked up and explained that the doctor would be in the office on Friday, when they would have open hours for patients.

He hung up and stared at the rest of the note that had been scribbled on the prescription paper: *AJS/8 Yetz et al.* Moran realized it must be some sort of article, so he looked for AJS on his computer. He found the *American Journal of Science* listed as AJS but could find no article under the name Yetz. But then he saw that there was an *Australian Journal of Science.*

He went onto that journal's site and scrolled until he found the August edition, which was what the number 8 referred to, and scrolled through the table of contents. There, he found an article by none other than Dr. Alexander Yetz, which he promptly clicked on. Moran silently read the title of the article: *Neurodevelopmental Disorders Linked to Antipsychotic Drug Use in Utero.*

The article was nearly impossible to follow as it went through the protocols of the experiment and the mechanism of the drug. One would need a PhD in chemistry to understand it, so he decided to skip down to the conclusion.

We will preface our results by saying that much more testing is needed and on a much larger scale to determine if certain antipsychotic drug use during pregnancy causes neurodevelopmental delays in offspring. Our protocol used the antipsychotic medication, Tyrmoxidine, and we believe this study implicates that it does.

In our study, children of mothers taking Tyrmoxidine while pregnant were .02 to .03 times more likely to have these issues. We feel this is a significant result and does establish a link between this medication and a developmental delay in infancy that can lead to cognitive difficulties in childhood.

But we reiterate: Much more testing will be needed to determine a direct association and prove that these are not just naturally occurring anomalies.

Moran leaned back in his chair, looked at the ceiling and wondered why Hannah Haskell would want to read such an article. Was she working on a drug like this Tyrmoxidine?

His thoughts were quickly interrupted, however, by Detective Ross who knocked on his door and entered his office.

"Normally, one waits to hear *enter* before doing so, Officer Ross," he admonished.

Ross turned purple, having fumbled again in the eyes of his superior. "I have an update on Hannah Haskell, sir."

Moran silently waited for him to continue.

"There doesn't seem to be anything out of the ordinary," he said, and handed the phone records to Moran.

"Looks like her husband was calling her as she was driving to Wellglad at around 4:07 p.m." He pointed to Captain Haskell's number on the call log. "Looks like he called her twice."

Moran also saw an outgoing call to a number at 4:10 p.m. "Who is this?" he asked.

Ross shuffled through his notes. "That's her lab assistant's number. He called her back later." Ross pointed to an unanswered call from that number a few hours later. "Guy named Ezekial Weintraub. And here's something interesting—he has a rap sheet."

"For what?" Moran asked.

"Possession, driving under the influence, vehicular endangerment. He almost killed a pedestrian. Had to drop out of school and do community service but went back and finished his degree and was working at Wellglad for Hannah Haskell. Oh, and from what I can gather from his PO, this wasn't his first offense, but I couldn't pull up the other records because it was in juvenile. Probably drug-related . . . if you ask me."

Moran was sure Ross was probably right. Kim Matsunaga had said that Ezekial Weintraub was close to Hannah. He also remembered her saying that he'd called in sick today and wasn't at the lab.

"Let's get him in here," Moran ordered. "Anything else?"

Ross nodded and read from his notes. "Found some DNA and a partial print on her neck, but we can't find a match in our database. But here's something really weird. They found a couple of hairs on her, and guess what they were from?" Before Moran could answer, he said, "The New Zealand white rabbit. I kid you not."

Moran recalled Geena in Randall's lab talking about the rabbit, OC-17, as Ross droned on about how weird it was that there was rabbit hair on Hannah Haskell, and that the Haskells didn't have a pet rabbit, so he wasn't sure how she ended up with that hair on her.

But Moran's mind was elsewhere. Specifically, on the man in the hat chasing the rabbit. Could that have been Weintraub? Could he have been doing his own experiments that day? Did he have a key to the South Building? Had he found something out, or was he trying to do something in the lab to show Hannah? Was that why she went there?

"Do we have a picture of this Weintraub?" Moran snapped, interrupting Ross's monologue on the New Zealand white rabbit. To which Ross replied by hurriedly handing him Ezekial's mug shot.

Moran scrutinized the troubled young man in the picture, with his dark hair and thick-lens, black-rimmed glasses. He definitely looked the part of the science nerd and not a drug-addicted felon, he thought. But his hair was black and not the red of the man in the strange hat.

"Very well, Officer Ross. Good work. Find Weintraub."

But all Ross heard was, "Good work," and his face lit up as he took his leave.

Chapter 35

After her strange encounter with Clark Van de Hout, Ella finished her sessions for the day and headed out to visit her aunt. Using Ubers was getting costly, and she decided to take the bus. She squeezed into a seat by an old man snoring and looked out at the rainy landscape. It was all so beautiful, she thought, looking at the meadow outside Bainbridge with its wild grass and shrubbery curling around the antiquated tracks. Was it real? she pondered. Or was it a picture of a light field or a hologram, as Clark had proposed?

She thought about how what Clark said intersected with what Malakhi had told her. Both spoke of energy, albeit in very different ways.

Malakhi had spoken in almost mystical terms as to the nature of life, and that it was in danger from some sort of invading force, which her aunt seemed to echo with her frantic warnings. Clark said light was the unifying force of the Universe. Malakhi had spoken of light and the Vanitan energy descending on Earth, consuming the light of the living. Her aunt had spoken of evil people taking your soul. Were they saying the same thing? For wasn't one's soul their light?

She pulled the little watercolor out of her bag and studied it. When she had first looked at the image, she'd seen the reflection of the pyramid with the two stars in the water. But now she turned the painting upside down and, upon further scrutiny, saw that it wasn't an exact reflection at all. It was a darker image of the landscape with much less detail. It was murky and looked more like a shadow to her now. Did this represent the *shadowverse* Malakhi was talking about?

If the pyramid wasn't in Egypt, as Malakhi had said, where was it? What was it he had told her when asked about the landscape? She closed her eyes and heard his words: *It was where we were many lifetimes ago.*

Well, if she thought about time in the way that Clark explained it, could the landscape in the painting be from someplace that both painters had lived in in another lifetime? Were they traversing the hologram or holograms, as the case may be?

She rubbed her eyes, letting the exhaustion overtake her, and realized that none of this made sense. But there was something about these fantastical stories they'd each told her that struck her as true, and she couldn't explain why—*she just knew it.*

Ella was quite familiar with the concept of gut feelings. She had relied on hers for most of her life. Her instincts had proven to be her strength in the work she did with her patients. But if she were truthful, she would have to admit that working with them made her feel less alone in the world too. Was that why she was taking what they said so seriously? Why she was trying to make it all make sense?

Perhaps it was because of her dream. Clark had spoken of dreams feeling real, and that had made Ella think of her dream about her aunt's house. The one Farber repeatedly pushed her to remember. She knew the dream was just reliving the horror of what had happened with her uncle. At the time, she'd become numb and didn't know what had transpired. It felt as if she weren't there. She remembered the gun going off. And the blood. His blood. She shuddered at this and told herself it was better not to think of that night now.

The bus pulled up to her stop and she gingerly stepped over the sleeping man and got off. She ran through the rain, entered Seaside Memory Care, and made her way down the hall, taking off her wet jacket as she went.

She opened the door and saw her Aunt Moira sitting up in bed. Her hazel eyes looked up quickly and smiled in recognition, and Ella breathed a sigh of relief.

"Hey there," she said and went to her aunt, who waited with outstretched arms. They hugged, and Moira held on to her longer than usual and whispered in her ear, "I love you, honey."

Ella responded in kind, put her things down, and lay on the bed beside her. She pulled the afghan over both of them just like they used to, and Ella asked about her aunt's day. Moira surprised her, remembering what she'd done, and asked Ella about her work at Bainbridge. Ella felt like crying. Her aunt was truly there, not lost in the haze of her disease.

Ella relayed some things about her day while Moira stroked her hair as she did when she was little, which made Ella's eyes well up. She didn't want her aunt to see her tears, so she looked off and wiped them away. And that was when Moira surprised her.

"You remember old Skeeter?" Moira asked.

Ella's breath caught as she looked back at her aunt and nodded, remembering what Moira had said when she'd had the episode the last time she visited. Something about *them* being all around her, and that they'd use her up like they had Skeeter.

"Whenever you were sad we would go down to the pasture and give ol' Skeeter some apples. Always made you feel better."

Ella sat very still, not wanting to lose this moment.

"I used to tell you he was a magical being—like the Navajo used to say. They thought horses were from the gods," Moira continued.

"I remember," Ella said.

"You loved him so," Moira said as she gazed off, remembering those long-ago days. "Remember how I'd put you on his back and we'd go walking up the old road of the mountain until we got to the spring up top? Then you'd go wading and Skeeter would stay in the shade?"

Ella nodded, fighting to control her emotions.

Moira smiled, remembering for a moment, and then her voice changed slightly. "I never told you what happened to him, did I?"

And she looked directly at Ella, who registered this shift in energy and shook her head. Moira looked at her for a second, then continued. "We sold him to the Sperlings, who had the ranch for the racehorses, because we needed the money. Those were tough times back then.

"Well, Ol' Joe Sperling loved Skeeter because he was fast for a gelding, and he was able to keep up with their stallion, Silver Dollar, who was crazy. Most of those racehorses were, and Ol' Skeeter, he was calm and sweet and the perfect companion horse.

"I called to check on him a couple of times, and they said he was doing fine, but then one day I was near their ranch and went to visit him and . . . and I didn't like what I saw. His big, soft brown eyes were kind of gray and tired, and he looked thin. I saw bite marks on him, and I knew they weren't treating him well. They were just running him into the ground and using him up."

Her voice caught, but she pushed on. "I knew how much you loved him, so I asked if I could buy him back, but we didn't have all the money, so I worked out a deal to pay a little every month until I could get him home."

Moira stopped and took a breath, finding it difficult to go on. "But after a couple of months, I went to see him again, and they said he was gone. I found out he'd been left out in a storm, and the next day, he was nowhere to be seen. Well, after they told me that, I drove all over, looking for him. I didn't think he could have jumped their high fence, but I guess that's just what he did. When I got home, I walked up the old road to the spring up top where we used to go, and that's where I found him. He'd gone up there to die.

"Your uncle and I buried him up there. And I never told you because I just didn't have the heart to. Not after what happened to your mom and dad . . ." Moira faltered here and began to cry.

Ella hugged her aunt to her. "It's OK. I understand."

After a moment, the two settled down. Moira looked at the girl she had raised as her own, took her face in her hands, and said something that would change Ella's life for good.

"I didn't know what he'd done to you, like I didn't know what was happening to Skeeter. I swear. I didn't know, but I do now," she whispered. "And I am not going to let anything else happen to you, hon."

Ella felt her heart stop. So, it was true. It had happened. How would her aunt know? She had never told anyone but Farber. Not ever. Not the police, or the psychiatrists at the hospital. No one. Especially not her aunt. She couldn't lose the one person in the world who loved her.

But now she was in her aunt's arms and heard her whisper, "You can trust me, Sugar. I love you forever. Do you hear me? I love you forever."

A wave of grief overtook Ella, and her body was racked by sobs from a pain that she'd buried long ago. Moira held her all the while and repeated her love for her over and over. They stayed like that until Ella, weak with exhaustion, drifted off to sleep. The two of them cuddled together like they used to when Ella was little, and the memories of the car crash gave her no respite.

Then something strange happened. At one point, Ella heard her aunt's voice. But she couldn't be sure if it was real or if she was dreaming.

"I am here, but I am not here. I am between realms," Moira said. "My body cannot hold this space much longer, so I must tell you—they are here. They are here, and they are going to steal the light. And we cannot let that happen, Ella. And you have a part to play in this."

And then Moira whispered something that Ella wasn't sure she heard correctly. "You must go back again, like you did before, and change what happened. Do you understand? You must go back, Sugar. It is time to remember. *It's time to run along the light.*"

Ella's eyes fluttered open, confused. What was happening? Was this a nightmare or a reality? She turned to look at the old woman next to her and saw that Moira's eyes were closed.

Ella felt her heart pound; she struggled to breathe. Was this happening? Had her aunt said that or was she imagining it? Was it a dream? But deep down, Ella knew what was happening. It had happened before, when she broke. When she broke into a million pieces.

Chapter 36

Moran entered his house that night to find his wife had made her famous roast chicken with the potatoes just the way he liked them—slightly burned and very greasy. He had never met anyone who could roast a chicken the way Marti could, and the smell that greeted him as he pushed the door open was divine.

He needed a break from all that was going on in his head after he visited Wellglad. It was a lot to process, and Moran found his mind had begun to get tired by five in the afternoon these days, which was something he attributed to age. Not to mention the physical exertion it took for him just to go anywhere, especially in the rain. His leg ached, and the pain spread to his lower back as the day progressed, so he had to take some anti-inflammatories to get into the car to drive home.

When they sat down to dinner and Marti asked about his day, he said very little, but she understood the demands his work placed on him. She didn't have to be psychic to see that, and she often told him he was working too hard and needed to slow down. Tonight, she added that he needed to reconsider his retirement date so that they could travel more before they got too old. He agreed amicably, as he always did, and helped himself to her chicken.

She then began to share the details about their upcoming trip to Spain in the summer. Marti looked forward to visiting the Alhambra, the red-walled palace and fortress in Granada, Andalusia. She explained that Alhambra meant *the red one*, and had been the residence of the sultan of Granada before Isabella and Ferdinand conquered the Moors and set up court there.

Moran, however, didn't hear a word she was saying. He was wondering who Hannah Haskell had last seen as she lay dying in that parking garage.

How had someone just left her like that? The human race never ceased to disappoint him.

"Paul, what is it?" Marti asked gently.

Moran looked at her, surprised. "What is what?" he replied.

"You're about a million miles away. What is troubling you?"

He knew better than to deny the accuracy of her observations, but he wasn't sure what to say, other than that the case he was working on was very consuming, and he was in for an uphill battle if what he thought was true had happened. He wanted to protect her and very rarely talked about what he saw and what people did to one another. Why bring that stuff home?

After dinner, they did the dishes and watched some television. But Moran couldn't stop thinking about Hannah Haskell's death and Dan's suicide. Two deaths happening around the captain in a matter of two days. Now that was strange.

And why had Dan chosen that particular day to kill himself? Dr. Westbrook and the others at Bainbridge seemed shocked by his actions, no matter how calm Westbrook tried to appear.

Paul Moran hadn't trusted the captain from the moment he met him. He just seemed off. He began replaying that night in his head, searching for something he wasn't sure of. Captain Haskell had become upset upon hearing the news about his wife and had gone to the bathroom in the entryway to be sick, closing the door behind him. It was a small thing, but that bothered Moran. Not that he'd gotten sick, but that he'd had the presence of mind to close the door.

And when Moran asked the captain if he could use the facility upon leaving, Haskell had shown him to the bathroom in the bedroom, saying that the entryway bathroom, the one he'd been sick in, was under renovation. That hit Moran wrong too.

He desperately wanted to speak with the captain, but his friend, Arthur Levine, his—and Wellglad's—attorney, had descended on them, and they'd been forced to escort the captain to Bainbridge. And so he had not ever truly been able to interview Captain Haskell.

There was also the question of the timeline. When he and Scarpetti had met him at his house to inform him of his wife's murder, they'd asked him about his whereabouts—including the time he and his wife had left the house. Captain Haskell had said his wife had gone to Wellglad around four p.m., which seemed to fit what they'd seen on the video. But Haskell said he'd left for his function at four thirty, and that was where things got confusing.

Scarpetti confirmed that Haskell arrived at the fundraiser around five ten p.m. Haskell's house was twenty minutes from the fundraiser and fifteen minutes from Wellglad. If Captain Haskell had left for his fundraiser at four thirty, why hadn't he arrived at the fundraiser at four fifty instead of five ten? Traffic was light that day. Had he left later than four thirty? Had he gone somewhere else before the fundraiser? Or had he followed his wife to Wellglad, which made him late there?

If Haskell had something to do with the murder, he would have to have left Wellglad at about four forty-five to make it to the event at five ten, and if he left his house at four thirty, as he said, he would have just arrived at Wellglad at around four fifty. Now, it wouldn't have taken long to attack and kill Hannah Haskell. She had been thrown to the ground and hit her head. But Hannah had walked back to her car at 4:31 on the video, which the detective trusted, and so would have been gone from the scene by four forty, or at least would have been driving out. Someone had accosted her at her car closer to four thirty-one p.m., Moran thought, because she never got inside the vehicle.

Moran asked Scarpetti to check with the neighbors to see if there were any cameras on their houses so that he could confirm when Haskell had left, but the they lived on a corner at the beginning of a cul-de-sac. So the only one who could have a camera facing the street and be able to see the Haskell house would be the neighbors who lived directly across from them, and they didn't have one. Nor did the neighbors next door, so they had come up empty-handed.

If Haskell had committed the murder, he would have left his house earlier than he'd said, followed his wife there, and lied to the police about it.

But then, where had he parked his car? They'd found no sign of any car randomly parked in the area that day.

And speaking of cars, what about the one in the South Building parking lot? It drove in at 2 p.m. and left at 4:51 p.m., according to the video. They'd tried to pinpoint what kind of car it was by using the headlights, but all they'd been told was that it was probably a midsize foreign model, like a BMW; the technician couldn't be sure.

If the people in that car had seen Hannah Haskell or heard anything, wouldn't they have called for help? Or had they had something to do with her death? Did that car belong to the man in the weird hat with red hair or was he a transient, a crackhead?

What about the manila envelope that Hannah Haskell took into the lab but came out without? What was so important that she had to get it there that day?

Where was Ezekial Weintraub, her assistant? Why had Hannah called him? And why had he called her back later? Was it just work, or was something else going on?

Why had the killer taken her ring and any cash she had and left the credit cards? Scarpetti and Ross imagined they wanted quick cash, but pawning a ring wasn't easy, and could get you caught just as easily as using credit cards.

After her sitcom ended, Martha got a call from a friend, so Moran turned off the TV and headed up the stairs alone to get ready for bed. He lay there for about a half an hour, going over his day. He remembered the little book he'd found in Dan's bookshelf. *The Basics of Universal Holographic Design* by Dr. Clark Van de Hout, PhD. Why would he have a book like that? Given the others in his room, it seemed a bit beyond him.

Martha soon joined him and took a bath, as she did most nights, then reappeared in her floral nightgown, kissed him on the cheek, and shortly thereafter fell asleep.

He was still ruminating over the case at one thirty a.m. when Martha rolled over and asked him why he was still awake. Moran apologized and told her that he was thinking about a book written by one of the patients at Bainbridge. She sat up, turned on her light, and waited expectantly.

"Apparently," Moran began, "the writer was a physics professor at Yale before he had a breakdown when his wife died. And what he writes seems interesting. He theorizes that the Universe is basically a two-dimensional hologram. And that all life exists in different portions of it at the same time. That we are in all portions at various points simultaneously." He allowed a beat to let her digest this, then continued. "So there is no linear time: no past or present or future. Your life is happening all at once at various points on the hologram at the same time."

Martha thought for a moment, then said, "I doubt we will ever really unlock the mysteries of the Universe. Remember the Nicene Creed?" And she quoted, "'We believe in one God, the Father, the Almighty, Maker of Heaven and Earth—*of all that is seen and unseen.*'"

Moran smiled. "You can take the girl out of the Catholic Church, but you can't take the Catholic Church out of the girl." He squeezed her hand tightly and looked at her with so much love it made her ask again if he was OK.

He nodded, kissed her hand, and put it to his cheek. And after a second, he asked, "How do you think you are able to see the things you see?"

This stopped Martha. In all the time that they had been together, he had never asked her that. Of course he had asked questions at times—what she saw, what she had to do to get images, things like that—but he had never wondered how it was possible.

"Wow. That book really affected you. The musings of a lunatic . . ." she teased.

"No, I'm serious. How do you think what you do is possible?"

Martha sighed. People had asked her that many times in her life, and usually she just answered, "I don't know." But Paul was her husband and best friend, so she answered as honestly as she could.

"I don't know where it's from," she said. "I just know if I get quiet and focus on the energy I need to look at, the information comes to me in images. And I follow them."

She saw that he was still confused. "It's like . . . I'm remembering. I'm remembering something that happened . . . even though it hasn't happened yet."

Moran was a skeptic, but he had to say that what his wife had just told him resonated with what Van de Hout had written about the Universe being a hologram and life going on at different points of it all at once.

"If you follow the energy or image, can you get to the source of it?" he asked.

Martha shook her head in wonder. "Look at you! The eternal skeptic who requires evidence for everything!"

He nodded, appreciating her point. "I'm sorry if I've been callous about what you do, Marti. It's my job, I guess. But have you ever tried looking past these memories to where they come from?"

She saw how serious he was and answered, "Of course I have. Several times."

"And?" he asked.

Martha sighed. "The best way I can describe it is that it's like you're in a dark room, and you see light coming from under a door, but when you go closer and try to see under the door to find the source . . . you become blinded."

"By what?"

"The light."

Moran felt the hair on the back of his neck stand at attention. "The light?"

He had neglected to mention to his wife that Clark's guiding principle was that light was the unifying force of all that was. He hadn't said a thing about that, and yet here she was, talking about light.

Martha nodded. "It blinds you, and I've never been able to get past it. It's like you get what you get, what you're meant to see, and that's it. If I try to get any more—I can't. The Universe is very prudent in deciding who can see what. But my grandmother used to tell me stories about people she had heard about from her grandmother. Legends about people who could go there. Into the light. People who could see all the . . . paths that a person could take. They were like witches or something, and they could play with energy and even change outcomes. But my family just has the gift of clairvoyance. So I just see what I'm given . . . or what will be."

She stopped and something about the way he looked at her must have puzzled her. "Paul? What is it?" she asked.

He shook his head, "Nothing," and then he kissed her hand again. "I love you, Marti."

She leaned over and kissed him. "I know you do. Now let's go to sleep."

She turned off the light, and the two lay in the darkness for a minute until Moran asked, "Yesterday, the girl and the rabbit—did you know that they were images of mine . . . or . . . from my world?"

After a minute, she quietly answered, "Yes."

"And did you get any more information?" he asked.

"I couldn't focus on them for very long," she answered.

"Why?"

Martha hesitated for a second, then said, "Because they ran into the light."

Chapter 37

Farber was quietly waiting for Ella to answer her question, but she was lost in thought. She told herself she couldn't be sure what Aunt Moira had said in the dream, and that it didn't matter. She'd been exhausted last night, and her mind was playing tricks on her. But as she sat, the reality of what was happening to her was getting harder to deny.

Ella had woken up at Seaside the previous evening when the nurse came in to check on her aunt and found Ella curled up beside the old woman. After kissing her sleeping aunt's cheek, she'd beaten a hasty retreat.

She checked during the Uber ride home but had no messages from Clyde. Instead of being angry, though, Ella felt nothing. It was as if he was an insignificant piece in the deadly board game taking place in her mind; just a part of her distant past, when she was an enamored resident, and not who she was now. Who she had always been, she supposed. And the strangeness of that thought scared her.

When she got back to her apartment, she doubled the dosage of her prescription medication and drifted into such a deep sleep that she'd almost missed her morning appointment. But here she was, with Farber looking at her intently.

"So, she knew what your uncle had done?" Farber asked again.

"I guess."

"Did she say how she knew or tell you anymore?" Farber asked with some urgency.

Ella shook her head.

Farber frowned and continued, "What happened after that?"

"I fell asleep, but I vaguely remember having a dream. A bizarre dream, where she was whispering to me. She said it was time to go back and remember. She said I had to go back and change the outcome. And . . ."

But Ella couldn't continue. It felt too awkward to relay the rest of what her aunt had said. How Moira had said, "They were here" and "They were stealing the light." How could she tell her therapist that her aunt was espousing things about evil beings stealing the light from you? Things that echoed what patients at the psych ward were saying to her at work? Things about an evil energy from some dark universe known as the Vanitan, and light traveling through a hologram and going back in time. She would be in a psych ward herself if she wasn't careful.

"What?" Farber asked.

Ella shook her head. "I don't know. It was just a dream."

Farber sat back, a frustrated look on her face. "Ella, I think we need to do something different. The dream where you're in your aunt and uncle's bedroom? The dream with the little girl crying from behind the closet door? We have to get you beyond that point. I think you should stop taking your medication. Maybe just for a few nights."

Ella looked at her, horrified. Not take her medication? With everything that was happening? At this point, it was the only thing keeping her together. Why would Farber suggest such a thing?

"I feel as if I'm losing my mind and you want me to go off my meds? Jesus Christ!" She stood, preparing to leave.

"Calm down and let me explain," Farber said.

Ella sat, trying to contain her anxiety.

"The reason I want you to get to the end of that dream is so that you'll be free. You need to express the truth here, Ella. You're safe in here. But you've never fully told your story, and we must make that OK for you to do—even if it means going off your medication for a night."

She stood and got Ella a glass of water and handed it to her.

"I would never want to hurt you—you *know* that. But sometimes, when things get a little too close to the truth—you get scared. And by truth, I mean, *the truth of who you are.*

"You've just told me that your aunt knew that you were sexually abused by your uncle. How long did she know? That's questionable, but she knew. You have repeatedly dreamed of yourself covered in blood, going through the house where you grew up. You go into your aunt and uncle's room and you hear the girl crying behind the closet door. But when you try to open it, you wake up. We need to find out what's behind that door, Ella. You need to set yourself free."

Ella felt her anger rise. Did Farber not understand what she was up against here? What was her preoccupation with Ella's dream?

"The real question is, why are you trying to get me to do that? Why is this so important to *you*? That I look behind the door and find my what? My inner child?" she said sarcastically. "That I embrace the wounded child who was molested and left to fend for herself? That I remedy the situation by holding that poor little girl?"

Farber didn't answer.

"Well, I remedied the situation long ago, and we both know how that ended. With me traumatized and my life forever altered, but you think that by remembering a dream, it will all magically go away! As if it never happened! As if I didn't shoot him over and over until his blood was everywhere. . . ."

There was a chill in the room. Farber gazed at her intensely. "Over and over, Ella?"

Ella stopped and looked at her. She hadn't said that, had she? No. She'd been ten years old when he died, and the gun had just gone off. It was an accident. Christ, what was she saying? She was confusing reality with her Goddam dream! What was happening to her?

"What? No. I . . . I don't know what I'm saying, you've got me so confused! But I do know that no amount of consoling that little girl in the dream will change what happened, Dr. Farber. I can't go back and change what happened!"

Farber looked at her and then very quietly said, "Oh, but you can. And you will."

Ella felt as though time stood still as a chill ran through her entire body. What was happening?

"Very well. Let's not talk about the dream. Let's talk about something else," Farber said. "Why do you think you're being warned by Malakhi and your aunt of this mysterious dark energy force?"

Ella sat there, stunned. "What?" she whispered.

She hadn't told Farber what Moira had said in last night's dream: that *they* were stealing the light, just as Malakhi had said. It was one thing to tell Farber what her patients were saying, but it was quite another to tell her about her aunt. Farber would think Ella was paranoid and delusional if she was getting the same message from everyone. And that was a slippery slope with a therapist. Even one as unconventional as Farber.

"Your aunt is apparently trying to warn you of evil beings sort of like Malakhi's Vanitan energy. Why do you think that is?"

"I didn't tell you that," Ella stuttered, unsure of herself.

Farber leaned forward and whispered, "Then how would I know it?"

Ella shook her head, confused. "I don't remember telling you my aunt said that. . . ."

"It doesn't matter," Farber snapped. "What's important is what these people are trying to tell you. Let's see if we can understand that. What do you think your aunt and Malakhi mean by the Vanitan stealing the light?"

But Ella was reeling from the fact that her therapist knew about her aunt saying something that she hadn't told her. The only explanation was that she *had* told her. *But Ella knew she hadn't.* So, either Dr. Farber was a mind reader or Ella was losing said mind. And that's when a terrible thought hit her: Was it happening again? Was she dissociating as she had before?

"Ella," Farber said gently, "you're overwhelmed. I understand that, and I'm here to help you make sense of what's going on. You're getting cryptic messages from people who have nothing to do with each other. We need to get to the bottom of this so you can have some peace. OK?"

"Get to the bottom of what?" she asked with trepidation.

"I think it's important to understand the message they're trying to give you, and then we can decide if it's real or not, and what to do about it."

When she heard that, Ella's worst fears were confirmed: Farber thought she was unwell again. She felt her pulse tick up.

Farber took her hand. "Ella, I promise you, there's nothing wrong with you, OK? You trust me, don't you?"

Funny; her aunt had told her to trust her too. Just last night.

"Yes," she heard herself whisper, but deep down she knew she didn't really trust anyone. She couldn't. Ella knew the frailty of reality in a way that only her patients seemed to grasp, which was probably why they trusted her. And why she felt safe with them.

But maybe now it was time to change that. Maybe it was time to take a chance, and who better than Farber to do that with? She had to. She felt as if she was slipping. She was afraid. Afraid of her own mind.

"I have no idea why my aunt and Malakhi are giving me similar warnings. Perhaps it's just a coincidence, but it's very strange." She paused. "I guess my interpretation of what is happening is important—especially if I'm in the midst of some psychotic break."

"I didn't say that," Farber retorted, and she squeezed her hand. Sort of the way a mother would. "If this is some sort of projection on your part, then maybe you're trying to warn yourself about the people around you. Do you remember the other day when we talked about the word *Vanitan*, and I spoke of antisocial disorders and the lack of empathy in people today?"

Ella nodded.

"Perhaps you've interpreted something that both Malakhi and your aunt have said to mean that you're in danger because you're surrounded by people who don't truly care about you. And they're the messengers because they do care." She looked at Ella pointedly.

"I don't think you're having a psychotic break. As a matter of fact, I know you aren't. But I also know that the world is changing quickly now. Sociopathy and psychopathy seem to be the new norm.

"It's like the apocalypse has happened—only it has to do with the death of our collective humanity and not our physical extinction on this planet. Perhaps—because of what you've gone through—you feel it more intensely. But Ella—I think it's time to be who you truly are, and I would like to help you do that. OK?"

And for the first time, Ella felt something she never had before: the desire to be understood and to understand herself. Perhaps Farber was right, and what she was hearing from her patients and her aunt weren't really warnings, though she'd interpreted them as such, because of all she'd been through. Maybe her intuition, which she'd always relied on, was being driven by paranoia. Maybe she was afraid to look at herself because she feared that she was irrevocably broken.

And it was at that point that she decided to take a leap of faith. She looked up at Dr. Farber, about to answer, only to be shocked by Farber's eyes, and how blue they were. She'd never noticed that before. *Almost as blue as mine*, she thought as she stared.

"Will you let me help you, Ella?" she heard Farber ask softly.

Ella felt as if she'd awoken from a dream. "Yes," she heard herself say.

But all the while she wondered how she had missed something so obvious. And she marveled at how much Dr. Farber's eyes . . . looked like her own.

Chapter 38

Ella walked down the hall to her office and noticed a large manila envelope in the message box on the door, but before she could see who it was from, she heard a noise coming from inside. She opened the door and found Sebastian pacing back and forth, muttering angrily to himself. He looked at her as she entered and blurted out, "I need to talk to you!"

Her hands full, Ella put the stack of mail on the desk, leaving the door to her office slightly ajar.

"Sebastian, what's wrong?" she asked, realizing she must have left her office unlocked when she left the night before.

"What's wrong is that I am being starved in this God-awful place! That's what's wrong!" he howled, looking as if he might burst into tears.

Sebastian had gone on a restrictive diet after he had done his annual because the doctor had warned her that his blood pressure and glucose were rising. So Ella had gone over a meal plan with him, which Sebastian had agreed to follow. But three months later, the orderlies were reporting that he had begun sneaking muffins and candy whenever he could.

She looked at his truculent face and said gently, "Sebastian, no one is trying to starve you. You agreed to go on a diet for your own well-being, and we've all been trying to support you. We want you to be healthy, that's all."

"Well, last time I checked this was a free country, and I can eat whatever the hell I want! If not—then maybe I should call Mama and see if I can find another establishment to hang my hat!"

They both knew Earline wouldn't care a bit.

"Did something happen? I thought you were doing well. Dr. Jimenez told me your glucose numbers were dropping. What's made you so upset?"

Sebastian looked off, choking back tears of frustration. "That bitch, Hilda, in the kitchen just told me I couldn't have waffles for breakfast because I was too fat! And then all the idiots laughed and laughed!" he moaned.

Ella immediately worried that Nadine may have appeared, but Sebastian knew what she was thinking and said, "Don't worry. I counted my deep breaths like you said, and she didn't come."

Ella got a box of tissues and pulled up a chair beside him, handing him the Kleenex. "I'm sorry you had to endure that," she said. "That was totally inappropriate of Hilda, and I will address it with her and the kitchen staff."

Sebastian blew his nose and wiped his face, somewhat mollified by her words.

"But," she continued, "we both decided that you were going to try your best to lower your numbers, Sebastian, and I hope that you're still doing that."

He looked at her petulantly and mumbled that he was trying, but that he hated dieting and exercise.

"I understand, but just do your walks in the garden. That alone will help, OK?"

He begrudgingly nodded that he would and blew his nose again.

And as she watched him, she had to fight the urge to ask if she could speak with Malakhi. She hadn't seen him since Dan's room and had desperately wanted to ask him questions. Especially after seeing her aunt last night. She wondered if she could coax him out of Sebastian but realized that now was probably not the right time. So she patted Sebastian's back and consoled him, lost in her own thoughts, when her office phone rang. She moved around the desk, knocking her bag to the ground as she picked up the phone, and saw Sebastian bend down to get it. She mouthed *thank you* as she listened to the person on the other end of the line.

"Dr. Kramer?" the voice asked. Ella was somewhat taken aback as she recognized it was Captain Haskell.

"Yes," she said.

"I hope I'm not bothering you," he offered.

"Not at all. No. Is everything OK?"

She turned her back to Sebastian. She had never had a former patient reach out to her like this.

"Well," he said, "as OK as it can be, I suppose. I just didn't get to say goodbye to you before I departed on Monday and wanted to let you know how much I appreciated your help, and that I was sorry not to have seen you before I left."

Ella was startled by this admission. She'd gotten the impression that he hadn't received any help from her and had had a terrible experience at Bainbridge. So much so that he'd felt the need to escape.

"I understand. I know you've been through a very trying time. How are you feeling?" she asked.

"A little lost, if I'm honest," he admitted.

This was said with such candor that Ella lost any suspicion she may have had and felt bad for him. The poor man was grieving. "I'm so sorry. That's to be expected," she said.

There was a long beat on the other end of the line before he said, "Listen, I know this is unorthodox, but would it be possible to talk to you in a private setting? As a therapist? I just feel as if I need some support right now."

"I wish I could," she said. "But we don't usually do that."

Just then, she noticed her door was ajar and went to close it. That was when she saw Clyde in the hall with a very attractive woman, and the gall rose in her throat.

"Dr. Kramer?" the captain said.

"Yes, I'm here," she said as she watched Clyde rub the woman's arm.

What a creep, she thought. A womanizing creep who may very well have stolen her friend's research. And what about the way he'd made her look on the Haskell case? Like some idiotic lackey who'd screwed everything up. And it suddenly occurred to her: Why shouldn't she see Captain Haskell for a follow-up? Why should she be penalized for Clyde's lack of interest in his case? It wasn't right, and she decided at that moment to finish the job she'd started.

"I guess I could make an exception, given the circumstances. Just to do a follow-up, which we didn't get to do," Ella said as she watched Clyde.

"That would be great. You can come here. I live at 450 Fenway. When were you thinking?" he asked gratefully.

"I have someone in my office right now, so let me call you back with some times a little later. What's your number?" She quickly scribbled down his information. "Very good. I'll call you in a bit." And with that, she hung up the phone and headed down the hall toward Clyde and the woman.

Ella could see the woman was upset, but since when did Clyde rub women's arms and escort them around the hospital? He usually made Alana do that. But this woman was quite striking, with her blond hair and surgically preserved looks, so of course he was taking her on a tour. By the time she reached him, she was apoplectic, and before Clyde could say anything, she snapped, "Where have you been? I've been trying to reach you for the past two days!"

Clyde's face went crimson as he tried to control his anger and turned to the woman. "Excuse me for a second," he said, and moved Ella a couple of yards away. "What the hell is wrong with you?" he hissed.

"I need to talk to you!" Ella hissed back.

"Well, that will have to wait. I am escorting Ms. Zimmerman out and will see you afterward, Dr. Kramer."

At the mention of Dan's last name, Ella realized the woman was Dan's sister, and her face flushed with embarrassment. She stood there, horrified by her behavior.

"Oh. Of course. I'm so sorry . . ." she stammered.

But Clyde was already escorting Ms. Zimmerman down the hall and out of the building. Ella stood there in shock. What was wrong with her? She had chased him down like a jilted teenager. She was so embarrassed, she didn't know what to do. She was surely in danger of losing her job now, and she felt a cold anxiety creep up her spine as her head began to throb.

She returned to her office and went to her bag in search of her pills. She would have liked to take Farber's advice and make it through the day without her medication, but that was out of the question now. She had just ruined whatever relationship she had left with Clyde, and things were probably going to get even worse from here on out. She found the pill bottle, but it was empty. *Shit*, she thought, she'd have to refill her prescription later. Advil would have to do in the interim.

She grabbed the Advil bottle from her desk drawer and noticed Sebastian looking at her aunt's little watercolor.

"It fell out of your bag," he said by way of explanation.

She nodded, lost in thought, took her Advil, and sat down. Clyde would want her gone now. And, if she were honest, it would probably be better for her, though what would she do? Where would she go? Even if Clyde gave her a recommendation, it wouldn't look very good that she wasn't staying at Bainbridge. Doctors were desperate to work there. Christ, what a fool she had been to get involved with him!

"Did you paint this?" asked Sebastian, interrupting her stream of consciousness.

Ella answered absent-mindedly, "No. My aunt did."

"Very good painter, your aunt," Sebastian said, and then he closely scrutinized the painting. "I bet it's Incan."

Ella cocked her head. "What?"

"The landing site," he said, referring to the painting. "Might be Incan. I can't be sure, but you know what I mean," he said, staring at the painting.

Ella felt the hair on her arms stand up. "No, I don't know what you mean."

"Your aunt didn't tell you?" he asked innocently.

Ella shook her head.

Sebastian turned the painting toward her. "Well, here's the pyramid, and as we know, they were always by pools of water—I suppose to keep things cool. Anyway, they were used as landing sites by our forefathers."

Sebastian noticed Ella's confusion, so he clarified for her. "Because you could see the pyramids from space. Right? So they used them like sort of signs. Anyway, once they got here, they built pyramids so that others could come here too. I guess because it was habitable because of the water." He turned the painting and stared at it quizzically. "I bet they used mercury."

"What?" she asked, feeling sick to her stomach. Was she imagining this? Who was he talking about coming here? Sebastian had never spoken like this before. What was happening to her patients? Well, not really her patients, she corrected herself; just to Sebastian, who was Malakhi. Christ, what was happening to her?

"Well, the gold here on the pyramid indicates there was mercury painted on the side. The ancients knew how to make gold from mercury. And sometimes it isn't water by them but pools of mercury to electromagnetically power the ships that came and went."

Then he shook his head and clucked. "We've regressed to the mental level of bugs on this planet. What a fucking joke! The only one who even came close to understanding how to use the energy around us was Nikola Tesla and look at how he ended up!"

He looked at the little painting again. "The enemy of intelligence is greed, Dr. Kramer. Never forget it! Christ, we're destroying this planet over it. Who knows where we'll end up next? There are pyramids everywhere! Even Ceres has a pyramid!"

Ella looked at him, baffled. Ancient landing sites? We had come to Earth from . . . somewhere else and left pyramids so that people following us could land in the same spot? She felt her chest tighten. Wasn't this akin to what Malakhi had said? About life moving from other places or other planets to a better place to survive?

"I . . . where are you getting all this, Sebastian?" she asked.

He raised his eyebrows and said, "Well, I guess I just know a lot of it without knowing how I know it."

Ella's heart skipped a beat before he added, "But there is this excellent show called *Alien Ancestors* on the History Channel, which I never miss, and it details a lot of this stuff."

And with the mention of the TV show, Ella felt herself breathe an enormous sigh of relief. She almost wanted to laugh. So, it wasn't one of those scary conversations about Vanitan energy. He'd gotten it from a cheesy television show. And this news made her feel infinitely better. Perhaps this show was informing Malakhi as well. *Christ*, she thought. Had she really been this gullible?

"I'll have to watch it," she said happily.

Sebastian wasn't paying attention, though. He was staring at the painting as if he was trying to figure something out.

"What is it?" she asked.

Suddenly, Sebastian smiled and said cryptically, "You promise you'll watch it? The show?"

Ella nodded, reassuring him. "Yes, I will."

"OK," said Sebastian. "After you watch a couple of episodes, I'm going to give you a little quiz. So you better!"

Ella doubted she'd ever watch it. "OK, well, I'll try to get to it as soon as I can, but . . ."

"No pressure, Dr. Kramer. It'll be fun. And just to show you how fun, let me give you a little preview!"

"A preview?" she asked.

"Yes!" And with that, he turned the painting toward her. "So, here's the pyramid and everything, and here it is in the water, right?"

She nodded, wishing he would just hurry up and leave. Her head was about to explode.

"So, your first quiz question is: why red?" and he couldn't help but snicker.

"*Why red?*" she asked.

"Yes, why did the artist—your aunt—cover the scene with red?"

Ella suddenly remembered the red color on Dan's painting as well. The damn paintings. How to explain them, she thought, and she shook her head. "Sebastian, I don't know and I really do have to get . . ."

"As I said, no pressure! Just think about it, and we can talk about it after you've watched the show."

With that, he stood up and lumbered to the door, where he turned and said, "Or you could just ask your aunt, couldn't you?"

Chapter 39

aul Moran liked puzzles. He enjoyed putting all the pieces in order and seeing the whole picture. But after his discussion with his wife the night before, he felt at a loss. He couldn't make sense of things like that and felt as if his brain had let him down, and he found himself in a fog the next day.

He decided the best way to cure that was to get to work. He spent most of the day following up on the vagrant with the hat in the parking lot. No one in the area had seen such a person and he came to a dead end. He then moved on to trying to find out if there was anything about drug testing in the Army's budget out of the VA for the last few years. But again his search was fruitless.

He then focused on Haskell's timeline. He'd asked Police Captain Jim Abbot about questioning Haskell, but Abbot already had agreed to give the captain until the following week for his interview. Moran thought that was a mistake. Memories faded as one got further away from the incident, and there was more time for the mind to confuse things. There were things Moran needed to know now. Things only Captain Haskell could tell him, and Moran decided to ignore his boss and pay a visit to the captain after lunch.

He reached over and took his phone out of the glove box as he waited at a light and dialed Detective Ross, who promptly picked up.

"Have you found Weintraub?" Moran asked.

"No. He didn't go to work again. Called in sick, but when I had patrol swing by his apartment, no one came to the door. Neighbor said she saw him at the bus stop outside their building with a duffel bag. Around eight a.m."

Moran frowned. "She see which bus he took?"

"No. It's a busy street, so several lines stop there. I mean, if he had a duffel bag, he was probably catching a plane or a train, right? Want me to call DHS and see if I can find out?"

Moran would need a pretty good reason to get the Department of Homeland Security involved. "Not yet. Let's see if any of the bus drivers remember him. Focus on the ones going to Marshall. See if any of them had cameras. Also, see if you can reach any family and ask if they've seen him."

"Yes, sir. Oh, there's one more thing . . ."

"What?" asked Moran impatiently.

"Can I close out the Zimmerman suicide? Spoke with Ernie . . ." and then he corrected himself. "Coroner Ernst, and he said it was definitely suicide. The family wants the body. Sister was here this morning."

Moran knew it was suicide, but for some reason he wished that he could hang on to Daniel Zimmerman's body just a little longer, and he wasn't sure why. It was as if he was one of the few puzzle pieces surrounding Haskell that was tangible, and as macabre as it sounded, he hated to part with him. He could hold them off, but if the family started complaining, that might piss off the brass, and right now he wanted to keep things quiet.

"Yes, go ahead," he finally said.

"Yes, sir," Ross replied, and hung up.

Moran riffled through his notebook and found Kim Matsunaga's number.

She answered, and after a few pleasantries, Moran asked if she had seen or heard from Ezekial Weintraub, to which she explained that he was taking another sick day.

"I see," said Moran. "He must be taking Hannah Haskell's death very poorly."

"Well, yeah. Like I said, he really looked up to her. Hannah gave him a chance when nobody else would, so this has hit him really hard for sure. Poor guy."

Moran had checked with security and knew Ezekial Weintraub hadn't gone into Wellglad on Sunday. And he hadn't seen him on the camera. He also knew that Weintraub didn't own a car, so the mystery car lights in the south parking lot probably weren't his. But Hannah's phone records showed she'd called him.

"Do you know if he met with her over the weekend?"

"I don't think so. She didn't say anything about it to me."

"Is it possible that they were working on something together?" he asked.

"I doubt that very much. Hannah was our boss, Detective. We didn't so much as work with her but *for* her, and she was very clear about those boundaries."

"I see," he said, and then switched gears. "One more question: Yesterday, when you were showing me the file on Lyprophan, what percentage of the test subjects would you say were from the Army?"

Kim hesitated. "I'm sorry, Detective. Um . . . I really shouldn't have showed you all that yesterday, and I could get into a lot of trouble for doing it. Maybe you should talk to Dr. Dowd."

"Of course. That would probably be best," Moran said.

"Well, I should be getting back to work."

"Very good. Thank you for your time. And if you hear from Mr. Weintraub, will you have him get in touch with me? I believe you have my number."

"Sure," she said, and hung up.

And Moran was left with the distinct impression that she had had a talking-to.

Chapter 40

Ella tried to find Clyde later but was told that he was still with Ms. Zimmerman, who was too distraught to make the funeral arrangements for Dan on her own. *Really?* thought Ella. And when was the last time this heartbroken sister had even seen her brother? The hypocrisy made her sick.

Of course, Clyde loved nothing more than being the hero of the day. Wasn't that what he had done with her? Swooped in and took her on as his resident? Bowled her over with his keen intelligence? He enjoyed playing the master, and little old Ella was supposed to just worship at his feet! The thought of it all made her cringe, and her head was giving her a horrible time. She reached into her drawer and took out some more Advil, then noticed her aunt's painting on her desk.

She remembered Sebastian's question: why red?

But before she had time to ponder an answer, Gary came into her office without knocking. He was very agitated and shut the door hard before blurting out angrily, "Well, I was right—I was scooped!"

"Oh Gary . . ."

"My brilliant light treatment for schizophrenia—scooped! And here's the clincher . . ." He looked at Ella with such intensity that she leaned back in her chair.

"According to my friends at *American Journal of Science* and *Psychiatry Today* it was presented by none other than Dr. Clyde Westbrook, head of Psychiatry at Bainbridge Psychiatric Hospital," and his eyes bore into her accusingly.

Ella was stunned. She'd been worried, but she hadn't thought it possible. She couldn't conceive of Clyde stealing from someone. Surely he wasn't that bad.

"Silly me! I thought he might help me get funding, but apparently, he decided to go ahead and do the research himself!" Gary spat.

Ella didn't know what to say, but she had to calm Gary down. "Listen, let me talk to him. There has to be some kind of mistake."

"Oh, there was a mistake all right! Trusting you was my mistake! You're the one who gave him my proposal! You're the one I told all about it! But see, I thought you were just his resident—not his fucking girlfriend!"

Ella bristled. "I can't control what he does or doesn't do, Gary! And for all we know, he was doing this research before you gave him your thesis. And need I remind you that I gave him that paper because you asked me to?"

Gary shook his head, disgusted. "You're right. And the sad thing is, if I'd given it to him through the proper channels, there would be a record of it. But now . . ." He looked as if he might cry. "I worked on that for years, Ella. Do you know the hours that went into it? For him to just take it . . ."

She felt horrible. "I understand, but let's just get more information, OK? Let me talk to him and find out what happened. Maybe . . . maybe he'll include you in the research . . ."

Gary sneered at that. "Oh, goody! Lucky me! I get to be included in my own research idea!"

Ella knew he was just working his way through his emotions and said calmly, "We need to find out exactly what happened. When was his proposal submitted to the magazine?"

Gary looked at her coldly. "Three months ago. About a month after I gave mine to you. And you wanna know the sickest part?"

Ella felt a growing fear in the pit of her stomach. What could be sicker than her boss and lover stealing the intellectual property of a co-worker and friend?

"What?" she asked.

"I think he was using Dan as his guinea pig."

Ella's breathing stopped as the fear quickly crept up her spine.

"The light hat that Dan was talking to Clark about?" he said, letting it hang there.

But Ella knew exactly what he meant. She felt her nails dig into her palm as she tried to maintain her composure. "Let me speak with Clyde, and we will rectify the situation, Gary. I promise."

"I sure hope you can, Ella. Because from my point of view, I would never have given it to you had I known you were dating. It wouldn't have looked right. No, I asked a colleague to deliver my research proposal to her boss. Not someone she was fucking, which, last time I checked, is a pretty big breach of ethical conduct." And with that, he left.

Ella stood to follow him but stopped at the door. What could she say that would lessen his anger? As she watched him walk down the hallway and into the sunlight beaming through the windows at the end of the hall, she noticed someone reflected in the window for a split second. The red-headed girl. She had seen the girl on the way to Dan's room the other day, but she was nowhere to be found when she looked. Instead, Ella had found Malakhi, and their strange conversation about the Vanitan had ensued.

It looked like the girl was standing in the hall staring directly at Ella, but it was hard to tell because Gary was blocking her view. But when he exited the hall and entered his office, the girl was gone, and Ella wondered if she'd ever been there at all.

It didn't make sense. Again, she wondered if it was a nurse. But the girl looked young, and she wasn't dressed like a nurse. No, she was dressed . . . more like a patient. But the women's wing, A Wing, was across the parking lot behind a fence.

Ella was about to go look for her but wondered what the point was of chasing down someone she wasn't even sure she'd seen. Even though she was. She rubbed her temples. The Advil was doing nothing.

What was wrong with her? She had to keep it together. But how could she? Was she seeing people or not? Were her patients warning her? Was her aunt? And what about Clyde, the person she fancied herself in love with; had he used her to hurt her friend? Was he capable of such a thing? But she knew the answer to that, she thought. She had all along, if she was honest with herself. Some part deep inside her knew, anyway, even if her mind pretended that he was something he was not.

How could one be in the world of people, knowing what one knew? It was as if life was a never-ending battle, a relentless war between her intuition and her mind. What was real and what wasn't. And it was wearing her out.

She stood there contemplating what to do before she quietly closed the door. The girl would have to wait. She needed answers from Clyde.

Chapter 41

Moran pulled into the Haskell driveway, knowing he'd be made to pay for this, though he didn't care.

Captain Oliver Haskell opened his door looking like he'd been painting; there were white splotches on his shirt and pants.

"Detective Moran," he said. And there was just a bit of an edge to his voice.

Moran replied politely. "Captain Haskell, I hope I'm not bothering you. I just wanted to tell you where we are with the case."

Haskell looked at him for a moment, sizing him up. "Of course. Come in."

It was a warm house, with apricot couches and white curtains. Not a lot of frills, but simple and elegant. Somewhat like Hannah Haskell, Moran thought as he settled himself onto one of the couches.

Captain Haskell held up his dirty hands. "I'm doing some retiling in the bathroom. Just let me wash up," he said, and he disappeared for a moment.

Moran looked around the room and saw takeout boxes and soda cans on the coffee table. Campaign and political papers marked with pen lay strewn around the floor. The captain hadn't wasted any time in keeping up with business, Moran thought.

And why would he? The polls had him winning by a significant margin before his wife's murder. They'd probably tapered off after the press got ahold of the fact that he went to the psychiatric hospital. No one would want a guy who'd had a breakdown in the Senate, Moran thought, but he hadn't heard if Haskell would continue his run or not. By the look of this room, he planned to.

Haskell came back in and asked the detective if he would like anything to drink. Moran declined, and the captain sat down and moved the takeout boxes off the table with, "Excuse the mess."

Moran shook his head. "Not at all. How are you doing, Captain?"

"I'm feeling better, thank you."

"Let me say again how sorry I am for your loss," Moran said.

The captain nodded. "You had something to tell me?"

"Yes. We know that there was a vagrant in the parking lot around the time of your wife's murder. We haven't identified him yet but hope to do so shortly. Your wife's credit cards were left in her wallet, so if it was a mugging, we think it got out of hand. Your wife may have defended herself, and her death may have been unintentional."

The captain sat there stoically, taking in his words.

"I know this is hard to hear, Captain Haskell," Moran said kindly.

"Is that all you came to tell me?" he asked the detective.

"No. I have a few questions too. They're just a formality, really. I wanted to be a little more specific as to certain parts of what you've said about your movements on Sunday." He consulted his notes. "When we spoke on Sunday night, you said you and your wife went tile shopping and were home around three p.m.?"

The captain's jaw tensed again. "Perhaps my lawyer should be here."

"If you like. I'm missing the time Dr. Haskell left the house for Wellglad on Sunday and am just trying to be thorough in my report," he said innocently.

After a beat, Haskell nodded and said, "Around four p.m." And then, without waiting for Moran to ask, he added, "And I left around four thirty."

Moran updated his notes with a bit of a flourish. "That's that. Thank you."

The captain nodded again.

But then Moran added, "The valet had you arriving at the fundraiser at five ten p.m., which means you were a little bit late. Now, when we looked at the route you said you took and the traffic that day, we estimated it would only take about fifteen to twenty minutes from your house to the function. Did you make any stops along the way?"

Haskell looked off, and Moran noticed that his jaw had tightened ever so slightly before he seemed to remember something and turned back to Moran.

"I didn't stop anywhere else, but I did come back to the house because I'd forgotten my speech, so that's why I was a little late," he said.

Moran wrote this down, then cleared his throat delicately. "And ... when was the last time you spoke to your wife, Captain Haskell?"

He looked at him strangely. "I don't know. I guess before she left here. Why?"

"We are trying to see if she was in contact with anyone else that day. Did she speak to anyone you know of, or see anyone else that you're aware of?"

The captain looked lost for a second, then shook his head. "Why are you asking? Do you think someone she knew did this?"

"No, not at all. Just trying to nail down what time she may have been accosted. That's all."

Haskell nodded, a pained expression on his face. "What about her phone? Were you able to get the password? I'm sorry I forgot it. I'm not very good at that stuff. But if she spoke to anyone else, it'd be on her phone. And now that I'm thinking about it—I called her a couple of times after she left here."

"You did?"

Haskell nodded. "I was trying to convince her to come to the fundraiser after she was finished with her work." He paused for a minute before adding, "But she never picked up." And he looked off sadly.

"I'm so sorry," Moran said. And then, very delicately, "I wanted to ask you about that. About her not joining you at the fundraiser. Was that somewhat odd, since her boss, Edward Dowd, was one of the hosts?"

Captain Haskell shook his head. "No. She was tired. And she went to very few campaign events. She didn't like them. In all honesty, I don't think my wife was happy about me running for office. She was a very private person, Detective."

"I see," Moran said kindly.

"Is that all?"

Moran looked at his notes. "Did your wife wear any jewelry other than her wedding ring?"

Haskell shook his head. "Her ring? Was that recovered?"

Moran shook his head. "I'm sorry. She wasn't wearing it when we got there." He looked down, respectfully quiet, as the captain took that in. And that was when Moran noticed his hands, and that he wasn't wearing a wedding band. There was, however, a pale shadow where one once resided on his left hand. Moran remembered the tiling the captain had been doing and decided it made sense he would take it off. And as his eyes looked at the ringless hand, he couldn't help but notice how long and elegant the captain's fingers were, and thought to himself that they looked more like a pianist's hands than a war hero's.

"I lost mine. A couple of weeks ago," the captain said, clocking Moran's gaze. "It was the last day we were in Hawaii. I left it on my towel at the beach and, sure enough, someone took it. I replaced it with my grandfather's ring. Someone from the campaign said I should, but ... it's not the same."

He paused, looking down at his ring finger before adding, "It's crazy. I've had that ring most of my adult life. Had it when I was captured in Afghanistan. I was a POW."

Moran nodded respectfully. "I remember."

Haskell looked at him. "The whole time I was there? I kept that ring in my mouth. Tucked it between my molar and my cheek. Never lost it ..."

But he couldn't continue the story and turned away from the detective, overcome by grief. Moran looked down again, knowing a man of Captain Haskell's ilk would not want to be seen crying. But when he glanced back up, he witnessed something that was almost imperceptible, it was so quick.

As the captain wiped his eyes, his head turned to the side, he took a quick glance out of the corner of his eye at Moran. It was only for a split second, but Moran saw it, and it made him feel as if he was the one being watched. Then the captain excused himself, and Moran sat alone.

Perhaps he was mistaken, but that look was strange, Moran thought. Something else didn't sit right with him, and that was when Captain Haskell said someone from his campaign had told him to get another wedding ring. Why had he shared that? What was the point?

Now, it made sense that if he lost his wedding ring and wanted to keep up appearances, he would replace it. And maybe someone in his campaign had told him to do just that, but why had the captain thought to tell him that? Was he preemptively answering questions that might come up?

When Moran had asked what time his wife had left the house, the captain had included the time he left the house without prompting. Was he just being efficient, or had he prepared what to say? Probably a mixture of both, thought Moran. But there was one thing he could say for certain: the captain seemed to like tying up loose ends.

But there was something missing when it came to the captain, and that bothered Moran more than anything. He could see it in the man's eyes, or couldn't see it, as the case may be. Captain Haskell could cry, and he could dazzle with a smile, but there was something robotic about him that made those moments seem questionable. Almost perfunctory. As if he was going through the motions of what someone in his situation would do, but there was no feeling behind them. His execution was quite good, nuanced even, and Moran doubted most people would notice it. But having been around a few psychopaths in his career had made Moran attuned to their lack of humanity. So, even though the captain was good at it, Moran wasn't buying it. No. In fact, he made Moran more uneasy as time went on.

His thigh began to ache from all the exertion, so Moran reached down to loosen the brace around his knee, and there, under the table, he spotted an article about the Captain.

It was from a newspaper, and there were pictures of him in it as well. Moran noticed that in one of the pictures, Haskell was smiling and waving to a crowd. Moran picked up the paper and squinted to see the date. It was from a rally the weekend before his wife was killed, the weekend after their Hawaii trip, and sure enough, there on the finger of his waving hand, he wore a wedding ring. He must have replaced it right away, thought Moran.

Then he noticed a blond woman standing behind Haskell. You could only see half of her face, but it was a face Moran had become quite familiar with, for it belonged to Hannah Haskell. She stood behind him, the dutiful wife. What was it Haskell had said about her not liking attending his campaign functions?

Captain Haskell reappeared and asked him if there was anything else he needed. Moran set down the paper, gathered his crutches, and pulled himself up. He told the captain again how sorry he was, and that they were doing everything they could to catch the murderer. Captain Haskell accepted this comment gracefully, bowing his head sadly and thanking the detective as he showed him out.

Moran slowly climbed into his car, willing the pain in his lower back to pipe down. But it was his gut that was really driving him crazy. His gut that wouldn't stop shrieking at him that something was amiss.

Chapter 42

Ella began to think Clyde had taken Ms. Zimmerman out to dinner, it was so late. She imagined him consoling her over a nice bottle of Merlot, the jerk.

She readied herself to leave her office just as she noticed the mail sitting on her desk. She picked it up and spotted the manila envelope. It was addressed to *Captain Haskell c/o Dr. Ella Kramer.*

She suddenly remembered the person on the phone, who Alana thought was a crazy paparazzo. He'd said that he was sending her something to give to the captain, and now this had arrived.

She would take it with her when she met him, she thought, as she put it in her drawer. She knew she owed him a call to set up their appointment, but that would have to wait. Right now, she needed to speak with Clyde. She headed down the hall and found his office door locked. She felt a pang of anger all over again.

She walked down the hall, ready to leave, when she saw Jenny putting on her coat. Ella was about to say good night when something suddenly occurred to her, and she stopped.

"Oh! Jenny, I was wondering if we had hired any new nurses? I thought I noticed one the other day and again this afternoon—a redheaded woman? She looks very young."

"Not that I know of, and I would know because I do the paperwork around here. Sorry, Dr. Kramer, you must be seeing things!"

Ella stared at Jenny for a second, wishing she could tell her what a miserable human being she was. That even her deceased husband had thought so, and was constantly berating her after he'd passed. And that only the prayers of a madman had pacified his pain. But instead, she bit her lip, moved on with a polite smile, and got on the bus to Clyde's.

Little did Jenny know that *seeing things* was exactly what Ella was afraid of. She rubbed her temples and admonished herself, again, to get a grip.

She got off at the bus stop closest to Clyde's house and walked the few blocks there in the cold night air, willing herself to calm down. She would have to be careful and not bruise Clyde's ego or there would be no convincing him to help Gary. Surely there was a logical explanation to all of this, and she would be able to smooth things over.

Clyde opened the door and looked at her, somewhat shocked. "Ella. What are you doing here?"

The way he said it immediately aggravated her. Hadn't they been lovers for the past four months? Had she just imagined that she was having a relationship with him?

"Can I come in?" she asked icily.

"Of course," he stuttered and opened the door.

She walked into the living room, half-expecting to find Ms. Zimmerman sitting on the couch, but only saw a bottle of bourbon and a glass on the coffee table.

"Would you like a drink?" he offered as he sat back down and poured himself another one. Ella could tell by the way he was speaking that he'd already had a few. That wasn't like him, she thought. It was a little early to be sloshed.

"No, thanks," she said tensely.

He gulped down his drink, and she noticed he looked older than she had ever seen him. It was as if the weight of the world was pressing down on him.

"Are you going to sit down?" he asked.

Ella remained standing and said tersely, "Where have you been the last few days?"

He stared at her for a moment and then rolled his eyes. "Oh Christ. I really don't have time for this, Ella."

She felt her face flush with anger. They hadn't spoken since Monday—and that wasn't even a conversation but rather a dressing down by him for the way she had handled Captain Haskell's case.

"Time for what? Time to explain to me, the person you have been seeing for four months, why you haven't called? What is going on, Clyde?"

He looked at her angrily. "It's been kind of a tough week. I lost a patient I've been working with for ten years, and you—you completely fucked up the Haskell case and I had to deal with the fallout! So—no! I really haven't been in the mood to talk to you! Sorry!"

He said it with such venom that Ella was left speechless. Then, without thinking, she lashed out. "But not too busy to escort Ms. Zimmerman around! Aren't you wonderful!"

Clyde slammed down his glass on the coffee table and stood. "Look, I can't deal with your petty jealousy right now, OK? I think it would be better if you left!"

Ella was furious, and any idea of having a calm conversation was gone.

"Oh, not to worry. I'll be going home very soon, but there's something I need to clear up with you before I do."

He looked at her impatiently.

"Gary Lester came to see me today. Remember the proposal I gave you? About his binary light treatment for schizophrenia? He gave it to me to pass on to you to get your feedback, but it seems that you've recently presented a paper on the same treatment to a couple of publications. He thinks you stole his work, Clyde."

Clyde stood silently seething before he became apoplectic. "What?!"

"He thinks you . . ."

Before she could finish, he yelled, "I heard you!"

He began pacing the room, muttering angrily under his breath, and Ella wasn't sure what she was witnessing. His eyes darted around frantically like a trapped animal in a cage, trying to escape. He tossed back another glass of bourbon.

"What a Goddam joke!" he hissed and refilled his glass, spilling some bourbon on the table.

Ella'd seen enough. "You're right. Maybe this isn't the time . . ."

"To what? Accuse me of stealing?" he snapped loudly.

She couldn't help but clap back. "Well, you'd have to agree that the timing is somewhat odd! And you refused to talk to me about it when I gave it to you! I thought you hadn't read it yet!"

"Do you know how many requests like that I get in a week? For fuck's sake! Gary Lester?" he roared loudly, getting in her face.

Ella stood her ground. "Yes, but I asked you to look at it as a favor and you never did anything about it. Ever! And then you have a paper about to come out with the exact same treatment? Don't you think that looks somewhat suspicious, Clyde?"

He looked at her contemptuously. "Get your head out of your ass, Dr. Kramer. I might fuck you, but that doesn't mean I think you're my equal when it comes to research. And I certainly don't think your pal, Lester, is, either."

He kicked back the bourbon, looked her in the eye, and slurred, "Why don't you just admit that you're jealous that I took care of Dan's sister instead of catering to your whiny bullshit and apologize for your childish behavior? Why don't you do that instead of attacking me with this garbage!"

Ella stood there unable to speak, she was so horrified. And suddenly it hit her—she couldn't be with someone like this. She couldn't allow herself to ever be abused again.

As Clyde began to pour himself another bourbon, she headed for the front door. She stopped at the stairway landing, remembering that some of her clothes and things were there, and she didn't want to have to come back to get them. So she headed upstairs.

"Where are you going?" he shouted, following her, completely inebriated.

"I'm getting my things," she yelled angrily.

He followed her up, stumbling on the landing before heading into his bedroom behind her. "Look, Ella, I'm sorry. All right? It's just been a horrible week. I'm under enormous stress. . . ."

But Ella wasn't listening; she moved around the room with purpose. She picked up her bracelet and earrings from the bedside table and threw them into her bag.

"You can't just come in here and accuse me of stealing, for God's sake! I mean . . ." he wailed plaintively as he stumbled, landing on the bed.

Ella went into his bathroom and gathered up the makeup and other toiletries she'd left there. She passed Clyde, who sat on the bed, his head in his hands.

"I'm sorry. OK? I've had too much to drink and . . ."

She continued into the closet, where she grabbed some of her clothes. She was about to open a drawer when something on top of the chest stopped her. It was a ring. A simple gold band. She picked it up. It looked like a wedding ring, but Clyde had never been married.

She heard him drunkenly slur more apologies from the bedroom. "Ella, you know how I feel about you. Can we just stop this now?" he pleaded.

She stared at the ring. Was this for her? Was Clyde going to propose? Was he this serious? Had her feelings for him not been in vain after all?

Then she did something without thinking and slipped it onto her ring finger and held up her hand to look at it. It was too big, but she was somewhat elated by the thought that Clyde, who was in the next room drunkenly protesting his love for her, might propose.

But she quickly checked herself. After the way he'd just attacked her, she knew she could never be with him. She shook her head as tears sprang to her eyes. Why had everything gotten so hard? Why had everything fallen apart? What the hell had happened to her life? She had to get out of there and think. She slipped off the ring and was about to put it down when something caught her eye. There was something inscribed on the inside. of the ring. She squinted and held the ring closer to her face and could just make out what it said in the dim light of the closet:

Hannah ❤ *Oliver 6/14/2007.*

Ella felt the ground move under her feet and her heart stop. She stood there as the blood rushed from her head, and she had a dizzy feeling that began to make her sick. *What the hell was this? What was he doing with this ring?*

Clyde had now moved to the closet doorway and was muttering drunkenly, "I didn't mean to say those things, Ella. You know how I feel about you."

She turned to him, and the look on her face silenced him. Even in his drunken state, Clyde could tell something was terribly wrong.

"What? What is it?" he asked.

With a feeling of dread and horror, she extended her hand with the ring lying on it.

"Where did you get this?" she asked him.

Clyde stared at the ring and involuntarily took a step back, almost as if he'd been burned.

"Clyde, where did you get the Haskells' wedding ring?"

He didn't say anything; he just looked at her, and she could see the fear and anguish in his eyes. He turned away from her and collapsed on the bed, where he buried his face in his hands and began to cry.

"I didn't know! I didn't know!" he sobbed as Ella looked on, terrified by what she might hear.

Chapter 43

Detective Moran pressed the Call button on the precinct elevator the next morning, and as the doors opened, what he saw made him chuckle. For there, in the car, was his partner, Detective Scarpetti, holding the handrail, in midplié.

"*Nutcracker?*" Moran quipped.

"Pretty sure it's in the bag this time," Scarpetti answered, which made Moran chuckle even more as he entered the elevator car, and the two headed up to their offices.

"I guess Ross told you about the rabbit?" Scarpetti asked.

Moran nodded.

"Well, I also had the guys run the partial print found on Hannah Haskell against Captain Haskell's prints, and it came back negative. Thought you should know, since you seem so keen on him."

Moran nodded again, unable to hide his disappointment. "Haskell explained the missing fifteen minutes to me. Said he went back home to get his speech, which he'd forgotten."

"That makes sense," Scarpetti said. "When'd you see Haskell?"

The elevator stopped, and the two stepped out and proceeded down the hall.

"Yesterday," Moran answered.

"I don't know, Boss. I'd be careful barking up that tree."

Before he could say more, they were intercepted by Detective Ross. "Detective Moran?" Ross said excitedly.

"What is it?" Moran asked.

"You have a couple of visitors. Dr. Westbrook and Dr. Kramer from Bainbridge. They've been here for about an hour and say they will only speak to you. I assumed it was about the inmate who committed suicide, but they wouldn't say. Just that they wanted to speak to you."

Moran frowned. This was odd indeed. "Thank you," he said to Ross, and he and Scarpetti headed to his office.

Upon entering, Moran was struck by the dread in Ella's eyes as she looked up at him. Both she and Westbrook looked exhausted, and he seemed to have aged a decade since he'd last seen him. Moran hung up his coat, and Scarpetti leaned on the cabinet behind the two visitors, the silent observer.

"Good morning," Moran said as he put down his crutches and sat at his desk.

Ella murmured, "Good morning," but Clyde looked down at his hands, saying nothing.

"May I offer you coffee or anything?" Moran continued, but both shook their heads. "How can I be of help," he finally asked.

Ella answered tightly, "Clyde needs to tell you something."

Moran turned his attention to Dr. Westbrook expectantly.

Westbrook struggled for a moment before he found his voice. "The other day, Tuesday, when I escorted you to Dan's room . . . I found something . . . I should have told you about it."

Moran nodded for him to continue.

Clyde looked at Ella, who gave him a comforting nod, and he pulled the ring out of his pocket and set it on the desk in front of Moran. "I found this in the plant in Dan's room. I wasn't sure what it was at first, but once I was, I should have come forward."

Moran picked up the ring and brought it close to his face for inspection. He noticed the inscription, opened his drawer, and took out a magnifying glass. He held it up to the ring, and what he read made his breath catch.

Hannah ❤ Oliver 6/14/2007

Scarpetti walked over to Moran, who handed him the ring and glass.

"Indeed you should have," he said quietly, while Scarpetti looked at it. Moran stared at Westbrook until Scarpetti headed to lean on the cabinet once again.

"Dr. Westbrook," Moran began, "would you like to have counsel present? I suggest you do."

Clyde looked at him, panicked. "Why would I need counsel? I didn't do anything wrong!"

"Obstruction of justice isn't nothing, Doctor," Moran replied.

Clyde looked as if he was about to come undone until Ella put her hand on his thigh reassuringly and said, "Just tell them what happened, Clyde."

"Again, would you like to have a lawyer present?" Moran reiterated.

Clyde snapped, "No! I just want to get this off my chest!"

Moran took out a recording device. "Do you mind if we tape you?"

Clyde shook his head, and Moran pushed the Record button and began. "Today is December 1, 2024, and we are speaking with Dr. Clyde Westbrook. Dr. Westbrook has declined to have counsel present. Can you reiterate that for me?"

Clyde answered, "Yes. I've declined counsel."

"Dr. Westbrook, you say you found this ring—which, for the record, appears to have belonged to the deceased, Dr. Hannah Haskell, with the inscription *Hannah* ❤ *Oliver 6/14/2007*, their wedding date, on the inside of the ring. You found it in Daniel Zimmerman's room on the day of his suicide. The day I met you. Is that correct?"

"Yes," Clyde answered quietly.

"And why did you take the ring and conceal it from me?"

Clyde shrugged. "I panicked. I didn't know what it was at first. . . ."

"That was three days ago, Doctor," Moran said accusingly.

Clyde became defensive. "Because I don't think Dan would do something like that! He was mentally ill, but he would never have hurt her! He wouldn't hurt anyone!"

Immediately, there was a chill in the room as Moran realized the weight of what Clyde had just said. Was Dr. Westbrook telling them that Daniel Zimmerman had been in the Wellglad parking lot with Hannah Haskell that day?

"Are you saying that Mr. Zimmerman was in the parking lot the evening Hannah Haskell was killed?"

Clyde nodded, looking down at his hands, which shook visibly. "I was too. I didn't see her, but . . ." Clyde stammered, ". . . we were there."

Moran sat back in his chair and waited for a beat. "Let's start at the beginning. What were the two of you doing in the parking lot of Wellglad on Sunday afternoon?"

Clyde swallowed hard and looked at Ella, who patted his leg again. "Well," he began, "I have been working on a new treatment for schizophrenia. It is banal but unique. It uses light to stimulate various parts of the brain. I won't go into the science behind it, but simply put—you put the subject under a sort of ring of lights of opposing wavelengths and rotate the ring around the head at different speeds. What I have found is that at just the right wavelength and velocity, it significantly decreases the activity of the brain in the affected areas and has quite a calming effect on the subject.

"I needed a lab that was set up for it where I wouldn't be disturbed. I needed to monitor the subject using brain scans called an EEG, and since there are very different areas affected, I wanted to develop something to monitor all of the areas at once, so I devised a sort of cap with electrodes to be worn by the subject while the light was being changed. So that the EEG could monitor the brain at the same time the light was going around the head." Here he waited a moment, then said, "Bainbridge isn't equipped to do that, but Wellglad is, so . . . that's what we were doing."

Moran flashed on the footage of Daniel Zimmerman running through the video with the weird cap on his head. And he realized the buttons were clasps for electrodes. He shot Scarpetti a look and saw he was on the same page. "So, you have access to Wellglad? To the laboratories there?" he asked.

Clyde nodded slowly. "Yes, Edward Dowd is a friend of mine. We went to school together. We've done a lot of work together over the years, and I have access to the laboratories in the South Building, where I've done research with small animals on certain drugs. I hadn't been there in a while, though."

Moran remembered the machines in the smaller lab in the South Building. In particular, he remembered the EEG machine Kim had pointed out.

Clyde mopped the cold sweat from his brow with his shirt sleeve. "This is the first time I tested something . . . on a patient, though. And since it was so minimal and noninvasive, I thought there would be no downside. I had already done a few experiments with rabbits, and it just . . . you have to believe me . . . I was just looking for a way to help people."

"Is this standard practice? To use patients for something like that?" Moran asked.

Clyde couldn't bring himself to answer and shook his head. Moran turned to Ella and saw a pained look sweep across her face.

"No, it isn't. We aren't allowed to do anything like that without the permission of the family," Ella answered.

Moran frowned at that. "Families sign off on letting their family members be used for experiments?"

Clyde blurted out, "It's not really an experiment! It's just light used in a different way! It may be a little disorienting, but it doesn't cause brain damage or anything like that, for God's sake! I mean, there are no chemical side effects!"

Ella put her hand on his leg to stop him. She then calmly explained, "If you present something as a noninvasive therapeutic treatment, then yes. Families are usually desperate to help their mentally ill relatives."

Moran saw how difficult this was for her. Whatever was going on between the two, what Westbrook had done wasn't good for either of them. He turned back to Clyde.

"Did you do this? Did you ask for permission?" Moran asked.

Clyde shook his head guiltily. "I was on a very fast track with it, and it was harmless, or so I thought. But it was just a stupid thing to do. This would be an enormous breakthrough in the treatment of mental illness, and such a simple one that I became obsessed with proofing it. I now realize how wrong it was, but I wanted to help and . . . well, there's no excuse. None." Then he added, "But I did speak with his sister just yesterday about the treatment. I was trying to let her know that we were doing everything we could to help Dan."

Here, Moran noticed Ella slowly removed her reassuring hand from Clyde's leg, and she seemed to become more withdrawn. Perhaps she was just spent, he thought, until he noticed a look of revulsion flit across her face before he returned to Clyde.

"Can you tell me what time you arrived at Wellglad?" Moran asked.

"About two p.m. Like I said, we made our way to the South Building . . ."

"What about Dr. Dowd? Did he know you were conducting these experiments there?" Moran asked.

Clyde shook his head again. "I've had a key to the labs in the South Building for a long time. I just came and went when I pleased. Ned knew nothing about it."

Moran felt he was telling the truth. "Where did you park your car?"

"I parked in the smaller lot closer to the South Building. There's no gate there."

Moran exchanged a look with Scarpetti, remembering the lights reflected in the kiosk's glass around that time. Lights from the south lot.

"So, you and Mr. Zimmerman arrived around two p.m. Then what?"

"I had been treating Dan with different light wavelengths and taking down data, and then we were getting ready to leave. . . ."

"What time was that?"

"About four thirty?" Clyde said.

Moran jotted that down and nodded for Clyde to continue.

"I was putting things away, and Dan was waiting for me in the lab with the rabbits, and I came out and . . . and he was gone. He just disappeared."

"Disappeared?" Moran asked.

"Yes. He liked the rabbits, and I let him visit them as I was getting everything squared away, and then he was just . . . gone."

Moran nodded, realizing that Westbrook could now be in very big trouble. "And did you find him?" he asked.

Clyde nodded quickly. "Yes! I went outside and heard him."

"What do you mean, *you heard him*?" asked Moran, slightly confused.

"He was crying and whimpering, and I realized he was in the parking lot because it echoed, and he just kept screaming my name over and over, *Dr. Westbrook! Dr. Westbrook*! And I could tell he was scared."

Clyde swallowed hard and looked as if he might break down, remembering his patient's dilemma, so Moran stood and retrieved a bottle of water from his refrigerator for him. Clyde took it gratefully, and Moran gave him a few seconds to drink it and calm himself before continuing.

"He was screaming your name and then what happened?"

"Like I said, he was in the parking lot, so I headed toward him, and all of a sudden, a rabbit . . . a rabbit ran across the road, and Dan was right behind it, chasing it. He was trying to catch it. And so I grabbed him, and he was a mess, crying and speaking gibberish . . ."

"What do you mean, gibberish?" Moran asked.

"He just kept saying *van, van, van*, and then something about the bunny getting hurt, and I didn't know what was happening. He was in a terrible state." Clyde took another swig of water while Moran waited.

"And then?"

"I calmed him down and got him back to Bainbridge," Clyde said.

Moran frowned. "You just brought him back? Didn't that raise questions?"

Clyde looked down at his hands again guiltily. "I made him lie down in the back seat as we drove through the gate, and then I brought him in—and out—through the doctor's lounge entrance. No one notices that exit. Anyway, I got him back to his room undetected."

Moran stared at him for a second, finding it difficult to hide his disgust at Daniel Zimmerman being used in this way. "When did you leave the Wellglad parking lot?"

Clyde shook his head, guessing. "I don't know. Probably around five p.m.?"

"And what kind of car do you drive?" Moran asked.

"A Mercedes sedan," Clyde answered.

Moran looked at Scarpetti, who nodded and made note of that so they could check it against the light pattern they saw in the kiosk's glass.

"Did Mr. Zimmerman say anything to you on the ride back to Bainbridge about why he was so upset?"

Clyde took another sip of water. "He just kept talking about the rabbit. That he wanted to save the rabbit, and that he had to hide or something. He was a wreck about what could happen to the rabbit."

"What do you mean, what could happen to the rabbit?" Moran pressed.

Clyde couldn't speak for a minute, and then tears welled up in his eyes and he began to cry. "I told him in the lab that the rabbits ... the rabbits weren't pets; they were there for experiments, and then they ..." Clyde stopped, unable to continue.

So Moran finished his sentence for him. "That the rabbits were used for experiments and then killed?"

Clyde nodded. "I told him that they were there to improve people's lives. I shouldn't have, but I didn't think ... I didn't think he would try to rescue them!"

Moran reached for a box of Kleenex and set it in front of Clyde.

"I didn't think he would do that," he murmured again and again.

Moran worked hard to remain calm in the face of Westbrook's cruelty and asked, "How long was he out of your sight, Dr. Westbrook?"

"It couldn't have been more than ten minutes or so. I don't know. I went in the other labs and the bathrooms before I left the building to look for him outside so, yes, about ten minutes."

Moran leaned in. "Did Mr. Zimmerman say anything about seeing Hannah Haskell in the garage?"

Clyde shook his head vehemently. "No! It was all about the rabbit and saving it from the van and rescuing it and hiding! He said nothing about a woman!"

"What exactly does that mean?"

"Dan used the term *van* to describe a bad person. When I first started working with him, I realized that he was associating the van that we used to transfer him to the hospital with something bad. So he called anyone trying to do something bad, in his opinion, a van."

Suddenly, Ella seemed to take a sharp intake of breath, but when Moran looked at her, she covered it with a little cough.

Clyde continued. "One time, when I was first working with him, Dan explained to me that the vans had tried to hurt him. I asked him which people had tried to hurt him, thinking it was the driver of a van or an orderly who had mistreated him, and he answered—I will never forget this because it showed just how truly terrified he was—he said that vans weren't people at all, but that they needed people to survive."

"They needed people," Moran reiterated. "For what?"

"For their energy. He said they sucked the energy out of people—no, their souls. *He said they sucked the souls out of people*."

Moran looked at him, not knowing what to make of this statement, as Ella's purse dropped to the floor with a loud thud. Moran turned to her and couldn't help but notice that she looked very pale as she scrambled to pick it up.

"Dr. Kramer? Are you all right?" he asked.

Ella nodded, but her face looked anything but all right, and Moran took a beat before he addressed Clyde again. "Sucked their souls out?"

"Yes. I mean—he was mentally ill, for God's sake!" Clyde explained. "But he wasn't a killer, if that's what you're thinking! I don't know if he found her body, or if the ring was dropped when the killer fled, but I know he didn't do anything to harm that woman! For God's sake, he was trying to save a rabbit!"

Again, Clyde dissolved into tears, holding his head in his hands, and Moran noticed that Ella didn't comfort him now as she had before. She just sat there looking as if she had seen a ghost. Moran couldn't quite make out what was going on with her, but he didn't have time to figure it out. He turned back to Clyde.

"Refresh my memory, Dr Westbrook: Didn't you tell me that Mr. Zimmerman was admitted to Bainbridge because he was violent with his sister?"

Clyde looked up, horrified by where this was going. "Yes, but he didn't hurt her! There was an argument and he pushed her, but she wasn't really hurt! He was schizophrenic, Detective, and that was why he was brought to Bainbridge."

Moran nodded, feeling the gall rise in his throat. "Are you aware of how Dr. Haskell was killed, Dr. Westbrook?"

Clyde paled. "Just what the paper said. That she was hit over the head during a mugging."

"The report said *blunt force trauma to the head*, Dr. Westbrook. What they didn't report, because they didn't know it, was that Dr. Haskell was shoved to the ground so violently that she cracked her skull on it and bled to death."

Clyde sat there, stunned. But after a moment, he rallied and defended Dan. "He didn't do it! I swear to you—he didn't!"

Moran had heard enough and turned his attention to Ella. "When did you become aware that Dr. Westbrook had this ring, Dr. Kramer?"

"Last night," she answered quickly.

"Dr. Westbrook told you about it?"

Ella didn't respond, and Clyde interjected, "What has that got to do with . . .?"

Moran snapped, "Hush!"

And Clyde did.

Moran resumed. "Dr. Kramer? How did you find out about the ring?"

Ella answered quietly. "I went to Clyde's house and was getting something from his closet, and . . . I found it."

Clyde looked at her accusingly.

"I see," Moran said, then folded his hands in his lap and thought for a second. After a moment of deliberation, he quietly said, "Dr. Westbrook, I am afraid you are under arrest."

Clyde sat there shocked but quickly became apoplectic. "But I came forward! I'm telling you everything!"

Moran was having none of it, though, and pulled himself up. "You will be charged with obstruction of justice for the time being. Detective Scarpetti will now remand you into custody."

And just like that, Scarpetti was at Clyde's side, pulling him to his feet.

"But I came here willingly! I didn't ask for a lawyer! I didn't hide anything!"

That was too much for Moran to bear. "You came here three days after you found a key piece of evidence, and I am not sure you would have come at all if Dr. Kramer hadn't made you! Detective Scarpetti will read you your rights and you will be allowed to call your lawyer. Do you understand?"

Clyde looked at Ella, completely shocked that this could happen to him. "Ella, you know I didn't do anything wrong. Tell him!"

But she sat there, stone-faced, unable to look at him.

"Ella, for God's sake!" Clyde wailed.

Scarpetti Mirandized Clyde and took him down the hall over his protests.

Moran turned his attention to Ella as she sat unflinching in the chair, staring off into space. What was happening with her? he wondered. Moran reached into the refrigerator for another water, handed it to her, and waited while she took a sip before asking, "What is your relationship to Dr. Westbrook, Dr. Kramer?"

"I've worked for him for the past three years. I started as his resident and then was offered a full-time position at Bainbridge," she said robotically.

"And?" he asked.

She looked at him as if she hadn't quite come to. As if half of her was somewhere else. Moran worried she might be having some sort of breakdown.

After a beat, she answered. "We have had a romantic relationship for the past four months, but recently things weren't good. I broke it off with him last night, and that's when I found the ring. When I went to get my things from his closet."

"And you knew nothing about his private work with Daniel Zimmerman?" Moran asked.

That question snapped the other half of her back into this reality quickly, and she said vehemently, "No. I did not." And the way she said it told him she was telling the truth. "Am I in some kind of trouble here, Detective?"

"No," he answered. And then he asked pointedly, "Westbrook made you the responsible doctor on the Haskell case, correct?"

"Yes," she answered, seeming confused as to why he asked.

But he said nothing further except, "I may have more questions for you later."

"Of course," she said.

"That will be all, Dr. Kramer," Moran said, and she gathered herself and headed out of his office.

He leaned back in his chair, contemplating what had just happened, but his train of thought was shortly interrupted by Detective Ross, who carefully knocked on his door.

"What is it?"

"Detective Scarpetti wanted me to let you know that Dr. Westbrook has been booked and his lawyer is on the way."

"Good," said Moran, and added, "The partial print they got off of Hannah Haskell's neck?"

"Yes, sir?" Ross said, looking at him quizzically.

"I need you to run it through the Psych Crimes database. If there isn't a match, I'll need you to see if you can get a print from Bainbridge for the patient Daniel Zimmerman, and see if it matches."

"Yes, sir," Ross said quickly.

"Where are we with Ezekial Weintraub?"

"Nothing from the bus drivers going to Marshall. I'm checking the footage from the buses with cameras. Bad news is, a lot of them don't have cameras. Oh, I also found out that both his parents are deceased. But he does have a sister, and I'm running her number down as we speak. You want me to go by his apartment again?"

Moran looked at him with a sense of urgency. If it was Zimmerman in that garage, then his suspicions about Haskell would be thrown out, and he didn't want that to happen. He knew that it was crazy, but he couldn't shake the feeling that Haskell wasn't innocent. He needed to speak with Ezekial Weintraub and find out what he knew.

"Yes. Find out if he caught a train or a plane anywhere as well."

"We'll need to go through Homeland then, won't we?" asked Ross.

If that partial print was Zimmerman's, the case was over. He had to move quickly. "Yes," was all he said to Ross, who nodded and left the office.

Chapter 44

Ella waited on the sidewalk outside the precinct for her Uber to arrive. The crisp air felt good on her face, and the blue sky above was very welcome after so many days of rain. She watched as people walked by, going on with their day as if nothing was happening. As if everything was normal.

Ella took exception to that word, *normal*. Always had. What the hell was normal when you really thought about it? All the word really meant was that which you were used to; what you'd grown up with; what was habitual; what was acceptable.

What about those, like herself, who'd grown up differently, so to speak? Or the people at Bainbridge? Why was it that their normal was discounted as abnormal or sick? She'd decided that normal was a relative term many years ago, and if she were truthful, it pissed her off that some people's normal was so damn good and hers was so tough.

Take, for example, the night she'd had to endure with Clyde. She knew that he was aware that hiding that ring was wrong but had to listen to his protestations and rationalizations for hours before he was able to admit to her what had happened. And even then, he hadn't told her half of what he'd told the police just now. He'd known it was wrong to use Dan but had made it sound like it had been an outing for the two of them and not the horror she'd just listened to in the police station. He swore that he was only trying to protect Dan. That he'd been in shock and would come clean to the police if she were by his side. He then began to profess his undying love for her, and a part of her still wanted to believe him.

It was at that point, however, that her inner voice, her gut, became incredibly loud. So loud that it began to drown out her other, reasonable voice, the one she always tried to listen to. *I've been telling you that he was a louse! When will you ever listen?* her gut screamed. And Ella didn't know what to think. It was as if each of her feet was planted firmly in a different reality.

Reasonable Ella stood by Clyde's side and supported him as she said she would. And now here she was, in a sleep-deprived daze, realizing what a horrible person he was, as *normal* people passed by her, unaware of the other realities going on all around them.

It was funny, she thought as she stood there, being in two realities at once. And frankly, she was amazed at how good she was at it. She always had been, she supposed. It was as if there were two of her in one body. That had made it easy to sit through all the questions in that room, because as she sat there as reasonable Ella, the caring girlfriend, she was also somewhere else, figuring things out.

But Moran was no fool. He was figuring things out too. As she was leaving, he'd asked her if she was Haskell's doctor. He knew she was, but now they both knew why Clyde had given her Haskell's case; so that he wouldn't have direct dealings with the captain but could still control things through her. Clyde didn't want to engage with Captain Haskell because he had been in the Wellglad parking lot around the time of his wife's murder. He wanted his visits to Wellglad to remain undetected but if anything were to come out about Dan and him being there, there would be no conflict of interest because Ella was handling Haskell and not him. But then he'd found the ring, and everything had blown up.

It also dawned on Ella why Clyde had spent so much time with Dan's sister. He was angling to have her sign off on Dan being his guinea pig. Clyde would need her help should it be found out that he was at Wellglad with her brother that day. If he could charm her into thinking he was only looking out for Dan's best interest, which he'd probably convinced himself was the truth, things wouldn't go as badly for him. Unfortunately for Clyde, if Dan was responsible for Hannah Haskell's death or was a witness to it, it wouldn't really matter what Dan's sister thought or sanctioned.

At one point during the interview, as the full weight of her observations hit her, a wave of revulsion overtook her, and she thought she might be sick. Fortunately, no one noticed. That was when the odd feeling of being two people in one had set in. And the notion that she'd been an imposter for far too long began to roam around her exhausted mind.

The Uber pulled up and she slid into the back seat, slamming the door shut.

The driver grunted, looking her up and down before he hit the gas and took off toward Bainbridge. She'd decided not to go home and change, even though she probably looked a fright. She pulled her makeup bag out of her purse and looked in her compact mirror.

She frowned at her roots. She hated having to dye her hair all the time, but she hated her hair color even more. What was it the other girls on the hall had called her? It had something to do with carrots, she recalled, remembering their cruelty. But, she thought, that was a long time ago, and it was better to leave those memories to the past, so she put on some lipstick instead.

The real dilemma was not having her medication, which she knew was potentially risky on no sleep, but with Clyde being detained, her patients and even some of his would need her to be there to give their lives normalcy—and she laughed at her use of the word.

Strangely enough, her head had stopped hurting somewhere midway through the interview, and even though she was worried an aura was coming on, she preferred thinking her real thoughts to being repressed. It felt good to have them back. She liked feeling her thoughts, and wondered where she had heard that before.

She took a deep breath and watched the scenery traveling by as they drove. She noticed the blueness of the sky again and marveled to the Uber driver, "It's a beautiful day, isn't it?"

To which he said nothing, and she found herself murmuring to herself softly, "The light looks so . . . different."

She opened the window to feel the fresh air, but the driver found his voice and told her to keep it closed, that it was cold, and looked at her like she was crazy.

She obliged and leaned back against the seat and let her mind drift back to the precinct, when Clyde was explaining the meaning of the word *van* according to Daniel Zimmerman. She thought she might pass out when he began recounting Dan yelling *van* all the time. And when he mentioned that Dan had told him many years ago that *vans suck people's souls out*, she had felt her hands and legs go limp and could no longer clutch the purse on her lap; it had fallen to the floor, surprising everyone, especially her.

It was at that moment that she realized that Dan *was* trying to say Vanitan. *Just as Malakhi had told her*. How could that be? Did those two have an imaginary world that they had made up together? With its own secret language?

But if that was the case, how had her aunt known about it? For her Aunt Moira had warned her during her visit on Monday, after her strange interview with Captain Haskell, that *they were all around her* and they would *suck the soul out of you*. Just as Dan had apparently told Clyde all those years ago.

She had felt herself sort of leave her body when her purse hit the floor, and was aware of Moran staring at her, but she'd covered pretty well. Just like she used to. She didn't say a word, but her heart pounded so loudly she thought he might hear it. Nor did she run out of the door as her legs so desperately wanted to do. Instead, she calmly guided herself to reach down, pick up her bag, and mutter some sort of apology, all the while trying to control the chaos that was raging inside her.

She was acting *normal*, and she was pretty proud of pulling it off. If only her patients could pretend to be normal, she thought, and hide the truth inside themselves as she had. Perhaps they'd never have ended up in a place like Bainbridge. It was all terribly unfair.

Malakhi and Clark would never do what Clyde had done to Dan. Never. They still had their decency, and a moral code. They wouldn't rob Dan of his humanity the way Clyde had.

Ella knew now that Clyde's narcissism had eaten away any core he may once have had. Of course he'd stolen Gary's idea. Because in Clyde's mind, Gary wasn't smart enough to have the light treatment idea, but he was. So Gary's idea was really his. Yet another rationalization, a feat in mental gymnastics, to make what he'd done OK. Just like convincing Dan's sister that he was helping Dan when he had been so blatantly used.

But Ella knew the truth. And that was that Clyde Westbrook was a shark consuming everything in his path with no care for the carnage he left behind.

She would have to tell Gary what Clyde had done, and that would be incredibly difficult. Hopefully, he would understand that she'd had nothing to do with it. It also dawned on her that she would probably have to inform the other doctors about Clyde as well. Christ, this was going to be a nightmare. The whole place would be turned upside down. Dating Clyde had probably destroyed any chance of *normalcy* she would ever have, and she dreaded what was to come.

She glanced out the window and saw her reflection, and thought she really had to get her hair fixed. It reminded her of too many feelings she would prefer to forget. And then she realized that her thoughts were taking another turn for the worse, so she rolled down her window defiantly and stuck her head out, hoping the winter chill would blow them all away.

Chapter 45

"D r. Kramer, I need to speak with you," Jenny said, beckoning Ella into an empty office. As she entered, Ella was taken aback by the look of fear that Jenny was desperately trying to hide.

"As I am sure you know, Dr. Westbrook will be taking a leave of absence. Dr. Levital will be assuming his duties, and I am sure he will want to speak with you shortly." She said this with such obvious distaste that Ella was speechless.

"We will be cooperating fully with the police, and I need you to make yourself available to them when needed."

Ella nodded, unable to think of anything to say, and Jenny motioned her head, as if to say, *That's all*, and turned her back on Ella.

Things were moving faster than Ella'd thought, and it took a second before she turned around and headed down the hall. The light inside Bainbridge looked different, the noises louder than she remembered them being. Gone was the sleepy monotony of the daily grind, to be replaced by a frenetic feeling that whirred down the hallway and vibrated along the walls.

Was Dr. Levital aware of her relationship with Clyde? Was he about to let her go? Did he know that she had been interviewed by the police? Probably. And now she didn't feel as free as she had in the Uber. Now she must reconcile herself to what was happening in the real world, and her old insecurities began to tear at her nerves.

Gary entered her office, and the look on his face made her feel even more afraid.

"What the hell happened? The police are taking Dan's room and Westbrook's office apart. And now I hear Westbrook isn't returning."

Ella could no longer contain herself, and tears began to stream down her face. Gary took her in his arms, murmuring, "It's OK, Ella. It's OK."

She cleared her throat. "I think you're right, Gary. I think he stole your proposal on the binary light treatment—all your ideas."

Gary stared at her for a second. "What?"

And even though she knew she shouldn't, the truth came spilling out. "He was there that day. With Dan. At Wellglad, when Captain Haskell's wife was murdered."

Gary looked aghast. "Westbrook?"

She nodded. "Apparently, he was treating Dan with some kind of makeshift light treatment in the labs there. At some point he lost Dan—who was in the parking lot when Hannah Haskell was killed. And now the police think Dan did it."

The weight of this hit Gary, and he said nothing for a moment.

"Oh my God . . ." he finally uttered, and Ella buried her face in her hands and began to sob.

Gary rubbed her back. "It'll be OK, Ella. It'll be OK." Then, "How do you know all this? Did he tell you?"

Ella laughed ruefully. "Of course not! I found her ring in his closet!" And she shook her head angrily, unable to continue, before noticing that Gary had no idea what she was talking about.

"I went to his house last night to confront him about your proposal on the light treatment. We got into a fight, and when I went to get my things, I found Hannah Haskell's wedding ring in his closet. He'd found it in Dan's room on the day he killed himself and said nothing!"

"Oh my God," Gary whispered.

"I'm so sorry, Gary. I didn't think he was capable of this. Any of this! I had to spend the night convincing him to go to the police. And now . . . I don't know! I just don't know what to do."

"So Westbrook knew that Dan was in the parking lot and had her ring and did nothing? Jesus Christ."

She nodded, and the two of them sat there for a second in silence before Gary offered, "I wouldn't think Dan was capable of killing anyone, would you?"

Ella remembered Clyde had said the very same thing, but she really hadn't thought about it because everything had moved so quickly. Before, she would say she didn't think Dan capable of murder. But she hadn't known that he'd fought with his sister and pushed her, injuring her. She hadn't known that was what precipitated his coming to Bainbridge. But

Clyde had. And the enormity of what Clyde had done by not coming forward with the ring, given everything, continued to haunt Ella. How had she ended up with such a horrible person? What was it in her that wanted to be blind to who he truly was?

"Ella?" Gary asked.

"What?" she said, forgetting what he had asked her.

"I just wouldn't think Dan capable of something like that."

Ella relayed the story of Dan pushing his sister down to Gary. "I think if Dan was focused on catching the rabbit, then he may have shoved her if she got in his way, and maybe she hit her head when she fell, but I don't know," she said.

But it was strange; in all the time that she'd been at Bainbridge, she'd never seen Dan get angry at anyone, let alone attack them. He would get scared of strangers and yell *van* over and over, but then he usually cried and ran to his room. He never hurt anyone.

Then it dawned on her: Hadn't Dan physically attacked Captain Haskell the morning after his arrival? Yes, he had. That was strange. That wasn't like Dan.

And hadn't Nadine showed up a few hours after Dan attacked the captain and gone after Haskell in the garden? Ella was with her aunt at Seaside when she'd gotten the emergency message. It was Gary who'd told her what had happened between Nadine and Elvis, and that Nadine had turned toward the captain afterward and hurled some insults at him. What was it he'd said? Wasn't it something that echoed what the others had said?

She turned to Gary. "What was it that Nadine said to Captain Haskell? Do you remember? When he was in the garden? He said something weird."

Gary looked at her, completely lost. "What? Why do you want to know what Nadine said?" he asked, confused, and she realized how strange that must have sounded.

"I . . . never mind."

Gary was staring at her oddly now. He took her hand and squeezed it reassuringly.

"None of this is your fault, Ella. None of it," he said, looking at her as if something was wrong with her. "You should go home and rest," he said.

"I'm OK," she said calmly. "The lack of sleep is hitting me, but I need to be here. Don't worry about me, Gary. I'm fine."

"You're sure?"

She nodded.

"OK, well, I'm right down the hall. Come find me if you need me," Gary said.

Ella stared at him guiltily. He was worried about her, even after what Clyde had done to him. "Gary, I can call the *Journal*. I'll pressure Clyde to hand the whole thing off to you. . . ."

Gary opened the door and said gently, "Let's not worry about that now."

She felt tears spring to her eyes. "Thank you for being such a good friend to me, Gary. Really." And as she said it, she couldn't help but get the feeling that she was saying goodbye to him.

"Of course. It's all going to be OK," he said, and closed the door.

And although Ella would have liked to believe him, she knew things were far from OK, and doubted that they would be anytime soon. She rubbed her temples and thought of Dan. Poor Dan, who'd been used so terribly. Maybe the light treatment had made him different. He'd never seemed like the type to commit suicide, either, but he'd done just that, hadn't he?

Ella looked down at Oliver Haskell's case file, still on her desk, and her thoughts returned to Clyde, who'd given it to her. Surely he would go to jail if they found any physical evidence linking Dan with Hannah Haskell's death.

She closed her eyes and steeled herself. She didn't have time for regrets, she thought. There were important battles left to fight.

She needed to save her career. Or what was left of it.

Chapter 46

Captain Abbot seemed pleased that they potentially had their killer in Daniel Zimmerman and became irritated when Moran asked him not to jump to any conclusions, saying they still had other avenues to explore.

Moran and Scarpetti, now feeling even more pressure, headed to Moran's office to discuss their next step. Scarpetti planted himself across from his partner and started throwing out other morsels of information he'd gleaned.

"I talked to Ernie in the morgue. Zimmerman's sister picked up his body yesterday and had it cremated so she could make her flight last night. So we won't be able to look for any DNA there. But wipes from his fingernails at the scene were kept, and I told him to hold on to them."

Moran remembered the call with Ross yesterday, when he'd told the young detective-in-training to close the investigation. Christ. Why hadn't he listened to himself?

"Did he find Zimmerman's print in the PsychCrimes database?" Moran asked.

Scarpetti shook his head. "But he got prints from Bainbridge, and the guys are looking at those now. And like I said, Ernie probably still has Zimmerman's DNA from the fingernails, so we can test some of it against what we found on Hannah Haskell's neck—so we should know soon."

Scarpetti watched as Moran's face ran through a gamut of emotions, eventually settling on disappointment. And he couldn't help but ask, "You still think it was Haskell?"

"I just don't think he *isn't* involved. And yes, I think he could have done it. Think about it: Zimmerman is described as very gentle, but he violently attacks Dr. Haskell in a parking lot while trying to rescue a rabbit. And why did he attack Haskell when he arrived at Bainbridge? Had he seen him in that parking lot that night? Was he scared of him? We'll never know what he witnessed, thanks to Westbrook!" Moran fumed.

"Zimmerman was a big guy. He hurt his sister, right? Maybe Hannah Haskell got in the way of him getting to the rabbit, and he didn't know his own strength and killed her," Scarpetti offered.

Moran didn't answer.

"OK, then, why?" asked Scarpetti, playing devil's advocate. "Why would Haskell kill his wife? Their family and friends all say they had a good marriage. No one knew of any problems."

Moran's mind was churning now. "Why didn't she go with him to the fundraiser? Especially given her company, where she'd worked for fourteen years, supported her husband's run? The CEO of Wellglad, Edward Dowd, was on the host committee that night. What made her stay away?"

"OK, that's odd, but according to her friends and colleagues, she was a very quiet person. Maybe fundraising and being a senator's wife just wasn't her cup of tea."

Moran remembered his visit to Haskell's house. "I saw a photo in a newspaper article a week before her murder. She was there with him at some rally."

He turned to his computer and typed *Haskell campaign photos* in the search bar, and several pictures came up. He zoomed in on two or three of them where Hannah sat beside Haskell. He turned the monitor toward Scarpetti.

"She was supportive of him. Except for that night."

Scarpetti shrugged. "I don't know. But it's a big jump from missing one fundraiser to murder."

Moran nodded, agreeing. "But what was so important that she had to go to Wellglad for fifteen minutes?"

Scarpetti thought about that. "She called her lab assistant from Wellglad, didn't she? The guy with the rap sheet? And now he's nowhere to be found. Now, *that* is suspicious."

Moran didn't think Ezekial Weintraub had anything to do with her murder. If Kim Matsunaga was to be believed, he adored Hannah. But why had Hannah called him from Wellglad? And why hadn't she picked up when her husband called her?

Scarpetti continued. "Maybe she found out Weintraub was on drugs again and went to confront him, and now he's gone." He looked at his notes.

"Ross said Weintraub's neighbor saw him leaving with a bag Wednesday morning. You tell him to check airlines and trains?"

Moran nodded. "He's checking with Homeland Security."

"I don't know Boss, but I think you're wrong about this one. Weintraub seems like more of a suspect to me. Haskell may be cold, but I don't think he's a killer. For starters, if he was in the parking lot, wouldn't we have seen him on the camera?"

"Not necessarily. He didn't have a key card to the lot. The camera only covered the west entrance. The lot was easily accessible from the east and north sides. He could have gotten in without a problem."

"OK, so he got there and waited for her to appear, and then shoved her so hard her head cracked? Why? What's his motive?"

Moran shook his head. "That's the million-dollar question."

He sat quietly for a moment and then began spitballing. "His wife goes to his campaign events—except for a fundraiser thrown by her boss. She takes a manila envelope into the lab but doesn't come out with it. She calls her assistant, but he doesn't answer, and then he disappears. The other lab assistant, Kim Matsunaga, swears that they were close. She said Hannah gave Ezekial Weintraub a second chance at life."

He shuffled through his notes that referenced Kim Matsunaga when something occurred to him. "When I was at Wellglad, looking at Hannah Haskell's computer files, I noticed that a lot of the test subjects for her antidepressant . . ." and he looked at his notes again, "Lyprophan— were in the armed forces." And he stopped, as if a light bulb had gone off.

Scarpetti stared at him. "What?"

"What if Captain Haskell helped with that? Members of the armed forces were paid for participating in the Lyprophan tests."

"And?" Scarpetti said.

"If Captain Haskell was helping get test subjects for Wellglad—if he brokered some kind of deal with the armed forces—then he probably would have known Edward Dowd. And Edward Dowd and Wellglad are big supporters of his campaign. But Dowd told me he didn't really know him."

Scarpetti looked lost, but Moran quickly began going through his notes.

"Armando Garcia said he took the camera to Dowd and showed him the footage late the next day. Monday."

"Yeah, and Dowd told him to go to the police," Scarpetti rebutted.

"Haskell was already at Bainbridge on Monday," Moran said. "And Wellglad's attorney is Arthur Levine, who is also Haskell's attorney."

Scarpetti shrugged. "Levine handles all the big muckety-mucks."

Moran followed the thread. "Yeah, but when Levine showed up that night when we went to Haskell's house, that's when everything changed. Levine spoke with Haskell and everything *changed*. Suddenly, Levine worried he was suicidal. But he didn't seem that way to me. Did he to you?"

Scarpetti thought for a second. "Not really. I don't know. We aren't really qualified to make that determination, are we?"

"Even Dr. Kramer didn't think he was suicidal."

"She said that?"

Moran shrugged. "In a roundabout way. And it was Levine who suggested Bainbridge, remember? Not the County Hospital but Bainbridge . . ."

"Welcome to the world of money," Scarpetti said.

"Then he's attacked by Daniel Zimmerman."

He looked at Scarpetti strangely. "I mean, why would Zimmerman attack him? Everyone says that he was gentle."

"I don't know—he's crazy?" Scarpetti smirked.

"What if Zimmerman recognized him? From the parking lot? What if Haskell was there and Zimmerman saw something?"

Scarpetti went with it. "So, Zimmerman saw Haskell kill his wife?"

"Maybe," mused Moran, lost in thought.

Scarpetti shook his head. "Haskell kills his wife and then goes to the exact hospital where the witness to his crime is? Why would Haskell go there? That's nuts—no pun intended."

Moran shrugged. "But it's a strange coincidence, isn't it?"

He thought for another beat and then remembered his visit with the captain, and how the captain would preemptively explain things. Moran had found that odd.

"Maybe he wanted to *tie up loose ends*," Moran said, more to himself than to his partner.

Scarpetti looked at him incredulously. "You mean he wanted to what? Get rid of Zimmerman? Get rid of the witness? So now Haskell's a cold-blooded killer? Geez, you really don't like this guy, do you?"

Moran looked him dead in the eye. "No, I don't. I don't trust a thing he says."

That stopped Scarpetti. He knew how good Moran was, so if he had a hunch, he'd better take it seriously.

"OK," Scarpetti started, "let's say he did go back to *tie up loose ends*. How would he know to go to Bainbridge? How would he know who Zimmerman was or where he lived if he'd just seen him in that lot?"

Moran's mind went back to Dowd. "What if Dowd knew Westbrook was working there with Zimmerman?"

"But Westbrook said he didn't tell Dowd about going to Wellglad. And I believe him."

Moran frowned and then remembered something. He suddenly pulled the tape recorder—the one he'd used to interview Westbrook—out of his drawer and started fast-forwarding through the interview, looking for something.

"What are you doing?" Scarpetti asked, but Moran held up his finger. Then he found what he wanted and hit Play.

Clyde: Yes! I went outside and heard him.

Moran: What do you mean, you heard him*?*

Clyde: He was crying and whimpering, and I realized he was in the parking lot because it echoed, and he just kept screaming my name over and over, Dr. Westbrook! Dr. Westbrook! *. . . and I could tell he was scared.*

Moran: He was screaming your name, and then what happened?

Clyde: As I said, he was in the parking lot, so I headed toward him, and all of a sudden, a rabbit . . . a rabbit runs across the road, and Dan is right behind chasing it. He was trying to catch it. And so I grabbed him, and he was . . . he was a mess, crying and speaking gibberish . . .

Moran: What do you mean, gibberish?

Clyde: He just kept saying van, van, van, *and then something about the bunny getting hurt, and I didn't know what was happening. He was just in a terrible state.*

Moran turned the recording off.

Scarpetti looked at Moran, lost. "OK . . . so?"

"He was screaming Westbrook's name. Over and over . . ." Moran took another breath before continuing. "What if Haskell got into a fight with his wife? After all, there was that fifteen minutes that he suddenly says is when he went back home for his speech. Maybe she was mad at him. Maybe he met her in the parking lot, they fought, and he pushed her and then ran. Zimmerman witnesses it and starts screaming Westbrook's name. If Haskell knows Dowd . . . he tells him . . ." and Moran stopped, not sure what to think next.

"And Dowd covers for him?" Scarpetti asked incredulously. "He goes along with the murder of his colleague? That's out there, partner."

Moran knew Scarpetti was right, but he couldn't help but feel that he was on to something. Especially after interviewing Edward Dowd. The man was hiding something.

Scarpetti, playing devil's advocate again, countered, "That still doesn't answer the question: Why does Haskell go to Bainbridge the next day? Especially if he did do it? There's nothing tying him to the murder, so why? Why would he go there?"

Moran shook his head, frustrated. "I don't know."

Scarpetti took a breath. "Look, I think we know what happened here. Westbrook was doing experiments on his patient, which is disgusting, and maybe that made Zimmerman more aggressive, and he hurt her. Accidentally, but nonetheless."

Moran listened.

"Then Zimmerman kills himself, which Haskell had nothing to do with. He'd left Bainbridge by that point. If Zimmerman was a gentle guy, maybe he felt guilty about what he'd done and just . . . you know . . . killed himself."

"Or he was so terrified of Haskell, he thought the only way out was to kill himself," Moran said, not letting go.

Scarpetti gave him a look. "Come on. I mean, Hannah Haskell's ring would eventually come to light. I don't think Westbrook would have held out on that forever. Zimmerman would have been investigated and charged."

Moran was about to disagree when something dawned on him.

"The ring . . . What if Haskell went there to plant the ring?"

Scarpetti frowned. "Again, Dowd would have to be in on it. Otherwise, Haskell couldn't find Zimmerman on his own."

But Moran slowly followed the thread. "So, let's say Haskell and Dowd did a deal using members of the armed forces as test subjects for Wellglad on this Lyprophan drug. And they both benefited. The Army got funding and Wellglad got test subjects.

"What if something went wrong and they fudged the data on the people in the services, or misrepresented something, but they kept it quiet because of the money? Or something like that, and Hannah found out. Maybe she wanted to blow the whistle . . . and her husband told her not to, because Wellglad was backing his campaign? He wouldn't want to piss off Dowd. They're partners."

"OK. Keep going," Scarpetti said, somewhat intrigued.

"What if Captain Haskell argued with his wife about it and followed her to Wellglad, and there was a fight? He pushed her, she hit her head

... and Zimmerman saw it all. So Haskell goes to the fundraiser and tells Dowd—saying it was an accident, which it probably was. And ... he tells Dowd about Zimmerman being there, and Dowd recognized Westbrook's name?"

"Wait a minute. So now Dowd sends him to Bainbridge that night to set Zimmerman up? That's crazy," Scarpetti said, ignoring the pun this time.

"If we say Haskell went there with the intention of setting Zimmerman up ... if he'd seen him in the lot, then he knew who to target. Right?" Moran said as he went through his notes.

"But how would Haskell or Dowd know that Zimmerman was in Bainbridge?" Scarpetti asked.

"If Haskell confessed to Dowd at the fundraiser and brought up some crazy guy screaming Westbrook's name in the parking lot ... then Dowd knows who Westbrook is. And remember, Dowd saw the footage before us. He saw Zimmerman. He probably knew what those buttons on his hat were for. Dowd can put two and two together. So he knew Westbrook was there with a patient."

Scarpetti frowned at the implausibility of all this. "Seriously? Why would Dowd risk everything to cover up a murder?"

"Money. Kim Matsunaga mentioned something about Lyprophan being the holy grail of antidepressants. Said their stock was way up and the sales projections," and here he read from his notes, "were off the charts."

Greed and passion were always the obvious motives for murder to Moran.

And if it was about money, then he needed to answer one question: What did Hannah Haskell know that would make her husband and her boss collude in such a deadly way?

Moran flashed on the OxyContin debacle, and how much havoc that had wreaked on the people who had believed Purdue's lies that it wasn't addictive. Purdue had to pay in the hundreds of millions to settle, and countless people had died. Moran could imagine a scenario in which Dowd would desperately want to avoid something like that. But again, this was all conjecture, and there was no solid evidence to prove any of it.

"She must have known something. Remember the way she looked up at the camera? She was scared," Moran said, and grew very quiet. "We have to find that manila envelope and her assistant, Ezekial Weintraub.

Something happened to make Dowd go along with the cover-up. Something at Wellglad. Something having to do with that drug."

The two men sat for a moment; then Scarpetti shook his head. "Sorry, Boss, this is all too circumstantial and puts us way too far out on a limb. Haskell and Dowd are in cahoots to kill his wife; Haskell feigns suicidal thoughts to get himself into Bainbridge and brings her ring—which, by the way, they would have taken off of him once he was admitted to the hospital. And for what? So Zimmerman takes the fall?"

He folded his arms and shook his head again. "There's no physical evidence to put Haskell at the scene of the murder. Everyone says they had a good marriage. I mean, I hate to say it, but what you're proposing is fantastical at best and kinda crazy, if I'm honest."

Moran grimaced at that. Scarpetti was right. What he was proposing had too many variables. He had nothing but his gut to go on, and yet he knew that he was on to something, no matter how bizarre it sounded. But his reverie was broken by Detective Ross knocking on his office door.

"Come in," he yelled, and Ross practically sprang into the room.

"Bingo," Ross said excitedly.

"What do you got?" Scarpetti asked.

"The partial print? It matches Daniel Zimmerman's. DNA will be in later," Ross said proudly.

Scarpetti patted Ross on the back and said, "Good work."

Ross smiled and looked at Moran, thinking he would be happy about the news, but Moran just grunted. "What about Weintraub?"

Ross looked flustered but answered, "Oh yeah, I sent you an email. Uh, heard from Homeland, and Ezekial Weintraub booked a flight to Toronto on Wednesday afternoon. Apparently, his sister lives there. I spoke with her, and she said he never arrived."

"Go by his apartment. Call it a wellness check," Moran said urgently.

Ross nodded, giving Scarpetti a bewildered look, which annoyed Moran, who said firmly, "Go."

Once the young detective was gone, he turned to Moran.

"Sorry, Paul. I usually go along for the ride because you're usually right, but I think Zimmerman probably did it. Accidentally or not, pretty sure he's our guy."

"Then why would he take her ring?" Moran asked quietly.

"Why take the ring? I don't know—he's crazy," Scarpetti replied seriously.

Moran nodded, realizing that the print was probably the end of the investigation as far as the department would be concerned. And he had almost no doubt that the DNA would belong to Daniel Zimmerman as well. Even if it was Haskell's, it would be dismissed because he was her husband and he had just been around her.

"What do I charge Westbrook with?" Scarpetti asked. "His lawyer is with him now, and after Abbot hears about the print . . ."

Moran frowned. "Keep it to obstruction for now. Once we get the DNA, we can change it."

He knew that Westbrook was in deep now, and that Abbot would end the investigation if it meant going after Haskell with the lack of evidence they had.

"You OK?" Scarpetti asked.

"I'll have to be," Moran said, and Scarpetti left the room.

Moran sat for a moment or two, staring at the wall, contemplating what could have transpired if the scenario he had presented to his partner were true. He leaned back in his chair and thought about Haskell's time at Bainbridge. When would he have planted the ring? he wondered.

Haskell had an altercation with Daniel Zimmerman in the morning, followed by another altercation with Nadine/Sebastian in the garden after lunch. He was checked out by Westbrook Monday afternoon. Moran mulled this over and remembered something. Something the nurse had said about the altercation in the garden. He began looking through his notes until he found it.

Nurse Bennet had said he'd shadowed Haskell but had helped take Nadine inside after the altercation, and had left Haskell alone for no more than a couple of minutes. When Nurse Bennet came back for him in the garden, Haskell wasn't there. Bennet had found him in the TV room, and Haskell said he was lost, which Moran had written was strange as his room was right next door. This was all at about two or two thirty p.m., and he noted Bennet said he wasn't *lost for long*.

Had Haskell gone into Zimmerman's room and planted the ring then? Wouldn't someone have seen him? Moran cursed that there were no cameras in the halls at Bainbridge, as there were in the county facility.

Then, something else struck him as he continued to read his notes. There was an altercation in the TV room over the remote, and Bennet had left Haskell alone and gone to help. And there was one phrase that caught Moran's eye. It was when Bennet said the altercation over the lost remote got loud, and it was *all-hands-on-deck time*. So the halls may have been empty of nurses, and Haskell could quite easily have snuck off to Zimmerman's room. But what if Zimmerman was there? Wouldn't he have reacted?

Moran flashed on his talk with Westbrook about Zimmerman. He had asked Westbrook if the electroshock could have triggered him. And what was it Westbrook had said about Zimmerman after the electroshock? He looked at his notes. *It would make him sleep for long periods of time after it was administered.* Bennet had said the same thing.

If Haskell took the remote after the fight in the garden—he'd been found in the TV room, after all—if he'd taken it to use as a diversionary tactic later and made it to Zimmerman's room when no one was looking, he very well could have planted the ring if he was asleep.

Moran rubbed his forehead, exhausted. How to prove that any of this was what happened would be impossible without an eyewitness who saw the captain sneak into Zimmerman's room, though. And even if there was a witness, if it wasn't a nurse or a doctor, they'd be discredited by reason of insanity.

Moran thought about the semicatatonic men watching TV in the TV room and suddenly paled as he recalled his conversation with the heavyset fellow with three personalities, Sebastian Crown.

What was it he had said? Moran looked through his notes, but apparently, he hadn't taken any during his conversation with Sebastian. Hadn't thought there was any reason to, but now he wished he had. He remembered feeling like Sebastian was toying with him during their tête-à-tête. Moran remembered thinking he seemed very intelligent and a little cunning. Although, at the time, he wasn't sure why he had thought that. He was too bowled over by the fact that the man had three personalities.

What was it Sebastian had said, though? There was something about the captain. He closed his eyes and tried to put himself back in that TV room. He remembered Sebastian talking about his terrible day, and how he was put on restriction, about how the others were baboons, about Nadine. And then he remembered Sebastian had told him about what had happened with the remote, and how someone always hid it, and it caused an uproar. But there was something else. And that was when Moran let out a little gasp, and his eyes flew open.

Sebastian had made it clear to him that he had warned Captain Haskell about just such an event. *That he had told Haskell to beware of the remote being taken because anarchy would ensue, and that the remote had been found in the bathroom, which Sebastian said was odd and not what usually happened.*

Moran sat straight up in his chair. Was Sebastian trying to tell him *he knew what Haskell had done?* But how? thought Moran. How had he known?

And it was here that he caught himself. Was he, Paul Moran, telling himself that this insane man, Sebastian Crown, had corroborated his theory of Hannah Haskell's death? Moran shook his head. That was a bit much.

Maybe Scarpetti was right, and Haskell really was having a breakdown the night of his wife's death. Perhaps he *had* thought of killing himself. Wasn't that possible? Scarpetti thought it was. Everyone thought it was.

But Moran hadn't. Moran had thought something else entirely that night. And to this day, he couldn't shake it. And that was that they had yet to meet the real Captain Haskell.

The captain's image was stellar, and he would want to keep it that way. So why would he have gone to Bainbridge? If he hadn't killed his wife, Moran doubted he would put himself into a mental facility. He seemed too in control for that kind of thing. Moran would think he would prefer to stay at home and let a specialist come to him.

And if he had killed her?

Perhaps Captain Haskell had felt that without definitive proof that Daniel Zimmerman was in the parking lot that night, the crime would forever be open-ended. Or maybe he worried that people would view him differently without a killer being caught. So he went to Bainbridge, planted the ring, and *tied up all the loose ends.*

Moran sat there, silently looking at the gold ring still on his desk. If Haskell went to Bainbridge to plant the ring, how had he gotten it into the hospital? Scarpetti was right—the ring would have been confiscated when he was admitted.

But then Captain Haskell's tear-filled tale about hiding his wedding ring in his mouth from his captors in Afghanistan flooded Moran's mind. *Surely he could've done the same thing the night he was admitted to Bainbridge.* But if he had murdered his wife and gone to all the trouble to incriminate Zimmerman, why would Haskell tell Moran that story? Making sure Moran knew that he'd hidden his ring in his mouth before. Wasn't he just incriminating himself by doing so? It didn't make sense.

Moran sat there staring at the ring until something slowly began to dawn on him.

He'd had dealings with people like this before. And one person in particular came to mind: Neil Hollingsworth.

Neil Hollingsworth was a serial killer who Moran had gone after thirty years before, when he was a new detective. Neil had shown great disdain for just about everyone's intelligence, and it had proven to be his downfall.

Hollingsworth was a mortician in Baltimore, and a necrophiliac. He started off sleeping with his dead clients but soon graduated to attacking older women in the suburbs, raping them after he killed them. He'd gone through seven women before the FBI were brought in to help, and what an education that had been.

Moran learned a lot from the FBI profilers. The most valuable lesson was the knowledge that there was true evil in the world, and he should never doubt that. Serial killers were a different species altogether. Moran would even go so far as to say that they weren't human at all and were hell-bent on destroying human life.

Neil Hollingsworth loved to play games, especially with the police who were looking for him. Neil was so arrogant that he began sending letters to the police task force on which Moran served. In hindsight, they'd seen that he'd even shown up at a couple of press conferences, pretending to be a journalist.

It was when Neil began to make calls to the police to leave tips that he was caught. He used one of his dead client's phones, and the FBI was able to trace it back to his mortuary, where they eventually dug up several body parts. It was such a stupid error on Neil's part, thought Moran, but that was Neil's weakness: the desire for attention to his brilliance. Neil thought himself so far ahead of them that he would never get caught, and liked taunting them with his superiority.

Had Captain Haskell thought himself so far beyond reach that he regaled Moran with that story because *he wanted someone to know how clever he was? Was he bragging?*

Moran flashed back to the moment in Captain Haskell's house, when he quickly looked at Moran out of the corner of his eye after telling him the story of hiding his ring. The look had sent a chill down Moran's spine, and he'd had the feeling that he was being watched. Was it because Captain Oliver Haskell wanted to know if he, Detective Paul Moran, was smart enough to see what he'd done? As if Haskell already knew that he had won.

For a minute or two, Moran struggled to catch his breath, he was so filled with adrenaline. Once he calmed himself, a determination steeled his fragile spine, and he decided to do what he did best: focus on the facts.

He picked up the ring on the desk before him and looked at it. What could it tell him? It was a simple ring. Neither masculine nor feminine. Just a simple gold band.

And then he noticed the ring wasn't that big, but it wasn't that small, either, and he remembered Captain Haskell's hands. Elegant hands, Moran had thought at the time. The hands of a pianist . . . *with long, slender fingers*.

Moran stood suddenly, knocking over his crutches. *Christ*, he thought, *Christ.* He knew he had to hurry. Hopefully, it wouldn't be too late, as it had been with Zimmerman.

He looked at the ring one more time before he pocketed it, grabbed his crutches, and set off to find out if he was right.

Chapter 47

As the day progressed, Ella was sure the staff knew about her relationship with Clyde, and that she was involved in his dismissal. As she made her rounds, she noticed the glances, and that everyone was walking on eggshells. The nurses, who were usually so forthcoming, seemed to avoid her altogether. It was as if she was floating outside herself, feeling what they were thinking, and she walked around in a daze until she received a summons to Dr. Levital's office.

Dr. Levital was a very officious man and came right to the point.

"Dr. Kramer, I have been made aware of the circumstances surrounding Dr. Westbrook's detainment and your . . ." and here he paused. "Your relationship to the circumstances. The Board has decided that it would be in the best interests of the hospital if you take a leave of absence, effective at the end of work today."

Ella was stunned. "For how long?" she asked.

"That hasn't been decided."

"But my patients . . ." she began to protest.

"I'm sorry, Dr. Kramer, but this is nonnegotiable. And concerning your patients, we do not want you telling them of your departure. We would like to keep things calm. Well, as calm as they can be. There's been enough drama for one day." And he looked at her condescendingly, which only affirmed her worst fears. They all knew.

"The doctor who takes over their cases will decide when and how to tell them."

And he said it with such finality, Ella was left speechless. "That will be all," he finished, and she walked out in a state of shock.

What would she do now? she thought in a panic. She had nowhere to go. She was almost to her office when she saw Sebastian napping in his favorite chair in the TV room. She felt a pang in her heart. She might never see him again. Or Malakhi. And the thought of leaving Malakhi made her incredibly sad.

Malakhi, who was kind and wise and had served a king in ancient Persia. Malakhi deserved to be told, she thought. She had always felt close to him and couldn't bear the thought of him thinking that she'd abandoned him. She wouldn't do that. She headed over to Sebastian and sat down beside him.

"Sebastian," she said quietly, and his eyes sprang open.

"Dr. Kramer!" And he sat up, somewhat flustered for being caught napping. "How are you? Have you come to tell me you've watched the show?"

Ella was momentarily confused by his question but then quickly remembered that she had promised to watch the *Alien Ancestors* television program.

"Oh! No, I'm sorry, I haven't had time. No, I . . ." And she stopped, not sure what to say. "I just wanted to see how you were doing."

He looked at her strangely and said that he was doing just fine, and began to talk about his diet, and how he wished his mother would stop sending him the saltwater taffy she so loved but that he had decided he would just throw out when it came, which Ella concurred was a good idea.

Ella praised him for all the good work he had done—especially when it came to Nadine—and told him how proud of him she was, which made Sebastian turn a little red, he was so affected. There was then a lull in the conversation, which Sebastian quickly filled. "Shall I give you another hint to the answer from our challenge yesterday?"

Ella smiled and nodded.

"OK," said Sebastian. "So, you're trying to figure out why your aunt painted that rusty red glaze over her painting of the pyramid yesterday, and when you watch *Alien Ancestors*, you will no doubt figure it out immediately, but here's another hint." And he cleared his throat and began singing, "'Twinkle, twinkle, little star! How I wonder what you are!'"

Then he abruptly stopped and roared with laughter. Ella sat there completely dumbfounded. Sebastian, observing her confusion, said, "Really think about it—especially the second verse—and if you don't get it, I'll tell you the answer. But really try!"

Ella assured him that she would, then said in a voice just above a whisper, "Sebastian, can you do me a favor?"

He noticed how serious she became, so he looked around the room to make sure there were no prying ears and said, "Of course. What is it?"

"I need to speak with Malakhi. It's very important."

And the moment she said it, she could see that he had taken it poorly.

"Well," he said, miffed, "I don't exactly see how I can help you with that, seeing as how I am not him! I don't care what stupid Clark says about the hologram. I am not him, and he is not me! He just visits me!"

Ella put her hand on his arm and looked at him lovingly.

"Sebastian, you know how much I care about you. But I care about the others too. And I need you to trust me. I just need to speak with Malakhi. It's important."

He looked at her for a long beat, wrestling with his emotions before his defenses fell, and he said, "I don't know if I can do that."

She marveled at how much he looked like a child, so young and vulnerable. A child who'd been left to defend himself.

"Sure you can," she said. "I'll help you," and she squeezed his hand reassuringly.

He looked at her with trepidation and then nodded his head.

"OK," he said, standing. "But not here. Let's go for a walk."

She followed him outside to the garden, which Malakhi loved so dearly, and Sebastian informed her that he was going to take a turn around it by himself. He instructed her to sit down on the bench next to the tomato plants and wait. She watched as Sebastian walked, nervously talking to himself, and she wondered if he would be able to summon Malakhi. She had never asked him to do this before, and it was a testament to her that he was willing to try.

And as she watched him, she realized it was not the other people who worked here that she would miss, except for Gary. It was the patients. She loved her patients, and they had made her feel loved in return. She felt a lump forming in her throat and couldn't stop a tear from trickling down her face. Not wanting Sebastian to see her and become distracted, she stood and walked off toward the roses near the wall.

There were no roses now, as it was winter, and all that was left was a large tangle of brown, thorny vines. But in the spring and summer, the wall was lit up with pinks, oranges, and reds and was truly something to behold. Judging by the size of the vines, Ella reckoned that they had been here a very long time, and as she moved closer, she noticed something. Something she had never seen before. Something behind the birdbath against the wall, buried behind the thorny vines, as if the roses were standing guard over it.

She went around the birdbath and carefully peered through the vines and saw a plaque that looked quite old. She could just make out the word on it, even though it was faded and cracked. And that word was *Millie. Who was Millie?* she wondered, before remembering that Wayne Bainbridge, the founder of the hospital, had had a daughter, Mildred. He must have put it there for her years ago.

Her vision began to shimmer, but she didn't have a headache, so she put it down to her crying. The tears were blurring her vision. And soon more tears came. Tears at the thought of Wayne loving his girl so much that he set her name in stone among his roses. A tribute to her mere existence. He was honoring her just for *being*, and this touched Ella to the core—almost as if it had been done for her. As if she were his daughter, and the name on the plaque had read *Ella*.

She reached out to touch it as if in a dream, but the shimmering had become so strong that she couldn't see clearly and her finger was pricked by a large thorn, and she immediately recoiled her hand in pain.

Then a gentle voice behind her said, "Are you OK, Dr. Kramer?"

And she turned to see Sebastian standing there. Only there was no playful smirk on his face, just a sweet smile. His hands were folded in front of him, and his shoulders were slightly hunched.

"Malakhi," she whispered.

He looked at her hand, concerned, for he could see the blood on her finger. "Is your finger OK?" he asked.

She laughed, embarrassed. "Yes, I was just careless," she said, wiping her hand on her coat. "I noticed this plaque on the wall and went to move the vines to get a better look, but . . ."

"You got pricked," he said, finishing her sentence for her, "That is Millie's plaque," he said, watching her carefully. "Wayne Bainbridge, the founder of the hospital and a very good man, had a daughter named Mildred. He called her Millie."

How had he known that? she wondered. Of course he had probably read about the Bainbridges, just as she had. He was so smart, she thought, and once again she felt like crying.

"I asked Sebastian to get you," she said.

"I know. And I am glad you did," he answered.

Ella gestured to the bench, where they moved to sit.

"I wanted to speak with you—there's something that I have to tell you," she said, rubbing her temple. The shimmering continued after she'd wiped her eyes, and she prayed it didn't turn into a full-blown headache.

"I'm going to be finishing up at Bainbridge today, and I . . . I won't be back for a while. I'm not sure how long, but I'll try to come visit you if I can. Something has happened, and I have to take a break. I just wanted you to know because I . . ." and she became too emotional to continue.

Malakhi took her hand gently and said simply, "I know."

She looked at him, surprised. "You do?" she asked.

"Of course," he said. "It is your karma to go. And by karma, I do not mean it is happening to you because you deserve it," he continued. "Although that is one of the translations of the word. But another way of looking at your karma is that it's a remembrance of all you've done or will do. For some of us believe that all of life is a memory. Do you understand?"

Ella said nothing. She just stared at him as the shimmering became stronger.

"It is hard to grasp if one is fully invested in being here, but it is the true reality of who we are. And you, you must play your part, and so you must go now."

"My . . . part?" Hadn't her aunt said that she had a part to play? Ella felt goose bumps on her arms.

He smiled at her and looked into her eyes lovingly. "Yes. You do have a part to play. You do know who you are and what you need to do. You only need to *remember*. Listen to me now and I will try to remind you, OK?

"Sometimes, when we are children who have experienced deep pain, we reach out to ourselves across the Universe and transcend time so that we may guide ourselves through the journey. You did that once. And you will do it again," he said.

Ella was having trouble breathing. She had done it once?

"It is time for you to do it again. It is time for you to be who you truly are, to acknowledge your true nature," he continued.

"My nature?" she whispered, somewhat terrified.

"Yes. Your nature. You can *see*, Dr. Kramer. For you are able to travel the light. Light that illuminates all. To remember the past, the future, and the present. For they are all happening at once."

Ella suddenly heard Clark in her head. *What if the only difference between people like you and me is that I know those voices or feelings are me? Me at various points along . . . my life and not some mental illness,* he had said.

Malakhi continued. "We hold in us the energy of life, of love, of compassion. We're in human form, which needs these energies to survive.

"In order to sustain life, we must uphold the light. The *shadowverse*, the Vanitan is descending onto this planet now. Just as it has descended onto the other planets in this galaxy, and left nothingness in its wake. It is here, and Earth is no longer able to protect us from this energy, and we may be destroyed by it.

"You will not see an invading army. It is a vibration slowly taking hold. You will see it in those you like to call psychopaths and sociopaths. But whatever name you choose to give them, it is the Vanitan slowly infecting humans. The Vanitan, extinguishing our very souls. But we can stop it. We must."

Ella remembered her aunt in her dream. *They are here, and they are going to steal the light . . . And we cannot let that happen, Ella. You must go back, Ella. It is time to remember. It is time to run along the light.*

Ella felt as if she were going mad. It had been a dream. *It was just a dream*, she told herself.

"Malakhi—this has nothing to do with me," she almost cried.

"It has everything to do with you! Everything! Just as the Christ said, 'I am the light of the world: he that follows me shall not walk in darkness but shall have the light of life.' *You are here to uphold the light! You who can traverse the land of darkness and light! You who can change the darkness to light! In ancient times, we called beings like you Light Runners! And that is your nature, Dr. Kramer. That is who you are!*"

She couldn't breathe. It was as if she were descending into a nightmare that wasn't hers. Like the void that she had once fallen into so long ago. The void that she had been determined to escape with all her being, and here it was again. She felt the urge to run, but her legs wouldn't move and she thought she might faint.

Malakhi's arm encircled her shoulders and held her. And the look of love on his face was so strong, she couldn't help but feel safe.

"It is the last time we will see each other. I will miss you," he said. "Perhaps one day, in another life, we will be together again." And he smiled at that. "But you have much to do. And you will know what to do. You just have to *remember*."

Then he kissed her hand almost reverently, and she saw he had tears in his eyes as he got up and shuffled toward the building. And as he walked away, he turned back, and she thought she heard him say goodbye, but it wasn't her name he used.

Ella looked around, but there was no one else in the garden.

And then it came to her. She looked at the dead rose vines guarding the faded plaque on the wall and realized who he had bid farewell to as the sun began to slip behind the buildings and the night descended.

He'd said goodbye . . . to *Millie.*

Chapter 48

Detective Ross had found him in the morgue with the coroner, Dr. Ernst, and Moran could see that Ross looked a little squeamish as they stood over Hannah Haskell's body. Moran asked what he wanted, and Ross had quickly informed him that Captain Abbot wanted to see him immediately. Moran quietly worried that the DNA had come back and been found to be Daniel Zimmerman's, which would mean that he would have to plead his case with Abbot—something he had never had to do before or, if so, very rarely.

Moran dismissed Ross and turned to Ernst. "Finish what you were saying, Dr. Ernst, before we were interrupted."

"I'm saying that even though the wedding band is loose on her finger, it's still not so large that it couldn't be accounted for by the loss of bodily fluids. After all, she's been embalmed, Detective."

Moran frowned. "You're sure of this?"

"As sure as I can be," Ernst replied.

Ernst had been doing this for thirty years, and he did not say anything that he didn't know to be factually accurate. Moran felt a wave of disappointment come over him and knew there was nothing more to accomplish here, so he thanked Ernst and headed off to see Captain Abbot.

He took the elevator to Abbot's floor, and as the doors opened, he was greeted by Arthur Levine, Captain Haskell's friend, preparing to enter it. He gave Moran a curt nod, to which Moran responded in kind and realized that his meeting with Abbot was probably going to be about his visit to Haskell. He soon found himself tapping on Abbot's door, only to be greeted by a rather angry "Come in."

He entered, and noticed how miserable Captain Abbot looked, and knew that his theory of the murder, which was a hard sale at best, would now be completely dismissed. Abbot asked him to sit down and began, "Arthur Levine was just here and was very upset that you went to see Captain Haskell yesterday unannounced. So upset, in fact, that he is now demanding that you be taken off the case."

Moran sat quietly, which irritated Abbot even more, causing him to bark, "What the hell were you thinking?"

Moran maintained his composure and said simply, "As the lead detective on this case, it was well within my purview to seek out Captain Haskell and do a follow-up interview. I hadn't thought it untoward and was merely doing my job."

Abbot waved this off impatiently, having known Moran for years. "You were trying to figure out if he had anything to do with his wife's murder and you went fishing. Come on! We both know it."

Moran again said nothing, which Abbot found unbearable. "He's running for the US Senate and is a beloved war hero who just came off a psych watch after his wife was murdered. Levine has been hovering over this guy since you told him his wife was dead! He made it clear to the department that he wasn't to be approached without his lawyer present until next week. Come on, Paul! You know better than to do something like this! Even if he was involved in her death—which he wasn't—Levine's argument would be that he was so emotionally fragile that he wouldn't know what he'd said to you! You could be formally reprimanded for this! I had to talk him out of filing a complaint just now, so stop it!"

But Moran was caught by something Abbot said. "What do you mean, he wasn't?"

"What?" asked Abbot, confused.

"You said even if Haskell was involved, *which he wasn't*. What do you mean by that?"

Abbot sighed, picked up a report on his desk, and handed it to Moran. "The DNA analysis came back and it's Zimmerman's DNA on Hannah Haskell. Along with his print and some rabbit hair. He did it, Paul. Pretty sure it was accidental, but he did it."

Moran looked at the report for a few minutes and felt his stomach drop before answering, "I don't think so."

Abbot sighed angrily. "OK, let's hear it. How and why did Haskell kill his wife in a parking lot while also being at a fundraiser fifteen minutes away?"

Moran had no choice but to lay out his theory as best he could for his superior, who listened patiently before asking, "And your evidence?"

"Sadly, I have very little," Moran said. "There's a time discrepancy with respect to the captain's arrival at the fundraiser. There seems to be almost twenty minutes unaccounted for."

Abbot rolled his eyes and asked, "Seriously?"

Moran became defensive. "Why were so many of the Lyprophan test subjects from the Army? If market analysis is correct, that drug is their bestseller. It's making a killing. And why did Dowd say he didn't know Haskell well, yet he helped host the fundraiser for him that night? And why didn't Hannah Haskell go to that fundraiser thrown by her boss *for her husband*? Then there's her lab assistant, who suddenly disappeared. The same lab assistant who she called from Wellglad that night seems to have packed up and fled—why?"

"The drug addict?" Abbot asked derisively.

Moran squelched the urge to shout and held up the ring. "And her ring? It's too big for her finger. I just tried it on her and . . ."

But Abbot was having none of it. "Oh, come on! She has no bodily fluids left, right? What did Ernie say?"

He could tell by Moran's defeated look that Ernst had said the same thing.

"Paul, Oliver Haskell didn't do it. And trying to put him in some kind of conspiracy with Edward Dowd seems insane! Over a new drug that is FDA-approved? Come on!" Abbot took a breath and then spoke calmly. "Daniel Zimmerman was there—we have him on camera. We have his prints and DNA, for God's sake! And—as if that's not enough—there's the history with his sister, who he apparently shoved and hurt many years ago," he said, holding up Zimmerman's admission report from Bainbridge, and Moran realized that Scarpetti must have shared the case file with Abbot.

"Even the doctors at Bainbridge didn't think he was suicidal. They let him move freely after interviewing him. Haskell could have planted that ring!" Moran said desperately.

"Oh, you mean the doctor who was experimenting on his patient illegally that night? The doctor who is about to be charged with negligent homicide? That doctor?" Abbot blurted out. "Look, you're the best detective this department has and probably ever will have, and I let you do your thing because you are that good, but . . ." and he lowered his voice "you're wrong on this one, Paul. I don't know what's clouded your judgment, or why you have such strong feelings about Oliver Haskell, but—you're wrong. The evidence points to Daniel Zimmerman killing Dr. Haskell. And the evidence is strong."

Moran felt like a balloon that had suddenly had its air let out. He realized everything Abbot was saying was true, but he still didn't believe their scenario was the right one. He also knew what he was saying seemed ludicrous.

He sat for a moment, coming to terms with what was happening, and looked down at the ring still in his hand. And his eyes focused on the inscription *Hannah* ❤ *Oliver 6/14/2007*, and it stopped him. *Hannah loves Oliver?*

Wouldn't that be inscribed on a ring Hannah had given to Oliver? And therefore wouldn't hers say *Oliver* ❤ *Hannah?* He became so still, his head bent down, staring at the ring, that Abbot mistook his silence for embarrassment.

"I'm sorry, Paul. Now, do I think it's weird that Haskell ended up in the same psych ward as his wife's murderer? Yes. But that's as far as it goes. It was a coincidence. A bizarre coincidence."

And as he said that, Moran realized that there were an awful lot of coincidences or convenient situations when it came to Captain Haskell. The way he ended up at Bainbridge with Daniel Zimmerman and Westbrook—the only two people in the Wellglad parking lot at the time of his wife's murder. His speech being left at home, which made him go back and took him the same amount of time it would take to get from Wellglad to the fundraiser. The test subjects being in the Army—just like him. The TV remote's disappearance just as he was leaving and the subsequent discovery of the ring. Even the story of losing his ring in Hawaii just before his wife was killed seemed a convenient explanation.

And if the last was a lie? If the ring he now held in his hand was Captain Haskell's? What did that mean?

"Can you give me a couple of days? I'd like to subpoena Wellglad's records and see if the test subjects had something to do with Haskell. I also think it's important that we wait until we find Weintraub to see what he gives us before we close this," Moran said.

Abbot just stared at him as if he couldn't understand why Moran wouldn't believe the facts placed before him and said, "I'm sorry, Detective. This case is closed. I suggest you move on."

Not happy with this response, Moran said, "I'd like to remind you that many of my cases have started off with hunches as to the true nature of the crime. And that is exactly what I am doing with this one. I do not feel we have the right person in Daniel Zimmerman. I would appreciate a few days to prove myself right or wrong. After all my years of service, it would mean a great deal to me, Captain Abbot."

But Abbot was resolute and shook his head. "I'm sorry, Detective Moran. I can't do that for you. I cannot conduct a police investigation of Captain Haskell based on a hunch without facts. That will be all."

Moran felt the gall rise in his throat at being dismissed like this. How many cases had he solved for this department? Cases that probably would never have been solved or taken years to do by another department. And after all his years of exemplary service, after he had suffered a debilitating wound in the line of duty, after all of that, they weren't willing to give him the benefit of the doubt. It was a bitter pill, one not so easily swallowed by Detective Paul Moran.

As he made his way down the hall, the other detectives looked up as they heard the *whoosh-thump* of his crutches and nodded respectfully. But Moran barely noticed. He was too busy making plans to trace the purchase of a ring and visit a doctor. Others had counted him out before and had lived to regret it. Such was the case with the criminal who had tried to kill him, and so it would be with Oliver Haskell, he thought quietly as he entered the elevator and watched as the doors closed.

Chapter 49

Ella spent the hour after her visit with Malakhi going on rounds and silently saying goodbye to her patients almost as if she was in a dream. She'd taken several Advil to combat the headache, which was looming even though the shimmer had abated. She would go to the drugstore for her medication as soon as she left work. And then? Who knew what she would do.

As she was packing up her desk, she found the manila envelope that had come in the mail the day before. She read the label addressed to Captain Haskell c/o Dr. Kramer with the Bainbridge address underneath.

She could give it to Levital but then thought better of it and decided to keep her communication with the captain quiet. She would forward it to the captain via the US Mail. She found the piece of paper with his address and quickly scrawled it on the envelope as her phone alarm went off. When she looked at the screen, she saw a reminder for her appointment with Otis and Carla in half an hour.

Christ, she thought, she had completely forgotten. She couldn't cancel. Carla would be devastated, and so would Otis. She would just have to keep the appointment. Who knew? It may be the last time she saw them as well.

She put the rest of her personal things in her bag, telling herself that she would come back to work at some point to get anything she missed. It was just a leave of absence, she told herself, grabbing the manila envelope.

It had all gone so fast. If people only knew how fast their lives would slip away, perhaps they wouldn't waste their time with all the games they played and the lies they told, she thought, and then wondered why she'd thought it.

She turned off the lights, then closed the door, and for some reason the noise it made when it shut felt ominous to her. Like a door closing on a part of her life.

After her conversation with Malakhi in the garden, she had sat for a while and watched the sun go down, inch by inch, as she slowly came to a decision: She could no longer afford to listen to his tales of evil forces, because even though she loved him, Malakhi was what he was. She reminded herself that he was a part of Sebastian, so it would make sense that he had been watching the television show, *Alien Ancestors* too. Who knew what they were seeing? She needed to move on.

A part of her raged at herself for making that decision, warning her that she was making a mistake. But she came to the conclusion that it didn't matter. Not here. Not now. So she'd watched the sun slip away while she wrestled that part of herself to the ground and made it stop battling her for space in her consciousness. She had to watch out for herself in *this* reality, not in some made-up one that her patients shared, she told herself. As for what her aunt was saying? Her aunt was clearly losing her battle with Alzheimer's and Ella would be left alone. Truly alone.

No, things were bad enough for her in her *real life,* and she couldn't afford to fall into any other realities right now, no matter how compelling they might be.

She saw the lights of the Uber by the gate and quickened her pace, putting more distance between herself and Bainbridge. She got into the waiting car, put on her seat belt, stole a look out the window, and saw the garden now shrouded in darkness. She felt her eyes sting as the driver headed off toward the fading light of the sun.

Soon she found herself being dropped off in front of the Raymond house. She saw Lance shooting hoops in the driveway and marveled at how tall he'd gotten. He had been twelve the last time she'd seen him, and it struck her again how fast the time had gone by.

"Hey Lance!" she called, "how are you?"

"Long time no see!" he responded. "You still don't drive?"

She laughed at that and shook her head. "How about you? You have your permit yet?"

"I should," Lance said. "But my mom's been really busy. I'll probably get it this summer."

Ella nodded, understanding how hard it was to be in a family with a special needs child.

"Otis will be happy to see you," he called over his shoulder, and Ella felt a pang of guilt at that, wishing she had kept up her relationship with the family.

The front door was swung open by Carla, who grabbed Ella and gave her a big bear hug. "Oh my God! How are you?" she squealed, and pulled her into the house.

Before she had time to answer, Carla added, "You look so tired."

Ella told her that work had been very busy the past few months.

Carla clucked at her to take care of her health and ushered her into the living room, which looked like a bomb had gone off in it. Thirteen-year-old Bonnie lay on the couch, staring at her phone, and Carla snapped at her, "Have you done your homework yet? Say hi to Ella," all without taking a pause.

Bonnie rolled her eyes and replied angrily, "Yes! I already told you like a million times! Yes! Hi, Ella," and went back to her phone.

"Hey Bonnie," Ella replied as Carla dragged her toward the staircase.

"Indignant teenage daughter. Lucky me," she quipped and started up the stairs.

"Otis is going to be so happy to see you. I told him on the way home from school, and you should have seen his face light up!"

Ella was about to answer when Carla suddenly stopped her ascent and turned, lowering her voice. "His evaluation at school wasn't that great. His teacher says that Otis still ignores everyone and refuses to participate in any of the games. I'm so worried, Ella. We really don't want him back in public school. That would be just the worst thing for him. Maybe you could talk to him about it. Push him a little?"

"Of course. I'll see what I can do," Ella said.

That satisfied Carla, who headed down the hall with Ella trailing behind. She stopped at Otis's door, smiled at Ella, gave her a thumbs-up, and opened it.

"Otis, honey! Guess who's here?!" she chirped.

Ella walked into the room and saw the maps along the walls and the constellations on the ceiling, all surrounded by blue, and felt like she had traveled back in time. She looked down at the boy in the middle of the floor building LEGOs. Gone was the chubby five-year-old, to be replaced by this bigger version, who seemed totally focused on the task at hand. He didn't respond as he pensively twisted his LEGOs into some exotic shape until Carla said, "Otie," and he looked up at her.

He noticed Ella standing behind his mother, and his face broke into a smile. And suddenly there was no distance from those days three years before, when she spent every afternoon with Otis. It felt good to be back. She felt less alone now that she was in the midst of this family.

Ella felt the tears well up but forced them back and sat down on the floor beside him. Her attitude was unemotional and friendly because that was how she knew he liked it. She and Otis had never bullshit each other. Even when he was little, she spoke to him like an adult, and that seemed to work best.

"Hey buddy," she said. "How are you?"

Otis smiled and nodded that he was good.

"What are you building?" Ella asked.

"A ship," he replied, focusing once again on his LEGOs.

Carla watched from the doorway, thrilled to see him so happy. "OK, well, I'll be downstairs making dinner. You two have fun!" She closed the door behind her.

Ella watched for a few minutes as Otis built his ship, then asked if she could help. Otis frowned and shook his head. Ella smiled to herself, remembering what he was like.

"Where is the ship sailing to once you're done with it?" she asked.

"It's not that kind of ship," he answered.

"Oh? Well, what kind of ship is it?" she asked.

"It flies," he explained without skipping a beat.

"Ahhh. Well, where will the ship fly to once you are done building it?"

Otis didn't answer. His ship seemed to take all his concentration.

"Maybe Wisconsin? To see your Grandma Ann?" she asked, trying to draw him out.

"No," he said simply. "Not to see her."

Ella watched him work and realized that Otis was completely focused on the LEGOs. Had going to the school made him better at insulating himself from the world? If so, that wasn't good. She pushed him a little further.

"If it's not to see Grandma Ann, then where is it going?"

"Someplace new."

"Are you going on it?"

"I can't."

"Why not?" she asked, and that was when Otis lost his patience.

"Because I'm saving a place here!" he said, slightly exasperated.

Ella stared at him for a moment. Hadn't her aunt said something like that? "Saving a place here?" she asked with trepidation. But Otis ignored the question.

She decided to move on. It was just a coincidence, she thought, and willed herself to get a grip. "How's school? Have you made friends?"

"No. I don't want any," he said.

"Why not?" she asked.

"Cuz they don't tell the truth."

Once again Ella was reminded of Otis's strict moral code, which he had had when he was a very little boy.

"Maybe they don't know the truth. Maybe you could tell them," she offered.

"I don't want to," he retorted.

"Why not?" she asked.

"Because only some people understand." He stopped and looked directly at her for the first time. "You understand," he said, and went back to his ship.

Ella felt herself falter. Understood what? Did he mean understand him?

"I think I understand you, Otis. Even if I haven't been here in a while," she explained. "You know we're still friends even though we don't see each other a lot. That's how it works with friends."

To which Otis said simply, "Uh-huh," and kept building.

Ella rubbed her head, remembering how frustrating it could be to try to draw him out. It had been a horrible day, and now she wasn't sure coming here was such a good idea. Not in the shape she was in. She looked around the room, trying to find something else to focus his attention on, and spied his coloring pad. She pulled it toward her and began to go through it.

"I like your drawings," she said, flipping through the pages. "Wow, I love this picture of the planets," she said. She turned a few more pages until she landed one that made her heart stop.

Time seemed to slow down, and Ella felt as if ice had been poured into her veins. For there in Otis's drawing book was the familiar tableau: the pyramid, the water beneath it with the pyramid's shadow, the two stars in the sky that looked like circles in Otis's drawing, all covered with a child's scribbling in rusty red.

It took her a second or two to catch her breath; then she looked up at him and whispered with difficulty, "Otis, what is this?"

He shrugged.

She tried again. "Where is this, Otis?"

But now he couldn't make something work with his ship and ignored her. Ella felt the cold perspiration on her forehead. "Otis, what is this a picture of?"

Now it was Otis's turn to be frustrated, and he threw some LEGOs down in disgust.

She pushed the drawing toward him.

Otis, recalling his mother's mistake that morning, blurted out defensively, "Well, it's not a mountain, and those are *not* stars!"

Ella felt her hands shake as she pointed at the drawing. "Is this a pyramid, Otis? Is that what it is?"

He seemed relieved that she'd got it right and nodded happily.

"And is this water?" she asked, pointing at the water beneath the pyramid. Otis nodded again.

Before she could ask another question, he reached over and pointed to the two orbs. "And those are moons! The small one is Deimos and the bigger one is Phobos. They are not stars!"

Ella sat completely frozen. Her mouth was dry and her heart was racing. She suddenly flashed on Sebastian, singing, "'Twinkle, twinkle, little star! How I wonder what you are!'" *How I wonder what you are*?

Was Sebastian trying to tell her that the orbs in her aunt's painting weren't stars? That they were moons, just as Otis had said? She remembered Sebastian had thrown back his head and roared with laughter, as if he had a secret. He said it was a clue about the painting. And now a chill ran through her entire body. This couldn't be happening.

"Where . . . where is this, Otis?" she said, terrified.

Otis looked at her quizzically, as if he thought she knew the answer. But then got an idea and smiled mischievously. He stood up, turned off the lights, and the room was plunged into darkness, all save the ceiling.

Otis extended his finger, pointing at something up above them. Ella looked up and saw all the pretty, glow-in-the-dark stars and planets that Carla had so lovingly placed there. She followed his hand until she saw what he was pointing at. A little reddish orb, the fourth planet from the sun. And suddenly it dawned on her.

"Mars?" she whispered, to which Otis smiled and nodded victoriously.

Ella worked hard not to show her fear and, looking down at the drawing with its rusty red crayon all over it, flashed on Sebastian asking, "Why red?"

She looked up at Otis. "That's why the red color?"

Otis nodded. "Well, it was black, but after all the explosions, the iron changed."

"Explosions?" she asked.

Otis cocked his head slightly, as if he was wondering if she was OK. "From the nuclear bombs." He pronounced nuclear as *newkular*, giving away his age. "The iron neutralized a lot of the radiation, but it changed the planet's color. It turned red." Then Otis used his hand to indicate a swirling motion over his drawing. "It's covered in red dust now. The wind is always blowing the red dust."

"Oh," she murmured. Hadn't Malakhi said that life had lived on many planets but been destroyed?

Then another thought seeped into her troubled mind: *her dream.* The dream Farber so desperately wanted to get to the bottom of. Her dream of being in her aunt and uncle's house. In the dream, she looked out the window and saw two bright lights nestled into the night sky. But they always seemed too close and too big to be stars. Could they have been the two moons of Mars? And right before she woke up, she would hear the wind howl as the windows flew open, and the dust would blow into the room. The red, red dust.

She sat there as these thoughts kept flowing to her when she heard her voice ask, "Were we there, Otis? You and I?"

Otis nodded, then cocked his head, again appraising her. "Don't you remember?" And he waited for her answer.

"Yes, Otis," she lied. "I remember."

For some reason, he didn't see through her lie. He just smiled, satisfied. Then he turned on the lights and resumed working on his LEGO ship as Ella tried to make sense of what had just happened, knowing all the while that she couldn't.

Whatever madness this was, she couldn't wish it away anymore. Farber had been right all along, she thought. She needed to look at that dream. But what was happening with Otis and the rest of them was just . . . incomprehensible. And now she wasn't scared as much as she was numb. As if her mind had come to a wall and didn't quite know how to scale it.

She sat, watching Otis work on his ship for a few more moments before something rematerialized in her overwrought consciousness.

"Otis, what did you mean earlier when you said you were saving a place here?"

"I have to save a place for others while I look."

"Look for what?" she asked.

"I told you. A new place to live," he answered.

Ella remembered the things her aunt had said so desperately. She remembered Moira saying, "Ask Otis. He knows."

"Otis, why do you have to hold a place?" she asked.

This question annoyed him. "Because if I don't, they'll take it. And since they don't see me, I can hold a place here and look for another one at the same time."

Ella felt her throat tighten. "Otis . . . who doesn't see you?"

"The *Light Eaters*," he said. "They can't get my light."

"The Light Eaters?" she whispered, feeling like she might pass out.

"Yeah. You know, the humans with the bad energy."

Ella heard her heart now as it loudly banged in her chest. "Why can't they get your light, Otis?"

"Because I bury it where they can't see it. And sometimes I'm not here—I'm out looking."

Ella felt her mind exploding. Everything the little boy was saying matched with what Malakhi and her aunt had said. Moira had said that those looking for a new place to live were brave, and that the children who were *here but not here* were the bravest of all. Was Otis one of those brave children her aunt had been speaking of? The sweet little boy who hated lying more than just about anything else? *Yes*, she thought. Otis was a very brave boy. A boy who refused to join others who didn't *know* the truth.

Her left eye began to shimmer, and she rubbed her temple. What was happening? Was this some collective form of insanity taking place? But insanity didn't spread like the common cold, did it? And then something dawned on her.

They were all telling different parts of the same story. And here was the kicker: *They were all telling them to her*. Why was that? Why was it making sense to her? Was she losing her mind? Was she just imagining this?

They were all coming at her with a vengeance now. One thought on top of another, until she felt as if she was drowning. The shimmer in her eyes became stronger. *Christ*, she thought, she had to get out of there, but she was too weak to move. She wished she had her medication with her. Why hadn't she picked it up on the way here? She had to stay calm and think. There had to be an explanation. But none was forthcoming, so she sat there watching Otis play with his LEGOs.

And as she watched, another thought surfaced. A memory, really. Of a name her aunt had used during her breakdown Monday night.

"Otis?" she asked. "How do you go out to look for a new place?"

He was somewhat preoccupied with his LEGOs and took a minute to answer. And when he did, he did so casually, without looking up at her.

"It's easy. I just *drift*."

Chapter 50

I t wasn't until the Uber sped off that she finally found herself able to breathe again.

She did nothing for a minute, her mind still reeling; then she pulled out her phone and googled *Mars Pyramids.*

Sure enough, within seconds the image of the D and M Pyramid popped up, with its rusty red color, in the region of Cydonia. She also verified Mars had two moons, Deimos and Phobos, and the latter was the larger one. She couldn't believe it. It was all too surreal.

She put down her phone on the seat, took a deep breath, closed her eyes, and began going over everything that Malakhi, Moira, and Otis had told her.

Basically, life had existed on all the planets and been destroyed by some evil universe called the Vanitan, which was now attacking Earth. Its energy was in human form now. Otis had called them the Light Eaters. They sucked the light or soul out of people. Pyramids were used as some kind of interplanetary road map that allowed other life forms to find life on other planets. Then there were people like her aunt and Otis, who were called Drifters. These people held spaces here while their souls were out looking for a new place to go. Holding space for life while they drifted. Between planets? she wondered. Or realities?

And this was the part that scared her. Wasn't that what she had done at one time in her life? Hadn't she descended into a completely different reality after the incident with her uncle? She'd had to stay in the hospital for a while but Ella couldn't remember that time. And when she tried, she conjured up only bits and pieces that didn't make sense. Other girls in the hospital; taking pills that made her sleep; and her Aunt Moira coming to visit her. Her aunt was always referring to her lack of memories as *losing time*, and told her it was nothing to worry about. But it did worry Ella. Very much.

She thought of Clark and his theory of time being coiled like a DNA helix, and of her aunt and Malakhi telling her to go back. Go back where? Somewhere else along the coil of time? Why? To change the outcome? That was crazy. If she could do that, she would have. She'd change everything, starting with her parents' deaths.

She wanted to ask Otis more about these things, but he was working off the premise that she already knew most of what he did. What was it he had said? That she understood? Hadn't Malakhi said the same thing? That she understood, and all she had to do was remember.

She'd lied to Otis when she'd said that she remembered being on Mars and was shocked she'd gotten away with that one. But what if she had been there and just didn't remember it yet? Sort of like her time in the hospital all those years ago.

And what about her dream of the little girl? What if it wasn't a dream at all but a memory of a life she'd lived before?

Suddenly, the implausibility of all of it hit her, and she clutched her head and let out a little gasp, terrified that she was entertaining these kinds of thoughts. She tightened her grip, pulling her hair as if her hands could somehow pull it all out of her terrified mind. And that was when the driver looked at her suspiciously.

"You OK back there?" he said.

Ella dropped her hands, thinking what a lunatic she must look. She nodded and said, "Yes." But what she wanted to say was, no, she was losing her fucking mind! Again! And it seemed as if a few people around her who'd already lost theirs were the only ones who knew! And she laughed at that a little, which freaked out the driver even more, because he asked again, "Hey. Lady, you OK?"

"Yes. I'm fine," she said, trying to pull herself together.

She looked down at her hands, which were clutching each other, then eyed the manila envelope sticking out of her bag on the floor. She had thought she would mail it to Captain Haskell. That had seemed the best course of action. But now she realized that by the time it got there, the captain would know that it was Dan in the parking lot that night. With Clyde, her boss . . . her boyfriend.

And now he was going to get some mail with her name on it without any explanation. Mail sent to him by the girlfriend of the man who was responsible for his wife's death. Ella felt a whole new panic overtake her.

What the hell was she going to do? Ella picked it up and felt how stiff it was. Photographs? What if someone had seen Clyde and Dan in the parking lot that night and captured them on film? *Oh my God*, she thought, if that was the case, she should've gotten these photos to him right away. Or to the police. She hadn't even told the detectives about the strange call. What if they thought she hadn't told them on purpose?

Would they think that she had known about Clyde and Dan's visits to Wellglad? What if they thought she was part of Clyde's scheme to steal Gary's treatment? Or, even worse, if they thought she knew about Dan hurting Hannah Haskell that night? And this thought struck terror in her heart.

She pulled her phone out of her bag, then frantically looked for the card the detective had given her Monday night. She found it and stared at it. If she told him about the envelope now, he would think that she had been withholding it, that she was a party to what had happened with Clyde and Dan. *Christ.* She sat back, closing her eyes. She had to think, she told herself, she just had to think.

Captain Haskell would probably be told of the latest development involving Clyde either over the weekend or on Monday, and she wouldn't have the opportunity to speak with him again.

She hadn't trusted Oliver Haskell. Couldn't figure him out. All the while, she had been dating the man who was responsible for his wife's death. Christ, what an idiot she'd been! And she'd never called him back about a follow-up session. She'd forgotten all about him in the nightmare of events that had unfolded.

She needed to apologize to him, tell him why she couldn't work with him.

She also needed to explain how she had come into possession of the envelope. *Before* he found out about Clyde, and about Clyde and her. She reached into her purse and grabbed the piece of paper on which she'd jotted down his number and address.

Should she call him? What if he had already been told about Clyde? Would he even take her call? No, she would just swing by and drop it off personally, and if he wasn't there, she would leave it on his porch with a note. Then she would be done with it, and that was what she desperately wanted, to be done with the whole thing.

If he was there, she would explain that she didn't realize she had the envelope until today; she would tell him about the man who had called the hospital, and also let him know that she couldn't work with him. And that would be that. She didn't want any of this blowing back on her.

Ella told the driver she had a new destination and gave him the address. He seemed only too happy to oblige because it was much closer than her apartment, and he was probably tired of keeping a wary eye on her.

She just had to keep it together a little longer. She would drop this off and then head to the drugstore for her medication, and then go to bed. She would sort things out with Dr. Farber in the morning.

All would be well, she told herself. *All would be well.*

But somewhere deep inside her, there was a lingering fear, a terrifying belief that everything in her world, her *reality*, was about to come crashing down for good.

Chapter 51

Detective Moran didn't like being in this part of town much, and seeing as the sun was now setting, he felt the need to be extra aware as he opened the lobby door of the dilapidated building. He looked down at the doctor's address in his notes and realized that the office was on the second floor, but at the elevator, he was greeted by a sign that said it was out of order. It figured, he thought.

Moran tightened his grip on his metal crutches and began to slowly climb the stairs. His arms were tired from all the running around he had done, and for a second, he felt a pang in his heart and wished that he could run up the stairs like he used to. Oh, to be free like that again. He hadn't experienced that kind of freedom for a very long time. In fact, it was in this very neighborhood that he had been gunned down all those years ago.

But it was better not to think of that now, he mused as he sweated with exertion. He had done a little research on Dr. Kimmelman and was somewhat surprised by what a renegade he was as far as pediatricians went. Kimmelman had set up his practice in the poor area of Baltimore and subsisted primarily off Medicaid cases for the last twenty years, with some supplementation from his role as an expert witness in malpractice lawsuits involving children. He'd had a stellar education and early career and was now an older doctor who'd decided to do things a little differently by declaring war on Big Pharma.

When he made it to the landing at the top of the second floor, Moran took his handkerchief out of his pocket and wiped his face as a mother and son passed him. He must make quite a sight, he thought, refolding the kerchief and tucking it into his coat pocket before heading to the office of Dr. Morris J. Kimmelman.

It was a comfy office, incongruent with the world outside. The receptionist, a stern woman with a mannish haircut, looked at him quizzically. He obviously didn't fit the profile of their usual clientele.

"May I help you?" she asked.

"I certainly hope so." He winced. "I am Detective Moran, and I am here to see Dr. Kimmelman." He paused to catch his breath. "About a case I am investigating. I would also like it if you could direct me to a water fountain."

The receptionist smiled, grabbed a bottle of water from a small refrigerator behind her counter, and handed it to him.

"You don't have an appointment, do you?"

Moran shook his head, gulping down the water. He wiped his mouth and said, "I do not."

The truth was that Moran didn't like making appointments with people he wanted to question; he didn't want them to predetermine what they would say to him. He found that the element of surprise had the nice side effect of making people more accurate and worse at lying.

More than anything, Moran was just happy that Dr. Kimmelman kept late hours because, given the changed direction of the case, he was worried Clyde Westbrook was about to pay for another man's crime.

"Hang on a second," she said, disappearing down the hall.

Moran watched her go and looked around. Kimmelman was a hippie, judging by the furnishings in the waiting room. Lots of chairs covered with Indian blankets and posters pushing the benefits of veganism and yoga.

Moran wasn't fond of yoga and that sort of thing, but he liked these old buildings that were built at the turn of the last century. For some reason, he felt less odd in them. Modern buildings always made him feel out of place, as if he was from a different era. An era that everyone had moved on from, which made him a little sad.

The receptionist reappeared shortly and led him down the hall and into Dr. Kimmelman's office. Morris Kimmelman sat at a big old walnut desk covered with papers. He was a large fellow with white hair pulled back into a ponytail and sporting a handlebar mustache. Moran put him near seventy, but his eyes had the twinkle of a much younger man.

"Detective Moran?" he asked.

"Yes. Thank you for taking the time to meet with me," Moran replied, and sat himself down with some effort.

"Of course," said the doctor. "But I'm afraid that I won't be able to give you any information on any of my patients without a court order."

Good Lord, Moran thought, *that was fast*. "Of course not, Doctor. No, I have a question about something else. I'm not sure if you have read the papers recently, but there was a murder a few days ago that I have been investigating. Hannah Haskell?"

Kimmelman nodded but said nothing.

"I found a prescription paper from your practice in her purse and was able to ascertain that she had made an appointment with you for this past Friday?"

Kimmelman nodded again but still said nothing.

"So, did you meet with her on Friday as scheduled?"

"I did," said Dr. Kimmelman.

Moran waited for a beat and then asked, "May I know what you discussed in that meeting? I don't need names or specifics."

Kimmelman scrutinized Moran. "I read that it was a robbery gone wrong."

"We are still investigating. I'm just trying to be thorough and am retracing her steps," said Moran, who thought back to the young Dr. Kramer saying the same thing when she met him Monday night at the Bell Jar.

Kimmelman sighed and said, "Horrible business. She was a lovely woman."

"Indeed, she was," said Moran, nodding in agreement.

"Well, I don't know what I can tell you. She sought my opinion on some research she was doing. I believe it involved children."

Moran frowned. Perhaps Hannah Haskell had started a new project that he didn't know about, but he found it odd that she would consult Dr. Kimmelman about anything. The two seemed like polar opposites.

"Why do you think she sought you out?" Moran asked.

"You mean as opposed to someone in a big, flashy office sitting in front of a computer monitor?" And here he smiled. "I'm not a typical doctor when it comes to children, Detective Moran. I'm a strong proponent of breastfeeding until the age of five. I believe in homeschooling and think the dairy industry should be abolished. As a matter of fact, I encourage veganism, and if that's not possible, I push vegetarianism. I also push herbs instead of antibiotics."

Moran raised his eyebrow. "Really?"

"Absolutely," Kimmelman said vehemently.

This guy was definitely outside the bounds of mainstream medicine, thought Moran.

"I despise what Big Pharma is doing to our children. I simply despise it, and that is why I have consulted on numerous lawsuits against the over drugging of kids in this country, which has made me Enemy Number One of the American Medical Association, which has branded me a quack. But most of my kids are healthy and thriving."

Kimmelman went to a small refrigerator and took out a bottle of water for himself, then extended one to Moran.

Moran raised the bottle in his hand. "Your lovely receptionist already gave me one."

Kimmelman took a few chugs and then sat back down in his chair. "So, why did she come to me? Well, before I started my own practice, I worked at the University of Maryland Hospital in the pediatric neurological department. Saw a lot of kids with brain injuries. Did a lot of screening for brain abnormalities—MRIs, CTs, and such. But as time went on, we saw more and more healthy kids with *behavioral problems*," he said, using the air quote gesture derisively, "that were being medicated.

"Basically, we were there to back up the diagnosis so that people could medicate kids so they wouldn't have to deal with them. But unlike most of my colleagues, I wouldn't take part in the mass sedation of children currently taking place in this country."

Moran decided to sidestep this topic and cut to the chase. "So, what did Hannah Haskell want your opinion on?"

Kimmelman looked at him and took a second to think. "I guess I'm not breaking any rules, as no names were mentioned. She brought in a couple of MRI scans of two different brains. One subject was aged seven and the other was five. She wanted my opinion on the scans."

Moran frowned. What the hell? "And what was your opinion?"

"Basically, the different parts of the brain correlate to different functions. In both scans, I noticed problems in the cerebral cortex; chief among them, there seemed to be an extreme deficiency of gray matter—meaning there was very low neural activity in the left anterior insula, to be exact."

"And what does that mean?" Moran asked.

"Well, I can't say for sure. Can't definitively say there is a problem." He took another swig of water. "But there is."

Moran was getting tired now. "What do you mean?"

Kimmelman tossed his now empty water bottle into the recycling bin. "Well, it isn't definitive, but when there's is low neural activity in the left or right anterior insula, you are usually dealing with a person who has low to—in this case—very low empathy. Potentially a person with an antisocial disorder—a sociopath or psychopath."

"And what would cause this in these children?"

Kimmelman sighed. "Impossible to know. Antisocial disorders like this are in a group of character disorders that are virtually impossible to treat, especially when they are extreme. It's also very difficult to pinpoint the cause. It's either genetic or environmental and probably a perfect storm of both."

Moran took this in. "What'd Hannah Haskell say when you told her the kids could potentially have this kind of disorder?"

Kimmelman looked at Moran pointedly. "She asked me if this could have happened in utero if the mother was on a mood-altering medication."

Suddenly, the hair on the back of Moran's neck stood at full attention. What was it that Kim Matsunaga had told him about the people who had dropped out of the Lyprophan trials? That two had gotten pregnant.

"And what did you say?"

Kimmelman shrugged. "I said absolutely. People may call me crazy, but I have long thought that pregnant women on any drug, especially mood-altering ones, could be negatively affecting their babies in utero. To be honest, I think women taking them preconception are running that risk as well but pregnant women? Definitely. Yet the FDA has declared many of them safe for pregnant and lactating women. Of course, they give warnings that the use of these drugs could—*in some instances*—lead to birth defects or low birth weights, but who knows what other problems they could cause? Ultimately, the risks are downplayed, and women are encouraged to take them. It's a joke. Take your pill but abstain from wine and coffee!"

"And in this case?" asked Moran, leaning forward.

Kimmelman sighed. "Look, it's just my opinion, but I think when a pregnant woman takes something that affects her own central nervous system and brain—surely it has the potential to affect the chemistry of the baby's brain and may even affect the development of the baby's brain structure. Unfortunately, there's no way to prove it. The data just isn't there. And here in the United States where they suppress any study going against Big Pharma, I doubt we'll ever see data that does support this kind of thinking."

"Did you tell Hannah Haskell this? That the drug may have caused these anomalies in the children's brains?" Moran asked.

"Sure, I did. But I had the feeling she was already on that track. I also gave her an article to read by a friend of mine in Australia that I thought might help, and then she left."

Moran remembered the article he'd just read. The one on Kimmelman's prescription paper by by Yetz et al, about antipsychotic drugs used by pregnant women affecting their babies in utero.

Moran sat thinking. What was it Kim Matsunaga had said about Lyprophan? That it had taken seven years to get it through the FDA, and one of the scans Kimmelman saw was of a seven-year-old, the other a five-year-old. What if these were the two test subjects who had become pregnant? If Kimmelman was right, that meant Lyprophan had potentially caused brain abnormalities in 100 percent of the pregnant patients' offspring. Kimmelman said there was no direct link as to cause with these drugs, but what if Hannah thought differently? This was turning into a horse of a different color.

Moran then asked, "Did she say how the children had come to her attention?"

Kimmelman shook his head. "No names or data were given."

So, the only way to get those names would be through Wellglad, and that would be impossible. Moran wondered why the parents of the children who'd had the scans hadn't come forward and talked about what Hannah had feared. What if they had? Perhaps the children had behavioral problems and had gone to Hannah for help. She'd probably reassured them that Lyprophan was safe and dissuaded them from thinking that it had any adverse effects. After all, there was no established link between mood-altering drugs and these types of disorders. That would be the responsible thing to do, and Hannah Haskell was nothing if not responsible. But Moran couldn't see parents just walking away like that. No, there would be lawsuits going on right now if they thought a drug company had harmed their kids.

It was more likely that Hannah had found something in her research that pointed to the drug causing these problems. Hadn't Kimmelman just said she was on that track herself? She'd probably asked the parents to do the scans as a precautionary step. She would have couched it in terms of doing a follow-up, and since the children were okay at this point, she didn't pursue it. Surely, she wouldn't alarm the parents, because no link had been established between antidepressants and these problems before.

But Lyprophan wasn't like other antidepressants. No, it was a revolutionary new drug, as Kim Matsunaga had told him. It was in a class all its own.

Why wouldn't she have told Dr. Dowd of her suspicions? He certainly wouldn't have been happy if she had, given how well Lyprophan was performing. But then Moran thought better of this. Hannah Haskell was a quiet, serious person. She'd probably been doing her investigating alone until she could definitively prove that the drug could have debilitating effects. She hadn't told Kimmelman which drug she was speaking about or given any data on how Lyprophan worked when she showed him those scans, so she was being very careful. He flashed on Hannah in the parking lot, and how worried she looked. What was going through her mind? he wondered. Was she preparing to blow the whistle, so to speak? He thought of her staring into the camera, visibly scared, and remembered she no longer had the manila envelope with her.

"How big were the scans she showed you?" he asked.

Kimmelman held up his hands to show the dimensions, which seemed to be just about the size of a large manila envelope. Was that what Hannah Haskell had carried back into the lab that night? Where were those scans now? And where was her lab assistant, Ezekial Weintraub? *Christ*, what the hell was he up against?

Just then, the receptionist poked her head in the door and pointed to her watch. "Your wife called, Doctor. Wondering where you are.

"Thanks, Louanne," Kimmelman said, looking at Moran. "We finished?"

Moran nodded and stiffly pulled himself up with a "Thank you for your time, Dr. Kimmelman."

As he turned to leave, he saw a framed newspaper article on the wall by the door, which read CHARTER HIGH STUDENT SETTLES WITH GANDION BIOMED. He moved closer and read the first line of the article: "With the help of Dr. Morris Kimmelman, Sandoval was able to prove that the medication, Meridal played a significant factor in causing the young man's seizures. The two parties settled for an undisclosed amount."

An undisclosed amount? Well, that was nothing to shake a stick at, thought Moran. Maybe Kimmelman wasn't a quack after all. He turned back to the doctor.

"Dr. Kimmelman, how many lawsuits have you been involved in as an expert witness?"

Kimmelman smiled. "'Bout a hundred. And given the odds against me, my batting average is pretty damn good."

And that was why Hannah Haskell came to see Dr. Morris Kimmelman.

Moran struggled down the last few steps of the stairwell and exited the lobby feeling energized by this discovery. He slid into his car with some difficulty and heard the iPhone ringing in his glove box. He pulled it out and answered. It was Detective Ross on the other end.

"Detective Moran?" he asked.

"Yes, what is it?" Moran asked.

"We found Ezekial Weintraub."

Moran was thrilled. Ezekial Weintraub could be his missing link. If he could confirm the scans were of children associated with the Lyprophan trials, Moran might be able to get somewhere. It would mean that Hannah Haskell was a whistleblower, and her murder would have to be looked at from a very different angle.

"He's dead, sir. In his apartment. Looks like a drug overdose. There's paraphernalia by the body, so that's what I'm assuming, anyway."

Moran sat, stunned. Weintraub had gotten on a bus Wednesday with a bag, heading to the airport to see his sister. What had happened? Dear God, what was this? Could he have been murdered too?

"Did we ever find out which bus he was on Wednesday?" he said, his mind racing.

"No, sir. I checked with the drivers of the two buses that go to the airport from Weintraub's stop and they don't remember him."

Moran thought for a moment. The airport was on the same side of town as the Haskells' house. The bus would have gone right by it. Had Weintraub gotten off before the airport?

"If he was on his way to the airport, we need to see if he got off at any of the stops along the way. Especially whichever stop is closest to Captain Haskell's house."

There was a pause on the other end.

"I don't think I can, sir," Ross said timidly.

"Why not?" Moran asked angrily.

"Captain Abbot said the Haskell case was closed and wants us to treat Weintraub as a drug overdose, given his history. He said we should wrap it up."

"I see," Moran said, feeling the walls closing in on him. "Thank you, Detective." And he hung up.

That was it. They had taken his case and closed it. He didn't want to believe this was happening. But it made sense. The big shots had won, as they always did.

And who did Moran have to back him up? A few mental patients and a young doctor who had just finished her residency and was sleeping with her boss. Whatever Ezekial Weintraub knew was now going to be buried with him. Moran would never convince Abbot to subpoena any records from Wellglad. Levine would see to that. And even if he did, what would he find? Kimmelman had said that there was no data to even prove drugs like Lyprophan caused birth defects.

But Hannah Haskell had still been willing to try.

Chapter 52

Ella got out of the Uber in front of Captain Haskell's house and pulled her coat tightly around her. The temperature had dropped and clouds were looming, and she worried that it might begin to rain again.

She hurried up the walkway to the front door, but right before she stepped onto the porch, she caught her heel on something, twisting her ankle, and fell, hearing a crunching noise as she landed.

A searing pain shot through her ankle. Crap, that was all she needed, a sprained ankle. She sat for a second, then stood carefully, hoping that it wasn't too bad. But as she bent down to rub her ankle, she saw something.

Something that had made the crunching sound as she hit the ground. Glasses. Dark-rimmed glasses with a broken lens. Ella picked them up and noticed how thick the remaining lens was. You didn't normally see lenses that thick anymore. Coke-bottle thick. Someone must have very bad eyesight.

Just as she was about to move to the front door, it opened, and Captain Haskell came out. He looked at her clutching her ankle and said, "Dr. Kramer? Are you OK?" And he quickly came toward her to help.

"Yes, I'm fine," she responded, embarrassed. "Just caught my heel on something and sat on these." She held up the glasses. "They aren't yours, are they?"

The captain took them from her and shook his head. "Probably belong to one of the workmen I've had here the last few days," he said, and pocketed them. "What are you doing here?" he asked.

And the way in which he asked made her think that he hadn't heard about Clyde being detained, thank goodness.

"I was just on my way home from work and I had some mail for you that someone sent to the hospital. I just wanted to drop it off. I hope it's not too late," she said.

"Not at all," he answered kindly. "Please come in."

He led her into the house and took her coat, and Ella immediately began to feel odd. She had never visited a patient at home before. Except for Otis, but that was different. He showed her into the living room, and she noticed the smell of paint in the house.

"Is your ankle OK?" Captain Haskell asked. "I could get you some ice."

"No, I'm fine," she lied, her ankle throbbing. She just wanted to get this over with.

"Would you like a drink?" he asked, and then added quickly, "I could make some coffee or tea."

Ella smiled at his kindness. "Sure. Some tea would be nice."

He went off to the kitchen, and Ella sat on the couch, rubbing her ankle. She looked around and couldn't help but notice the articles from magazines and newspapers everywhere. She looked at a few on the coffee table in front of her and saw that all of them were open to an article about the captain. One was devoted to predicting if he would stay in the race for senator, which Ella found odd, given the events of the past week.

"Is chamomile OK?" he called.

"That would be great," she called back.

She sat, studying the pictures of Haskell and his wife in various articles when she saw the paper from Monday. The one with the front-page headline that read HANNAH HASKELL, WIFE OF SENATE HOPEFUL, CPT OLIVER HASKELL, MURDERED. She picked it up and scanned it again.

Dr. Haskell is known for her work leading the team that developed Lyprophan, a revolutionary new antidepressant that has only been on the market for a few months but has met with much success.

And there was the picture of Hannah with Edward Dowd, who, of course, was a friend of Clyde's, and the rest of her team, which was just three other people. A woman named Kim Matsunaga, an older gentleman who was a visiting professor named Burt Salvey, and a young man named Ezekial Weintraub.

It was on Weintraub that her eyes now rested and couldn't move, for one of the most interesting features of his face didn't happen to belong to his face at all but was an accessory resting upon it: his glasses. His dark-rimmed, Coke-bottle-thick-lens glasses. The kind you don't see anymore. Ella held her breath for a second. But then she heard Haskell coming back into the room and quietly put the paper back in its place.

He casually sat across from her. "It should be ready in a minute."

She heard herself thanking him as she shifted uncomfortably in her seat.

"You said you brought some mail for me?" the captain asked.

"Oh! Yes," she said, pulling out the envelope and handing it to him. "Now, I need to tell you about something," she started, and the captain looked at her expectantly.

"A man called the hospital Tuesday. Looking for you. He wouldn't give his name, but he said something about your wife, and that he was going to send something to me to give to you. I'm sorry, but I didn't see it in my mail until today and thought it might be important."

Haskell's eyes narrowed. "What did he say about my wife?" And his tone of voice was cold, as were his eyes, which seemed to pierce right through her.

"Nothing. He just said he was sending me something for you and hung up. Honestly, I thought he was a whack job or a paparazzo," she stuttered, unnerved by his sudden change in demeanor.

The captain stared at her for a second, almost as if he was trying to assess the veracity of what she'd said. Then, seemingly satisfied, he excused himself and walked over to his desk, his back toward her. Whatever was in the envelope must be important, she thought.

She heard him open it, but before he could take out the contents, his cell phone rang, and he answered it with an "Uh-huh." He must be familiar with the caller, she thought. He held up a finger, mouthing, *Gimme a minute* as the kettle began to whistle, and he headed into the kitchen to turn it off.

The whistling stopped, and she heard Captain Haskell talking on the phone, but she couldn't make out what he was saying as his voice got farther and farther away. He seemed to be heading down the hall to another part of the house, where she suddenly heard a door shut.

What was going on? Ella wondered as she sat staring at the envelope. Something wasn't right. She remembered the man calling the hospital that day, and how cryptic he was. Almost as if he was scared of getting caught. That was strange. And why had Captain Haskell gotten so intense with her when she mentioned the anonymous call? He'd treated her as if she was lying about something, or concealing something from him. That was strange too. And now her concerns about Captain Haskell began to resurface.

She hadn't been able to get the captain. There was an aloof quality that she hadn't trusted. The detective hadn't trusted him, either.

Then it occurred to her: Why had he wanted to see her privately for a session, anyway? He hadn't seemed to worry about leaving Bainbridge without speaking to her, and in all honesty, he didn't seem like the type who would want therapy. Quite the opposite, actually. Why the sudden change? What was going on?

Ella stared at the envelope and wondered if the answers might just be within her reach. *What was in that envelope?*

She decided to find out. She quickly stood and winced from the pain in her ankle but hobbled over to his desk and the manila envelope. She picked it up, looking over her shoulder before she quickly pulled out the films. They weren't the kind of pictures that she had thought they might be, but they were pictures of a sort. They were MRIs. And they appeared to be of children's brains.

She read the sticky note attached to one of them: "*Z—Hang on to these re: Lyprophan—Hannah.*" Lyprophan? That was the antidepressant that Hannah and her team were involved with. So this was probably something to do with Hannah's work. Z? Was that short for Ezekial? It must be.

She glanced at the brain scans. They seemed normal enough upon inspection, but then something struck her as odd, and she held them up to the light for a second. *And a chill ran through her.* There, in the left anterior insula on both scans—there was much less gray matter when compared to the rest of the cortex in both children. Much less was an understatement; it was as if both children had no gray matter in those areas at all, and therefore . . .

Farber's words rang in her ears: *Wouldn't it be remarkable if one day we just ran MRIs on people before doing therapy to determine if a person had these disorders? Certainly would save a lot of time.*

Ella stood there suddenly feeling quite cold. Hannah had given these to Ezekial, and Ezekial had wanted her, Ella, to give these to the captain. So, that meant that Ezekial was the one who had called her. And he was scared on the phone; she was sure of it. But of what? she wondered.

Then another thought occurred to her. If he was Hannah's colleague, why hadn't he given them to the captain himself? Surely he could have come here just as easily as she had. It didn't make sense. And then she flashed on the glasses she'd found on the walkway, with their broken Coke-bottle-thick lenses.

What had the captain said when she gave them to him? That they probably belonged to one of the workmen? But Ella didn't think so. Those glasses were too different. One never saw glasses like that anymore. But she had. Just a minute ago in the paper. Resting on Ezekial Weintraub's face. So that meant ... *Ezekial Weintraub had been here.*

Just then, she heard a door open. She quickly put everything back into the envelope and barely made it to the couch before he entered, saying, "I'm sorry. I had to take that."

He looked somewhat happy, she thought. Relieved. As if there was some kind of good news from whoever was on the phone.

"Oh!" he said before sitting down. "Your tea." And he went back into the kitchen to retrieve it.

Ella's mind raced. What had happened to Ezekial? Had he just dropped his glasses there by accident? And if he'd already been here, why had he wanted her to give the scans to the captain?

"Here you go," he said, placing the tea in front of her.

She watched as he moved to his desk and pulled the scans out of the envelope, giving them a quick once-over. He stopped at the note for only a second and then very unceremoniously put the scans back in the envelope and shoved it in a drawer.

"Everything OK?" she asked, referring to the envelope as she desperately tried to stop her hands from shaking.

He returned to the seat across from her.

"Whack job," he said, shrugging it off. "You get a lot of that when you're in the public eye."

And just like that, Ella was transported out of her body and into a state of utter terror. *Whack job*? Is that what he said? *Why would he say that?*

And suddenly there was a cacophony of voices assaulting her, starting with Nadine's: *Go suck the light outta somebody else!*

Otis: *The Light Eaters. They can't get my light.*

Aunt Moira: *They'll steal your soul!*

And now she heard Dan yelling *Van* while Malakhi's voice said, *That was not what he was saying, and you would do well to remember in whose company he said it!*

Ella felt a scream forming in her throat. A scream she knew she must contain. Her vision began to shimmer. She had to get out of there. Now.

"You know, I really don't want to take up any more of your time," she said very *normally,* trying to control her urge to run. "I just wanted to come by and tell you that I don't think I will be able to counsel you, Captain Haskell. If you call Bainbridge, they have a list of doctors who see patients outside the hospital, and I'm sure you'll find someone you like."

Haskell looked at her, confused. "Do you want to at least drink your tea?" he asked.

"It's been a long day, and I just wanted to get you your mail," she said, and went to stand, but winced in pain, clutching her ankle.

The captain took her arm supportively, and Ella jumped at his touch, which he seemed to clock. "You're hurt. Here, sit down. I'll get you some ice," he said, and went to the kitchen.

But once he was out of the room, Ella grabbed her bag and started toward the front door. She'd almost made it when she heard the captain behind her.

"Where are you going?" he asked.

Ella eyed the bathroom near the entry and ducked into it. The bathroom smelled of new cement and paint. "I just need to use the lavatory," she said quickly, and shut the door behind her.

She heard him call out, "I'm regrouting the tile in there, so if it smells bad, that's why."

She slumped to the floor, her ankle killing her.

If Ezekial had wanted Haskell to have those scans, if he thought they were important, why would the captain say he was a whack job? What did those scans mean? Did Lyprophan cause the anomalies in the brains she had seen on the scans? And if it did, had Hannah known about it? Had she tried to do something? And if she did . . . had something happened to her? What were Ezekial's glasses doing here? *What had Captain Haskell done?*

Her breathing was coming short and quick now, and she began to feel dizzy. Her field of vision grew smaller as the shimmer in her eyes expanded. Why had Dan attacked Captain Haskell? Why had he yelled *van* in Haskell's presence? Why had he yelled it in the parking lot? Had he seen Haskell there that day?

Suddenly, her phone rang, and she jumped before she answered quietly.

"Ella, it's Polly, honey. At Seaside," the voice on the other end of the line said.

"Polly," Ella started, willing herself to say something more.

But Polly interrupted her. "Honey, I hate to tell you this over the phone, but . . . Ella, your aunt passed. I went in to bring her dinner and she was gone. I'm so sorry, honey."

Ella sat there, stunned. Moira was gone? Moira, who had loved her like a mother? Moira, who forgave her for what she'd done to her uncle and stayed by her side? Moira, who had gone to bring Skeeter back to her.

"Ella, you OK?" Polly asked.

"Polly . . ." Ella heard herself whisper but couldn't continue.

"Oh, Ella, the coroner's here. I'd better go. I'm so sorry, hon. Come as soon as you can," she said, and hung up.

Ella couldn't breathe. The aura was taking over her field of vision, but strangely enough, her head didn't hurt at all. She closed her eyes, and all she saw were her aunt's hazel eyes looking at her lovingly. She sunk down until she was lying on the floor.

No, no, this cannot happen. She had no one now. No one . . .

She felt the cold floor as the room spun and the light became whiter. She felt as if she was no longer tethered to this planet.

There was no one here who loved her.

She fought to breathe, her ankle throbbing as she curled herself into the fetal position, staring at the side of the toilet base with the limited field of vision she had left.

There was no one here who loved her . . .

As she stared at the base of the toilet that the captain had just regrouted, she saw that he hadn't resealed it in one spot, and there was a gap between it and the floor. She struggled to control her breathing, but the grout smell was making her want to vomit as she stared at the little space under the toilet.

No one here who loved her . . .

Her eyes were shimmering, and the light was getting whiter as she struggled to maintain consciousness, blinking her eyes hard, trying to clear her vision.

And that was when she saw something shiny and gold in that little space under the toilet. No one would see it unless they were at this angle, lying on the floor, and she wiggled her little finger in the space and pulled something out. Something small and round and gold. She brought it close to her face within the small window of vision she had left, and saw the inscription inside the ring, which read:

Oliver ❤ Hannah 6/14/2007.

Of course . . . it was Hannah's ring. And before she knew what she was doing, she slipped it on. And it fit. Unlike the other one she'd found in Clyde's closet. So that one belonged to Captain Haskell. But how had it gotten into Dan's room, where Clyde had found it . . .

No one here who loved her . . .

Then she heard the captain loudly banging on the door. Of course, she thought. *Of course, it was him.*

No one here who loved her . . .

And suddenly, all in an instant, the red-haired girl was sitting beside her, and she reached out and took Ella's face in her hands and whispered lovingly, *Yes, there is.*

Ella stared at her, wondering if she had died, when the girl said, *We have to go. They're here.*

And before Ella drifted away, as the light became whiter, as Captain Haskell began to break down the door, Ella stared at the girl's face and was struck by how blue her eyes were . . . . . .

And how much they looked like her own. . . .

Chapter 53

etective Paul Moran had seen a lot in his long career, but this case had proven to be something else entirely.

After he had gotten the call about Ezekial Weintraub on Friday evening, he joined Ross and Scarpetti at Weintraub's apartment and examined the scene. There were no prints other than his, and just as Ross had said, there was drug paraphernalia: a syringe and a spoon beside his bed, where he had overdosed on crystal meth.

That was where things got a little odd. Moran asked Ross to bring him Weintraub's records when they'd returned to the precinct that night. He read it front and back, handed it to Scarpetti, and said, "Nothing about him shooting any kind of drug into his system. Smoking it was his preferred method. I checked his arms and feet, and they were pristine. As a matter of fact, the only puncture wound in his arm seems to be from the fatal one."

"Guy's an addict. Maybe all the pressure and Hannah Haskell's death pushed him to go further."

Maybe, thought Moran, but he'd noted another interesting anomaly upon searching the apartment: Weintraub's glasses were nowhere to be found. And yet they appeared in every photograph of him. Even his mug shots.

"Where the hell are his glasses?" Moran asked.

"People lose glasses all the time, Boss."

But Moran wasn't buying it.

Then there was the matter of the manila envelope. He had scoured Weintraub's apartment looking for it but had found nothing. If Hannah had left the scans for him at the lab, as Moran suspected, where were they?

The following day, Saturday, Dr. Ernst let them know that Ezekial Weintraub's meth had been laced with fentanyl, which was what had killed him. He put the time of death at some time on Wednesday. Ezekial's neighbor had seen him at the bus stop Wednesday morning at around eight a.m. He had booked a flight to Toronto that afternoon at noon to be with his sister. Why hadn't he made his flight?

And where were those scans? Hannah had gone into the lab with them but hadn't had them when she came out. She had gone to work for fifteen minutes on a Sunday afternoon to leave those scans. Why hadn't she waited until the following day, Monday? And why hadn't she joined the captain at the fundraiser thrown, in part, by her boss? Had something happened between her and the captain that afternoon that made her want to put the scans in a safe place?

Had she left them for Ned Dowd and not Weintraub? Moran decided that she hadn't, because if she had, there would be no need for Dowd to cooperate with Captain Haskell and be complicit in Hannah's murder. Because if Dowd had the scans, he would have the proof that Lyprophan hurt unborn children in his possession. He wouldn't necessarily need the captain.

The only thing that made sense was that she left the scans in the lab for Weintraub. She had called him right before she was killed. Perhaps to tell him where they were. Had she also told him what those scans meant? And if she had, why hadn't he gone to the police?

But Moran knew the answer to that: He was scared. Ezekial Weintraub was in trouble with the law before and didn't want to be again. So if he knew those scans could hurt Lyprophan, what would he do with them? Who would he give them to?

Once again, Moran's mind turned to the captain. Weintraub would have no way of knowing that Haskell was involved in Hannah's death. And if he had given them to the captain, then Haskell had a little insurance policy to keep Ned Dowd in place. Haskell may have committed murder, but Dowd was making a lot of money creating a potential generation of psychopaths.

The more Moran thought about it, the more likely it seemed to him that Ezekial Weintraub had gotten off the bus before the airport and gone to the Haskell's. Why would he leave his apartment at eight a.m. if his flight was at noon? Moran could see leaving two hours before but four?

Moran went to the bus stop that was closest to the Haskell house on the route he would've taken and saw that there was only a gas station nearby. Moran asked to see their cameras, but unfortunately, they were only inside the station. He showed the attendant Weintraub's picture and asked if he remembered seeing him get off the bus on Wednesday morning. The attendant said that he'd worked that day, though he didn't remember him, but he would ask the mechanic who'd been there as well. Moran left the attendant his card and texted Ezekial's picture to him and asked that the mechanic give him a call if he recognized him.

Moran waited the rest of the day only to receive a call sometime after his dinner break from the mechanic, who hadn't seen Ezekial Weintraub either.

On Sunday, Moran went to Captain Abbot's house and pleaded with him for more time. He told him about his meeting with Dr. Kimmelman, and how he thought Hannah Haskell was a whistleblower. He explained that from everything he'd seen regarding Weintraub's death, he was sure it was part of a cover-up.

Moran begged Abbot for warrants and subpoenas. He wanted the names of the Lyprophan test subjects who had become pregnant; he wanted access to Haskell's financial records. He wanted to see if there was an agreement between Wellglad and the Army brokered by Haskell, and he wanted all communications between Captain Haskell and Dr. Dowd, between Hannah Haskell and Dr. Dowd, and between Hannah Haskell and Ezekial Weintraub.

Captain Abbot refused all Moran's requests across the board. "I cannot understand how, even after the DNA evidence we have, you want to pursue this vast conspiracy theory, Paul. This isn't like you," Abbot admonished.

"No, it isn't. And that should tell you something. May I remind you, the case against Daniel Zimmerman is circumstantial as well. I know I'm right about this, Jim. My gut is right."

"I'm sorry, Paul. This case is closed. You did a good job. We have the right man. Go home," Abbot said, and showed him out.

Paul Moran drove home, where he sat in his backyard, thinking of what was to come. People would surely vote Haskell into office now that they knew he hadn't been involved in his wife's death. Maybe a few would scratch their heads that he had ended up in the same sanatorium as the killer, but that would soon be forgotten. That was how the public was. And Captain Haskell was easily the most dashing, the most charming candidate Maryland had seen in a long time. He was a war hero, after all.

And then his thoughts turned to Hannah Haskell. Hannah, who'd been barking up a tree that would probably never bear fruit. But she had done it, anyway. And the enormity of the challenge she'd faced and what she had tried to do suddenly hit Moran. What a remarkable woman, he thought. Too remarkable for this world.

Chapter 54

Ella woke from a deep sleep and looked at the window, with its heavy screen and bars. The room was white, and there was an IV hooked up to her and a monitor behind her. Where the hell was she? she wondered groggily. She looked down at the hospital gown she wore and tried to remember what had happened.

Her ankle was now heavily bandaged, and she remembered twisting it, but she was not quite sure how. A doctor entered her room. He was a tall man with a long face, and Ella seemed to be aware that she knew him, but she couldn't place him. Her mind felt so groggy, and she looked at the IV again and realized she'd been drugged.

"Hello, Ella. I'm Dr. Saltz," said the man kindly.

"Where am I?" responded Ella.

"Bainbridge Psychiatric Hospital," he replied. "The infirmary."

She blinked hard. What was going on? "I work here," she said.

"Yes. We've met a couple of times. The paramedics brought you here after the ER."

Ella looked at him, confused. "The ER? I was at the ER?"

He nodded his head.

"Why?" she asked.

But he avoided this question. "You don't remember the ER?"

She shook her head again.

"What is your last memory, Ella?"

She thought for a minute. "I was at Captain Haskell's house, and I hurt my ankle. I think I fainted."

"Ella, are you under the care of a therapist or psychiatrist at this time?" Dr. Saltz asked.

Ella found the question incredibly intrusive but nodded.

"May I ask that person's name?" he continued.

"Dr. Eleanor Farber," she replied, becoming worried.

Saltz wrote down the name and then asked, "And are you on any medication?"

"Just for migraines. Eletriptan," she said.

"Who prescribed it?" he asked.

Ella looked at him oddly. What business was that of his? "My internist. I've used it for years."

He wrote that down and then pulled up a chair next to her bed, patting her hand. "You had an episode, Ella. You were hysterical in the emergency room and very combative, so they called for a psychiatric evaluation. The attending psychiatrist saw your ID and let us know, and Dr. Lester arranged to have you brought here. We've given you some medicine to keep you calm. You've been sleeping on and off for the last couple of days."

"An *episode*? What do you mean, an *episode*?" she asked quietly, afraid to hear the answer.

Saltz patted her hand again before saying, "It seems as if you had some sort of psychotic break. Dr. Lester explained that you have been under an inordinate amount of stress, and that your aunt just passed. These things can trigger a break with reality, as you know. But you are here now and should be feeling better soon."

Ella felt a chill in the room. She'd lost time again. *Oh Christ*, she thought, *please don't let it happen again.* "I think I may have hit my head. Maybe that made me . . . react strangely," she said, struggling to focus.

"Yes. We spoke with Captain Haskell, who called the paramedics. He said you were acting very strangely. That you came over uninvited, demanding to see him. He said that he found you in his bathroom in a catatonic state, and when he tried to help you, you became combative and violent."

Ella gasped. "That's not true."

And now bits and pieces of what happened with Captain Haskell were starting to enter her memory: Ezekial's glasses, the MRIs, and the way he had said it was a whack job who had sent them. And Moira, her beloved Moira . . .

"Captain Haskell . . . you can't believe him," she stuttered.

"Why is that?" Saltz asked pointedly.

But she didn't answer; she didn't want to look paranoid. And she realized again how hard it was for her patients to be thought of as crazy, to be doubted and dismissed. Just the way Saltz was looking at her now, as if she was some child who was telling lies. It infuriated her, but she couldn't let him see that.

"I'd like to go home, Dr. Saltz. I'm feeling better now, and I need to plan my aunt's funeral and go back to work," she said evenly.

"Dr. Levital explained to me that you are on leave. He also explained the situation with Dr. Westbrook and the Haskell murder. Terrible thing to be caught up in," he said somewhat smugly, patting her hand again.

Ella struggled to keep her fear in check. "I think I need to go home now," she said and moved to get out of bed, but his voice stopped her.

"Unfortunately, you are on a 5150, an involuntary hold, Dr. Kramer, so that we may ascertain your state of mind. Captain Haskell has filed a complaint against you and sought a restraining order. I implore you to stay calm, and with any luck, you will be out of here in a few days. Please, don't put yourself up for any more scrutiny, and don't put the hospital through any more scandal than you already have." And now there was a certain acidity to his tone that wreaked of contempt.

This enraged Ella, who'd had enough and snapped, "Who the hell are you to talk to me like that? You have no idea what's going on! I'm leaving!"

She started to pull the IV out of her arm, but Dr. Saltz grabbed her hand and hit the buzzer by her bed. Ella looked at his hand, restraining hers. What was he doing?

Suddenly, a nurse was there with a syringe, and Ella realized they were going to knock her out again.

"*No!* Wait! Please! I need to speak with the police! You can't do this! You don't know what's going on! Captain Haskell is . . ." But she felt her voice getting heavier and heavier. "I . . . I . . . found her ri . . ."

But it was too late. The Haldol had hit her system and taken control, rendering her into an almost comatose state. She lay there listening as Dr. Saltz instructed the nurse to increase her Haldol frequency, and, if there was any problem, to use restraints. And then he left, and Ella felt her thoughts quietly slip away until there was nothing but light.

Chapter 55

She dreamed she was walking down a hall at Bainbridge. She heard voices, and looked up to see some girls walking toward her. Teenage girls. They were all in blue hospital jumpsuits. She looked down and saw she was wearing the same thing. As they got closer, they snickered and called out to her as they passed.

"Hey, Carrot Head!" they taunted.

One began hopping like a rabbit, saying, "I'm hungweeee," until the others laughed and pulled at her hair.

Suddenly, a nurse appeared and told the girls to move along, then turned to Ella and said gruffly, "What are you doing, Ella? Get back to your room. Lights out."

Ella did as she was told and headed down the hall, unsure of where she was going. Why had the nurse spoken to her like that? As if she knew her? She moved quickly, and as she passed a door with a glass pane, she caught her reflection in it. But it wasn't her reflection at all, though, was it?

Ella stared at the face looking back at her. The girl's hair was red, and she wore the same blue jumpsuit as the others, but there was an innocence to her. Especially in her eyes. Her blue, blue eyes . . .

But then she realized that the reflection in the window was her. Her at fifteen. But how could that be? She felt a chill run through her and moved away from the door, shocked. She couldn't move; she couldn't speak. She wanted to wake up. She had to get out of here . . . and that was when she heard his voice.

"Ella . . ."

She struggled to open her eyes, and there he was, sitting on the edge of her bed. Gary Lester, her friend. She was so happy to see him that she began to cry. Gary ran his hand across her forehead gently.

"Hey there," he said softly and smiled. "It's OK, Ella. It's going to be OK."

"Gary, I have to go. I don't belong here," she whispered.

Gary looked at her sadly. "I think it's best if you just stay here for a bit. Just until you're feeling strong again."

Ella pulled herself up into a sitting position. She had to make him understand that Captain Haskell was not who he appeared to be. Gary knew she wasn't crazy.

"Gary, I'm fine. It's Captain Haskell, he's . . ."

Gary looked down, pained at the mention of Haskell's name. Ella remembered what Dr. Saltz had said. That Captain Haskell had taken out a restraining order and said terrible things about her.

"What? What did he say?" she asked.

Gary looked at his hands and shook his head. "I think right now you just need to . . ."

"What did he say? I need to know."

Gary relented. "He said you came to his house in a rage. That you began yelling at him and blaming him for what had happened to Westbrook. That you just . . . lost it."

Ella sat there, stunned. Blamed him for what had happened to Clyde? How did that make any sense? Haskell hadn't even known about Clyde's connection to the case when she went there, or at least she hadn't thought he did. Then she remembered his phone call, and the way he had seemed relieved when he ended it and rejoined her in the living room. Someone had told him. Told him that Clyde was probably going to take the fall for his wife's death.

She looked at Gary and took a deep breath. She had to get him to listen to her.

"That's not true. I went there to give him some mail that had been sent to him at the hospital, and to explain why I couldn't take him on as a client."

Gary looked at her dubiously.

"It's true! He called me and said he wanted to do a follow-up session, and I . . ."

"You can't do that. You know that's against hospital policy. Just stop, Ella. You're digging yourself into a deeper hole with everything you say, and the hospital's up in arms as it is. Haskell is threatening a lawsuit. This is serious," Gary said.

Ella was stunned. So Captain Haskell had gone on the offensive to protect himself, had he? Well, she had no intention of staying quiet. She wasn't letting Clyde take the fall for Hannah Haskell's murder.

"He killed her, Gary. He killed his wife," she said as her head began to throb. She waited for him to reply, but he shook his head sadly.

"What?" she asked, scared. "What's wrong?"

"Ella, they found Dan's DNA and prints on her. He did it. They think it was an accident, but Dan did it. And Westbrook is in real trouble," he said slowly.

Ella felt as if she'd been hit in the stomach, then realized, "Dan must have tried to help her! He must have seen him! Remember, he was yelling *van* in the parking lot? Well, he was yelling it at Haskell! He's been infected by the Vanitan! Don't you see?"

As soon as she said it, she realized her mistake. The Haldol was making her mix them up. And then it dawned on her—what she'd just thought—*It was the Haldol making her mix them up.* And what was *them? Her realities.*

Gary looked at her oddly. "What is the Vanitan?"

She rubbed her forehead. She had to keep things straight. She mustn't seem crazy or she would be stuck in a place like this for the rest of her life.

"Nothing," she said quietly, and she noticed a pained look cross Gary's face.

"Gary, you know I'm not crazy. You know that," she whispered urgently.

"It's not up to me, Ella," he murmured quietly.

She wondered what he was talking about. And why he looked so guilty.

"What do you mean?" she asked, fear gripping her.

"Look, Ella, you've just been through a bad string of stressors that have caused you to react poorly, and given your history, I think it's best if you just let us help you until all of this blows over."

Ella's breath caught. "My *history?*" she asked, cocking her head slightly. "What do you mean, my *history?*"

But Gary seemed to want to flee and was about to stand when she grabbed his hand. "Gary? Please. We've been friends for a long time. Tell me."

After a beat, he began. "When I found out you were in the ER, I went there, and it was bad, Ella. You were ... violent. We got you here, and you've been better, but it's been four days, and we needed to know what we were dealing with, so ..."

"So?"

"Because the episode kept going for such a long time, Levital looked at your medical and mental health history. There was something. He petitioned the courts and was able to access . . . your records."

He stopped there, staring at her sadly.

"They know about what happened when you were young, Ella. About *the incident.* And the aftermath. They have your mental health records. You just have to be calm. Please. For your own good."

Ella felt herself floating above her body. Sort of the way people described doing during a near-death experience. That was sort of how she felt right now. Near death.

Dr. Levital knew. That meant he would be devising a strategy where Bainbridge wasn't liable for anything she had done because they hadn't been aware of her mental health problems when they hired her. So of course their hands were clean.

"Those records were sealed," she said quietly.

"Ella, the head of the hospital is up on manslaughter charges, for God's sake. Bainbridge is terrified of a lawsuit, and then you have this breakdown. They're scared. They brought you here and are trying to help you. They genuinely care. A lot of people at Bainbridge care about you."

"I'll bet," she scoffed. "They just want me quiet."

"Well, I care about you," he said, a quiver in his voice, and Ella knew he meant it. But right now she was angry. Angry and embarrassed.

"So, what did it say? *Ella has dissociative disorder. Intermittent episodic psychosis?*" She shook her head, turning away from him, ashamed. Couldn't stand the pity in his eyes. "So, now you know all my dirty little secrets. That my uncle abused me for years, until one day I worked up the courage to kill him. Well, good for you. That must feel good!" And she felt the hot tears stream down her face.

He took her hand in his. "No, Ella, it was an accident. You were ten years old, and we know what happens when kids have access to firearms. There was no mention of abuse. It was an accident. And no one blames you. Least of all me." He gently squeezed her hand, trying to comfort her, but she just looked at him, lost.

What was he saying? Who was he talking about? "No, I killed my uncle when I was fifteen, Gary. I shot him. I unloaded a gun into his chest! It was self-defense, but I ended up in a place . . ." She looked around as if for the first time and said haltingly, ". . . like this."

Gary shook his head slowly. "No. I read the report, Ella. You were ten, and you were playing hide and seek; you hid in the closet, where you found his gun; you picked it up and . . . it accidentally went off."

And now she felt her mind starting to spin. What he was saying was what she'd been told. That it was an accident. *But she didn't remember it that way now. No, she didn't remember it that way at all.* What the hell was happening to her?

"I don't understand," she murmured, confused.

She began to have trouble breathing. What the hell was going on? She rubbed her forehead and closed her eyes, trying to calm herself. Her mind was playing tricks on her. She knew the truth. She knew she was remembering it correctly. Dear God . . . what was happening? She had to get out of here. She moved to get up, and Gary held her in place.

"Ella, we are going to help you. OK? We're going to make sure that you're OK. You just need to rest."

Suddenly, a nurse was by her, administering more Haldol.

"Double it," Gary said quietly, and the nurse nodded.

"No!" Ella pleaded. "No more drugs! I need to think! Please!"

And then she remembered something. "Call Dr. Farber! She knows my history—please, I saw her almost every day! Please, Gary . . ."

Gary just looked at her sadly, and she felt the lilting fog of the Haldol take over.

"Dr. Saltz—did he find her?" she asked as her eyes began to flutter.

Gary shook his head no.

And as she drifted away, she could have sworn she heard him say, "There is no Dr. Farber, Ella. Not in Baltimore."

Chapter 56

On Monday it was released to the press that the police had solved the case. The morning paper featured a black-and-white picture of Dr. Clyde Westbrook that horrified Moran.

The speed with which they were moving was something he'd rarely seen and let Moran know that the decisions were coming from much further up the food chain. Probably corporate heads and politicians who didn't want Haskell, their golden boy—or goose, as Moran was sure he would prove to be—hurt in any way. He had witnessed corruption before in his long career as a police officer, but never in a murder case, and never to this degree.

It was also on Monday that he'd found out that Dr. Kramer had had some sort of breakdown at Captain Haskell's house on Friday night. Haskell had called the police, and the paramedics had taken her away in restraints.

He didn't believe what Haskell's lawyer, Levine, had told the department: that she had come over and belligerently blamed the captain for Clyde Westbrook's imprisonment and then locked herself in the bathroom, refusing to leave and even becoming violent. Again, there were just too many convenient coincidences around Captain Haskell. Too many pieces on the board being removed.

He had called Bainbridge and been told she couldn't have visitors. When he called on Tuesday, they fobbed him off again, so he took matters into his own hands and went there on Wednesday.

Dr. Gary Lester, a colleague of Ella's, greeted him, and they sat outside her room and discussed Ella's case. Lester informed him that she was on an involuntary psychiatric hold, and when Moran pushed to interview her, Dr. Lester became extremely nervous, and lowered his voice as he tried to explain what was going on with her.

"Ella isn't well, Detective. She is extremely agitated and combative. We've had to medicate her pretty heavily." He looked around again. "She's become very enmeshed with her patients, which is a danger when one is in practice," he said. "She's taken on their problems and beliefs as if they were her own." And here he lowered his voice ever so slightly. "She's even gone so far as quoting Dan Zimmerman in her sleep. She's been thrashing around saying *van* inexplicably, which was something Dan did. I think she feels a lot of guilt about what happened with him and Dr. Westbrook."

Moran again pushed to question her, and that was when Dr. Lester did something that completely obliterated any ethical boundary he was supposed to have. He spoke urgently, almost as if he was pleading with Moran. His face showed nothing but fear.

"We recently found out that Ella had a history of mental illness, and that she was in the juvenile justice system as a young girl. She'd had some sort of breakdown. It will probably be Bainbridge's position that she was dealing with ongoing psychiatric issues during her tenure here that they were unaware of. They're going to use that to avoid liability, and it'll all become public if Haskell sues the hospital. That will ruin Ella, Detective."

Moran looked at him, horrified. "How did they get ahold of this information?" he asked.

Dr. Lester shrugged. "I don't know. But I'm sharing this with you because I'm very scared for Ella. Please don't push her about this whole Haskell thing. She's going to face enough trouble as it is, and she's too mentally fragile right now. She needs time to rest and get better."

Moran nodded sympathetically. "What happened to her as a child?" Moran asked.

"I can't share that with you, but suffice it to say that it was violent, and I think her mental health suffered greatly."

Moran took that in. "I understand your fear for your friend. I know you are trying to protect her, and I commend you for that. But would it be possible for me to see her for a few minutes? Off the record? I feel very badly for her and would just like to make sure she's OK."

While this was true, he failed to mention that he was positive that Ella had seen something at the Haskell house. Something that would incriminate the captain, and Moran desperately wanted to know what that something was.

Dr. Lester looked at him quizzically. "You know Ella?"

Moran nodded. "I spoke with her at Bainbridge, and she was very helpful and sweet. I can assure you, nothing she says will ever be shared."

It was the only time that Paul Moran remembered lying that blatantly to anyone. Of course he would try to keep Dr. Kramer's input out of his investigation, but if she knew something that proved Haskell was involved, he was going to use it.

Lester shook his head. "I'm sorry, Detective. She isn't well enough right now. Call me in a few days and I'll see what I can do. Thank you for your concern." Then he added nervously, "And please keep what we spoke about between us."

"Of course," Moran said reassuringly. "I'll reach out in a few days."

The two shook hands, exchanged cards, and then Moran noticed his umbrella leaning against the chair he was sitting in. He made a decision, stood to go, and left the umbrella where it was.

He walked to the elevator, where he pushed the Down button, then slowly turned around and saw Dr. Lester head up the hall in the opposite direction. That was when he moved to retrieve his umbrella and, after glancing both ways, entered Ella's room.

Chapter 57

She wasn't sure what time it was. The hum from the fluorescent lights and the whir of people walking down the hallway distracted her, and she couldn't focus long enough to make out where the sun sat in the sky behind the bars. She followed the hum and the whir and drifted in and out of consciousness until she saw him sitting there. In a chair beside her bed, his metallic crutches leaning against the wall behind him. He stared at her intently, and she recognized something in his eyes that she hadn't noticed before—a flicker of light. A light she seldom saw in people. But there it was in Detective Paul Moran's eyes.

She felt like crying, but for some reason, she couldn't. He took her hand in his, and she tried but wasn't able to make her hand clasp his back. And then it dawned on her that they must have just administered the Haldol that ruled her body and soul. It was as if she was a prisoner in her own skin, and she was desperate to get out.

Or was this another dream? A manifestation of her mind that had concocted this scenario to lure her into thinking she was being saved. For surely Moran knew what she knew. Surely he didn't think she was crazy, as the others did.

"Would you like some water, Dr. Kramer?" he asked gently, and raised a cup of water to her lips.

Ella felt herself lift her head with his help and take a sip of the water. That was when she noticed the woman sitting in the corner of the room. An older woman, about Moran's age, with gray hair, wearing a floral print nightgown. Yes, she was sure it was a nightgown. Who was that? She must be a patient, dressed like that, she thought.

Then she heard Moran speaking again. "How are you feeling?" he asked.

But the hum of the fluorescents seemed to grow louder, and Ella found herself transfixed by them and couldn't answer.

"Your friend, Dr. Lester, says you are better now," Moran continued.

At the mention of Gary's name, it hit her that all of this could have been avoided if Clyde hadn't taken Gary's idea. If he hadn't, then he wouldn't have been at Wellglad that day and he wouldn't be in jail now; Dan wouldn't be dead and she wouldn't be here, lying in a psych ward.

"Cly . . . too . . . Gus . . ." she said with effort, and saw him frown.

She was trying to say, "Clyde took Gary's light treatment." But not for the sake of letting him know that. That wasn't the point she was trying to make. Her point was how incredibly intertwined their destinies were, but the hum of the fluorescents made it hard to focus on that now.

Moran looked as if he was worried that she was drifting off and moved in closer. "Can you tell me what happened?" he whispered with some urgency.

She stared at him for a moment, confused by the question.

"At Captain Haskell's . . ."

She felt another nurse whir down the hall, but it didn't distract her what he'd said seemed to have opened a door in her mind and a cold terror rushed in.

"Hask . . .?" she said, frightened.

She remembered his face, twisted and angry, as he was breaking down the door. The monster who had killed his wife.

"*Li . . . oh . . .!*" she gasped with difficulty. But the *r* in *liar* was too much for her sleeping tongue.

Moran looked at her, dumbfounded, when suddenly there she was at the foot of her bed: the woman in the floral nightgown. She reached out and put her hand on Ella's leg and patted her, as if to say, *There, there. You can do it.* And she looked at Ella with such reassurance that Ella found herself, for the second time that day, wanting to cry.

"Did you find something at his house, Dr. Kramer?" Moran whispered.

Ella stared at him, trying to process what he had just asked, but the fluorescents were humming so loud now, she had to fight to keep herself there.

Yes, she thought, she'd found plenty, and she began to push back against the hum that drowned out the voice in her head.

"Ezee . . ." she muttered, trying to tell him that Ezekial had been there. But she could see by his face that he didn't know what she was talking about.

Before she could continue, a nurse came into the room, and Ella felt her vibration banging off the walls.

"Excuse me," she said to Moran somewhat officiously. "You aren't supposed to be in here." And she put her hands on her hips, as if to emphasize what she'd said.

Caught, Moran stood, grabbing his crutches to steady himself.

"I am Detective Moran with the Baltimore Police Department," he said, and started to pull out his credentials.

The nurse was having none of it and shook her head angrily. "This patient is not supposed to have any visitors, Detective. We have already made that quite clear to law enforcement. I'm sorry, but I will have to ask you to leave." And she stood there, resolute in the fact that he had to go.

Moran nodded, then turned back to Ella. "I have to go, Dr. Kramer," he said softly.

His voice was muffled now by the whir of the nurse's energy. The Goddam nurse, she thought. She was sending him away. Ella had to tell him before he left. But . . . what was it she had to tell him? she wondered, struggling to feel her thoughts. Suddenly, it came to her. Yes, she had to tell him that she'd found Hannah's ring. She had to tell him about the . . .

"*Weee* . . . *!*" she blurted out, unable to get out the *r* in *ring*. The Goddam *r*!

Moran stopped and looked at her, but the nurse ordered him to leave again. So he smiled sadly, patted her arm, and headed out. Strangely enough, he didn't seem to notice the woman in the floral nightgown at the foot of the bed and walked right by her on his way to the door.

There was no time. She panicked as the whir of the nurse and the hum of the fluorescents began to drown everything out. She felt her eyes flutter and knew she was about to drift away, but the voice inside her screamed at her, *Tell him about the ring under the* . . .

"*Tiiiile!*" she gasped out loudly.

Moran stopped, turned around, and looked at her one last time, and after a second, she saw the flicker in his eye, the light, grow stronger. She got the distinct impression that he understood what she'd said and, even stranger, that he was thanking her. He gave a little nod and was gone.

Ella felt her eyelids become heavy, and just before they closed, she caught a glimpse of the woman in the floral nightgown, who was still standing at the foot of her bad. Before the white light flooded her mind and the hum of the fluorescents carried her away, Ella felt the woman pat her leg one more time and heard her say softly, *Try as you might . . . you can't outrun your destiny.*

Chapter 58

Detective Moran hadn't been aware of how much stuff he had accumulated over the years, but it was proving to be a fair amount. As he picked up yet another box and moved it near the door to his office, he stopped and looked at the room where he had worked the last thirty-five years and felt a tug at his heart. He reminded himself that he had done a lot of good in this office, and that he should be excited to start the next chapter of his life. But the truth was, he was not. Perhaps if he had left on different terms, he would feel better about his decision to retire, but too much had transpired.

He was now sure that Hannah Haskell's death had not been caused by the person they had in custody, Dr, Clyde Westbrook, who would probably make a plea deal but still spend some time in prison. He was certain that Captain Haskell had been in the parking lot that night, and that he was the one who pushed his wife down, killing her.

When he'd gone into Ella's room yesterday, he was immediately struck by how fragile she looked, and he understood her friend Dr. Lester's concern. She was terribly young, he thought. Too young to endure this sort of thing. She should be out dancing with friends or . . . anything. Anything but lying there in that state, in that place.

He'd sat by her bed for no more than a minute when her eyes opened, and she'd looked at him so strangely. Almost as if she'd known he would come for her, which made his heart ache.

At first, he wasn't sure what she was mumbling; the drugs they were giving her had reduced her to spouting gibberish. But as he walked to the door, he heard her blurt out one word—*tile*. And suddenly he realized that everything she had been trying to say *meant something*.

As he'd walked to the Bainbridge parking lot, his mind reeled, and he'd sat in his car in the dark trying to piece it all together.

She seemed terrified after he mentioned Haskell's name, and when he asked if she'd found anything at his house, she'd grunted, *Easy* a couple of times. And it dawned on him: Was she trying to say Ezekial? Surely she hadn't seen him there? And if she had, how would she have known him? Or had she just known he was there? He racked his brain for a few minutes, and then Ezekial Weintraub's glasses came to mind. His dark, thick-lensed glasses that were a signature for him. Had she seen them there? They still hadn't been found. But why would they mean anything to Ella Kramer? Why would Ezekial Weintraub mean anything to her?

But it was the word *tile* that most intrigued him.

Captain Haskell and his wife had bought the tile on Sunday, the day of the fundraiser, the day of her murder. Moran had smelled the grout when he and Scarpetti went there to inform the captain of his wife's death. Then he remembered something else—that Captain Haskell had gone into that bathroom and been sick after he'd been told of his wife's murder. Or at least he'd said he'd been sick.

Had Captain Haskell hidden something in that bathroom? Say under the tile? Brain scans would fit very nicely there, and no one would be the wiser. But if that was the case, why would he want to keep the scans in the first place?

Assuming Weintraub had brought the scans to Haskell, had Ella found them in the bathroom? *Under the tile?* Was that why she had struggled to get that word out before he left her room? But how would Ella have known the scans meant something? Very probably she would have no idea of their importance.

So if Ella hadn't found the scans under the tile, what could she have seen that made her so upset? What had made her lose control as she had?

Then it came him. Of course, he thought: *the ring. Hannah Haskell's wedding ring.* That would be the only thing that Ella would have knowledge of that would incriminate Captain Haskell.

Moran was quite sure that the ring the police had in their possession belonged to Captain Haskell. Haskell, with his long, slim fingers, could have worn the ring that had been a little too big on Hannah Haskell's finger at the morgue. Moran didn't think it had to do with fluid loss.

There was also the business of the inscription. The ring that was found and given to him by Westbrook read *Hannah ♥ Oliver 6/14/2007.* If one gave a ring to one's betrothed, it would usually start with the name of the person doing the giving. Ergo, *Hannah ♥ Oliver 6/14/2007* would have been the ring she had given to him. The ring she wore would read *Oliver*

❤ *Hannah 6/14/2007* because it came from Captain Haskell. He knew he was right about that, even though Ross had come to a dead end when he tried to track down the rings.

So if Ella had found Hannah's ring in the bathroom, how had it gotten there?

Perhaps Captain Haskell had taken his wife's ring off her as she lay there in the parking lot to make it look like a burglary gone wrong. Then why hadn't he taken her credit cards? he wondered. Well, perhaps he'd been interrupted by Daniel Zimmerman, wearing his bizarre hat, chasing a New Zealand white rabbit.

But if he had taken her ring, why hadn't he brought it to Bainbridge to plant on Daniel Zimmerman instead of using his own? Moran had racked his brain trying to figure that one out but hadn't, for the only answer was that the captain didn't have Hannah's ring on him when he was admitted to Bainbridge.

He sat there in the parking lot as the sun began to go down, trying to figure this out, when another thought made its way to him. The night of Hannah's murder, he and Scarpetti had arrived at the Haskell house at the same time the captain had. So perhaps he hadn't had time to get rid of Hannah's ring if it was on him. Upon entering and informing him of his wife's death, Captain Haskell went into the bathroom and became sick. The same bathroom that Ella had the breakdown in.

Had Haskell hidden his wife's ring in there in a state of terror of getting caught by the police? Or had he lost it in there in that state? Either scenario worked, but Moran found the last possibility more likely, for surely if he had hidden the ring in there, Captain Haskell would have gotten rid of it when he returned home from his stay at Bainbridge, and Ella would never have found it.

Or had he wanted to keep it? Like Neil Hollingsworth, who had kept some of his victims' trinkets. Perhaps he had hidden Hannah's ring under the tile so it would always be near him, he thought, and shuddered.

But Moran thought it was more likely that Captain Haskell had lost the ring when Moran and Scarpetti descended upon him that night. Maybe, in his panic, the ring slipped away in the bathroom under renovation and he couldn't find it. He wouldn't have had a lot of time to look for it with two police detectives on the other side of the door. Maybe that was why Haskell made Moran use the other bathroom that night.

And why had Haskell returned home from Bainbridge and begun retiling his bathroom immediately? It didn't make sense that right after his wife was killed, he continued with a renovation they had planned together. That was incredibly strange. But if he'd lost the ring in there the night of the murder, maybe what he was actually doing was tearing the bathroom apart, looking for it.

But Ella had found it first.

So, if Ella Kramer had found the ring, she would have gone into complete alarm, realizing that she had helped put her boyfriend away for a murder committed by Oliver Haskell. Had she locked herself in the bathroom in terror?

He was told Haskell had broken the door down. And what had he said? That she'd been screaming at him about Clyde being taken into custody? That it was his, Haskell's, fault? But why had he broken the door down at all? thought Moran. Why hadn't he just called the police? Was he worried about what she'd found?

Moran was convinced that Ella had found the ring. He had to speak with her to verify that this was what she was trying to tell him. He reached into his glove box, pulled out his phone, and rang Dr. Lester, who answered immediately.

"Detective Moran, I have nothing left to say to you," Gary said angrily. "The nurse informed me that you ignored me and went into Ella's room."

Moran interrupted him. "I am very sorry, Dr. Lester, but it is imperative that I speak with Dr. Kramer. She divulged some information to me about the Haskell case that I must follow up on."

Gary Lester was having none of it. "And I am telling you that nothing she says will help you! For Christ's sake! I told you she wasn't OK! I begged you to leave her alone!"

"I need to know what she saw at the Haskell house. . . ."

"What she saw? It doesn't matter what she saw!" Gary said almost hysterically. "She's delusional, Detective Moran. Nothing she says will matter! The doctors here are inches away from declaring her incompetent. I told you she had an episode when she was a child; well, she doesn't remember it. She's come up with a completely different story instead!"

"I'm not concerned with what happened in her past, Dr. Lester."

"Well, you should be! Because it has caused her to completely break with reality!" And here he whispered urgently, "She thinks she's been seeing a therapist on a daily basis, Detective Moran. A therapist who doesn't exist. Do you get it? Nothing she says will help you! It will only destroy her! I'm begging you, leave Ella alone!" And with that he slammed down the phone.

Moran sat there in the parking lot, Lester's words ringing in his ears. *Christ*, he thought. What had happened to the vibrant young woman he met? What had pushed her over the edge like this? If what Dr. Lester told him was true, it didn't matter what Ella Kramer saw or found. She wouldn't be able to bear witness against anyone.

But how on Earth had Bainbridge been able to go back and not only find Ella Kramer's records in the juvenile justice system but also get a judge to unseal those records so quickly? He had worked in law enforcement all his adult life and knew that to be a nearly impossible feat.

The incident between Ella and Haskell had happened Friday evening. How had they been able to find her records and unseal them in five days? Three, if you excluded the weekend. It didn't make sense. That never happened.

Then he realized the answer to that was quite simple: Only money and power had that kind of reach.

And then it all made sense.

Haskell must have been terrified by his confrontation with Ella. He would have called Levine immediately. He'd probably called Ned Dowd as well. And because it was undeniably true that Dr. Kramer had had some kind of breakdown that night, those two had probably decided to do a little digging to see if they could find anything else with which to smear the young doctor and protect Captain Haskell. Dowd would certainly have a judge or two in his pocket.

Suddenly, Moran felt sick at what the girl was facing. He was sure Levine had shared her history of mental illness with Bainbridge and threatened legal action. And so Bainbridge was now in the position of doing damage control, hoping to avoid liability and litigation. It already looked very bad that Dr. Westbrook had conducted an unapproved experiment on a patient who allegedly ended up killing Captain Haskell's wife. Moran doubted that they would survive that.

But imagine if word got out that a doctor who was mentally ill had been in charge of the captain during his stay at their hospital. And that she had been dating the doctor who had conducted the unapproved experiment and inadvertently caused his wife's death. That would be catastrophic.

So they were going to silence the young doctor. Anything she saw or found that night would never hold up because she wasn't mentally sound and probably hadn't been for years. He now understood why Dr. Lester was terrified.

It was here that Moran paused, realizing what was to come.

There was no way he could go above or around Abbot. And even if he could, Abbot wasn't the one he needed to get around. It was the powerful pulling the strings to help Haskell. And there was no way of getting Haskell without destroying young Dr. Kramer.

In the end, it wouldn't really matter. Moran didn't have enough physical evidence to prove it was Haskell in the Wellglad parking lot when Hannah Haskell died. Haskell had probably destroyed his wife's ring by now, and there were no witnesses.

And none of this mattered anyway because, after everything was said and done, proving drugs like Lyprophan would cause brain damage would take years, if ever.

It was at that moment that Paul Moran made his decision to walk away.

From all of it. He couldn't bear the injustice he was witnessing. The lives that had been destroyed. The system had failed Hannah Haskell, Ella Kramer, and Clyde Westbrook. Not to mention Dan Zimmerman and Ezekial Weintraub. He couldn't be part of a system like that. Not anymore.

He drove home and told Marti what he was going to do, which, of course, didn't seem to surprise her. She set about consoling him as only she could, and it wasn't until after they'd gone to bed that he realized that Marti had known what was going to happen.

She'd already seen it.

Chapter 59

Ella woke to see the moon shining brightly through the barred window of her hospital room and saw it was fuller than before. How long she'd been here she couldn't remember anymore; her mind was so muddled from the drugs.

She seemed to remember thinking that Detective Moran was in the room. But she saw now that he wasn't, and she felt incredibly odd; his presence had seemed so real to her. As had their conversation.

She vaguely remembered telling him—or trying to tell him—about Ezekial Weintraub, and how she'd found Hannah's ring. She'd hoped that he would help her, but deep down, she knew he couldn't. And it really didn't matter anyway. It was just a dream.

Hot tears stream down her face. She missed her Aunt Moira. She hadn't been able to plan a funeral for her, or even go to it. Seaside had handled everything, which made her feel like a nonperson. As if anything she said or did was meaningless, and she knew she would probably spend years in a hospital again.

Just as she had before.

She'd tried so hard to make something of her life, only to see it all destroyed for committing the simple crime of *knowing*.

Captain Haskell was infected by the energy of the Vanitan. A *Light Eater*, as Otis had called them; or a *van*, as Dan had cried. She doubted the captain knew he was such a thing as he'd probably convinced himself of his righteousness long ago.

If one could kill many people under the guise of a righteous war, how hard would it be to convince oneself that protecting a drug that helped people wasn't righteous as well? Though Lyprophan would help no one in the end. It would spawn a generation of psychopaths by destroying the area in their brain responsible for empathy. It would render millions of innocent babies soulless.

And Captain Haskell had done it all for his own glorification—to make sure he became a US Senator. But he hadn't acted alone. Wellglad must have sanctioned the killing of his wife, and that of Ezekial Weintraub, to make sure nothing happened to their precious money.

Indeed, the Vanitan was descending; infecting people with its energy as it had infected other life forms on other planets. Turning them against their own humanity, which would ultimately lead to their destruction and that of others. Until there was nothing left. Until Earth looked something like Mars. Cold and empty; devoid of life.

Ella had had a lot of time to think over the past few days, and even in her drug-induced state, it had all become clear to her, but so had the tragic fact that she could do nothing about it. No one would believe a word she said.

Only people in her dreams, with strange companions in floral nightgowns, would give countenance to anything she had to say from now on. And with that, she drifted helplessly back to sleep.

Chapter 60

The next time she awoke, Dr. Eleanor Farber was sitting beside Ella, patiently waiting for her to wake up. Ella reached out her arms and hugged the doctor. Much to her surprise, Farber, who was usually reserved, held her tightly.

"It's OK," Farber admonished gently. "It's all going to be OK."

"They told me they couldn't find you! They said there wasn't a Dr. Farber in Baltimore!"

"Ella . . ." Farber started.

"You can tell them I'm not lying! That he killed his wife and that poor young man! You'll tell them, won't you?" Ella pleaded. "It all makes sense! What the others were trying to warn me of! Even you were trying to warn me! The scans—remember you said that one day we may be able to judge psychopaths from looking at scans? Well, they're going to create them! It is the Vanitan! Malakhi and Moira and Otis! They were right!"

But Dr. Farber put a finger to her lips, gesturing for Ella to be still. "We have very little time, and you must be quiet."

Ella looked at her, panicked. "What do you mean, we have very little time? You're not leaving, are you?"

"I'll never leave you," Farber reassured her gently. "I never have."

"Then you'll tell them. You'll tell them I'm telling the truth. You're a psychiatrist. They'll listen to you!" Ella begged.

Farber, seeing her panic, quickly did something that shocked Ella to her core: She covered Ella's mouth with her hand and whispered, "If you are too loud, they will come in, and we have much to do. Be quiet. Promise you'll be quiet."

Ella felt terror creep up her spine, but she nodded in spite of it. Dr. Farber removed her hand and gently brushed Ella's cheek—almost as a mother would.

"Are you registered in Baltimore?" Ella asked quietly.

Dr. Farber shook her head.

"So you're not supposed to be practicing here," Ella surmised before another thought occurred to her. "Are you even a psychiatrist?" she asked.

Farber nodded her head. "Indeed I am just not in Maryland. I live in Seattle, and that is where my practice is," Farber said.

"So you moved but didn't get your license to practice here?"

"I didn't move here," Farber replied. "I still live and practice in Seattle."

Ella's brow furrowed, confused. "But you've been seeing me for the last three years. What are you talking about?"

Ella had moved to Baltimore to start her residency at Bainbridge when she was twenty-seven. Her aunt was diagnosed the prior year, so she'd brought Moira to Seaside because she could no longer live on the ranch by herself, and she would be close to Ella.

But almost immediately she'd started having her headaches again, and the dream. Ella'd found her medication wasn't enough, so she began to see Dr. Farber shortly after her arrival. How on earth could Dr. Farber live and practice in Seattle and still see her?

Farber put her hand on her arm, comforting her, as Ella continued to stare at her. Her mind reeled. She had seen Dr. Farber very early, every morning before she went to work. Sometimes, just as the sun was rising. There was only one conclusion. *Ella'd been dreaming. Dr. Farber was a dream. . . .*

"So you're not here, are you?" she whispered.

"No. Not physically. But I am here for you. I'm visiting you. But I am also asleep in Seattle," Farber said.

Ella felt as if her mind was coming completely undone. How did any of this make sense? And then a creeping suspicion entered her thoughts as she locked eyes with Farber. Eyes that looked conspicuously like her own. She'd noticed it before, in their last session, though so much had happened, she hadn't had the time to give it much thought. But now she did. Dr. Farber's face too. Weathered and wrinkled, her hair grayer, but still . . .

"You're . . . who are you?" she asked, holding her breath.

Farber smiled gently. "I am you, Ella. You, at sixty-four years of age. I live in Seattle, where I now lay in my bed, asleep. Seattle, which is three hours behind, and where I will be waking shortly and going to work at the hospital. And the year there is 2058." She paused, allowing this information to flow into Ella's consciousness before asking, "Do you understand?"

Ella lay there feeling as if she must have died. The impossibility of it all was staggering. She vaguely remembered her conversation with Clark. Hadn't he tried to explain that time was like a coil on itself? That the past, the present, and the future were all happening at once? And if he was right, then couldn't what Farber was saying be . . . true?

"So Dr. Van de Hout was right? We can travel back and forth . . . along time?" she asked, shocked.

Dr. Farber nodded slowly. "Some of us can. For that's our nature."

And her blue eyes—Ella's blue eyes—looked at her lovingly, waiting to see if she understood.

And then Ella remembered the red-haired girl in Captain Haskell's bathroom. Hadn't the girl had the same eyes? It had struck Ella when the girl was telling her that *they were here and they had to go.*

"And the red-haired girl . . . she's me too?"

Farber nodded. "She's been waiting for you. All these years. Like me, she is here to guide you."

Ella's mind was moving quickly now, fluidly. Almost as if it was expanding. Seeing things for the first time. As if boundaries were dissolving and she was seeing it all at once. What was it Malakhi had said? That she was a Light Runner? Was that what was happening to her? Was she traveling along the light?

"And Malakhi and my aunt, Otis . . . they were all telling the truth? About the Vanitan?"

Farber nodded again. "Yes. They were warning you. For you have a greater destiny to fulfill."

"A greater destiny?" she whispered. And her aunt's and Malakhi's words that she had *a role to play* rang in her ears.

Farber nodded. "You have always *known* it. But now it is time to *claim* it. And there isn't much time left; the window is closing."

And suddenly Ella was in the crash again. Reliving it. She saw the glass fly everywhere as her mother was thrown out of the car, and she felt someone covering her young body, holding her in place. Could it have been . . . *her?*

"Do you understand what I'm saying, Ella?" Farber asked.

And now she *knew.* As Malakhi had said, she would discover her true nature. She felt a sense of calm descend upon her. Just as she had in the car accident that so tragically changed her life. Of course she understood. She had understood for a very long time that she had been playing a role here. And now she would play a new one. The role of who she really was.

"I'm a Light Runner," she said simply, claiming it for the first time.

"Yes," said Dr. Farber. "And you can go back and forth along the light, and you can change the outcome. And we need to do that now. As the Vanitan energy descends." She took Ella's hand. "We must go back to your dream now, Ella. For that is where the red-haired girl is waiting. Where she's been waiting for a very long time."

Ella's eyes teared up as she realized that nothing would be the same. That she would no longer have the life she had now. She thought of the red-haired girl. "What happened to her? What happened to me?"

Dr. Farber slowly began. "Your uncle was abusing you. It began when you were ten, and when you were fifteen, you took his gun . . . and you killed him. You were taken away to a mental hospital. Do you remember?"

Ella nodded slowly.

Farber continued. "I began to visit you there. I told you how to go back. How to go back and remember everything differently. And so you did. You went back, and you went to yourself at ten—before he hurt you—and there was the accident with your uncle's gun. But it was no accident. Do you understand?"

Ella nodded again.

"The red-haired girl is you at fifteen. She shot your uncle and left the gun with the ten-year-old you, who was too young to understand what was happening, and so she broke. But your aunt's love saved you, Ella. Your Aunt Moira saved you. And you became whole again."

At the mention of her aunt, Ella began to cry. "Will I see her again?"

"She has her own destiny. Moira is a *Drifter.* As is Otis. They have played their role in keeping the Vanitan at bay. For their energy holds a place for light and love here on Earth. But they are seeking a place that may not be found.

"Malakhi was right. Life has existed everywhere, but now it is threatened here, and we must fight, lest the energy of the Vanitan vanquish it for good. Do you understand?"

"How can I change anything? What is it I'm supposed to do?" she asked.

"The soul is the light, Ella. If one has a soul, one is a Light Being. Captain Haskell and Wellglad have the ability to destroy children, rendering them soulless. They must not be allowed to succeed. Hannah Haskell saw that. Hannah Haskell must be protected, Ella. She mustn't die. You must go back now. To your uncle's house. To the red-haired girl who waits there for you. She will guide you."

"But how? How do I go back?" Ella asked, confused.

"You must go back to your dream, Ella. To that terrible night. You must open the door to the light and remember it all differently. Follow the light, and remember Hannah Haskell being alive. Remember saving her. Can you do that?"

Ella felt herself shiver, scared. "Will you help me?"

"Of course I will," Farber said lovingly.

Dr. Farber gently closed Ella's eyes with her hand, and she heard her voice whispering to her to go back to sleep. And something about the way she said it made Ella very tired. As her eyes got heavy and her thoughts began to dissipate, she heard Farber.

"Go back to your dream and open the door. *It is time to remember.*"

Things would never be the same again, Ella thought. And the play on words made her want to laugh as she realized *she would be going back to the past to realize a new future—again.*

And that was when she let go, and Dr. Farber's voice led her into a vast, unknown chasm . . . *of light.*

Chapter 61

There she was again. In the dream she'd been in countless times. The dream that used to scare her into sleepless nights. She was in her aunt and uncle's bedroom. There was their bed, with the afghan covering it, the pictures of her as a child, and Aunt Moira's slippers by the bedside. Everything was the same. She looked down and noticed there was no blood on her hands, and they were younger. They were the hands of a teenager. She was fifteen again. She was the red-haired girl. And without knowing how, she knew what she must do.

The wind howled, and Ella looked out the window and saw the moon shining brightly through the trees. Only one moon, for they were here on Earth. She listened carefully and could just hear the little girl behind the closet door. She saw the light under the door grow brighter as she reached out her hand and opened it.

There she sat. Ella at ten. The little girl looked up at her as she stepped into the closet, closing the door behind her. Ella saw her uncle's gun on the shelf above the clothes. The gun she had taken down before—for surely the little girl couldn't reach it—the gun she had used to defend herself. She gazed down at scared little Ella and knelt in front of her, smiling gently. She looked into her eyes and touched the girl's face.

"You must be very brave now," Ella told her.

The little girl nodded, full of trust. Ella hesitated for a second, knowing all the pain she was to endure, but she must do what she had set out to do, she told herself. There was no going back now.

"Remember to forgive her. Aunt Moira. She loves you. OK?"

Slowly, the little girl nodded, not fully understanding.

But before she could explain, they were interrupted by a voice. The voice of her Uncle John, calling out to little Ella to come out from her hiding place.

Ella stood and told the girl to close her eyes; then she turned, putting herself between the door and the little girl, and waited. Suddenly, the door swung open, and there was her Uncle John, the man who had ruined her life. A look of shock crossed his face as he saw her standing there in the bright white light.

But before he could utter a word, she shot him in the chest, over and over, until he fell dead. She looked down at him, her hands covered with his blood. Blood that had spattered everywhere. This was as it should be, she told herself, looking down at the man who had destroyed so much. The man who had been a part of her destiny. And when she turned around, she found that the little girl was gone. There was no one there but her. Ella at fifteen.

Suddenly, the windows blew open and dust began to fill the room. It moved toward her in the closet and began to surround her as the white light grew brighter and brighter. And soon, everything in the closet began to dissolve into dust. Ella watched as her aunt's clothes and shoes began to dissolve; her Uncle John's suits began to dissolve. And then the walls and the ceiling and everything *real* began to dissolve. Until there was nothing between her and the light but the dust. It wasn't red as it was in her dream, for that was a different place and a different time. And she found this as funny as it was untrue. For it was all happening at once.

In the light, the dust looked like little crystalline fragments that shimmered as they floated in the air, and Ella laughed at the idea that she'd had auras and headaches. No, her vision had shimmered as the truth drew nearer to her as the light from the other time dimension seeped into her reality.

It all made sense now, she thought, as the dust began to swirl around her until she became encapsulated by it. Until Ella felt herself begin to dissolve too. She watched as she felt bits and pieces of her fall away, and her memories shimmered in the air. She flashed on her life as Dr. Kramer, with Malakhi, Clyde, and Sebastian; with her aunt and Gary and Otis. For a brief moment, fear gripped her, but some part deep inside her told her to focus on the light.

So she did. She focused on the bright white light that was blinding her now. And as she did, she felt herself become a part of it. Until there was no Ella and there was no time.

There was nothing but a distant memory of a fragmented dream.

Chapter 62

She was walking down the hallway. A hallway much like the ones at Bainbridge, except that there were women in the rooms she passed, in various stages of getting ready for bed. As she passed by one room, she couldn't help but stop and stare at her reflection in the door's glass panel.

The woman reflected had the same face and the same age as the Ella who had worked at Bainbridge. The same crow's-feet surrounded her eyes, and the same smile lines adorned her mouth. All was the same except for one striking feature: her very red hair, which was now long, according to her reflection. Then she looked down at the blue hospital jumpsuit she remembered the other girls wore. The girls who had made fun of her hair.

"It's almost lights out, Ella," she heard behind her, and she turned to see a nurse walking by. Ella nodded and started walking, hoping that she was headed in the right direction. As she looked around her, she marveled at how like Bainbridge this place was. The paint was somewhat different, but the lights above still buzzed the same monotonous tune, which felt eerily familiar to Ella.

She came to a bend in the hallway with full-length windows much like Bainbridge, and something she saw as she looked out the windows stopped her. There, in the parking lot, was a Mercedes. It was dark out, but she was sure of it. The car was black and sleek, and she had ridden in it countless times, for it was Clyde's Mercedes. Slowly, she began to realize that she was in the women's wing at Bainbridge. The A Wing. Next door was the B Wing, for male patients, where she had worked, and behind them both, next to the train tracks, lay the C Wing for the criminally insane.

Ella began to smile, astonished by the journey she was on. She walked farther down the hall and into the TV room, where a few of the patients were watching the news. It was all so familiar, she thought, but it wasn't. She was about to leave when something the newscaster said stopped her.

"Tomorrow, Captain Oliver Haskell will be attending his last fundraising event before the election in two weeks. The cocktail event is being hosted by Wellglad Pharmaceuticals, JM Biometrics, and other pharmaceutical companies who support Haskell in his bid for the US Senate. Many have said that Haskell is too heavily backed by corporate donors, but the people of Baltimore seem to love the war hero. His polling shows that he could handily defeat his opponent . . ."

And she watched as they aired footage of Haskell walking and smiling as he waved to the crowd. And there, demurely by his side, was his wife, Hannah Haskell.

Ella felt her heart jump. The fundraiser was tomorrow night. Dr. Farber was right, there wasn't much time. The window was closing.

"Hannah Haskell must live," she heard herself say.

Ella exited the room and began walking. What could she do? Was it too late?

But the answer presented itself, as it always did in the Universe, with a group of women rounding the corner toward her. They looked familiar to Ella. Like older versions of the girls who had been so nasty to her when she was fifteen.

One of them, a particularly large woman, shoved her out of the way, muttering something about carrots as the others laughed. Normally, Ella would let this kind of thing go. Especially with someone as menacing as this; but not now. Now she remembered what happened next.

"Touch me again and I'll kill you!" Ella snapped.

The fight probably would have lasted longer if Ella had fought back instead of just provoking the woman, taunting her to keep fighting, which the woman was only too happy to do. But she didn't. She knew where she needed to go, and this was her way to get there.

She woke up in the infirmary, where Dr. Saltz informed her that she had a concussion and would remain there for the night.

She waited until it was near dawn, then snuck out to the garden, where she hoped she would find what she had asked Dan's grandmother to tell him to leave for her. Just before he had committed suicide in the other reality.

A Wing was just over the wall from B Wing, so Ella scoured the border in search of what she hoped to find.

There it was. In the back, by the wall on the other side of the rose garden at B Wing, she found a coat rolled up on the ground, under some bushes that were tangled and gnarled. A coat that was much too big for her because it belonged to Dan. And when she unrolled it, she found a crowbar. And not just any crowbar. Clyde's crowbar from his Mercedes. Dan had been able to steal it just as she knew he would.

But now came the hardest part. She threw on the coat, tucked the crowbar inside it, and headed to the back of the property. Her head throbbed from the concussion, but she ignored it and hurried on, knowing that she wouldn't catch it if she didn't. As she rounded the corner, she saw C Wing to her left and the high fence in front of her. She steeled herself and began to climb, hoisting herself up and over the tall fence. At least there wasn't razor wire at the top, as there was on the fence surrounding C Wing, she thought as she went.

She began her descent as she heard the train whistle and moved faster, knowing she had to make it. Three-quarters left to go, and she saw the train in the distance. There was no time to lose, so she jumped the rest of the way, landing with a thud. She picked herself up and began to run. She ran as if life depended on it.

For someone's life did—Hannah Haskell's.

Chapter 63

She made the train without a moment to spare and rode in the empty boxcar until she saw Wellglad just a few miles down the track. She'd hid in the woods, dozing off at times as the pain from the concussion dulled her senses. When the sun lowered in the sky, she made her move. She headed for the pharmaceutical company's parking lot, scaled the low wall, and found an alcove in the back, where she waited quietly in the darkness. She heard a homeless person roll their grocery cart by, talking to themselves, but other than that, the lot was quite deserted.

Her head hurt more and more as time passed. The beating she had taken was a bad one, and her head felt like it was cracked wide open. The pain was searing, and it became more difficult to focus and stay awake.

After waiting for an hour in the small alcove, she couldn't help but close her eyes, and she felt herself drifting off when the car entered the gate. She roused herself and peered around the wall as Hannah Haskell got out of her sedan carrying a manila envelope. The one Ella had taken to Captain Haskell's house. The scans, she thought. Hannah was taking them to Ezekial Weintraub for safekeeping.

Hannah walked toward the entrance of the building, her footfalls echoing in the empty lot until there was silence. Ella waited anxiously for what seemed like hours, and began to wonder if what had happened would happen. Maybe Captain Haskell wasn't coming. Maybe in her travel back through time, his fate had changed just as hers had. She hoped this was true.

She saw no sign of Clyde and Dan, which, at first, shocked her. But then she realized that Clyde had been given Gary's light treatment proposal by her, and so she had *rewritten* that action by going back in time.

There was no proposal given to Clyde, for there was no Dr. Kramer to give it to him.

Her reverie was cut short by the sound of Hannah Haskell quickly walking back toward the parking lot a few minutes later. And as she walked past the kiosk, Ella noticed Hannah did something strange: She slowed down and looked up very purposefully at something inside the kiosk. This confused Ella, who was now having trouble with her vision. She didn't understand why she would slow down like that, but she didn't have long to dwell on it because Captain Haskell had just entered the lot.

He leaped quietly over the wall next to her, like a cat, and Ella jumped back into her alcove, praying she'd escaped his view. He moved quickly, toward his wife, who had just reached her car.

Ella stepped out of the alcove and began to move quietly toward them, glancing over the wall to where his car was parked behind a sign. She heard them begin to argue, and she quickened her pace as best she could, the concussion making her stomach sick.

"You can't do this!" she heard Haskell hiss at his wife. To which Hannah Haskell told him that she had to. Captain Haskell demanded that she give him the scans, but Hannah ignored him and got into the car, and that was when things changed.

He became enraged and grabbed the door, holding it open as Hannah shrank back from him, shocked. Ella tried to quicken her pace, but her head was spinning, and it was difficult to see. She worried that she wouldn't be able to do what she'd come back to do.

She heard Hannah protest as he grabbed her and pulled her out of the car.

"Where are they? Where are they?" he snapped, looking through the car.

Hannah decided to flee and began to run as he flew out, grabbed her, and began shaking her violently before he threw her down to the ground.

Ella moved with all the speed she could muster, terrified that he had killed her. She was a few feet away when he sensed her presence and turned to face her, the rage still burning in his eyes. He moved toward her threateningly.

But it was too late. Ella removed the crowbar from her coat and swung it with all her might, cracking him over the head. For a second, the two just stared at each other as he stood there. As if they recognized each other and knew that this was always the way it was destined to be. And then blood trickled down the side of his face and began pouring out of his mouth, and Captain Haskell collapsed to the ground, dead.

Ella dropped the crowbar and rushed to Hannah Haskell's side. There was blood on her head, but she put her ear to her heart and heard it beat. Ella's sight was blurred as her head throbbed painfully. She didn't know what to do. She mustn't die like this. She mustn't let Hannah Haskell die and leave the world behind her. She must help Hannah do what she was meant to do. Hannah Haskell was to play a part in saving humanity. By saving the living. By defying the Vanitan. Hannah Haskell must not die.

Ella grabbed Hannah's purse and struggled to pull out her phone. Her right eye was completely blind now and her left was dimming, but she willed herself to keep going. She pushed 911 on the phone and saw that a word looking like *Emergency* popped up at the bottom of the screen, and she pressed it.

Hannah Haskell must live, she told herself. *She must live.*

Suddenly, a voice on the other end asked what the emergency was, and as Ella fought to remain conscious, she gasped out their location and what had happened.

The last thing she remembered was the coolness of the ground as her head hit it. So cool, like a pool of water. Like the banks of the mountain spring at Aunt Moira's.

The cool, cool water was all around her now, and she saw Skeeter grazing in the distance. And as she heard the sound of the sirens, she focused on a voice that she recognized. A voice that whispered to her as she lay by the spring watching Skeeter. A voice full of love, saying, over and over, "I love you, Sugar. I love you forever."

Chapter 64

D r. Clyde Westbrook left his office in the B Wing of Bainbridge Psychiatric Hospital and moved quickly across the grounds until he came to the entrance of C Wing, where a guard unlocked the gate and allowed him to enter. He walked to a waiting area, where he was met by two police detectives who had been handling the Hannah Haskell case, Detectives Alonso Scarpetti and Paul Moran. He escorted the two men into an office and sat down with them.

"As you know, we are here to interview Ms. Kramer," Detective Moran said. "It's been a week, and Dr. Saltz thinks that she is sufficiently well to speak to us now."

"Yes," Clyde replied. "I have spoken to Dr. Saltz, and he said that she's lucid and doing well. May I ask if we will need our legal representation present as well? We've never had an escape from Bainbridge, and I must protect the hospital."

"That won't be necessary," Moran responded. "We're just tying up loose ends."

This was literally music to Clyde Westbrook's ear; he could hardly contain himself. He'd been shocked to hear that Ella Kramer had escaped. She was a docile patient who had lived here for fifteen years without any trouble. She'd even been found to be very helpful with the other patients, and was a favorite of the nurses in A Wing.

He felt badly about the beating she'd endured, and Lord knew that wouldn't look good if it was made public, but he doubted that would have made her kill Captain Haskell. He wasn't sure what was going on but was glad to hear that neither Hannah Haskell nor the police were going after her in an aggressive way.

"Can you tell us about the young lady?" Moran asked.

Clyde, having just reviewed her file, began to explain Ella's life to the two men.

"She's been at Bainbridge since she was fifteen years old. It's rather a tragic story. Her parents were killed in an automobile accident when she was eight, and she went to live with her aunt and uncle. Apparently, the uncle began molesting her when she was ten, and at fifteen, she shot him. She spent three years here, after which we tried to settle her back at home with her aunt, but it was no use. There were too many episodes of psychosis, to the point where she didn't know who she was, and she would lash out angrily at her aunt. She's a schizophrenic and tends to live in a world of her own creation. We brought her back here, and she has lived in the women's ward, A Wing, for the past fifteen years. Her aunt was so heartbroken, she ended up committing suicide. Truly tragic. Under our care, she's been doing pretty well—until recent events, of course."

"With the exception of her uncle, has she displayed any other signs that she was violent?" Moran asked.

"She's had some squabbles with some of the other patients over the years, but never anything violent until a week ago, when she got into a fight with four other patients, and they beat her pretty badly. Ella was in the infirmary with a concussion when she crawled over the fence, caught the train, and got away. We think the concussion may have triggered a trauma response, which caused her to do what she did in the parking lot, so we're keeping her here in C Wing, which has maximum security."

Clyde sat for a moment, then couldn't help but ask, "The police have told us very little about what happened in the parking lot that day. Would you be able to enlighten me?"

"We believe that she came upon the Haskells during an argument and tried to help Dr. Haskell. But we will know more after we speak with her," Moran said.

Clyde nodded, then stood. "Very well. Shall we?"

The two men followed him out of the room and down the hall to the visitation area.

Chapter 65

Ella sat quietly at the table, waiting for whom she didn't know, her hands and feet restrained. There was a guard in the room standing in the corner behind her, and Ella thought it ridiculous that there was all this security for someone like her.

Indeed she must have looked small and somewhat fragile sitting there all by herself. The bruises on her face had healed but were giving her complexion a yellowish hue, making her seem a little sickly, which only added to her air of frailty.

She heard the door open and turned her head to see Dr. Westbrook escort the two detectives into the room. She'd never met Detective Scarpetti, but she remembered Detective Moran and was secretly happy to see him and hear the *whoosh-thump* of his metal crutches. He must have noticed her joy at seeing him, for he looked at her curiously, and she quickly averted her eyes lest she give herself away.

They sat down at the table, and Dr. Westbrook introduced Ella to the two men. She nodded quietly, taking it all in, but wanted to say that she knew exactly who they were and that she'd even had a drink with Detective Moran one evening not too long ago. Instead, she remained quiet until she was asked question after question, which she answered perfunctorily.

Yes, she felt better.

Yes, she understood who they were.

Yes, she remembered what happened.

"Would you mind sharing with us what that was?" Detective Moran asked. And so she told the detectives about being beaten up by the other patients in A Wing. She had wanted to leave, so when she was in the infirmary, she decided to catch the train that passed by every morning at six a.m.

Detective Scarpetti asked her why she got off just a couple of miles away at Wellglad instead of staying on the train and, as he put it, "really getting out of Dodge."

That was when she realized the blessing of being mad and told them that the woods looked so inviting, she'd decided to walk around the trees for a while, so she'd gotten off and done just that. Scarpetti bought it, but Moran's eyes narrowed ever so slightly, which intrigued her. What was he thinking?

She was then asked about the parking lot and what had transpired there. She told them the whole thing—that she had heard angry voices and had crept over the wall just in time to see a man assaulting a woman, so she ran over to help.

"Where did you get the crowbar?" Scarpetti asked.

"I found it there in the lot," she answered, remembering how she had carefully wiped off the crowbar lest Clyde or Dan's DNA be found on it. Scarpetti nodded, seemingly satisfied, but Moran just stared at her. And there was something so piercing about his gaze that she felt a little exposed, for lack of a better word.

"What were they arguing about?" Moran asked.

This question thrilled Ella, as she must make it known that Wellglad was creating a potential disaster for mankind in the form of Lyprophan.

"He kept screaming at her that he wanted the scans. She said that she couldn't give him the scans because they were proof."

"Proof of what?" Scarpetti interjected.

"You'd have to ask her," Ella responded.

"Did he attack you?" Moran asked.

Ella nodded. "Yes. He moved toward me after he threw her down, so I hit him over the head."

"So you had the crowbar with you at that point?" Moran asked.

Ella wanted to smile. *Good question, Detective.* This was rather a fun game.

"Yes, I did. I saw it when I came over the wall, just lying on the ground, and he was very scary. The way he was treating her was scary. She was in danger, so I took it with me, and I helped her."

They asked a few more questions until the two men looked at each other, satisfied. She noticed Clyde seemed downright thrilled by what had just transpired, as he asked them somewhat gleefully if they were finished. Detective Scarpetti told them they were and stood, ready to go, but Moran remained seated, staring at the young woman.

"Detective?" Dr. Westbrook asked.

"I would like to speak to Miss Kramer alone for a couple of minutes, if that's all right with you, Doctor?" he asked.

This didn't seem to thrill Dr. Westbrook, but he acquiesced, happy that Haskell was the villain and not her, Ella thought. As a matter of fact, she mused, it must thrill Clyde that she had come off rather heroically, intervening the way she had.

As they headed out, Moran told the guard that he could go as well. The guard looked to Dr. Westbrook for guidance, and Clyde somewhat reluctantly nodded, and the three men left the room.

Moran watched them go and then turned back to Ella.

"You're a brave young woman," he said simply. "Very few people would have stepped into that situation."

"Well, I know what it's like to be scared of being hurt," she replied simply.

To which he nodded, and then looked at her for a moment with such an odd expression on his face that Ella was half-expecting him to tell her that he remembered her from the Bell Jar, when she had introduced herself as Dr. Kramer. But of course that wasn't meant to be.

"I'm sorry. I just had the strangest feeling of déjà vu when I came in and saw you. Have we ever met before?" Moran asked.

She looked at him for a second, wishing she could tell him everything: how much it had cost her to come back here, how much she would rather be a doctor working with Sebastian and Malakhi and the other patients she had so loved. How she wished that Captain Haskell had been a loving husband who supported his wife instead of being someone with no ability to care.

She wished she could explain that she had come back because while she wanted to do the right thing—she'd also had no choice in the matter. Her life had been destroyed in her other reality, and now all she could do was help others by staving off the rapid rate of infection and destruction by the Vanitan energy taking hold of the world.

But instead, she said simply, "No. I don't think so."

Moran nodded and began to stand to leave when he winced in pain and grabbed his lower back.

"Are you OK?" Ella asked, concerned. "What happened to your back?"

And he was pleasantly stunned by her forthright honesty.

"I was shot many years ago. The bullet was lodged very close to two vertebrae. I had the choice of leaving it in, which would have left me using crutches for the rest of my life. Or of having it removed and, if successful, I would walk. But if not, I would end up in a wheelchair. I chose not to do the operation and have been on crutches ever since. The two vertebrae have fused, which is irritating, but, as you can see, I can walk."

"That must have been scary. Making a decision like that."

"It was," he admitted, now finding her honesty refreshing. "But I listened to my wife. And she said that no matter what, I was destined to be here with her for a very long time, and crutches or not, she saw me walking out of the hospital." And he smiled at the memory.

"Destined?" Ella whispered as the hair on her arm stood up.

"Yes. She's a big believer in destiny, my wife. She always says that try as you might, you can't outrun your destiny."

Suddenly, Ella was transported back to the hospital bed, with Detective Moran asking her about Haskell and the woman in the floral nightgown patting her leg so kindly. The woman had told her the exact same thing. So, was that Moran's wife?

"What is your wife's name?" she asked.

He looked at her a for second, then answered, "Marti."

"And what does Marti do?" she asked, trying to figure out why she was in her dream.

He looked at her and seemed to be mulling something over before he answered, "She's a clairvoyant."

Ella smiled. That made sense, she thought. That made a lot of sense. And she was now sure that the woman in the floral nightgown was Moran's wife.

"Do you believe in that stuff?" she asked.

Moran smiled at the word *stuff*. "Well, I didn't use to. But she's been right about too many things too many times not to believe in it. I met her working on a murder case, and she guided us to the killer."

"How does she explain what she does?" she asked, intrigued.

"She has an unusual take on it. She says that it's sort of like remembering. When she sees things, things that are going to happen, she says she feels like she's remembering them."

Ella felt a chill go through her. That was exactly what it was, she thought, and she wished that Marti was here with them right now.

"And is she right all the time?" she asked.

"Well, she's more right than wrong." Then he smiled, adding, "She says she can't see something unless it's definitely going to happen, and in my experience, if she doesn't know it, she doesn't say it."

Ella felt a wave of excitement run through her. "So, are there other outcomes that are possible, but she just can't see them?"

Moran looked at her intensely, as if that was a very insightful question. If only he knew.

"According to my wife, there is such a thing as destiny. There are just several paths to getting there, I guess. But she's also said that there are some people who can change destiny, though they are very rare."

Ella nodded and suddenly felt like she might cry. Moran looked worried by her sudden change and leaned forward, patting her arm gently.

"I shouldn't say this, but Hannah Haskell isn't pressing charges. She is actually very grateful that you came along when you did. And as far as we're concerned, you were acting in self-defense."

With that, Moran was about to stand when she said in a small voice, "Did your wife say anything about me?"

The look in his eyes let her know that Marti had indeed mentioned her. Moran hesitated for a second and then nodded.

"What did she say?" asked Ella.

"First, I must tell you, I almost never ask her about my cases. But there was something about what you did, Miss Kramer, that struck me. I cannot explain it, but it affected me to the core."

He took a breath before saying, "She said that when she looked at what happened in the Wellglad parking lot, there was someone there. Someone protecting Hannah Haskell. She said that she couldn't see who it was because they were . . ." He stopped for a second before continuing. "They were surrounded by light."

Then he gazed into Ella's eyes as if he was looking through her to her soul and said, "She said you were sort of like an angel, surrounded by light."

Tears welled up in her eyes, but she quickly wiped them away and thanked him for telling her that. "I would like to meet your wife one day." She smiled.

He stood to leave and thanked her for her time. And just as he was about to open the door, he looked back at her and said, "Oh, she also said that there was a rabbit in that lot with you and Hannah Haskell. She couldn't figure out what it was doing there, but she kept getting the image of a rabbit running around. Sort of like *Alice in Wonderland*."

And here he paused before saying, "I don't know why, but I thought you'd like that."

Ella smiled, delighted for reasons he would never know. He bid her farewell and left.

Ella sat, thinking of the rabbit, and laughed out loud. There had been no rabbit in this reality when she had killed Oliver Haskell. No, Marti was picking up on a piece that came from the other reality. The one she had erased with Dr. Kramer. So Detective Moran's wife was better than even she knew.

The guard came in and took her down the hall toward her cell, for the rooms in C Wing were more like prison cells than hospital rooms. It pained Ella to know that this was probably going to be the way she lived for the foreseeable future.

As she rounded the corner, she looked out the window and saw Detective Moran walking toward his partner, and she slowed down long enough to see him stop and look back at her. She gave a little wave, and he nodded just as he had done in her dream, when she told him about the tile, and then he was off.

The guard opened her cell, and she went inside and sat on the bed and wondered what would become of her now. Her head still ached from the concussion, so she lay down and pulled her blanket around her, positioning her face so that it fell in the path of the sun, which was streaming in from the small window above.

And soon, its warmth lulled her into a deep sleep. One uninterrupted by memories of Dr. Farber or red-haired girls or Captain Haskell. One that allowed Ella to float away and dream of the March Hare and the Mad Hatter and tea parties where they talk about *time* not being an *it* but a *him*.

Chapter 66

Ella wiped the sweat from her brow as she finished her work in the Bainbridge cafeteria. It was July now, and six months had passed since she landed in C Wing after her ordeal with Captain Haskell. She was allowed to work in the kitchen and was given more free time, but they still wouldn't let her go back to A Wing for fear she would escape again.

She was looked at as sort of a celebrity by the other inmates for her daring escape, and she'd noticed that the hospital had put razor wire on the fencing now, even the ones surrounding the A and B Wings, in an effort to thwart any future attempts. But they'd probably be surprised to know that Ella wasn't planning anything. She didn't know where she would go even if she did leave. Her aunt was gone, and any friends she might have had in her life as Dr. Kramer wouldn't know her now.

She tried to counter her growing depression by reminding herself that she had a purpose; that she indeed did have a role to play. Two months after she was put in C Wing, her faith in humanity was renewed when she saw a small blurb in the newspaper stating that Lyprophan had been pulled from the market for unspecified reasons. Hannah Haskell had played her part. Just as Ella had.

She thought a lot about Otis and what kind of world he would inherit. She remembered her conversation with him. How he had informed her that they had lived on Mars together.

Curious, she began digging around in the library, reading all the articles on the red planet that she could find. With new imagery, they had shown that the D and M Pyramid on Mars had evidence of what looked like collapsed brickwork, and the nearby Face at Cydonia Mensa showed a nose, a mouth, eyes, and even helmet ornamentation that was comparable to artifacts from ancient Egypt.

Some scientists believed there was evidence that there were very large thermonuclear reactions on Mars similar to the ones created here on Earth. It was quite feasible, then, that there had been life on Mars that had come to an end because of some thermonuclear event. How had living beings changed so drastically over time? she wondered. And why would living beings create their own extinction? But she knew the answer to that.

More than anything, she was lonely. She'd had no more visits from Dr. Farber, and she hadn't seen Malakhi or spoken to anyone else she'd known in her other life, which resulted in her feeling isolated and sad. She even began to wonder if maybe it was all a dream. Maybe she'd been locked up since the death of her uncle fifteen years before and her mind had made up this fantastical tale to help her escape from what her life had become.

She'd finished washing the cooking pots and pans and went to take out the trash to the dumpsters when she saw him standing at the fence that separated B and C Wings which now had razor wire at the top. There he was, and her heart skipped a beat as he waved her over. Would he remember her? Did he know what had transpired? These questions stormed her mind as she found herself hurrying over to him.

"Sebastian?" she asked quietly, her voice shaking with anticipation.

"Ha! You look a little worse for the wear and tear, Dr. Kramer!" And it was said in a very thick Brooklyn accent accompanied by a sneer. Ella's face flushed, and her eyes welled up at the mention of her old self. She had never been happier to see someone in all her life. Especially not . . .

"Nadine?" she asked.

"Yeah. It's me. Look at you! You're one of us again, huh?" Nadine quipped. And this simple statement flooded Ella with anticipation. Nadine knew that Ella had been here before. She seemed to know that Ella had gone back in time and changed that reality and become a doctor—but was now back and one of them *again*.

"You know," Ella murmured, shocked.

"'Course I know," Nadine said unceremoniously in her rough Brooklyn way. "So did Malakhi. Although I would venture to say that I knew what you were before he did. Anyway, he told me to find you. To help you out."

"Malakhi sent you here?" Ella asked.

This bothered Nadine. "No one sent me anywhere! Malakhi asked me to look out for you, so I will. He's a stand-up guy, so I'm gonna do you a solid. Got it?"

Ella remembered Nadine's temper and nodded. "Where is Malakhi?"

Nadine shrugged angrily. "He got chased off by that damn light machine of Dr. Lester's! Freaking thing wipes people away! Malakhi disappeared right after the first treatment, and now poor Sebastian can barely remember him at all. Christ! Well, I'm not going anywhere! The Goddam bastards!"

Ella couldn't believe what she was hearing. Gary's light treatment was being used on the patients at Bainbridge? And wiping away their memories?"

"I don't understand. What do you mean, he disappeared? Is Sebastian losing his memory of you and Malakhi?"

"You really aren't the sharpest tool in the shed, are you?" Nadine retorted. "Sebastian barely acknowledged us, but he knew we were around—and I will say, he's gotten better at listening to me since Malakhi left. Maybe it just gave me more room to be louder. Who knows?" She stopped and cleared her throat before continuing. "What I mean is that *the memory of who Sebastian was before* has been wiped out by that freaking light hat. That's why Malakhi's gone. The light forces us away."

Ella looked at her, dumbstruck, and repeated Nadine's words: "The memory of who Sebastian was before?"

Nadine lost her patience now. "Hard to imagine you was ever a doctor! Malakhi and me were Sebastian *before*! Get it? Malakhi was from way the hell back in Persia, and I was born in Brooklyn, New York, in 1915, and then killed by that Goddam husband of mine in 1945! *We are both Sebastian! Get it?*" And she stood there looking at Ella crossly.

Ella nodded slowly, sort of shocked by the explanation.

"So, you and Malakhi are Sebastian's past lives?" Ella asked.

"You can use the word *past* if ya wanna, but I prefer to say we are just his *Others*. Sounds classier." Nadine replied.

Ella stood there, stunned. "So . . . you're like me?"

"What?" Nadine exclaimed. "You think we're like you?" And she threw back her head and laughed as Ella watched.

"No, doll! Not everyone can travel back and forth like you! No! We're just visitors, so to speak. We can't go back . . . or up or down, for that matter. Once we're here, we're here. Malakhi was already with him, so lucky for me, Sebastian already knew how to get out of the way and make space," Nadine said.

And then a dark cloud seemed to pass over her face, and she explained angrily, "He didn't have a soul lookin' out for him! So, when I heard the poor kid screamin' again as that son-of-a-bitch father beat the hell out of him—I moved that kid out of the way and took care of the bastard. I've stayed with him ever since, and no one will ever hurt him again! Not as long as I'm around!"

And she looked at Ella, who looked back at her almost reverentially.

"I see," Ella said quietly, mentally adding yet another piece to the board: *Drifters, Light Runners, Light Eaters,* and now *Others.*

"Oh, do ya now?" Nadine snorted. "Well, good for you!" she said and looked around suspiciously, remembering that she was on a mission. "So here's the deal. You ever see Fletcher over in C Wing?"

Ella remembered the old man she occasionally had seen in the lunch line. He must have been eighty years old and seemed to have trouble getting around, but she was pretty sure he was called Fletch.

"I think so. Women and men live on different floors, but I think I may know who he is."

Nadine rolled her eyes impatiently. "Well, anyway, Fletch is an old friend of mine, or I guess I should say Sebastian's, and he likes his fires. So, this morning, I spoke with him, and he's gonna help you."

Ella wasn't sure how such an old man could help her, but she didn't want to seem ungrateful, so she asked, "What exactly is he going to do?"

Nadine mimicked Ella with a hoity-toity voice. "*What exactly is he going to do?* Christ! You still think you're a doctor, dontcha? He's gonna light a birthday cake for me! That's what he's gonna do! I asked him for seven candles on my birthday cake and slipped him a pack of matches. You understand? So, when you see the fire and smell the smoke, you head to the back. . . ." And she pointed toward the woods to the back of C Wing ". . . and run like hell."

Ella stood there dumbfounded by what Nadine was proposing—was she saying this Fletcher was going to help Ella escape?

"Nadine . . ." she began.

"I don't have a lot of time, honey. You do what I say—got it?"

Ella nodded her head and gratefully whispered, "Thank you, Nadine."

Nadine primped her hair a little. "Don't thank me! Malakhi said you got a lot to do. Although how he thinks a girl like you can stop the Vanitan, I will never know! Light Runner or not!"

Funny, thought Ella, that was just what she'd been thinking. But before she could say anything else, Nadine turned and headed back to B Wing. Casually tossing over her shoulder as she went, "Oh, and by the way? My birthday is tonight!" And she was gone.

Ella stood there shaking. She had waited months for something to happen and it finally had. In the shape of a six-foot-three-inch, 250-pound man named Nadine.

Chapter 67

t was well past midnight when she heard the first sirens go off, letting everyone know that there was an emergency in C Wing. She grabbed the blanket from her bed, wrapped it around herself, and waited. A few minutes later, the guards ushered all the inmates out of their cells and down the hall.

Because of the smoke, they had to be rerouted to the front staircase, which was normally off-limits to the inmates of C Wing. From there, they were ushered down into the lobby, where Ella huddled with several other patients waiting to be evacuated.

She noticed the old photos on the walls that showed Bainbridge throughout the ages, with little placards beneath each, detailing its history. Ella had never seen these photos, and one in particular caught her eye. She moved closer to get a better look, and saw that it was a picture of the Bainbridge family. It must have been taken some time in the 1950s, and it showed Wayne and his wife, Marie, seated in comfy blue armchairs, with a little girl of about eleven sitting on a rug on the floor in front of them. She read the name on the placard and saw that this was Mildred Rose.

But it was the little girl's hair that stopped her. Most of the photos she'd seen of them were in black and white and very rarely included Wayne's daughter. But this one was in color, and the girl's hair was a striking shade of red. Ella looked at her eyes. They were blue, and there was something about them that reminded Ella of her own.

This was Millie. The same Millie that the plaque in the garden paid homage to. The same Millie Malakhi had said goodbye to. And now a thought crossed her mind, and she couldn't help but wonder: Was the little girl with the troubled face before her *her*? *Was she Millie?*

Suddenly, the guards barked at everyone to get into a line and start moving out of the building. But Ella didn't move. She couldn't. Her eyes desperately scanned the picture until they settled on Wayne Bainbridge holding his cane, staring defiantly into the camera. And for a fleeting moment, she was reminded of Detective Moran, with his steel crutches and his deep, intelligent eyes. But it was when she looked at Marie Bainbridge that she was *certain*. Her heart stopped for a moment as a flood of feelings overwhelmed her.

Feelings of recognition, of sorrow, of love descended upon her all at once, and Ella somehow *knew* that this woman was her mother. She stared at the stranger who had died a tragic death all those years ago and felt hot tears fill her eyes. She reached out to touch the woman in the photo when her hand was roughly grabbed by an orderly, who pulled her forward toward the exit and out of the building.

Once in the yard, she looked up at the devastation of C Wing and noticed that, true to his word, Fletcher had already set six of the seven fires he'd promised to Nadine. Each in a different part of the building. The guards and orderlies were struggling to get the inmates out of danger and keep them under control. Ella decided that she would run the minute they weren't looking, and she slowly began to back away toward the fence.

Her moment came when a seventh room was set ablaze at the far end of the building, and several of the guards sprinted off. That was when Ella turned and ran to the back of C Wing and headed for the woods.

Of course there was the matter of the new fence with its razor wire at the top, but Ella had brought her blanket to help mitigate some of the damage. It was heavy and woolen, and Ella tied it around her waist and began to climb. As she neared the top of the fence with the knifelike wire ready to shred her skin, she pulled the blanket over her head and wrestled her way under it, using the blanket as a shield to, she hoped, blunt the sharp edges as she climbed to the other side. The wire prevailed in a few places, but, by and large, she made it over unscathed.

As soon as her feet hit the ground, she headed toward the woods. In the morning, she would catch the train and make her way out of Baltimore to God knew where. But it didn't matter. Ella knew that she had a purpose. That all her pain and suffering had not been in vain. She knew deep within her that she was here to fight the energy of the Vanitan. To illuminate the shadow that was now encompassing Earth, infecting the living with its poisonous energy. She didn't fully comprehend how she would do it, but she was intent on finding out. And she trusted that Malakhi and others like him would guide her and help her find her way. Just as they had already.

She continued along the edge of the woods in the moon's shadow, never losing sight of the train tracks that would guide her out of the city. She stopped and rested, nestled under the trees for a while until she saw the sun began to rise, and watched as it changed the sky from purple to red.

She stood, basking in its glow as the sun rose higher. Until soon its golden rays beckoned her to follow her destiny, and she set off once again.

Toward a place they couldn't catch her.
Toward a new life.
Ella set off . . .

Toward the light.

About the Author

Ally Walker was a budding biochem-
ist with a BA in biology from UCSC
when she stumbled into show business.
Spotted by a producer in an LA eatery,
she was cast in a small film and continued to make her name as an actress
for the next thirty years, starring in
Profiler, *Universal Soldier*, *While You
Were Sleeping*, and *Sons of Anarchy*, to
name a few. She produced and directed
an award-winning documentary on LA County's foster care system, then
penned and directed the film, *Far More*, which won Best Screenplay at the
Milan International Film Festival. She lives in LA with her husband, three
boys, and two unruly bulldogs. *The Light Runner* is her first novel.